D0383602

"And can your fancy man provide *this?*"

Cameron's hand flashed out and circled Meg's wrist. Its cast-iron grip spun her against the edge of the tub, where his other hand waited to seize her waist and continue the momentum, wrenching her over on top of him.

Meg struggled like a wet cat. "Let me go, you—"

The rest of her words were lost against Cameron's hard, angry mouth.

She dangled over the tub's rolled edge, feet kicking in midair, nightgown trailing water as he kissed her—kissed her with a ruthless, dizzying fury. His hand cupped her head, pulling her into the tub in a wild tangle of knees and breasts and floating cotton lawn. Meg's hand clawed water, then, incredibly, found flesh.

They clasped . . . and clung.

Dear Reader,

April brings us another great batch of titles!

Readers of contemporary romance will surely recognize Judith McWilliams. In her first historical, *Suspicion,* she pens a tale of intrigue and danger in which young Lucy Langford must team up with Colonel Robert Standen in order to find a would-be killer.

Popular historical author Elizabeth Lane brings us *MacKenna's Promise.* Meg MacKenna travels to East Africa to get a divorce from her estranged husband, Cameron. But when tragedy strikes, they must band together to save their family and their love.

When ruthless businessman Oliver Keane inherits part of a Barbados plantation, he learns how to love from Alexa Fairfield—a woman he's been raised to despise. *Island Star* is by Kit Gardner, one of the 1992 March Madness authors.

In *The River Sprite* by Kate Kingsley, Serena Caswell is determined to take over as pilot of her father's steamboat. But handsome riverboat gambler—and half owner of the boat—Nathan Trent has other plans.

We hope you enjoy these titles. Next month look for four brand-new releases from your favorite Harlequin Historical authors!

Sincerely,

Tracy Farrell
Senior Editor

Please address questions and book requests to:
Reader Service
U.S.: P.O. Box 1325, Buffalo, NY 14269
Canadian: P.O. Box 1050, Niagara Falls, Ont. L2E 7G7

ELIZABETH LANE

MacKenna's Promise

Harlequin Books

TORONTO • NEW YORK • LONDON
AMSTERDAM • PARIS • SYDNEY • HAMBURG
STOCKHOLM • ATHENS • TOKYO • MILAN
MADRID • WARSAW • BUDAPEST • AUCKLAND

If you purchased this book without a cover you should be aware
that this book is stolen property. It was reported as "unsold and
destroyed" to the publisher, and neither the author nor the
publisher has received any payment for this "stripped book."

ISBN 0-373-28816-6

MacKENNA'S PROMISE

Copyright © 1994 by Elizabeth Lane.

All rights reserved. Except for use in any review, the reproduction or
utilization of this work in whole or in part in any form by any electronic,
mechanical or other means, now known or hereafter invented, including
xerography, photocopying and recording, or in any information storage
or retrieval system, is forbidden without the written permission of the
publisher, Harlequin Enterprises Limited, 225 Duncan Mill Road,
Don Mills, Ontario, Canada M3B 3K9.

All characters in this book have no existence outside the imagination of
the author and have no relation whatsoever to anyone bearing the same
name or names. They are not even distantly inspired by any individual
known or unknown to the author, and all incidents are pure invention.

This edition published by arrangement with Harlequin Enterprises B. V.

® and TM are trademarks of the publisher. Trademarks indicated with
® are registered in the United States Patent and Trademark Office, the
Canadian Trade Marks Office and in other countries.

Printed in U.S.A.

Books by Elizabeth Lane

Harlequin Historicals

Wind River #28
Birds of Passage #92
Moonfire #150
MacKenna's Promise #216

ELIZABETH LANE

has traveled extensively in Latin America, Europe and China, and enjoys bringing these exotic locales to life on the printed page, but she also finds her home state of Utah and other areas of the American West to be fascinating sources for historical romance. Elizabeth loves such diverse activities as <u>hiking</u> and playing the piano, not to mention her latest hobby—belly dancing.

For Tanya

Prologue

Darlmoor, Scotland
October 17, 1894

A sparrow had flown in through an open window of the kirk. Frantic for escape, it fluttered back and forth above the empty pews, its plight ignored by most of the small, grim wedding party below.

Cameron MacKenna watched it out of the corner of one eye. Poor, trapped creature. Aye, he knew how it must feel. He was feeling much the same way himself, and there was nothing to be done about it.

The wool of his stepfather's dress kilt scratched Cameron's bare legs. The traditional costume had been yanked out of storage an hour before the ceremony, and it reeked of mothballs. Cameron felt like a bloody organ grinder's monkey in it. The jacket seams strained against his shoulders. The linen shirt was yellowed with age, and the sporran looked as if it had been chewed by rats. But for the past sixty years, all the MacKenna men had been married in it, so there'd been no arguing. Not even with his mother. It was an honor, she insisted, especially since Cameron was a MacKenna in name only.

Cameron's bride stood an arm's length away, a small, silent bundle of misery. A drab lace veil obscured all but the tip of her nose. Aye, poor little Meg. Not yet seventeen, and to have this happen.

At twenty-three, he should have known better. It had been a chance encounter between them, a teasing dare that had erupted into passion almost before they'd realized what was happening. Now, unbelievably, Mary Margaret Owen, the judge's pampered only daughter, was carrying Cameron's child.

The sparrow had exhausted itself for the moment and settled on an open rafter of the kirk. Cameron gave it a last sympathetic glance as the preacher—ancient and doddering, like everything else in this wretched town—cleared his throat to begin the ceremony.

"Dearly beloved, we are gathered here in the presence of God and these witnesses . . ."

Aye, these witnesses, blast them. Cameron could feel their eyes boring into his back. He could feel their rage, their contempt. There was old Judge Owen, who'd have sent him to the gallows if he could, for ruining his precious daughter. "You'll give my grandchild a name, and that's all, MacKenna," he'd rasped furiously. "Once the wedding's done, you're to be gone from here. Meg can stay in my house and raise the babe without you. I'll not have you hanging around this town, making more grief for her with your profligate ways!"

And there was Cameron's own stepfather, big Jock MacKenna, whose bitter words still rang in Cameron's ears. "I've tried to make a decent man o' you, a good farmer like my own blood sons. But it's all come to naught! Well, you've disgraced the family for the last time, Cameron! You've been beggin' me to let you go to Africa and get a job on that lunatic railroad line. I've got the money for a one-way steamer ticket right here. Marry the blasted girl, get Judge Owen off my neck, an' it's yours! Aye, go to Africa! Go to the devil! I don't care if I ever see your face again!"

The old preacher's voice droned like a bullfly in the narrow space of the kirk, interspersing little homilies about love and devotion with the phrases of the traditional ceremony. Cameron shifted uncomfortably, the rough linen collar chafing his throat. His three older stepbrothers stood behind him, stalwart clods who cared for nothing but the land and the dull, bleating sheep that grazed it. They wouldn't miss him, Cameron knew. They'd never understood his need to know what was between the covers of a book or what lay beyond the next valley. Even though he'd been a mere babe when Jock married his mother, they had never accepted him. They never would.

Only Cameron's mother had truly cared about him. Even when, in his desperate aloneness, he'd taken to hell-raising, fighting and drinking with wild companions, she'd tried to understand. He could hear her now, a fragile, pretty woman, weeping softly into her lace-edged kerchief. She was the only person he would miss.

"Will you, Mary Margaret Owen, take this man to be your lawful wedded husband, to have and to hold from this day forward..." The old preacher plodded through the words, unconscious of their mockery.

Cameron glanced covertly at his bride. Her veil had fallen back a little, revealing a few loose tendrils of dark blond hair. Little Meg. Lord, he scarcely knew her. He'd thought she was a child that night, when she'd come upon him swimming alone in the cove. Laughing, he'd flung out a challenge for her to shed her clothes and join him. He'd fully expected her to turn and bolt back up the path. She had not. And the slender body that slipped through the moonlight and into the water had not been a child's at all.

Cameron could feel the tension in her as the old man finished speaking. He could almost feel the pain in her tight throat as she drew a quick, sharp breath and spoke her answer.

"I will." The words emerged as a whisper, scarcely audible in the hollow space of the kirk.

"And will you, John Cameron MacKenna, take this woman to be your lawful wedded wife..." The old preacher's delivery was as perfunctory as before.

Cameron could hear the sparrow again, fluttering against a windowpane. He could feel his own heart struggling against his ribs.

"I will," he muttered hoarsely.

The ring—Cameron fumbled for it in his pocket. His mother had given him the thin gold band only this morning. It was hers, he'd realized, saved from her first marriage to his own father, who'd perished at sea before Cameron was born. For her to sacrifice such a treasure...

His fingers found the tiny gold circlet. Meg had turned a little to face him, and he was able to truly look at her for the first time that day.

Heaven help him, she was still a child, her slight body lost in an ornate Victorian wedding gown that was far too big. Wisps of hair straggled from a lopsided pompadour to hang damply around her small, square face. Her wide violet eyes were bloodshot; they burned with reproach, but there were no tears. Maybe she had none left.

In one reckless moment, Cameron realized, he had changed this girl's carefree young life forever. He ached to speak to her, to tell her how sorry he was; but this was neither the time nor the place for it, and in any case he knew she would not listen. Her father had made it clear that Meg never wanted to see him again.

Well, she would soon get her wish. Before nightfall, he'd be on the road to Aberdeen. From there he'd be catching the next steamer with connections to Mombasa. God willing, he'd be gone for years. Maybe for good.

Meg's small hands, nails chewed to the quick, clutched a few hastily plucked sprigs of heather. She trembled as she shifted the sad little bouquet and, fingers spread, extended her left hand. Quaking himself, Cameron slid the ring down over her knuckle joints. Amazingly, it settled into place as if it had been fashioned on her finger.

Cameron was dimly aware of the bird, still floundering in the rafters, as the old preacher cleared his throat again.

"By the authority vested in me by the Kirk o' Scotland, I do pronounce you man and wife!"

The expectant silence that followed was broken only by the flurry of desperate wings. Suddenly, Cameron realized he was supposed to kiss the bride. He hadn't kissed her—hadn't even touched her—since that frenzied night on the beach. Now, to take her in his arms here, in front of everybody...

He made a slight, awkward move toward her. But Meg would have none of it. Her arms clung rigidly to her sides. Her head remained lowered, mouth set in a stubborn line.

Well, he bloody wasn't going to force her. Half relieved, half angry, Cameron turned away. Aye, it was over. They'd done their duty now, he and young Meg. For whatever it was worth, their child would not carry the stain of bastardy. Beyond that, there was nothing to be said.

The family members were stirring in their seats, some already rising. Cameron hung back long enough for Meg to reach her father's side, and for the two of them to start back up the aisle. Then he followed a dozen steps behind, lost in brooding silence.

Inside, he felt as black as the storm clouds that seethed across the moor. He had wasted most of his life in meaningless frustration, he realized, despising not so much the town, not so much his stepfather and dull stepbrothers, as himself. Now he'd capped it off by fathering a child he couldn't raise, by a girl who would never have chosen him as a husband. Well, he'd done enough damage here. It was time to be gone, before he could do more.

Only the thought of Africa buoyed his spirits. *Africa.* Open and untamed. Waiting for him like a tawny, perfumed mistress. Hours, days, and he would be on his way. Weeks, a month or two, and he would be there, free to wallow in her sweet savage splendor....

The sparrow had crashed into a glass windowpane. Cameron heard the sound, saw the small bird reel and plummet, to land with a soft thud between the pews.

Meg had seen it, too. With a little cry, she spun away from her father and plunged, stumbling on the lace hem of her gown, toward the spot where the bird had fallen.

"No!" Cameron growled impulsively. "Leave it be. I'll see to it."

She froze where she was. Her violet eyes flashed him a stricken glance as he slipped between the pews and bent to scoop up the bird. It lay dazed and warm in his palm, its tiny heart quivering through its feathers.

He could feel her questioning gaze as he probed it with a finger. "Aye, it's only stunned," he muttered. "Go on with your father, now."

Judge Owen had caught Meg's arm and was pulling her toward the door. Her eyes caught Cameron's in a last, fleeting glance. In their purple depths, he glimpsed anguish, tenderness, a desperate, helpless rage. Then she veered away and was gone.

Cameron's breath pushed out of his tight chest. For a long moment he stood there between the pews, his eyes still seeing her, holding the image of his bride, the mother of his child. Faintly, as if from another world, he could hear the shuffle of boots as his stepfather and brothers came tramping up the aisle. He could hear his mother, sobbing openly now.

"Well that's over and done with!" Jock MacKenna boomed. "Let's be gettin' back to the farm. There's work to be done!"

The bird had begun to stir. It was struggling now, in the cup of his hands, wings straining against his fingers.

Gently, Cameron carried it outside and set it free.

Chapter One

East Africa Protectorate
February 24, 1899

The island town of Mombasa steamed drowsily under a torrid African sun. Heat waves shimmered above coral walls and orange tile roofs, their mosaic broken here and there by the jade cupola of a mango tree or the twisted purple arms of a baobab. In the harbor, low-slung Arab dhows skimmed the water like lazy dragonflies, chased by light breezes that stirred the drooping palms along the shore.

A mile out of port, Meg Owen MacKenna stood at the crowded rail of the *S.S. Horatius,* eyes squinting under the brim of her felt-lined *terai.* The air was heavy with heat, the shoreline a blur through the blinding sunlight. The long rains would not begin until March or April, and the sapphire air glittered with African summer.

An aroma that blended oranges, frangipani and dried fish rose from the island to float out over the water. Meg inhaled, her senses quivering. Even from offshore, the land beckoned, teasing her with a sensual languor that puckered her nipples beneath the proper twill traveling suit. Blindfolded, she would have known she wasn't back in Scotland.

"I want to see!" The little girl's hand tugged at Meg's skirt. Meg scooped her daughter up in her arms and lifted her above the rail. "What's that?" the small, clear voice piped like a lark's. "Is it Africa?"

"Yes, Jenny, it's Africa." Meg hugged the child close, laughing to mask the nervous apprehension that was almost choking her. It was over at last, the grueling five-week voyage from Tilbury to Suez, through the sweltering Red Sea and around Africa's great, dry horn.

What lay ahead, she feared, would be even worse. But she had vowed to succeed. She would not leave this land until she had found Cameron MacKenna and obtained what only he had the power to give her—her freedom.

"I want to see elephants! When will we see elephants, Mother?" Although not quite four, Jenny spoke in succinct phrases, like a miniature adult.

"Not yet." Meg smoothed the tousled blond curls, wondering where her daughter's hat had gone to this time. Jenny was always losing her felt-lined straw helmet. She did it on purpose, Meg suspected. Not that it seemed to matter. Over the past weeks, the tropic sun had turned Jenny's skin golden peach and bleached her hair to the color of ripe wheat. The effect was stunning.

"Why not yet? I want to see elephants now."

"We'll be in a town, sweetheart, and elephants don't live in towns," Meg explained. "Oh, but we'll be staying at the Emir's house. There'll be monkeys and parrots, even peacocks!"

"But no elephants?" Jenny gazed up at Meg with eyes as blue as the African sky. Cameron's eyes.

"No, dear, no elephants." Meg swallowed hard, remembering Cameron as she had last seen him, towering sullenly in his stepfather's kilt, his black curls tumbling over his forehead, his cobalt eyes blazing in silent fury. She'd given him no warning that she was coming to Africa. Certainly he would be shocked, and probably angry, as well—angry still, after four long years.

He had written to no one except his mother. Through that frail, kindly woman, Meg had kept track of Cameron's whereabouts. Through his mother, as well, he had sent money for Jenny, every shilling of which Meg had set aside for the child's schooling. But between Cameron and herself, not a word had passed since the day of their wedding.

Even last year, after her solicitor had mailed him the divorce papers to sign, Cameron had not responded. Month after frustrating month, Meg had waited. Her father, perhaps, might have eased the matter through the courts, but he had died a few months after Jenny was born. Meg was alone, striving to make do on the small inheritance he had left her.

At last, despite her stretched finances, she'd resolved to go and confront Cameron face-to-face. It was time they ended this farce of a marriage, time they freed themselves to go on with their separate lives.

The ship was chugging through the *mlango*, an opening in the coral reef that rimmed the outer harbor. Within the reef's circle, calmer waters mirrored the jewel-like sky. A lighthouse rose like a minaret from a distant landpoint. Beyond it, Meg could see the ramparts of an old stone fort.

Maybe she would find Cameron right here in Mombasa. His mother had said he was still working for the railroad. The process could be as simple as getting his address from the railway office and presenting herself at his door with the papers in her hand.

But no, Meg knew better. She had watched Cameron secretly for years in the town where they'd grown up, and she knew that nothing about him was predictable. Cameron craved adventure the way some men craved whisky or opium. He could be anywhere.

But no matter, Meg swiftly reminded herself. She was not leaving Africa until she'd found him.

"So, we're arriving at last!" The old Arab's silvery voice broke through Meg's reverie. His long *kaftan* rustled silkily as he glided to the rail. The Emir, he called himself. Once, he claimed, he had governed half a kingdom. Now he lived in Mombasa, in comfortable exile with his three wives.

He had boarded at Suez, a slight, wizened man whose regal bearing offset his small stature. In his flowing robes and embroidered *tarbush,* he was as exotic as a figure from the *Arabian Nights*—too exotic for the upper-class British passengers. Although he spoke charmingly stilted English, they'd kept aloof from him. Snubbing the old man, they had left him to wander the deck alone, save for the cadaverous bodyguard who floated behind him like a shadow.

Not so Jenny. In her trusting young eyes, the Emir was a bearded Merlin from storybook land. She had marched right up to him, tugged at his robe and demanded to know his name. By the third day out, the two had become fast friends. Meg, trailing her daughter, had swiftly followed suit.

Some passengers had viewed the innocent liaison as shocking, especially when it became known that the Emir had invited Meg and her daughter to be his houseguests in Mombasa. But Meg had shrugged off their disapproval. The old man was her friend. And flying in the face of convention was nothing new to her. Her quiet rebellion had begun that moonlit night when she'd slipped bare and trembling into the water with wild Cameron MacKenna. In her own prim, quiet way, she'd been rebelling ever since.

"If you need help in finding your husband, I have friends," the Emir was saying. "The sort of friends who know how to get information."

Meg stared down at the ripples that slid along the steamer's wet, black flank. "That's kind of you, but I'll try it on my own first. If Cameron is working for the railroad, they should know his whereabouts. After that..." She sighed, already bracing herself for the confrontation that would come when she found him.

The old Arab shook his head. "This unhappy matter of the divorce.... Why not put it aside until you see the kind of person your husband has become? Perhaps there is still a chance—"

"No. There's no chance." Meg spoke softly, but there was steel in her voice. The Emir knew only part of her motive for divorcing Cameron. Meg hadn't told him the rest. She hadn't told him about her need to give Jenny a secure, respectable future. She hadn't told him about Arthur Tarrington-Leigh, the man who could provide just that.

The ship had halted in the middle of the harbor, its anchor splashing into the depths. A fleet of motley-looking skiffs was converging on them from the docks.

"You see, little one, this big ship cannot go all the way in to the shore," the Emir was explaining to Jenny. "The water is too shallow. Those little boats are coming to carry us to land."

Jenny was only half listening. Still in Meg's arms, she had stretched across the rail to wave at the crew of a passing dhow. Entranced by the golden child, the ragged Arab sailors were grinning, waving back at her.

Meg tightened her grip on the sturdy little legs. She'd agonized for weeks over the decision to bring her daughter to Africa. Night after sleepless night, she'd pondered the alternatives. Cameron's mother was in poor health. Arthur had offered to take Jenny in, but he had a large, silent home with a shrewish housekeeper who disliked children. And in any case, Meg had no wish to be obligated to him. Not yet.

In the end, there'd been no choice except to bring Jenny along. So far, at least, Meg had no regrets. The little girl had thrived on sun and sea air and made friends all over the ship. Even the problem of what to do with Jenny while Meg dealt with Cameron had been resolved by the Emir's invitation. Meg was relieved and grateful. There were some things in which a child should have no part. This divorce was one of them.

Meg gazed at the shoreline through the simmering air. It would all work out, she told herself. Cameron had no reason to fight her. He would welcome the chance to be free of a marriage he'd never wanted in the first place.

A shadow had fallen across the rail. Sensing a presence behind her, Meg turned sharply and found herself staring up into the pockmarked face of Hassan, the Emir's bodyguard.

She stifled a gasp. He was looking intently down at her, his long, hollow cheeks drawn inward, his eyes as black as anthracite in their sunken orbits. A dagger the size of a five-pound carp, its handle fashioned of rhino horn, hung in a beaded scabbard at his waist.

He smiled now, thin lips stretching over tobacco-stained teeth, one of them gold. His pipe-stem body flowed forward from the waist in an unctuous bow.

Meg took a deep breath and willed her pulse to slow to its natural pace. Hassan, for all his politeness, was an unsettling creature. His face seemed to break into a smirk whenever she looked his way. And this wasn't the first time he'd floated up behind her on his big, silent feet, startling her when she turned around. It happened so often, in fact, that she'd begun to suspect the poor man was sweet on her.

"Yes, what is it?" she said, trying to sound relaxed and pleasant.

Hassan's toothy grin broadened. His black eyes narrowed to slits of pleasure as he drew an object from behind his back.

It was Jenny's missing sun hat.

Meg's nervousness dissolved in chagrin as she muttered her thanks. Accepting the straw helmet, she thrust it onto Jenny's blond head. What a goose she'd been, letting Hassan startle her so when he'd only meant to be kind.

Hassan bowed again, then straightened to his full, gaunt height and glided away. She would learn from this incident, Meg resolved; next time, she would not be so quick to judge.

The ship's crewmen were rigging tackles on the starboard deck to lower passengers and cargo into the waiting skiffs. Men and women were gathering up their hand baggage. Hassan had taken the old Emir's arm.

Meg set Jenny down and took a firm grip on one damp little hand. With the hand that was free, she caught up her leather Gladstone. It held copies of the unsigned divorce papers and a few essentials for Jenny and herself. The rest of their things, packed into her steamer trunk, would be unloaded later.

Passengers were already queuing up for the boats. They were civil servants and medical personnel mostly, bound for duty at customs posts or the new government hospital in Mombasa. Many had served in India. A half dozen of them, in fact, had brought their wives, formidable women, who'd given Meg hours of advice on what to wear in the tropics, what to eat, what medicines to take for malaria and dysentery, and how to keep the natives in their place.

Meg stepped into line behind one of these women now, tugging Jenny close to keep her from getting jostled. As the queue inched along the deck, she sensed, suddenly, the awful weight of what she was about to do. It had been easy enough, planning her divorce at home, with half a world separating her from Cameron. Even on board ship, the distance had been there, and the safe barrier of the ocean.

But this was different. This was now. This was here. And once she set foot on African soil, there would be no turning back until she had faced him.

"When will we see my father?" Jenny's birdlike soprano piped above the murmur of the crowd.

"Truly, dearest, I don't know." Meg's fingers tightened around her daughter's hand. She'd told Jenny, as gently as she could, about Cameron and the divorce. Real understanding would take years, she knew, but at least the child would have no devastating surprises to deal with later on.

"What will he look like?" Jenny persisted. "When will I see him?"

"We'll worry about that after we've found him. Be careful, now." Meg sidestepped a jutting capstan. Her answer had been evasive, but it was the best she could give. The question of Cameron's meeting his daughter was something she had yet to resolve. Seeing him could satisfy Jenny's curiosity and strengthen her as a person. It could also break her trusting, young heart.

The first skiff, weighted to the gunwales, was already pulling for the dock. Meg kept Jenny close as they approached the creaking tackle for their turn at the chair. Farther up the deck, a hefty English matron tittered nervously as another tackle swung her past the rail and lowered her out of sight.

"Can we do that?" Jenny bounced with anticipation.

"That's how we'll get off the ship. You're not afraid, are you?"

The wheaten curls danced. "It looks like fun!"

Meg held her daughter tightly as the crewmen buckled her into the canvas seat and tucked the Gladstone alongside. Then they were dangling in midair above the water. Looking down, Meg could see the Emir waving up at her from one of the skiffs. The stalwart Hassan was posted beside him. The tackle whined as they sped downward. Seconds, and they had reached the level of their own skiff. By that time, however, the low boat had drifted back a yard or so. Meg and Jenny had come down just short of it. They were skimming water.

"Hang on—" A young clerk leaned over the gunwale, arms outstretched. "Pass me the little girl first. Then we can catch your hands and pull you in."

The idea made perfect sense, Meg was to recall later. Holding Jenny by the waist, she thrust her into the stronglooking hands. Yes, he had her. It was all right. Meg let go.

Then the nightmare struck.

As Meg released her hold, the skiff drifted against the hull of another waiting boat. The collision was no more than a bump, but that, with Jenny's added weight, was enough to upset the young man's balance. Still clasping her, he toppled headfirst over the gunwale and into the water.

He sank momentarily, then came floundering to the surface. "Help!" he blubbered, churning the water. "Help! I can't swim!"

Suddenly, Meg could not see Jenny anywhere. Only her straw hat floated on the waves, bobbing up and down as the young man struggled to stay afloat.

"No!" Meg felt herself screaming. Her hands clawed at the strap that held her to the canvas chair, unable to release the tight buckle. "No! Jenny!"

Frantic, she flung herself one way, then another. The chair danced crazily with her motion, but she could not get free. Someone in the skiff had caught hold of the drowning man, but there was no Jenny—no Jenny anywhere.

Then, swiftly, there was the splash of another body hitting the water. Something flashed like a shark in the blue depths, and in the next instant Jenny was thrust to the surface. She was spitting and choking, her nose drizzling water, but she was alive. Alive!

Hands reached out from the boat to take her in. Meg felt tears streaming down her face. She breathed her thanks for that one person with the presence of mind to dive after Jenny, to push her up to the life-giving air before time ran out.

That one person. And suddenly Meg realized who Jenny's rescuer had been. She knew even before she looked down into the water where the swimmer had surfaced. She knew, even before her eyes found Hassan's wet, grinning face.

Jenny was sleeping, curled in a cocoon of satin quilts on the far side of Meg's bed. Her damp hair lay fanned on the pillow. Light from a flickering oil lamp pooled soft shadows on her face.

Earlier in the evening, the Emir's wives had tiptoed in to gaze at the slumbering child, to touch her hair and whisper over her beauty. Meg had met all three women on her arrival at the Emir's house, and warmed to them at once. Imposing, gray-haired Halima had been with the Emir since his youth. Aziza, of the dark, sad eyes, had woven the exquisite tapestries that hung throughout the house. Jehani, young, plump and quick to laugh, was the mother of two lively little boys. None of them spoke English, but their nuances of gesture and expression transcended the need for words. Meg had no fears about leaving Jenny in their care tomorrow while she went to the railway office.

Her shadow loomed on the stuccoed wall as she crossed the floor. It was late, and she was exhausted, but her taut nerves would not let her rest. Every time she paused in thought, her mind saw the dark water and Jenny's hat bobbing on the waves.

The ordeal was over, Meg soothed herself. She was tired, that was all, and worried about tomorrow. She needed something else to occupy her thoughts.

Her steamer trunk, which had arrived before dinner, sat locked in the middle of the floor. She would open it and do some needed rearranging, she resolved. Maybe by the time that was finished, she'd feel relaxed enough to sleep.

After rummaging for the key, she unlocked the trunk, raised the lid and began lifting out the hastily packed garments. She tried to keep her mind on the task, to concentrate on refolding each skirt, each waist, each chemise, and placing it in the appropriate pile on the rug. She was doing well enough until she remembered Arthur's letter.

He had slipped it into her hand as she and Jenny were boarding the *Horatius*. "Read this later," he'd whispered, his mustache prickling as he kissed her chastely on one cheek. "You can give me your answer when you return. I'll be counting the days."

The letter remained unopened.

Oh, Meg knew what it would say. She even knew what her answer would be. Arthur Tarrington-Leigh was a catch worthy of a duchess. A widower at forty-two, he was handsome, courtly and distinguished. He was liberal enough to tolerate Meg's independence, and he was wealthy—wealthy enough to provide a secure future and a place in society for Jenny.

So why had his letter lain untouched for the past five weeks?

It was a matter of rightness, Meg reasoned. In Britain, she'd kept all men, including Arthur, at proper arm's length. In this one thing her resolve had never wavered. She was a married woman, and she was determined that no scandal of that sort should touch her daughter.

Even the divorce—it was an ugly matter, but necessary. Only when she was no longer Cameron's wife would she feel free to open the letter and consider Arthur's proposal.

Meg stared at the sealed envelope, at her name, penned in Arthur's elegantly slanted hand. Arthur was a good man. She liked him. Maybe in time, she would even grow to love him.

She suddenly lost interest in unpacking the trunk. Jamming the letter deep into one side, she spun away and began to pace the flowered Persian carpet, her mind in turmoil.

What was troubling her? It couldn't be Arthur. Arthur was the answer to all her needs, and he was hers for the taking. All she had to do was sever her ties to a wastrel who had never loved her, and she'd be free to accept him. It was that simple.

At least it had been simple back home. Why not now?

Meg could not rest. She felt confined, the room suddenly too small, the walls too close. She felt a wild urge to be outdoors, where she could breathe and see the stars.

Jenny was sleeping soundly, one arm flung outward across the pillow. Meg paused to smooth back a lock of damp hair from her daughter's cheek. Then she stole from the room and closed the door softly behind her.

The Emir's house was a maze of chambers and courtyards, its whitewashed rooms laid with oriental carpets and hung with Aziza's rich tapestries. Its gardens overflowed with hibiscus, bougainvillea and slender date palms.

Meg's room opened onto a secluded patio with an orange tree and a tinkling fountain. She drifted toward the fountain now, cupped water in her hands and splashed its coolness on her throat.

The night was black and moonless. Stars lay like bits of shattered crystal against the velvet sky. An inland breeze whispered in the high palms, its perfume stirring the warm, dark air. Meg felt the sensual caress of its touch.

She unpinned her hair and shook it loose, feeling its weight down her back. She closed her eyes and took deep gulps of wind—wind that had ruffled the mane of a lion and blown the dust from an elephant wallow. She filled her lungs with Africa.

Cameron's Africa.

Meg sighed in defeat. All day she had been fighting Cameron, resisting every urge to remember him. Now she was too exhausted to resist any longer. Helplessly, like twigs in a current, her thoughts drifted back to that fateful summer, a time so remote it seemed like a dream.

She had loved Cameron then—had loved him, in fact, from the earliest stirrings of her childish passion. But he was already grown to a man's size, and she'd been far too young for him to notice. For years she had watched him, envying girls who were ripe enough to catch his eye, until one day she was sixteen, and it was her turn.

She had by no means planned it, that warm summer night, walking home late from a friend's house, deciding to take the isolated path that skirted the cove. She'd thought herself alone with the full moon and the black-rippled water until her ears caught the sound of splashing from below the rocks. Caution told her to run; but for all her quiet, bookish manner, there was a side of Meg's nature that ignored sensible warnings. That recklessness spurred her now, as she hiked up her skirts and began to scale the jutting rocks that screened the cove from the path.

Reaching the crest, she crouched low and peered down at the tideswept beach. Suddenly, her lips parted in wonder.

Cameron stood naked at the water's edge, moonlight flowing over the contours of a body that was sculpted like that of a Roman god.

Meg knew she should turn and run, but she was mesmerized by his astounding male beauty. Her teeth pressed into her lower lip as he bent to sluice the water from his skin. Each drop that remained gleamed with its own reflected moon as he straightened again to stand erect and motionless, staring out to sea.

Meg's breath came in shallow gasps. Her eyes caressed every inch of his body, tracing the outline of each muscle, the arch of his lean, straight back and the taut, curving moons of his buttocks. Something deep inside her had begin to throb with an ache so sweet it almost made her dizzy.

But even as she gazed at Cameron, Meg sensed his smoldering frustration. She knew that for years he'd wanted to leave Darlmoor, and that his stepfather would not hear of it. Now, as he stared toward the horizon, she could almost feel his trapped anger, and she knew that sooner or later that anger would explode. How soon, she wondered, before he lashed out at the hidebound world that held him prisoner? How soon before he bolted and vanished for good?

Cameron's shoulders rose and fell in a broken sigh. Slumping, he turned toward the beach where his clothes lay in a careless heap on the sand.

Meg had been staring at his back. Now, suddenly, she found herself looking squarely at his naked front.

There was no reason to be shocked, she told her benumbed mind. He looked like a photograph she had once glimpsed of Michelangelo's *David*, that was all. But she had never seen a man's body before, and her eyes could not stop staring . . .

She did not realize she had made a sound until he looked up and saw her.

With a grunt of surprise and a frantic splash, Cameron was back in the water. Now would be the time to run, Meg thought; but her legs might as well have been concrete pilings, driven into the ground.

Waist-deep in the swirling waves now, Cameron looked up at her and laughed. "By thunder, it's young Meg, the judge's bairn! What are you staring at? Haven't you ever seen a man before?"

Meg tried to think of a smart and witty retort, but her tongue felt as if it were glued to the roof of her mouth. She could not answer.

Cameron's reckless laughter echoed above the sound of the surf. "Well, don't just stand there gaping! It's a right fair night for a swim! Come on, lass, take off your clothes and join me!" Meg's cheeks flamed hot in the darkness. Oh, she knew his game. He was bluffing. He thought she was a silly child who would giggle and run away. But she wasn't a child at all. Why couldn't he see that?

"Well, what's it to be?" he taunted. "Are you coming in, or will you go on home so I can get out and get dressed?"

Slowly, Meg stood up. For years she had ached to have Cameron notice her. She had watched him, dreamed of him, spun endless romantic fantasies around his black curls and riveting cobalt eyes. She was damnably, miserably in love with him, and fate had finally given her a chance to do something about it.

Maybe the only chance she would ever have.

"What are you waiting for?" Cameron teased. "Come on, I dare you!"

She moved. Her feet found the path that led down from the rocks to the beach. As she walked, one trembling hand began undoing the buttons down the front of her waist....

Meg wrenched herself back to the present. It was over, she reminded herself. She was in Africa. She had traveled more than six thousand miles to undo what had begun that night.

Except it could never be fully undone, because that night had been the beginning of Jenny.

Leaving the dark garden, Meg tiptoed back inside and locked the door behind her. The bedroom was filled with the sound of Jenny's soft breathing, intermingled with little sucking sounds. Aching with tenderness, Meg leaned over the bed and tugged the wet, pink thumb from her daughter's mouth.

As she lingered, looking down, she felt a surge of fierce, hot mother-love, and she knew there was nothing she would not do for her child. She would fight, she would steal, even kill if it came to that. And she would marry Arthur Tarrington-Leigh.

But first things first, she reminded herself as she sank down on the foot of the bed and began to unfasten her high-topped shoes. Tomorrow she would go to the railway office and inquire about Cameron. With luck, he would be close by. If not . . .

Meg took a deep, sharp breath. She would find him, she resolved. If she had to trail Cameron MacKenna all the way across the Dark Continent, she would find him and do what had to be done.

She would do it for Jenny.

Chapter Two

The clerk behind the counter of the Uganda Railway office glanced up as Meg walked in. His ink-stained hands paused in shuffling a disorderly sheaf of papers.

"How may I help you, madam?" He peered at Meg over the wire rims of his spectacles. His straight, black hair and coffee-colored skin spoke of India, but his khakis and clipped haircut were Western. A pencil was thrust behind one ear.

Meg cleared her throat. "I'm looking for a man named Cameron MacKenna. I understand he works for the railway."

"MacKenna?" There was no spark of recognition in the clerk's jet-bead eyes, and Meg's heart sank. The rail line from Mombasa to Lake Victoria was a massive project, she knew; but most of the workers had been shipped here from Bombay. Surely a tall, blue-eyed Scot like Cameron would be remembered.

"What work does Mister MacKenna do?" the clerk asked.

"I don't exactly know. But you must have a record—"

He abandoned the sheaf of papers with a harried sigh. "All right, I can look. Are you a relative of Mr. MacKenna's?"

"He's..." Meg hesitated, then plunged ahead. "He's my husband. I have to find him. I've come all this way."

The clerk nodded brusquely and turned his back to rummage through a drawer full of files. Feeling awkward, Meg wandered away from the counter, sidestepped a turbaned Indian swabbing the tiles and paused before the survey maps that were tacked along one mildewed wall.

The maps showed the progress of the railway over the past four years, from Mombasa to the Tsavo River and up toward the Uganda border in a slanting, northwesterly line. Even on the most recent map, the tracks stretched little more than halfway to their goal.

Meg had followed articles in the *Times,* describing the incredible hardships—drought, disease, floods, even maneating lions—that had plagued construction of this "Lunatic Line." As life-loss figures crawled into the thousands, she'd shared Cameron's mother's relief in the arrival of each terse letter. Her estranged husband was not a man of many words, but at least Meg had known she wasn't a widow.

"Mrs. MacKenna." The clerk's tinny voice broke into her thoughts. "Your husband's record is here. He's part of the engineering division. That would likely put him at the railhead, somewhere near Machakos Road."

Meg stared at the map, her heart sinking. "But that's—"

"Yes. Almost three hundred fifty miles up the track."

Meg's mind had begun to spin. "You're sure that's where he is?"

"That is where he's assigned."

"And how often does he come back to Mombasa?"

The clerk flipped through the open file in his hands. "Mr. MacKenna's pay goes directly into his account in our bank. But I do not think he comes here often. Otherwise, I would certainly know him. I know most of the English by sight." He glanced up at Meg again, his eyes a little less impersonal than before. "We won't have a working telegraph until the next shipment of wire comes in. But the goods train will be leaving here tomorrow morning. You could send a letter. Surely if Mr. MacKenna knew his wife had arrived—"

"No!" Meg's protest was swift and vehement. Cameron, for reasons unknown, had ignored her solicitor's letters. If he got word she was in Mombasa, he might try to evade her, as well. Her only sure ally was surprise.

She strode back toward the counter. "I have to be on that train! If you'll be kind enough to sell me a ticket."

The clerk's face froze. "Quite impossible. We won't be taking passengers until the line is finished."

"But surely there'd be room."

"Please understand, madam. Tomorrow's train will carry supplies and workers, all on open flatcars. Even if we were to allow it, no Englishwoman could travel under such conditions."

"But—"

"And the camps, madam, you cannot imagine. Dust and tsetse flies, the water filthy to drink. And lions—lions everywhere. You have heard, no doubt, of the two man-eaters at Tsavo who devoured more than a hundred of our workers?"

"I understand both lions were shot last month," Meg answered coolly, remembering talk she'd heard at the customs house.

"Yes, but only those two. There are others."

"If you please, I would like to speak to your supervisor," Meg said.

The clerk shrugged. "As you wish. His office is up those stairs. But you are wasting your time, madam. You will only hear again what I have just told you." He returned to his task of sorting papers.

Meg strode toward the iron stairway, then hesitated with one foot on the bottom rung. The clerk was right. His supervisor would not help her, either. Worse, he might even warn Cameron that she was looking for him—men tended to stick together in such matters. There had to be another way.

Meg stepped out onto the veranda of the railway office, her mind churning. From where she stood, she could see the forbidden train. It lay along a siding at the far end of the depot, its string of flatcars already half-loaded. Indian coolies, wearing turbans and long cotton tunics called *kurtas,* lounged in the shade, idling away the time. At dawn tomorrow, they would board the train, wedging their bodies into spaces among the cargo for the ride to the railhead—the almighty railhead where no Englishwoman was allowed to go!

Petticoats swished beneath Meg's twill skirt as she strode down the platform. Somehow she had to be on that train. Her only other choice would be to wait for Cameron in Mombasa while her patience and her money trickled away to nothing.

The railway office was located at Kilindini, on the outer side of the island where a new deep-water harbor was being built. Meg had traveled the three-mile distance from old Mombasa by *gharri,* a two-seat trolley that was pushed along its narrow track by a pair of strapping Swahili youths. She'd planned to return the same way, but now she found herself too charged with nervous frustration to sit down.

It was too hot to trek back across the island on foot, especially in her best shoes. But she needed to think, and her thoughts flowed best when she was walking. She would explore the town, Meg decided. Maybe that would get her mind working.

Not that Kilindini was much of a town. The harbor itself was little more than high-piled raw timbers and sweaty workmen raising warehouse walls in the sweltering heat. Only the Indian bazaar that sprawled like a blight off one corner of the railway office held any promise of interest.

Holding her skirts above the dust, Meg meandered through the maze of open-air stalls arrayed with brassware, tin pots, straw mats, cheap cotton *'mericani* cloth, oranges, and sticky-looking sweetmeats that drew swarms of black flies. Spindly children peered at her with curious

chocolate eyes. A vendor thrust a jangling string of bracelets into her vision. Meg shook her head and moved on, lost
in thought.

Maybe the clerk had the right idea after all. Why
shouldn't Cameron come to Mombasa if he knew she was
here? He could have any one of a dozen reasons for not
having sent back the divorce papers, including the possibility that he'd never received them. Why should he avoid
her? Why should he refuse to set her free, when he'd never
wanted her in the first place?

If she had any sense, she would go back inside the railway office and write him a letter, or even send a copy of the
papers with the morning train.

But the soft voice of reason was already fading, drowned
out by a clamor of urgency. Meg had run out of patience.
She had to resolve things with Cameron once and for all,
and she had to do it now. She *had* to be on that train tomorrow morning.

Her gaze moved down the line of grubby little shops,
searching for something, a clue, an idea, lying like a missing key on the fringes of her awareness.

Suddenly, her plan fell into place. It would be the most
dangerous, daring thing she had ever done, but she knew
at once there was no other way.

Everything was arranged. Meg took the *gharri* back to
Mombasa and spent the rest of the day in a state of quiet
agitation, puttering around the bedroom, chatting with the
Emir and watching Jenny romp with Jehani's small sons.

Jenny had settled happily into the Emir's household. The
three women adored her, and the two little boys, delighted
to have a new playmate, had drawn her into running, gig-
gling games that needed no common language.

Even now, as the day cooled into twilight, Meg could see
them darting through the shadows, their laughter blending
with the chirp of crickets and the hum of cicadas. She
shifted restlessly on the marble bench where she sat. Jenny

would be all right, she reassured herself for perhaps the tenth time. The Emir would be here to speak with her in English; his wives would care for her; his sons would amuse her. And if any kind of danger threatened—yes, there would be Hassan.

Meg glimpsed Hassan now, keeping vigil from a doorway beyond the garden. His mouth slid into an unctuous grin as their eyes met, and she swiftly looked away. Hassan had saved her child's life—he had even rescued Jenny's soggy sun helmet. She was forever in his debt. But all the same, his darkly fawning gaze made her squirm inside.

The children had chased a pet monkey into one of the palms and were trying to coax it down with slices of mango. Meg heard the rustle of silk as the Emir sat down beside her. She turned and smiled at him.

"Jenny seems so happy here. Thank you again for letting me leave her with you tomorrow."

The old man settled his robes with a sigh. "Your daughter will be safe with us. Have no fear of that."

"I have none. But there's something I need to give you." Meg rummaged in her skirt pocket and drew out a sealed envelope. "It's a list of instructions—what to do, who to notify if anything happens to me—" She broke off, thinking she must sound like a fool. She had told the Emir she was leaving on the morning train, but he knew nothing about the circumstances. No one did, except for the Kilindini shopkeeper and his wife, who would help her carry out her scheme.

The Emir frowned. "Are you sure you want to undertake such a dangerous journey? It would be easy enough to send one of my servants."

"No, I've thought it all out. I have to find Cameron myself. It's the one sure way."

The old man's sigh was tinged with irony. "My dear young woman, there is no 'one sure way.'"

"You're trying to tell me I'm wrong?"

"Not wrong. Only very young. And young people think they have to bend life to their own wills. They shut themselves off from the possibilities of surprise."

Meg shot him a puzzled glance. "I've always thought it a good thing to be in charge of one's own destiny."

The Emir chuckled. "But who would want to be in charge? Life's unexpected twists and turns are so much richer than anything one would plan. It's the *unplanned* that makes us wise and strong—the *unplanned* that teaches us the true meaning of happiness."

"You're speaking in riddles."

"Am I? Look at my own life. Would I have planned the uprising that forced my family from power? Would I have planned to settle here in Mombasa, an exile from my homeland? Of course not. Yet, here I am, talking with you in this beautiful garden, and I feel, somehow, that both of us were meant to be here."

Meg nodded, comprehending, but still not agreeing. Life was what one made it. She watched as the monkey left its perch in the palm tree. Snatching a slice of mango, it bounded toward the kitchen, with Jenny and the boys in shrieking pursuit. Meg laughed. "And those two little bundles of mischief—did you plan them?"

"Oh, no indeed. Nor did I plan their mother. That is just my point. Of my three wives, only Halima was planned. Our marriage was arranged when we were no more than children."

"She's a lovely woman," Meg commented, picturing Halima's erect figure, rich gray hair and sharp, intelligent eyes.

"A dutiful wife, Halima. She gave me three daughters, married and gone now, and a son who died in war. But understand this, we are very different, Halima and I. She is my strong right arm, and I would not be parted from her, but ours has not been a passionate marriage." The Emir sighed deeply, his narrowed eyes fixed on the emerging stars. "Now, Aziza..."

"Aziza was not plánned?" Meg prodded gently.

"She was the daughter of a friend. I glimpsed her in his house, without her veil. Our eyes met, and we both went wild with love. I had to have her—our customs allow that, you see, and Halima did not object. Passion..." He fell into a dreamy silence, the memories flickering over his expressive face, but when he spoke again, his voice was tinged with sorrow.

"Seven times she conceived. Seven times her babies died at birth. The last time, Aziza nearly died, as well. After that, I resolved to spare her..." His words trailed off.

Meg remembered Aziza's tragic, dark eyes, remembered the exquisite tapestries that hung throughout the house. Yes, there was much she had not understood.

"And Jehani?"

"It was as you might guess. Not long after we had arrived in Mombasa, my two wives came to me. 'It's lonely here,' they said. 'The laughter of children is what this sad house needs.' And so, for all our sakes, I took Jehani. As you see..." The Emir's words ended in a contented sigh.

Meg smiled her affection for the old man. "It still doesn't make sense—not for me, at least. I know what I want for Jenny and for myself. And I know that I can't just wait for those things to come. I have to strike out and go after them."

The Emir nodded wisely. "As I said, you are very young."

"I do agree with you about one thing," she said, shifting to safer ground. "You've found a paradise here. Your house is beautiful."

"Thank you. I was fortunate to find it. The place was for sale at the time I arrived in Mombasa, its previous owner having been beheaded by order of Sultan Barghash in Zanzibar."

"Beheaded!" Meg gasped. "Whatever for?"

"Bad judgment, let us say. The man—Mustafa, his name was—had made his fortune in the slave trade. When the sultan and your British government signed the treaty declaring slavery illegal, Mustafa lacked the wisdom to obey the new laws. The sultan, I was told, chose to make an example of him.''

"Slavery." Meg felt as if a sinister shadow had invaded the night. It was hard to believe that with time moving into the twentieth century, there were still corners of the world where humans were rounded up and sold like animals. "Tell me, does it still go on?" she asked.

"Yes, I fear, though at greater risk. In the old days, slaves taken in the interior were marched to the coast and carried by sea to the markets at Zanzibar. But the treaty ended all that. Zanzibar's gone to the ivory trade, and the waters are patrolled for slave boats. That's how our friend Mustafa was caught, for which I have no regret. Not only did the rascal deserve his fate, but I acquired a fine house and a capable servant in the bargain."

"Servant?" Meg felt a prickle across the back of her neck.

"Hassan was Mustafa's majordomo. I kept him on as my bodyguard. He has long since proven his worth."

"Yes, I know." Meg remembered Hassan's flashing dive, and Jenny's golden head breaking the water's surface. Even now, the memory made her quake.

She fidgeted with her skirt, trying to put the incident out of her mind.

The Emir yawned wearily. "I hope you will excuse an old man who needs his rest."

"Of course." Meg rose with him. "I'll be leaving before dawn. I'll try not to wake anyone."

He had started to walk away, but he turned back toward her, his sharp profile etched against the lamplight. "Be careful," he said. "Do not tempt fate by taking foolish chances. If you change your mind—"

"My mind is made up. I have to do this."

"Then, child, may Allah protect you."

* * *

Machakos Road
February 27

The railhead camp lay like a blight on the yellow landscape, a teeming, dusty sprawl of tents, cookfires, lumber, thorn enclosures and rubbish heaps. Steel hammers rang out from beyond the rise, where the rails crawled their way across the high grassland. The morning air, still blessedly cool, carried the tang of coffee, woodsmoke and last night's stale curry.

Cameron, as always, had been up since first light with the work crews. Even now, he would have been at the gully where the track ended, supervising labor on the half-finished bridge; but the train was due in camp that morning with a cargo of supplies and fresh coolies. It would also be bringing more timbers for the bridge. He'd be needed here, to see to the unloading.

The train was late. Cameron strode restlessly to the edge of the camp. Hands thrust into his pockets, he gazed out across the rolling expanse of dry savanna, dotted with acacia and thornbush. A mile off, a herd of wildebeest flowed like a dark brown shadow across the plain. Far to the south, the dazzling cone of Mount Kilimanjaro rose against a sky of flawless blue.

The unclouded sky was good, Cameron noted. Every day without rain meant more track bed prepared, more sleepers laid, more rails hammered into place. If the bloody rains would just hold off until April—

His thoughts were shattered by the shriek of a train whistle. Shading his vision against the glare, he peered toward the horizon, where the squat, wood-burning locomotive with its short string of flatcars was toiling into sight. The wildebeest herd paused in its motion, then wheeled and melted into the pale distance.

Cameron strode back toward the tracks. By his own admission, he was an impatient man who fumed at delays, chafed at inaction and ground his teeth at the incompetence of others. He was happiest—if that was the word for it—when the work was forging ahead and he was in the thick of it, making things happen. Now, as the train hissed to a stop in front of him, he felt a prickle of anticipation. He pictured the massive timbers swinging into place, the bridge taking shape little by little.

A hundred or so Indian coolies had arrived with the train. They were clambering groggily to the ground, sore and exhausted after twenty-four hours of clinging to the rattling open flatcars. Cameron gave them a cursory appraisal. Most looked to be in decent condition. He'd give them a couple of hours to rest, eat and settle their gear. Then they would join the work crews at the end of the track.

The last two cars on the train carried the bridge timbers, roped and bolted into place. Cameron strode toward them, then stopped short as a slight, turbaned figure wriggled out of the space between two huge logs and dropped unsteadily to the ground. A boy, Cameron surmised, though the slender back was turned, hiding the face below the oversize turban. The lad looked to be about fourteen, and not very husky at that. Lord, why would they allow such a sprout on the train? Maybe he'd sneaked aboard, to be with a father or elder brother.

As Cameron stared, the youth tugged a battered rucksack from its hiding place and crept out of sight around the far side of the flatcar. Muttering, Cameron was about to start after him, when something else caught his eye.

It was Kumar Dass, the stonecutter's assistant, strutting like a cock between the tents. Kumar Dass, who that very morning had been too "sick" to get off his pallet for work call.

The lazy wretch needed a lesson, and it was Cameron's job to give it to him. Wheeling in his tracks, he charged after the malingering coolie. The boy, for now, would have to wait.

* * *

Meg leaned against the edge of a loaded flatcar, her legs wobbling like licorice strings. Her whole body throbbed from the long, bone-jarring ride. The brown stain the shopkeeper's wife had rubbed on her skin was splotched and smeared. Her scalp itched miserably beneath the tightly wound turban that covered her hair. But it was all right. She was here. She had made it safely to the railhead.

As far as she could tell, no one had seen her get off the train. But she knew she couldn't hide for long. Sooner or later her identity would be discovered. When that happened, she would have to be ready.

Meg glanced down at the baggy *kurta* that hid her tightly corseted curves. It wouldn't mean the end of the world, being found out now, she reminded herself. The coolie disguise had served its purpose. All she really needed to do now was find Cameron.

But where, in this sea of people, could he be? Forcing her cramped legs to walk, Meg wove her way through the swarm that milled around the train. Everywhere she looked, she saw turbans and brown faces. There were tall, proud Sikhs with bristling beards, hawk-faced Pathans and wiry Punjabis. There were even a few women in the crowd, draped in ragged saris, their jaded eyes smeared with kohl, their arms jangling cheap brass bracelets.

But Meg saw no one who looked like Cameron— no one, in fact, who even looked as if he might speak English. The knot of fear that had formed in her throat began to tighten.

Suddenly, over the heads of the crowd, her eyes caught sight of a tall, lean man in a khaki shirt and broad-brimmed *terai*. He was standing on the step of the locomotive, talking with the engineer. Meg stared at his back, her mouth dry. It had been so long; could this really be . . . ?

He turned and swung down from the step. No, Meg realized, her heart sinking, it wasn't Cameron, after all. This man was blond, with a thin face, prominent nose and watery eyes. But at least he looked as if he might speak English. She could talk to him. She could throw herself on his mercy and beg his help in finding her husband.

She plunged through the crowd. Surely the man would take pity on her. Surely he would—

She froze at the sound of a voice, coming from somewhere behind her, a voice raised in anger.

For the first few seconds, Meg could not move. Her ears strained for words, catching none. No matter, it was the voice that held her. The tone, the timbre, even the rage, jolted her memory. She had not heard that voice in four years, but even without thinking, she knew....

Trembling, she turned around.

There was no one in sight except the Indians she'd already seen. Beyond them, however, lay a row of tattered canvas tents. The voice was coming from somewhere on the other side.

Forgetting to breathe, Meg edged toward the sound. The tents were closely spaced. She slipped between two of them, stumbling over ropes and clutter. Suddenly, there he was.

He had not seen her. His back was turned, and he was dressing down a whimpering coolie, raging at the man in unintelligible phrases that Meg could only guess to be Hindustani. The coolie cowered like a dog, cringing, whining, all but rolling onto his back in submission.

Meg crouched alongside the tent, her heart hammering her ribs. She had yet to see his face, but there was no mistaking the broad shoulders straining against the threadbare khaki shirt, or the dark hair curling low on the back of the frayed collar.

The chastised coolie, still pleading for mercy, had begun to back away. At Cameron's snap of dismissal, he wheeled and scurried off in the direction of the railhead. Muttering angrily, Cameron swung back toward the tents. Only then did Meg see his face.

She stifled a gasp.

The right side was as she remembered—older, yes, and weathered by the sun; but that much did not surprise her.

No, it was the left side of Cameron's face that caused her to fall back against the tent, her knees unable to hold her.

A raking scar ran from Cameron's left temple to the center of his chin, skirting his eye and puckering the corner of his mouth into a hard, downward twist.

It was the cruelest-looking face Meg had ever seen.

Chapter Three

Cameron swung back toward the train, his anticipation soured by what he'd just had to do. Damn this bloody railroad, he groused. Damn the heat and the flies and the chigga bugs. Damn all malingering coolies, like the one he'd just caught and dressed down. And damn himself for not having given the sluggard worse than a tongue-lashing. With the push on to reach Nairobi before the rains, every fit man was needed to lay track. Those who hung back on flimsy pretenses made everybody's job harder. Kumar Dass was one of the worst offenders. This would have been a good time to make an example of him. Now that chance was gone.

Cameron glared after the departing coolie, then turned back toward the track. He'd see the timbers unloaded. Then he'd hotfoot it back to the gully before the work slowed down again. Any day now, the rains could come sweeping across the highlands, washing out bridges and making a quagmire of the track bed. The work would go on, yes, but at a miserably slow pace. Now, while the skies were clear and the earth still dry, was the time to drive the crews to their limits.

As he strode between the tents, he caught sight of a figure huddled among the gear. Cameron sighed irritably. He'd forgotten about that blasted boy from the train. Now here the little wretch was, crouched behind a big rope coil, as if he were trying to make himself invisible.

This time Cameron had a better view of him. The slim, effeminate youth looked as if he'd never swung a hammer in his life. Lord, why did they let these half-grown children on the train? He'd be doing this one a favor if he grabbed him by the scruff of the neck and tossed him back onto the train.

He was about to do just that when he heard shouts and glimpsed men running toward the tracks. Cameron swore under his breath. Only a fight would stir up that kind of excitement. He'd seen enough fights to know. He knew, too, that if somebody didn't stop it fast, the whole camp would be taking sides, and there'd be no peace for days.

Forgetting the boy again, he plunged into the open. He could see the antagonists now—two hulking Sikhs who'd hated each other for months. They were circling each other with drawn daggers, egged on by the swelling crowd.

Bowman, chief engineer on this part of the line, had jumped onto a flatcar and was barking orders to desist—orders that no one was hearing. Bowman was an Oxford graduate, but he didn't have the experience to handle this kind of trouble. Only one man in the camp did.

Cameron took a deep breath. Then he lowered his head and bulled his way into the crowd.

Meg huddled in the shadow of the tent, limp with relief. Cameron had not recognized her; but he would have in another second or two, and judging from his mood, their encounter would not have gone pleasantly.

She took a gulping breath and exhaled slowly, trying to calm her galloping pulse. She would have to reveal herself soon, she knew. But she needed a time of her own choosing, a time when she could feel some sense of control.

As Meg stumbled to her feet, an image of Cameron's face thrust into her mind, and once more her legs would not hold her. The scar... dear heaven, what horrible thing had happened to him? Why hadn't he told his mother, told anyone?

But it would be like Cameron not to tell, she reminded herself. And even if his appearance had shocked her, she couldn't allow herself to pity him. It would show in her eyes, and Cameron would know.

Steeling her resolve, Meg scrambled to her feet. The sounds from the track had risen to a roar. Caution warned her to stay clear, but she had come all this way to find Cameron. She could not afford to lose sight of him now.

Warily, she peered from between the tents. At first she could not see him at all. Then she caught a flashing glimpse of his dark, bare head above the swarm of turbans, and her heart stopped. Cameron had waded into the very center of the fray.

Without thought, Meg was running. Still clutching her bundle, she clambered atop a heap of broken sleepers and wood scraps piled near the track. The added height gave her a clear view of what was happening.

The two antagonists—huge, bewhiskered Sikhs—faced each other across the open circle, fists clutching long, curved daggers not unlike the one Hassan wore. Blood dribbled down the side of one man's face and oozed into his beard. The other man crouched low, red soaking the sleeve of his *kurta*. The hatred emanating from the two was so intense that even Meg could feel it, like heat from a raging bonfire.

Between them, alone and unarmed, stood Cameron. He was glancing from one to the other, speaking in a low, hard voice. Again, Meg could not understand his words, but she inferred from his tone and gestures and from the murderous glares of the two Sikhs, that he was grating out insults of the vilest sort, goading either of the two to fight him.

Meg's mouth had gone dry. Cameron was taller than the Sikhs, but not the equal of either in weight and bulk. He was facing two raging, armed brutes, with no weapon of his own.

She shifted her position on the woodpile to get a better view. Cameron had to be bluffing. Yes, that was his strategy. As long as neither man moved against him...

A gasp rose from the crowd as Cameron spat out another epithet. Now he'd gone too far. The Sikh with the wounded arm, forgot his antagonist and hurled himself at Cameron with a savage bellow, his blade glinting in the midmorning sun.

Cameron's fist shot out like a battering ram, catching the Sikh alongside the jaw. Knuckles cracked bone. The Sikh dropped his dagger. He reeled and fell backward, spitting blood and clutching a jaw that could only be broken.

The second man had sheathed his knife. He backed away, eyes bulging with fear, as Cameron turned on him. Meg's protest strangled in her throat. The fight was over. Wasn't that enough?

Cameron's blue eyes blazed with the coldest fury Meg had ever seen. The second Sikh was still pleading for mercy when Cameron's fist slammed into his midsection. The breath exploded out of him. He doubled over, gasping like a fish as he collapsed in the dust.

Without another look, Cameron turned and strode away. Subdued now, the spectators parted to let him pass. Meg felt a leaden sensation in the pit of her stomach. It was not so much because of what he'd done; clearly, the two Sikhs had deserved their hard lesson. No, it was the way he'd done it, with an icy deliberation that was nothing like the impulsive, hot-tempered Cameron she remembered.

Meg felt sick and lost.

She closed her eyes for a moment in an effort to focus her thoughts inward. It wouldn't do to get emotional, she reminded herself. All she needed was Cameron's signature on a piece of paper. Then she'd be gone from his life for good. What he'd become would no longer be her concern.

When she looked again, Cameron had reached the edge of the crowd. She was about to scramble down from the woodpile when she saw the man with the broken jaw lunge for his dagger. Suddenly, it was in his hand. His arm was poised to fling the blade at Cameron's departing back.

The cry ripped from Meg's throat before she could think. "Cameron! Look out!"

Cameron whipped around. Instinctively, he dived to the earth. The knife whistled above his head and thunked into the side of a telegraph pole, where it hung quivering.

Cameron was up and moving again. He crashed into the husky Sikh with angry force. Two crunching blows, three, and the man was down again, a bloodied, unconscious heap in the dust.

Breathing hard, Cameron turned and glanced up at the thin, blond Englishman, who stood on the flatcar. The Englishman nodded. "The blackguard will be no good here. Tell them to tie him up and throw him on the train."

Cameron growled an order at one of the onlookers. Someone appeared with a rope. Meg, who'd been gazing horrified at the scene, suddenly remembered her warning shout. She was in full view, still crouched atop the woodpile.

She shifted her weight and groped for a lower foothold. If she could get out of sight before he noticed her... But it was already too late. Cameron had turned toward the woodpile, fury still twitching across his ravaged face. And now he seemed to be looking directly at her.

No—she wasn't ready to face him! Not here! Not like this! Panic bursting inside her, Meg leapt off the back of the woodpile, stumbled and began to run.

Cameron squinted up into the bright sun, sweat trickling down his face. Maybe he was losing his mind. He could have sworn it was a woman's voice he'd heard warning him—a woman's voice, speaking English and calling him by name.

But that couldn't be. This was the middle of Africa, almost three hundred miles from nowhere. The only women in camp were a half-dozen Bombay whores who'd followed the men here and, providing they survived, would go home as rich as maharanis. Not one of them spoke a word of English. No one here spoke much except Bowman and his other assistant.

He suddenly caught sight of a figure sprinting away from the woodpile. Cameron cursed under his breath. It was that blasted boy again, the one he'd resolved to send packing for Mombasa. The greasy little rascal must have read his mind. Clearly, he was doing his best to get lost until the train left.

"You, boy! Stop!" Cameron bellowed in Hindustani. But the boy had already vanished into the space between two tents. Cameron plunged after him. Emerging on the other side, he glanced swiftly ahead. Aye, the young idiot was still running. He was headed straight for the boundary of the camp. If he didn't stop, he'd soon be out on the open plain, where he'd be hyena bait within the hour.

Cameron redoubled his speed. The boy had already gained open ground. Fifty yards ahead, Cameron could see his red turban bobbing above a ridge of long, yellow grass.

"*Stop!*" Cameron roared again, but he was out of breath himself, and again the boy ignored the command. A hot tide of exasperation welled up in Cameron as he plunged ahead.

The boy was nimble, but he seemed to be getting tired. Little by little, Cameron was gaining on him. He swore under his breath as he pounded closer. Before he was through, the young whelp was going to wish he'd never set foot in this camp.

The boy gave a high-pitched yelp as he stumbled over a rock. Closing the gap between them, Cameron made a flying lunge. His momentum sent them both tumbling into the grass.

"Hold still, damn you!" Cameron was too riled to bother with Hindustani. The body in his arms was all motion, twisting, struggling, arching. But somehow it didn't feel like a boy's body at all. His hands clutched the taut, inward curve of a corseted waist. The alarming softness of a breast brushed his palm. This was definitely no boy.

He sat up. "What the devil—?"

The words died in his throat. In the struggle, the red turban had come loose and fallen aside, releasing a mass of tawny hair. Cameron found himself looking down into a pair of startling violet eyes.

Maybe he was hallucinating, he told himself. In all his life, he'd only known one pair of eyes that color. And the last time he'd seen *those* eyes, they'd been glaring up at him from beneath a veil of limp ivory lace.

What was happening to him?

"Hello, Cameron."

The voice—still shy, but huskier than he remembered— jarred his senses. He blinked away the dots of light that filled his vision. Meg. Real. Warm. Solid. *Here.*

Cameron's head was spinning. None of this made sense. Meg didn't belong in Africa. She was part of that other world, the one he'd thrown off like the weight of a heavy cloak when he boarded the steamer for Mombasa.

Oh, he'd known that sooner or later he'd have to deal with having a wife. But, now? Here? The shock was like a blow from a cosmic fist.

Scrambling to his feet, Cameron squared his hands on his hips and assumed a bravado he did not feel.

"By thunder, it's young Meg, the judge's bairn," he declared in the same mocking tone he'd used that long-ago night on the beach. "What the blazes are you doing in that tomfool costume, spying on me?"

Meg struggled into a sitting position. Watching her now, Cameron found it hard to believe he could ever have taken her for a boy. Even in that idiotic disguise, there was nothing boyish about her. The baggy *kurta* could not quite hide the evidence of sensuous female curves. The face that scowled up at him, even beneath that ghastly brown paint, was every bit as pert as he remembered.

"Well, bairn, the least you can do is tell me what the blazes you're doing here!" he demanded.

Meg's chin lifted like a queen's. "I'm a bairn no longer, Cameron," she answered with icy dignity. "I've come on important business. Once it's done, I'll be on my way, and I'll never trouble you again."

Her words and manner sobered Cameron. He stretched out his arm in an unspoken offer to help her up. Meg hesitated, clutching her dusty rucksack as if it were precious. Then her left hand, its weight no more than a butterfly's, reached out to clasp his wrist. Her fingers were as cool and fine as porcelain against his skin—a sensation alien to his raw, rough existence. Aye, four years was a long time. They'd grown worlds apart since their wild coming together on the beach.

Still overwhelmed, Cameron gazed at her. Young Meg. How old would she be now? Twenty-one, or close to it. His child bride had grown up.

He glanced at the small, dye-stained hand. Something twisted inside him as noticed his mother's gold ring on the third finger. "I see you've stopped biting your nails," he commented wryly.

"I stopped a long time ago." Her hand lifted from his arm. Her head barely came past the middle of Cameron's chest, but he sensed that she was not intimidated. Even in that shabby coolie costume and ridiculous brown paint, there was a presence about her, a sheen of tempered steel in his Meg. But she was not *his* Meg, he reminded himself. She'd never really been his, not even then.

Her eyes, even in the glare of the sun, were a deep, cool purple, their centers as dark as English pansies. And they did not flinch, as most people's eyes did, when she looked into his face. Whatever she'd felt on seeing the scar, she hid it well.

She cleared her throat. "Cameron, there's something I need to discuss with you. If there's someplace where we could have some peace and quiet for a few minutes."

Something to discuss. Cameron glared down at her. Aye, she'd said she'd come on business.

But peace and quiet? Cameron thought of the dusty clutter in the tent he shared with Hal Cummings, Bowman's other assistant. No, that wouldn't do. Nor would anyplace else within the bounds of the noisy, squalid railway camp.

"Come on," he growled. "I'll pick up a rifle at the tent. Then we'll go find some shade."

He strode back toward the middle of the camp without another word. Meg hesitated, then followed him at a trot, taking two steps to his one. Cameron tried not to look back at her. Even in that ludicrous disguise there was something disconcerting about the swing of her legs and the way her breasts bounced against the thin fabric of the *kurta*. Even after four years, damn it, he was not immune to her. Little Mary Margaret, the judge's bairn. The mother of his child.

He was still thinking about his daughter when they stopped at the tent to retrieve the .450 Martini rifle that Cameron always carried outside the camp. He'd never quite been able to imagine himself as a father; the money he'd sent was as much as he felt he could do for the poor little mite. Still, he'd occasionally wondered what it would be like to have a small girl sitting on his knee, looking up at him with adoring eyes.

Adoring eyes? Hell, with a face like his, he'd probably scare her to death.

"How's little Jennifer Jane?" he asked casually. "My mother says she's as pretty as a new penny and twice as bright."

Meg had caught up with him at the tent. From there, he'd slowed his pace so she could walk alongside him. "Jenny's beautiful," she said softly. "Whatever else happened between us, Cameron, she's the one thing I've never regretted."

The one thing. Implying, of course, that she regretted everything else. "You don't have a photograph of her, do you?" he asked in a detached tone.

"No, I'm sorry. I should have thought of it. She's—" Meg bit off the rest of the sentence and lapsed into a sudden, awkward silence.

"She's what?"

"Nothing."

They'd passed beyond the camp's boundaries by now. The yellow plain, dotted with scrub and acacia, rolled before them like an ocean of grass, its vastness broken only by the misted outline of blue hills on the horizon. A herd of Thompson's gazelles drifted across the distant landscape, their black-striped sides flashing like beacons in the sunlight.

"What happened to your face?" she asked.

So that question, at least, was in the open. "Lion," he said. "At Tsavo, not quite a year ago."

Meg's breath caught. "How? It attacked you?"

"Not exactly. The other way around, in fact. The brute had broken into a tent at night and grabbed one of the coolies. The poor devil was screaming, and no one would help." Cameron shrugged. "I made the mistake of going to his rescue with nothing in my hands but a shovel. The lion finally dropped him and ran off, but not without getting a good swipe at me first."

Meg swallowed hard. Cameron had no trouble imagining what was going through her mind.

"And what happened to the coolie?" she asked weakly.

"Died the next day. The pain he was in, it would've been a mercy to let the bloody lion do the job. As it was, I came damned near to dying, too. There's nothing filthier than what's under a lion's claws. Infection put me in the hospital for a month."

A visible chill passed through her. "I'm sorry."

"It's done and past. Come on." He led the way to a fallen limb that lay in the mottled shade of a low-spreading thorn tree. After a pause to check the overhead branches for leopards, he motioned for her to sit.

A silence had fallen over Meg, and Cameron noticed that her eyes no longer met his. Still clutching her rucksack, she lowered herself gingerly onto the limb's far end.

Cameron took his seat a few feet away. Aye, he told himself, it was time to face up to things. Meg would not have come all this way for a simple chat. Whatever she wanted, it was bound to be unpleasant.

But then, what did he expect? He hadn't exactly done well by the poor girl. Lord knows, she couldn't have had an easy time of it, all alone after her father's death, and with a baby to raise. Maybe it would make things easier if he was the one to speak first.

"Meg, if it's more money you're needing, I can spare a little. I know I've not provided as well as I should have—"

"It's not money."

"No?" Something black stirred inside him, like a crocodile beneath the calm surface of a pool. "What, then?"

She stared at him, her eyes wide and startled. "You mean, you don't know?"

"You're talking in riddles. Don't know what?"

"You didn't get the papers from Edwin Parkhurst?"

"What bloody papers? And who is Edwin Parkhurst?"

Meg's brown-smeared face had taken on a look of desperation. "Edwin Parkhurst is . . . my solicitor."

The blackness stirred inside Cameron again, revealing glimpses of something he'd known all along. He'd known it, he realized, from the instant Meg said hello. What else would have brought her all this way? Not loneliness. Certainly not love.

"All right," he said quietly, "tell me about the papers."

She drew a sharp breath. "Cameron, I'm petitioning for divorce."

For a long, painful space, Cameron did not speak. His gaze wandered out over the shimmering plain to the dim, purple mountains. Aye, there it was, he thought. No more denials. No more evasive games. And why, after all, should he care? Had he ever loved little Mary Margaret Owen? Had he ever wanted their marriage?

He could feel Meg's eyes on him. She was waiting, braced for his response. He could hear the buzz of insects in the long, yellow grass. He could hear the ring of hammers from the distant railhead. To hell with it, he thought. To hell with everything.

Meg felt as if every drop of emotion had been wrung from her body. The worst was over, she told herself. She'd found Cameron. She'd told him. Now they could get on with whatever came next—if only he would look at her. If only he would say something. Even curses would be better than this leaden silence.

He was staring into the distance, with a lost, frustrated look that reminded her of the way he'd stared out to sea on that long-ago night. Even now, Meg found herself wanting to touch him, to brush the curve of his shoulder and smooth the dark hair at the nape of his neck, where it curled down over the frayed collar.

But what was she thinking? He was no longer hers to touch. Cameron had never been hers, not even then. She could do nothing except wait, and leave the next move to him.

After what seemed like an eternity, he stirred. Fumbling in the pocket of his khaki trousers, he fished out a rumpled handkerchief. "Here," he growled, thrusting it toward her. "You can wipe off that paint now."

Meg accepted the handkerchief numbly. "Cameron—"

"You've got no more reason to hide from me."

"Cameron, for heaven's sake..."

He drew in a hard breath and exhaled slowly, his broad chest rising and falling. "It's all right, Meg. I should've expected this sooner or later. It's no kind of marriage we've had. You need the freedom to go on, to make a decent life for yourself."

Meg felt a chill of relief. It was resolved, then. Cameron didn't care enough to fight her. All along, he'd never cared.

The silence between them was cold and heavy. "Then you really didn't get the papers from Edwin Parkhurst," she said, groping for a way to fill its emptiness. "If you had, I suppose, you'd have signed them, and sent them back."

"What else could I have done? Do you think I'd hold you against your will?" Cameron stared down at a dung beetle that was toiling to roll its burden through the grass at his feet. "When did your friend Parkhurst send the papers?"

"Almost a year ago—the ninth of March, it was—by registered post, of course."

"Meg, I'd have been in the hospital then, out of my mind with fever. The camp was moved twice, there were floods. It would've been a wonder if I *had* gotten the bloody papers!" Cameron's breath rasped impatiently, but when he spoke again, his voice was low, with only a slight edge. "You could have posted a second copy and saved yourself a trip."

Meg stared at the ground. Cameron was right. She could have made more efforts to contact him. In fact, she certainly should have. But when the original papers didn't come back...

Oh, what was the use lying to herself? She'd *wanted* to see Cameron again. She'd wanted to know his reason for not returning the papers. Well, now she knew.

"I have a copy right here," she said, touching her rucksack. "All I need is your signature. Then I'll be right back on that train."

Cameron cast her a black look. "You've got a pen? An inkpot? I'll sign right now," he growled.

"Of course I haven't. How much do you think I was able to pack?"

He stood up, the rifle swinging lightly from one hand. "There'll be pens and ink in Bowman's tent. The train should be pulling out in an hour or so. You'll have time for a decent meal first."

He'd begun to walk away, but he stopped abruptly and turned back to where Meg was still sitting. "I'll see that they let you ride to Mombasa in the engine, like a proper lady. But for that, you'll need to *look* like a proper lady. Where's that kerchief?"

Meg had been twisting Cameron's handkerchief around her fingers. Remembering now why he'd given it to her, she made a wad of it and began to scrub at the brown stain on her face.

He watched her a few seconds, scowling. "That won't do. You're just smearing it. Here—"

Two long strides carried him back to her. He propped the rifle against the tree. Then, taking the kerchief in one hand and lifting Meg's jaw with the other, he began to wipe the color from her skin.

Meg sat icily still, gazing up into his ravaged face with unflinching eyes. She would not tremble, she vowed as she willed her frantic pulse to be still. Whatever happened on the inside, she would not let him know that his appearance, or his nearness, had any effect on her.

Cameron's fingertips, bracing her chin, were as tough as rawhide, and he smelled like a working man, pungent with sweat. He plied the handkerchief with rough, downward strokes, pausing to moisten it every few seconds with the tip of his tongue. There was no gentleness in his touch, only the brusqueness of wanting to get the job done.

Meg willed her emotions to freeze, willed her eyes to see only the surface of him. Now that she was forced to stare straight into his face, she saw it as it was, the one side touched only by time and the burning African sun; the other with its terrible, raking scar. The two sides blended, forming a whole that, ironically enough, seemed to suit the person Cameron had become.

What would Jenny think of him? But, then, Cameron would not be meeting his daughter, Meg realized as the decision fell into place. She could not allow it, and for reasons that had nothing to do with his appearance. Back in camp, she'd watched Cameron batter two men into bloody submission with his ruthless fists. Jenny was too young, too tenderhearted, to be exposed to that kind of brutality.

"Shut your eyes," he grated.

"What?"

"You've got paint on your eyelids."

"Oh." Meg closed her eyes and felt the rough pressure of spit-dampened linen against her lids. Now that she could no longer see Cameron, the sense of his nearness was even more acute. She could feel a subtle pulse in his fingertips and hear breath rasping in and out of his chest. She could smell the salty man-warmth of his body. She steeled herself against feeling, against remembering . . .

"All done!" he growled. "Now stand up and unbutton your collar."

Meg's eyes shot open. Seeing their startled expression, he laughed roughly. "Your neck, dear lady, is as brown as a Masai's. Unless you'd prefer to leave it that way. . . ."

With a little huff of exasperation, she began fumbling with the wooden buttons of the high-necked *kurta*. There would be no need to unfasten it far—the shopkeeper's wife had only smeared the stain as low as her collarbone—but Meg's fingers were trembling, just as they'd trembled that night on the path to the cove. She could not undo so much as the first button.

"Here—" Cameron's big, callused fingers brushed her hand away. Meg stood like stone, her heart hammering as he bent closer to deal with the stubborn buttons. No, she hadn't anticipated this, his hair brushing her chin, his breath warm on her neck, her senses swimming in his warm male aroma. She could see the rise and fall of his shoulders through the sweat-soaked khaki shirt, and she realized her own breath was flowing in and out to the same rhythm.

Cameron, too, seemed to be having trouble with the buttons. He was sweating, uttering half-spoken curses under his breath as he twisted and tugged. Meg could sense the frustration building in him, a growing anger that had little to do with a few trivial wooden buttons. And she had seen what Cameron's anger could do.

Suddenly half-fearful, she twisted away from him. "It's all right," she muttered, seizing the handkerchief. "Here, I'll just wipe it myself for now." She began to rub furiously under her chin and around behind her ears. "There, does that look better?"

Cameron's only answer was a long, tense sigh. He bent and picked up the rifle. "Come on, let's get back to camp and find a pen," he said.

Meg kept silent pace with him. The sun blazed torridly through the thin upland air. She could see her shadow moving ahead of her along the ground—an unearthly outline cast by her frowzy, uncombed hair, which had half fallen from its pins. She felt hot, achy, dirty and itchy, and she probably looked even worse. Was it any wonder Cameron hadn't argued about signing the divorce document?

"One thing," he was saying. "The money for little Jenny. I know it isn't much, but I'd like to keep on sending it. It may be the only thing I can ever do for her."

"I'll put it where I've put the rest, into a special bank account for her schooling." Meg brushed a lock of hair out of her eyes. This didn't seem the time to mention Arthur Tarrington-Leigh, or the idea that if things went as planned, Jenny would never want for anything again.

It probably wasn't a good time, either, to ask Cameron what had become of his plans to make a fortune in the ivory trade. Here, in this squalid camp, with his ravaged face and worn, dusty clothes, Cameron had the look of a man who had long since lost sight of his dreams.

They had come into the camp again, a more settled place now, with people going about their business as if the fight between the two Sikhs had never happened. Those coolies who were off shift dozed in the shade or bickered over cards and *pachisi.* Haunches of meat sizzled over the cooking fires. The train sat empty on its track, deserted by its crew and passengers.

The tall, bony Englishman Meg had seen earlier came trotting toward them, his watery eyes blinking incredulously. "By Jove," he muttered over and over. "By Jove, what's this, MacKenna? You've been holding out on us!"

Cameron sighed wearily. "Meg, I'd like to present Anthony Bowman, chief engineer. Bowman, this is...my wife."

"By Jove!" Ignoring Meg's costume, Bowman swept off his *terai* and bobbed gallantly over her hand. His khakis were immaculately creased, his thinning hair carefully combed over the bald spot at the crown of his head. "I'll confess to being surprised. Your husband doesn't talk much about himself. I didn't even know he *had* a wife! So you've come to pay your husband a visit, have you, Mrs. Mac-Kenna?"

Meg smiled, feigning an ease she did not feel. "I'm only here on business, I'm afraid. When that train pulls out, I'll have to be on it."

"Which I understand will be within the hour," Cameron interjected brusquely.

"Within the hour?" Bowman's thin, homely face suddenly brightened. "Not this time—say, you two are in luck! The crew wants to stay for some early-morning bird-shooting. They won't be taking the train out till late tomorrow morning. You'll have the night here together!"

Meg felt Cameron stiffen beside her. "We hadn't made any plans..." he began awkwardly.

"Now, there'll be no arguing!" Bowman's voice carried the proper tone of magnanimity. "MacKenna, you and your wife can have my tent for the night. I'll bunk in your tent with Cummings."

Meg felt the color flooding her face. "Oh, but we couldn't put you out—"

"Nonsense! You've got to sleep someplace, dear lady!
Mine is the only clean tent in the camp. And incident-
ly..." Bowman paused before dangling the pièce d'résist-
ance. "I've also got the only genuine copper bathtub this
side of Mombasa!"

"Oh," Meg breathed. The idea of a bath sounded like
heaven, but no, things were moving out of her control.

"I don't feel right about your going to so much trouble,
Mr. Bowman," she protested. "Surely I could sleep on the
train...." Her words trailed off uncertainly. Bowman
wouldn't know, of course, about her relationship with
Cameron. He was offering his tent out of politeness, on the
assumption that a man and wife, long separated, would
want to spend the night together. But to Meg, the idea of a
night alone with Cameron was enough to send her into
flights of panic. Anywhere, even the open bush, would be
preferable to—

Cameron's gruff voice broke into her thoughts. "The
train wouldn't be safe. It's too unprotected. Bowman, your
offer's right generous. Much as we dislike putting you out,
it's the only sensible choice. We accept."

Meg's heart lurched against her ribs. "But we can't
just—"

"Now, Meg, darlin'," Cameron laid a familiar hand on
her shoulder. His fingers gripped hard, but his voice oozed
honey. "Look, sweetheart, would you rather squeeze into
a dirty little tent between Cummings and myself? Bowman
here has made us a very kind proposition. The way I see it,
we've no choice except to take advantage of his hospitality."

"Your husband's quite right, Mrs. MacKenna," Bowman insisted. "And I guarantee you wouldn't like bunking
with Cummings. The chap snores like a bull rhino!" He
chuckled at his own joke.

"Oh...very well." Meg gulped back her indignation. She
was cornered, and she knew it. She shot Cameron a barbed
glance. If he so much as touched her— But then, he

wouldn't, she reminded herself. He was only putting on a facade for Bowman and the other men. Beyond that, he didn't care. He'd never cared about her; she'd known that much all along.

"Well, then, it's settled!" Bowman declared. "I'll just get a few of my things out, and then the place will be—"

He broke off as another Englishman, this one squat and bandy-legged with a sooty growth of beard, arrived panting from the direction of the railhead.

"Blimey, MacKenna, you'd better get t' the bridge! They was swingin' up one o' them big timbers an' the bloody tackle line snapped. The wood's in pieces, Pooram Singh's got a broken leg, an' the Jemadar's ready t' murder the tackle boys. I tried to calm 'im down, but 'e'll only listen t' you!"

Cameron sighed. "All right, Cummings, I'm on my way." He turned to Bowman. "Coming?"

"I'll get your wife settled in first, then I'll be right along. But you'd best get up there, MacKenna, before things get any worse."

Meg felt a sudden rush of urgency. "Cameron, the papers—"

"They'll have to wait!" He wheeled without another look and was gone, sprinting off along the tracks to where the rail line disappeared over a yellow rise.

As Meg watched him go, she could feel the uncertainty building inside her. Everything had seemed so simple out there on the plain when Cameron had agreed to the divorce. Now, suddenly, the whole situation seemed to be slipping out of her control, and there was nothing she could do about it. It was as if some hidden force had snatched up her carefully laid plans and was scattering them like dry leaves to the wind.

Cameron raced along the track, concerned about the accident at the bridge, but grateful, too, for the reprieve. Seeing Meg again had churned up a maelstrom of emotions inside him. He needed time to come to terms with what was happening, to sort things out for himself, away from those cursed, recriminating purple eyes of hers.

Damn her, he thought. If she'd contacted him about her plans, he would have been all right. He'd have had time to accept the news, without this gut-wrenching shock. But with her showing up like this—Lord, he was reeling. He felt as if he'd been kicked in the side of the head.

But what else could he have expected, Cameron asked himself. He'd behaved like an ass when Meg had told him she was with child, and he'd not behaved much better at the wedding. Then he hadn't written to her, not even once, in four years. If he was in pain now, he had no one to blame but himself.

Oh, he'd always meant to write sooner or later, in spite of what old Judge Owen had told him. At first, it had been anger that held him back. Later, it had simply been a matter of not knowing how to begin. More recently still, it had been his accident— and the dawning awareness that the fortune he'd dreamed of finding in Africa was a will-o'-the-wisp. He had nothing to offer Meg or any other woman.

For a time, he'd hoped that the money he was sending—not much, but all he could spare—would open doors between them. He should have known it would not. Women needed more than money. They needed words. And even now, Cameron had no words to give.

He strode down the hill toward the bridge site, his thoughts still churning. What had possessed him back there, putting on that idiot performance for Bowman? Meg would probably be ready to fend him off with a pistol by the time he got back to the tent. Well, he would spare her the trouble. He'd sign the bloody divorce papers and then find an excuse to take himself somewhere else for the rest of the night.

Work at the railhead had come to a halt. The massive timber lay splintered in the dry wash bed. The injured man, an excellent worker, was moaning on the ground, his leg bound by a makeshift splint. Cameron felt the tension in the air; he could see that the tackle crew and the carpenters were on the verge of coming to blows.

He strode calmly into the explosive situation, assessing the damage, growling orders. Before long, things were moving again. A stretcher was improvised with poles and clothing. The carpenters were sent off to find another suitable timber, the tackle boys to fetch fresh rope.

Crises like this one were all in a day's work for Cameron. He had trained as a surveyor, but his employers were quick to discover that his greatest strength lay in managing the Indian work crews. He'd learned both Hindustani and Swahili with a facility that amazed even himself. And he seemed to know instinctively which situations called for tact and diplomacy and which ones demanded action. His reputation as a troubleshooter had spread up and down the line. Supervisors like Bowman, a brilliant engineer, but too fastidious to get his hands dirty, had come to rely on him.

Now Cameron hurled himself into the work of replacing the broken timber. The burning sun hammered his bare head as he labored alongside the coolies; sweat drizzled down his body, salting the shirt to his back. Dust caked his face, arms and hair. Once the huge log grated over the end of his finger. He cursed but kept on pulling. The pain was trivial compared to what he was feeling inside.

Forget her, he lashed himself as he strained his raw flesh against the ropes. *Sign the bloody papers and let her go. She's probably got some fancy man waiting back in Britain. Why else would she come all the way out here?*

The sun crawled across the sky. Bowman came and went. The tackle slipped and sent the new log careering into the wash. Cameron was there to drag it up the slope, to adjust the rigging, to see it swung, at last, into its place.

By then the sun had settled behind the dark horizon, leaving a vermilion sky in its wake. Grimy and exhausted, Cameron abandoned the work and trudged back down the track with the others. Aye, he'd put things off as long as he could. Meg would be waiting, and he would have to deal with her.

The camp blazed with cook fires, where men squatted in circles, eating and smoking. The flickering light of oil lamps danced against canvas walls. Cameron went first to his own tent. Raising the flap, he saw Cummings stretched out on the far bunk. His own side of the tent had been cleared out and swept, the cot made up with clean sheets.

Cummings grinned. "Blimey, what you doin' 'ere, MacKenna? Bowman's already moved your gear to 'is tent, an' your wife's waitin' for you there. If I was you, an' she was mine, I wouldn't be wastin' any—"

Cameron jerked the flap down again, cutting off the sight of the little cockney's leering face. He sighed raggedly as he turned toward Bowman's large, new tent. He'd be happier walking into a leopard's den, he told himself; but it made no sense to put off the confrontation any longer.

Bowman was nowhere in sight. The flaps of his tent were tightly closed, but Cameron could see the flicker of light through a thin gap along the ground. Aye, she would be there.

He hesitated. From all sides he felt the knowing stares of male eyes through the twilight. Cameron cursed under his breath. Then, steeling himself, he separated the flaps and slipped inside.

He heard a gasp, then Meg's icy voice. "The least you could do, Cameron, is announce yourself!"

He blinked for an instant, dazzled by the light. Then he saw her. She was curled in Bowman's big copper tub, her shoulders bare and glowing. Soapy water, gilded by lantern light, rippled around the rich satin curves of her breasts.

Chapter Four

The water, pleasantly warm an instant before, suddenly chilled Meg's skin. She sat shivering, trying to appear calm while Cameron's raw gaze raked over her bare shoulders.

At first, he'd only appeared startled. But, now, his mouth had taken on a hard set that had nothing to do with the scar. His blue eyes glittered with annoyance.

"All right, Meg," he grated. "Suppose you tell me what kind of game you're playing!"

"Game?" Meg tried to sound detached, but a quiver in her voice betrayed her. "I don't know what you're talking about."

"The devil you don't. First, you show up with divorce papers. Now, I walk in here and find you naked as a sea-siren."

"Oh!" Meg's indignant gasp cut him off. She sat bolt upright in the copper bathtub. "Of all the presumptuous ideas—" she sputtered. "Cameron MacKenna, if you think I'd try to *seduce* you—"

His gaze dropped, then jerked perceptibly upward again. Meg glanced down and realized her bare breasts had emerged from the water. Soap bubbles were dripping from the raspberry points of her nipples. Color stained her face as she shrank back into the suds. She glared at him, wishing she could dissolve and disappear. Cameron might be her lawful husband, but she was unused to having *any* man see her like this. And as for her having arranged it . . .

"You've had all day to bathe," he growled. "Why now?"

"Do you think I planned your walking in on me like this? I'd have settled for a sponge bath, but your well-meaning friend Mr. Bowman insisted I take advantage of his tub. When I accepted, I didn't realize it would take the rest of the afternoon for the coolies to carry the water and strain it and heat it—"

"Strain it? Heat it?" Cameron exclaimed. "This is Africa, woman! Do you have any idea how precious that much water is?"

Meg made an elaborate show of soaping the washcloth and dribbling suds along her left arm. What she'd told Cameron was true. But she could see that in his present state, the truth made no difference. Her only defense against his hostility now was to pretend she didn't care.

"I thought it a very gracious gesture on Mr. Bowman's part," she said lightly. "And if you don't like it, Cameron, you're certainly welcome to leave. In truth, I wish you *would* leave. I'm accustomed to bathing in private."

Cameron wheeled away from her, muttering, and took a step toward the lowered tent flap. Then, abruptly, he halted, cursed and turned back toward her.

"What's the matter now?" she asked.

He glowered at her in mute frustration, and Meg sighed her understanding. Scores of eyes had watched Cameron step into that tent. For him to come slinking out moments later, tail between his legs, would cause a loss of face with the men, something his male pride would never allow.

Meg sighed. "Stay, then. Just don't stand there looking at me like that. Look somewhere else."

For a moment, Cameron did not move. Then he rumbled low in his throat and turned his back on her, to glower at the brown canvas wall.

Meg scrunched down in the tub until the soapy water came up to her chin. She would have given anything to be back in Mombasa with Jenny, or better yet, back in Darlmoor, safe in her own room. But she had to look on the bright side, she told herself. She'd found Cameron. He'd agreed to sign the papers. Everything she'd set out to achieve was within her reach.

All she had to do was share this miserable tent with him for one night. One single night, that was all. Then she would be free.

Cameron prowled the confined space like a caged animal. He tried to keep his eyes averted, his thoughts elsewhere, but it was no use. Even behind his back, Meg's image swam in his senses like a delectable pink mirage.

He could hear the tinkle of water as she dipped the washcloth, the satiny shift of her bare buttocks against the tub's copper bottom. And she was humming under her breath, some maddeningly half-remembered ditty that his ears could not quite catch. The scent of Bowman's finemilled English soap, innocuous enough on its owner, was spicily seductive where it lathered on Meg's slick, wet skin.

Seductive? Blast her, what was he thinking? The woman had come here to divorce him. Cameron mentally shrugged. Sign the papers, then; what difference did it make? Damn all women, anyway!

His gaze darted about the tent. Bowman usually kept his writing supplies on the camp table that stood in one corner. Incredibly, they were gone.

"Where the devil—?"

Meg's humming stopped. "The pen and ink?" she asked with the innocence of a stage ingenue. "Your friend Bowman took them. He said he had some letters to write." There was a long, quiet pause. "Cameron, why don't we just tell him the truth? It would make everything simpler."

"The truth," Cameron growled, "is none of Bowman's business, or anybody else's."

"Your manly pride is worth that much?" Her voice was as brittle as thin ice.

"Damn it, Meg." Bursting with frustration, he jerked around to face her. She was leaning forward in the tub, her shoulders gleaming where they emerged from the soapy water. Her lion-colored hair was pinned atop her head, with loose tendrils curling damply around her small, scrubbed face. Her eyes, the irises blazing purple in the lamplight, met his gaze in open defiance.

A gentleman would have kept his back turned, Cameron reminded himself sardonically. But then, he was no gentleman, and Meg, for all her airs, was no lady. He, of all people, ought to know that. He'd seen her cavorting buck-naked in the surf the night their child was conceived. Lord knew how many had seen her that way since, but in any case, he'd be damned if he was going to treat her like Queen Victoria.

He glared at her. "I'm the one who has to work here. You want my signature on those papers, fine, you'll get it. But it's to be private, you hear? Between you and me."

"All right." Meg leaned back in the tub with a resigned shrug. The tops of her breasts gleamed like two ripe pears above the bubbles. "As long as we're stuck here, then, we may as well be civil with each other. Bowman's expecting us to join him for dinner. He'll send a boy to tell us when it's ready."

"Decent chap, Bowman," Cameron muttered, turning away from her again. The bunk, he noticed, was laid out with the clothes she'd brought in her rucksack. There was a white waist with a high, lace-trimmed collar, and a tan twill skirt with matching jacket. Proper costume, Cameron supposed, for the lady traveling to Africa to get rid of an inconvenient husband. His eyes flicked over the sturdy walking boots and thick, brown stockings, deliberately avoiding the cream-colored, satin corset cover, the lace-edged camisole and drawers.

"Maybe—" The word stuck in his throat. Cameron swallowed and tried again. "Maybe you ought to be getting dressed, since Bowman's expecting us for dinner."

A shadow of hesitancy flashed across Meg's face, but she masked it with a shrug and a quick laugh. "Why, yes, I suppose I should. If you'd be so kind as to hand me that towel, Cameron, and after that—yes, I really must ask you to turn your back."

Annoyed by her flippancy, he flung the white Turkish towel at her outstretched hand. "Aye, turn my back and think of England. You're still my wife, Mary Margaret, and you've nothing I haven't seen, unless you've gone and gotten yourself a bloody tattoo on your—"

Meg's eyes widened sharply. Something flickered in their violet depths—something fragile and wounded that was gone almost before Cameron saw it. Then her glance dropped to the water, and when she looked up at him again, her face had taken on the closed, stubborn expression he remembered from the day of their wedding.

"Cameron, I won't have that kind of talk, and I won't have you leering at me," she said in a small, cold voice. "Either you turn your back, and keep it turned, or I shall stay right here in the water until you leave."

Cameron turned his back. As he glared at a hole in the brown canvas wall, his breath eased out in a long, exasperated sigh. In truth, he was more angry with himself than with Meg. The idea that he'd be brute enough to make her get out of the tub with him watching—hell, it had never entered his mind until he'd blurted it out. But Meg didn't know that. She probably thought he was a lecherous beast.

Well, let her think what she bloody well pleased. Tomorrow she'd be on the train with his signature on her precious divorce papers, and she'd never have to set eyes on him again.

The gleam of a whisky bottle, left on the table with two clean glasses, caught Cameron's restless gaze. Aye, that would be Bowman's doing again. There was no wine to be had out here; it tended to go bad in the heat. But at least the chap had done his best to be a good host. Meg didn't appear to have touched the whisky, and probably wouldn't, but by damn, Cameron thought, *he* would. Usually, liquor was something he could take or leave, but if he'd ever needed a drink in his life, it was now.

He edged sideways toward the bottle, keeping his face carefully averted from Meg's direction. A scant three paces behind him, he could hear trickling sounds as she stepped out of the bathtub. The fragrance of her damp skin crept around him like a warm, mauve blanket. Cameron's thoughts swam into unbidden images of water jewelling on her breasts and sluicing down her bare thighs to trickle into puddles around her toes. He could feel the respondent heat-surge in his loins, the maddening strain at the crotch of his khakis.

If he were to turn around right now . . .

Damn the woman!

His fumbling hands found the glass and the bottle. He poured himself a finger of the amber liquid and swallowed it in a single gulp. The whisky burned its way down his throat, making Cameron's eyes water and shocking him back to his senses. He'd need steel nerves and an iron will to get through this night without touching Meg, but he had to try. Weakening would buy him nothing but humiliation.

She was struggling into her clothes now. Cameron could hear the rustle of fabric, the subtle click of hooks and buttons, the soft, feminine grunts as she fastened her corset. He stared down at the empty whiskey glass in his hand, hesitated, then jammed the stopper into the bottle and replaced it, with the glass, on the table. It would be a fit night to get roaring drunk, but he would spare Meg that, at least.

Not that it would make much difference, Cameron mused bitterly. Drunk or sober, this night was bound to be one of the longest of his life.

* * *

Dinner promised a welcome respite from the tension-fraught evening. Bowman had set up a table between the tents, within sight and warmth of a crackling fire. Four camp stools served as chairs. The meal of spit-roasted topi, rice, tinned beans and Indian *chupatti* bread was plain but appetizing in the night-cooled upland air.

Meg had eaten as ravenously as her tightly laced corset would allow. Everyone, in fact, had been too hungry for much conversation during the meal. But now it was finished. The cook boys were clearing away the plates. The men, Cameron, Bowman and Cummings, were sipping warm beer out of battered tin cups. Meg had asked for, and gotten, tea. She swallowed it cautiously. It was no longer hot, but at least she could hope the water had been strained and boiled.

Outside the orange ring of firelight, the camp was settling into quiet. A solitary mule—Bowman's—stirred and nickered within its *boma,* a protecting enclosure built of thornbushes piled higher than a man could reach. Bowman had mentioned that back down the line at Tsavo, the men, too, had slept inside *bomas.* Even then, the determined lions had found their way through the thorns to wreak havoc and terror.

Here on the game-rich plain, however, no one seemed worried. Coolies smoked and dreamed by the light of their own fires or huddled over cards and pachisi. From somewhere beyond the tents, a woman laughed. Meg remembered the jangling bracelets and kohled eyes. She wondered if Cameron had ever...

But that made no difference. Not anymore.

She took another sip of the lukewarm tea, closed her eyes and tried to float her awareness outside the camp's squalid boundaries and into the shadowy darkness beyond. Her ears picked up the whine of insects in the long grass and, farther off, a yelp that might have been a jackal or a hyena, followed by a crescendo of ominous grunts that made the hair rise on the back of her neck. The night tingled with mystery and danger, and Meg was suddenly grateful for the camp's protecting circle and the bright, warm fire. She thought of Jenny, tucked safely away in the Emir's house. Tomorrow, she thought. Tomorrow the train would start back for Mombasa. Soon they would be together again.

She opened her eyes to see Cameron staring morosely into his tin cup. Cummings had fallen into a doze, chin on his chest. Across the table, Anthony Bowman leaned back in his seat, regarding her pleasantly.

"I still can't believe a lady like you would smuggle herself on to that train disguised as a coolie," he said with a conversational smile. "You must have been extremely anxious to see your husband, Mrs. MacKenna."

"Oh, yes. Yes, indeed I was," Meg murmured, aware that Cameron's gaze had shifted, and he was now watching her intently.

"If you'd sent word, he could have met you in Mombasa," Bowman said. "It's true, we're hard-pressed here, but under the circumstances, I would certainly have let him go for a few days."

Meg forced herself to smile sweetly. "That's very kind of you, but I did want to surprise him."

Bowman glanced at Cameron. "The offer's still open, MacKenna. You could take the morning train back to Mombasa with your wife. That would give you a couple of days together before the return trip."

Cameron swiftly shook his head. "You'll be needing me at the bridge. And my going wouldn't sit right with the men, not when I've pounded it into them that we need every hand."

"But surely once the bridge is done, you could be spared," Bowman persisted doggedly. "Mrs. MacKenna, you could find quarters in Mombasa until—"

"No, really, it's not possible. I can't stay in Africa." Meg felt herself crumbling under Bowman's barrage of polite intentions. Her eyes darted toward Cameron in a silent plea.

Bowman blinked. "My dear lady! You can't mean that you've come all this way to spend one night with your husband!"

Cameron's fingers toyed with the tin mug. His face wore an expression of sardonic amusement. "It's not that simple, old chap. Meg's come on a matter of urgent, private business. And much as we'd enjoy more time together, she's got to be getting home as soon as it's done. We have a young daughter, you see, left behind with friends—"

"A daughter!" Bowman exclaimed. "Good heavens, MacKenna, what a secretive fellow you are! First a beautiful wife, now a child! How old is the little nipper?"

Firelight glowed devilishly on Cameron's scars. "Not quite four. And quite the little beauty herself, or so Meg tells me."

"You didn't bring a photograph, Mrs. MacKenna?"

"I'm afraid not." Meg stared into the amber depths of her tea, weighing the strain of the conversation against the ominous prospect of going back to the tent. She hadn't exactly lied about Jenny's being in Africa. But then, she hadn't corrected Cameron's assumption, either. The dark seed of deceit had been planted, and was taking root. If she didn't pluck it out now . . .

But she was only protecting her daughter, Meg reminded herself. If he knew the truth, Cameron might insist on seeing his child. And Jenny, with her tender, impressionable mind, would carry her father's brutish image with her for the rest of her life. That image would color her perception of who she was.

No, it wouldn't do. It wouldn't do at all.

Meg glanced covertly at Cameron, trying to reconcile what she saw with the restless young man she'd loved in that faraway world. She remembered their wedding day, when he'd rescued a fallen sparrow from between the pews, cradled it in his hand and set it free outside the church. What had happened to that gentleness? Where had it gone?

It wasn't simply his appearance that troubled her. Cameron had come by his wounds bravely enough. No, it was the man *behind* that face. It was the poison he seemed to carry inside himself, as if those vile claws had ripped to the core of his being and festered in his soul.

He was sitting now with his elbows on the table, gazing toward the fire as he listened to a story about Bowman's college days. He'd splashed a little of Meg's bathwater on his face and slicked back his hair, but his jaw was dark with stubble, and his khakis were dust-grimed from the day's work.

Even now, Meg could not look at him without having to suppress a shiver. If she'd met this man as a stranger, alone on some dark street, she realized, she would have gone cold with fear.

Bowman had finished his story, a humorous incident involving the Oxford rowing team. Meg laughed politely, though, in truth, she'd been too distracted to listen. Cameron drained his tin mug and set it on the table with a metallic clunk. The sound jarred Cummings awake. The scruffy little cockney blinked and yawned. Then he quaffed his own beer, belched lightly and wiped his mouth on his sleeve.

"W'ot say we turn in, eh? Bloody sun'll be up early as ever t'morra an' just as 'ot."

As if by common consent, his words signaled an end to the gathering. Meg rose, steeling herself to endure the rest of the night. Bowman and Cummings stood up at the same time, and finally Cameron, too, eased himself off the camp stool.

"It's been a pleasure, truly, Mrs. MacKenna." Bowman nodded his acknowledgement to Meg's thanks. "If there's anything further I can do—"

"Oh, you've done more than enough, old fellow," Cameron muttered, covering a yawn that Meg could have sworn was faked. "We'll take it from here."

"'Evenin', mum. Sleep well, now." Cummings quirked a sandy eyebrow in Cameron's direction, and Meg's face flared hot. For all she knew, every man in the camp would be imagining the goings-on inside Bowman's tent tonight. Well, let them! They would all be wrong!

"Coming, Meg, darlin'?" Cameron offered his arm with a mocking smile. Not wanting to cause more talk, Meg laid a hand on his sleeve and let him guide her back through the maze of the camp to Bowman's tent. She held her head high, conscious of the knowing eyes that watched from the shadows. Never mind. Tomorrow it would all be over. Tomorrow she'd be on her way back to Mombasa with the signed divorce papers in her pocket, mission accomplished.

The tent was dark. Cameron raised the flap, waiting as Meg hesitated, then squared her shoulders and strode inside.

"Oh—" She yelped with pain as her knee banged something solid. She'd forgotten about the tub, still filled with water. She stumbled to the edge of the bunk and sank onto one corner.

"You're all right?"

"Yes. Only that blasted tub. It's taking up most of the floor space. Maybe you could push it outside and empty it."

Cameron's laughter pierced the darkness like a blade. "Push it out and empty it? All that lovely, precious water? Why, Mary Margaret, darlin', I haven't had a real bath since the last time I was in Mombasa!"

"You—you're going to bathe?"

"Aye, that I am. In the dark, of course. Wouldn't want to offend your maidenly sensibilities, now, would we?"

"Oh, stop it, Cameron!" Meg huddled on the edge of the bunk, clutching her throbbing knee and fighting the urge to hurl something—anything—in the direction of his voice.

"There, now. Of course, if you like, you'd be more than welcome to light the lamp—"

"Are you drunk?" she asked coldly.

"On a sip of whisky and a mug of beer? Not bloody likely. Would that I were, Meg, my girl."

"I'm not your girl."

"Oh?" His voice was suddenly, unexpectedly razor-sharp. "And whose girl might you be?"

Meg's breath caught in a gasp that, small as it was, filled the dark stillness of the tent. For the space of a long breath, neither of them spoke.

Then, abruptly, Cameron turned and lifted the tent flap. "I'm going to my tent for some clean underclothes," he growled. "You can use the time to undress and get in bed if you like. Oh, and don't worry about having to share the bunk. I'll spare your precious virtue and sleep on the floor."

He stalked out of the tent without another word.

Meg stared after him, feeling as if she'd just been slapped. It wasn't fair, she fumed as she unpinned her hair. Cameron had no right to play the part of the wronged husband. *He* was the one who'd gone off to Africa and left her to raise their child alone. In four long years, he hadn't even tried to contact her. What did he expect after all this time, a wife who'd lick his feet like a dog?

Her hands shook as she unbuttoned her waist, slipped out of her clothes and tugged the sheer cotton lawn nightdress out of her rucksack. The fabric flowed down her body, soft and cool against her skin.

Wasting no time, Meg groped for the covers, jerked them aside and scrambled into bed. When Cameron returned, she would pretend to be asleep. That way, at least, she wouldn't be forced to endure any more of his taunting sarcasm.

She tugged the sheet and blanket up to her chin and lay rigid in the darkness. Through the thin canvas walls she could hear, dimly, the sounds of the camp—a half-drunken laugh, the snort of the mule, the muttered curse of a coolie stumbling over one of the tent ropes.

Minutes crawled by. Maybe Cameron had changed his mind about coming back. Maybe he meant to leave her alone in this camp full of men, in the wild, dark African night. Oh, blast him! Blast him!

Cameron stepped into his own tent just long enough to yank a clean union suit out of his duffle bag and grab a spare pillow. Cummings was already snoring like a steam calliope. Bowman lay quietly in the opposite bunk, making a noble effort to sleep. Cameron departed as swiftly as he'd entered, relieved that neither man had spoken to him. He'd been putting on a front all evening, but he wasn't capable of that anymore. He was too churned up inside.

He wandered an aimless path through the camp. Soon, he knew, he'd have to go back to the tent and face his tawny-haired tormentor once more. He'd have to freeze his face into an iron mask again, while she tore bloody little pieces out of his heart. He needed some time first, to become sufficiently numb for the ordeal.

A cook fire, abandoned at the camp's edge, had burned down to red coals. Cameron tossed on a few dry sticks and stood staring emptily into the flames. It wasn't Meg's fault, he reminded himself. He hadn't wanted her in the first place; worse, he'd let her know it. And he'd never been any kind of husband to her or any kind of father to their little girl. She had every reason to demand her freedom.

Why, then, couldn't he just let her go? Damn it, why now, when he was about to lose her for good, couldn't he look at her without wanting to grab her in his arms and do things to her that would make that night on the beach look like a bloody Maypole dance?

A bat-eared fox, scavenging the rubbish heap, yipped in the darkness. From somewhere out on the plain, the cough of a hunting lioness echoed like dim thunder. Aye, he'd delayed long enough. Cameron took a deep breath. Then, with an attitude of weary resignation, he turned his steps back toward the tent.

Eternities seemed to pass before the flap opened again and Meg saw the outline of Cameron's bulky shoulders against the stars. Relieved in spite of herself, she closed her eyes and slowed her ragged breath to a semblance of sleep. She heard him step into the tent, heard the whisper of canvas as he lowered the flap and tied it into place.

"Meg?" His voice was a low rasp in the darkness.

Meg kept her eyes tightly closed, her lips pressed together.

"Asleep already, are you?"

He paused a few seconds, waiting. When she didn't respond, he turned away with a little mutter. Meg heard the muffled *flump* of his pillow landing on the floor. She heard the thud of his boots coming off, one, then the other, followed by the unmistakable clink of his belt buckle as his trousers dropped around his ankles. Then there was silence, warm and breathless in the dark space of the tent.

A memory from that night on the beach sprang up afresh in Meg's mind—Cameron poised at the water's edge, surf swirling around his bare legs, moonlight defining the platinum contour of each muscle in his beautiful male body.

Heart pounding, she willed the image to dissolve, but her mind would not obey. The vision shimmered, then blurred, only to take shape again, this time with heightened clarity. And with Cameron here, so close, Meg sensed—all but knew—that if she opened her eyes, she would see him that way again, and perhaps even—

No! She shuddered at her own audacity. Her whole future was at stake, not to mention Jenny's. To follow a

foolish whim, then go home and have to lie about her con-
duct to Arthur, that would be unthinkable!

Still, the tantalizing image lingered, teasing at the reckless streak that simmered below Meg's prim surface. A
quick peek with just one eye. What harm could it do? She
experimented with a cautious slit.

The tent was dark, but not so dark that an accustomed
eye couldn't make things out. Meg could see Cameron
standing at the foot of the bunk, dressed in a ragged, sweat-
stained union suit, unbuttoned to the waist.

His head was down, his hands fumbling with the rest of
the buttons. As Meg watched through half-closed eyes,
those hands paused. His shoulders rose and fell in a weary
sigh, and he began to speak.

"We didn't give it much of a chance, did we, lass?" His
voice was a whispery rumble that Meg would not have
heard if she'd truly been asleep. "One crazy time together,
and then me going off like that. A fine fix for a young girl
like you, not even grown."

He drew a long breath. Meg lay rigid, trembling as if an
ice jam were threatening to break up inside her.

"I know it's too late for apologies now," he muttered.
"Even if you could hear me, you probably wouldn't listen.
But for whatever it's worth, I want you to know I'm sorry.
A man does stupid things when he's young, and what I did
to you was beyond stupid. But blast it, Meg, I couldn't have
stayed in Darlmoor, not even for you. I was losing my mind
on that farm, and in that hidebound little town...."

Meg could not keep still. Bursting with emotions held too
long in check, she lifted her head. Cameron's breath caught
in his throat as he realized she had heard him. He stood
awkwardly above her, his big hands poised at his side as if
he were preparing to defend himself.

Meg trembled as she looked at him. She could sense
something inside her, struggling for release. But how could
she let it go when she didn't even know what it was?

"I understand how you must have felt, Cameron," she said in a low, tense voice. "But I didn't understand it then. When I told you about the baby, and you looked at me that way, almost as if you hated me...."

"No," he whispered. "It was never you I hated, Meg. I felt trapped, that was all. It was like having irons clapped around my legs, chaining me to that damnable place forever."

"And I was so naive." Meg sat up in bed, arms clutching her knees. "I thought my having your child would make a difference, that you'd be content to stay. I should have known better." She drew a long, ragged breath. "You can't imagine how much you hurt me, Cameron. But that's done now. It's over, and we can't undo it."

Cameron sank onto the foot of the bunk, his face unreadable in the shadows. "You heard me say I was sorry."

"I accept your apology. But that doesn't matter anymore. It's too late."

"Aye, I suppose it is." He fell into a silence that grew blacker with each heartbeat. Meg sensed a slow storm brewing inside him. She steeled herself against its eruption. She would not let Cameron intimidate her, she vowed. Whatever the cost, she would be honest, direct and unafraid.

He swallowed, then took a sharp breath. "There's someone else. That's why you're here, isn't it?"

"Yes."

He turned away from her in the darkness and stood up. His hands resumed the slow unbuttoning of his union suit, to the hips, then the crotch.

"I can see you quite well, you know," Meg said.

"I don't give a damn. Close your eyes if you want."

He turned his back and peeled the dirty union suit down to his ankles. Meg, watching out of sheer contrariness, glimpsed a body that was huskier and more mature than she remembered, with massive shoulders tapering to a powerful back and trim, tight hips. Even his buttocks were more muscular than she recalled. They stood out in the darkness as he stepped out of the union suit and climbed into the tub. Water sloshed onto the tent floor as he accommodated his length to its cramped contours.

Reaching for the soap on the washstand, he dipped it between his knees and began to work up a lather. "So tell me about the man who's waiting in line for you, fair Meg. Is he someone from our village? Someone I'd remember?"

"No. He's English. From London. But he keeps a summer house on the hill above the loch." Meg spoke coolly, with no expression in her voice.

"A summer house!" Cameron's fist hit the water. He laughed harshly. "Don't tell me little Mary Margaret's snared herself a *gentleman!*"

"More gentleman than you'll ever be, Cameron Mac-Kenna."

He laughed again, a rough, angry sound. "Aye, with fine manners and money, to be sure. Such a catch, Meg, darlin'! Oh, but you've got to get free of me first, before he slips through your fingers!"

"That's enough, Cameron!" Meg felt her ire building like steam in a closed teapot. Without thinking, she was out of the bunk, looming over him in her nightdress. "You don't know how hard things have been since my father died! The scrimping, the worry. Why, I've had to take boarders into the house and cook meals for them to make ends meet. Strangers, who treat me like dirt. I've done their washing, their ironing, their mending—"

"I sent you money." He glared up at her from the confines of the copper tub, soap bubbles gleaming darkly on his tawny shoulders. "Granted, it wasn't much, but you could have put it to use."

"No! Every shilling of that money is for Jenny! She's going to have a proper education, Cameron! She's going to have proper clothes and proper friends, and when the time comes for it, she's going to have a proper marriage!"

"Not like yours, I take it, darlin' Meg?"

Adrenaline surged through Meg's body. Pinwheels of rage, their fuses smoldering for four long years, rocketed off in her head. "Damn you for that, Cameron! What chance has the child got now? She's got no father at home, no money, no prospects—"

"And your gentleman friend can provide all those things. Isn't that so, Meg?" Cameron's eyes glinted like a leopard's in the darkness.

"Yes!" she hissed. "That and more!"

"And can your fancy man provide *this?*"

His hand flashed out and circled Meg's wrist. It's cast-iron grip spun her against the edge of the tub, where his other hand waited to seize her waist and continue the momentum, wrenching her over on top of him.

Meg struggled like a wet cat. "Let me go, you—"

The rest of her words were lost against Cameron's hard, angry mouth.

She dangled over the tub's rolled edge, feet kicking in midair, nightgown trailing water as he kissed her—kissed her with a ruthless, dizzying fury. His hand cupped her head, pulling her down to him, pulling her into the tub in a wild tangle of knees and breasts and floating cotton lawn. Meg's hands clawed water, then, incredibly, found flesh. They clasped . . . and clung.

Fight, you fool! her mind screamed; but even now, her body would not obey. Her heart was crashing against her ribs like the pounding surf on that long-ago beach. Desire forked through her body like lightning through a black night sky as Cameron's relentless lips drained away her will.

No—he was mocking her, testing her, Meg's frantic mind shrilled. But no other part of her was listening. Her mouth had gone molten against his. Her fingers clutched at his soap-slicked shoulders and, as he rose from the tub, with her still in his arms, she could not stop one hand from sliding down the muscled curve of his back to linger on the flat diamond at the base of his spine, within enticing reach of his lean, wet buttocks.

His lips tantalized her, tortured her. Meg groaned out loud as he nibbled his way across her cheek and down the curve of her neck. Her fingers taloned in his hair, cradling his face in the moisture-beaded cleft between her breasts. She felt the rough stubble of his beard, felt his rough tongue tip licking the tiny water drops from her skin. His mouth grazed lower to tease her nipples through the thin, wet cloth, to suck, to bite with a tenderness that was agonizing in its restraint.

Meg's head fell back as she gave herself up to the exquisite puckerings. Tiny ripples of ecstasy radiated from his touch, to shimmer through every part of her. Low in her body, her muscles tightened and quivered in their readiness to welcome his invasion. No man had touched her since Cameron. And she had forgotten...forgotten...

She would never forget again.

Cameron's arms, imprisoning her in their powerful clasp, were no longer necessary. Meg clung to him of her own accord, wild with the feel of his skin through her soaking gown. But even as he held her, she could feel the angry resistance in him. He was bronze against her fire, rock against her flowing, liquid passion—unyielding, even where the marble ridge of his maleness jutted against her thighs. *Struggle,* the frantic inner voice urged her. *Don't let him do this to you!* But Meg was beyond hearing.

Cameron's lips seared a path up the hollow of her throat. Then, with a movement that was too swift, too sure, he recaptured her lips in a savage kiss. She groaned as his tongue pillaged her mouth. She arched her body to his, wanting only to be close, wanting only to be loved....

Suddenly, with a savage, wounded sound, he thrust her away from him. Meg hung between his hands, stunned and bewildered as he glared at her.

"Aye, you little wanton!" he grated. "You'd cheat on your gentleman friend just as fast as you'd cheat on me!

Well, I'll not be a party to it, Mrs. MacKenna! Your fancy Londoner can bloody well have you."

In a final burst of anger, he flung her onto the bunk. Meg lay there for a moment, hurt and dazed. Then her own temper ignited like flame touched to gunpowder. She sat bolt upright.

"Why, you beastly, brutish, arrogant—"

"Go to sleep, Meg." Cameron, his anger gone as swiftly as it had come, had stepped out of the tub and was pulling on his clean union suit. He sounded weary now, drained of emotion. "It's no use, lass. We've said all there is to say. There's nothing to do now but get some rest and finish this wretched business in the morning."

"Cameron..."

He did not reply, and Meg sagged in the bed as the full weight of exhaustion descended upon her. She was too tired even to change her wet nightgown. Yes, Cameron was right for once. They had nothing more to say to each other. The sooner she went to sleep, the sooner this miserable evening would end.

Pulling the blanket up to her chin, she closed her eyes. At first she was too angry to relax, but soon the arduous journey and trying day began to take their toll. Her thoughts began to drift and swirl. By the time Cameron stretched his weary, six-foot length on the floor beside her bunk, Meg was breathing deeply, fast asleep in the sultry African night.

Chapter Five

Sunlight, streaming through a sliver-sized rift in the tent flap, woke Meg with a jolt. Her eyes shot open, their gaze darting this way and that in bewildered panic. Where was she? Where was Jenny?

Then she remembered. The long train trip. Finding Cameron, spending the night in Bowman's tent. Yes, it was all right. It was morning. Cameron would sign the papers; then she would get on the train and go back to Mombasa. And this time she wouldn't have to disguise herself or ride on a flatcar. Cameron would see to it that—

Cameron! Where was he?

Meg leapt out of bed so fast that it made her vision blur. She staggered against a tent pole, groping for balance as her head cleared and her equilibrium righted itself. Her eyes swept around the tent once more. The bathtub was gone. So were Cameron's clothes. So was Cameron.

She sank back onto the edge of the bunk. Panic would be silly at this point. She'd overslept, that was all. Cameron had responsibilities at the railhead. He would be there now, doing his job. All she had to do was get dressed and find him.

She struggled into her clothes, and used water from a handy canteen to splash her face and clean her teeth. A few brush strokes, a practiced twist and a half dozen strategically placed pins secured her hair in its loose knot atop her head. That done, she snatched up a spare hat and stumbled out into the morning.

The air was still cool, the sun a ball of white light on the flame-blue horizon. Meg's ears caught the ring of hammers from the railhead, and the myriad calls of African songbirds. The trampled grass was beaded with dew.

She glanced anxiously around the camp. The tents and fires were deserted, except for a few cook boys cleaning up after breakfast. Meg's lurch of dread dissolved in relief as she saw the train, still slumbering unattended on its track. Everything was all right. From the looks of things, in fact, the engine wouldn't be pulling out until much later. She would find Cameron now and bring him back to sign the papers. After that, there'd be nothing to do except bundle up her things and wait.

She struck out up the long slope, following the rails. It was not far, but the raw-cut ground made the going rougher than she'd expected. By the time she reached the top of the rise, Meg's hiking boots, handed down from a friend and not yet broken to her feet, had already begun to pinch.

She sank down on a boulder to loosen the laces, her lungs burning in the thin, sharp air. From where she sat, she could see the end of the track, where swarms of men labored like ants to span a deep, dry wash. She could see the massive timbers that had hidden her on the flatcar. Tackles were hoisting them onto braces, where they would be anchored to become part of the bridge. Cameron's bridge, she thought, with a twinge of unexpected pride.

Her hand froze on the laces as the memory of last night, the memory she'd forced to the back of her mind until now, crashed in on her with the force of a tidal wave. Shame seared her face as she relived Cameron's brutal kiss, her own explosive response and the final humiliation of being flung onto the bunk like a piece of unwanted baggage.

What a silly little fool she'd been!

She raised her hands to her flaming cheeks. Oh, yes, Cameron had done it on purpose. He'd *wanted* to bring her down, to show her how powerless she really was. And she had let him. She had played right into his hands!

Meg stood up again, ignoring the pain in her toes. Never again, she vowed. Never again would she allow Cameron, or any other man, to catch her with her guard down. Never again, *never,* would she risk the kind of mortification she'd suffered at Cameron's hands last night.

She strode down the hill toward the bridge, the agony in her feet only feeding her fury. One more time, she reminded herself as she reined in her emotions. One last confrontation; then she would never have to face Cameron MacKenna again.

As she drew closer, her eyes scanned the work gangs milling around the bridge work. She could not see Cameron, but he would be there. And this time, when she found him, she would be in control. She would not show one flicker of emotion. She would be as cold as a winter's day on the Scottish moor.

A khaki-clad figure was striding uphill to meet her. Meg's heart sank a little as she recognized Anthony Bowman's lanky frame beneath the oversized *terai.* Bowman waved, then motioned her to stay where she was while he climbed up to where she stood.

They exchanged pleasantries while the minutes crawled by. Meg's eyes darted past Bowman, searching for Cameron and not finding him.

At last, Bowman noticed her distraction. "Forgive me, Mrs. MacKenna. You'd be looking for your husband, of course. I'm afraid he's not here."

"Not here?" Something inside Meg sank.

"Oh, he was here earlier, yes, but he had to dash off. One of the meat-hunter chaps came in with a story about finding a body out on the plain. MacKenna took a couple of the boys and went back with him to investigate."

Meg felt the weight sinking deeper. She forced herself to be charming. "Oh, but surely he'll be back before the train leaves! I can't possibly go without saying goodbye to him!"

"Of course not." Bowman frowned in polite under-standing. "I'm sure he'll make every effort to return in time."

Every effort. Meg churned with unbearable agitation. Why should Cameron make *any* effort to get back before the train left? After last night, why would he even want to see her, let alone cooperate with her?

"Oh, but couldn't we go and look for him?" She clasped her hands in a convincing show of helplessness.

Bowman sighed. "My dear Mrs. MacKenna, that's quite impossible. I can't leave the railhead until the bridge timbers are secured, and there's no one else I'd trust to take you out in the bush." He gazed down at her, his expression blending sympathy, dismay and the pained wish that this fluttery little woman would take her troubles else-where.

"I'll tell you what!" he said brightly. "Hike back up the hill with me. You can see the Machakos Road from the top."

"Is that where Cameron went?" Meg fell into step with him, her throbbing feet forgotten for the moment. They reached the crest again, and Bowman pointed north into the yellow distance. "There. See it? It's not really a road, of course, just an old caravan trail, but there'll be wagons on it soon, now that the railway's here. Just think of it, Mrs. MacKenna! Wagons, settlers ... civilization! And we Brit-ish the ones making it possible!"

"That's where my husband went?"

"It is. Now, if you'll just wait in the shade of this thorn-bush, you'll be able to see him coming back."

"But how soon will the train be leaving?"

"Don't worry, there's plenty of time." Bowman took a few steps downhill, then paused. "You should be all right here. Shout if you need anything. Cheerio, now." He turned and strode jauntily back down the slope.

Meg plopped down in the meager shade. She stared morosely over the parched landscape, at the barely discernible trail that meandered off toward the north horizon.

Oh, she knew what Cameron was up to. He'd seized the chance to run out on her without signing the divorce papers. Right now, he was probably laughing as he imagined her frustration. And it wasn't because he wanted to keep her for himself. No, Cameron would do it out of sheer, cursed spite.

She stood up again, her mind seething. She would go after him if she could, she thought. But she'd never be able to catch up with him, especially in these miserable boots. Once more she was at Cameron's mercy, with no choice except to wait, fret and hope.

The sun was getting higher now, and hotter. Meg wiped a trickle of sweat from her cheek. The heat had awakened torpid insects in the dry grass. Their high-pitched whining only heightened her agitation.

She shaded her eyes to watch a pair of vultures, riding an updraft, their black wings etched against the sky. What would she do, she wondered, if Cameron didn't return before the train left? Could she bear to stay, and leave poor little Jenny to wait and worry in Mombasa? Could she go, and abandon her whole reason for coming here?

Meg's balled fist struck her leg. No—both choices were unthinkable! Whatever it took, she would find Cameron. Whatever the cost, she would be on that train when it left, with the signed divorce papers in her hand.

Thrusting out her chin, she stalked down the brushy hillside, in the direction of the so-called road. Her cramped feet screamed with each step, but she ignored the pain. Pain didn't matter now, she told herself. Not when her daughter's future was at stake.

Meg had gone no more than two dozen steps when an ominous snort from behind a clump of brush sent her reeling wildly to one side. Her ankle twisted on a slippery stone. She lost her footing and went down.

Panic seized her as the scrub crackled with the weight of a large animal. She clawed at the grass in a futile effort to scramble away. Her legs tangled in her petticoat. It was no use. Her constricted throat would not even let her scream for help. She was going to die right here, on this miserable African hillside, trampled to a bloody pulp by some—

The breath whooshed out of her as a big brown mule ambled into the open. Bowman's mule, trailing its bridle reins on the ground, wearing a saddle, with a rifle in its leather scabbard slung on one side.

This was too good to be true.

The mule paused in its grazing and regarded Meg with quizzical brown eyes, as if inviting her to climb on its back. It had likely gotten loose from where Bowman had left it tied, she reasoned. He was bound to come looking for it soon. But maybe not too soon.

Meg scrambled to her feet, grabbed the dragging reins and hauled herself into the saddle. It wasn't very mannerly, repaying Bowman's hospitality by absconding with his mule. But this was no time to fuss about etiquette.

She jabbed her pointed boot toes into the mules's flanks. Forsaking its stubborn nature, the animal shot forward, and they rocketed down the hill toward Machakos Road.

Distances, Meg was learning, could be deceptive in the diamond-clear African air. From the hilltop, the road had looked very close. In reality, the distance was a good three miles. By the time they reached the narrow, rutted trail, the mule had slowed to an intractable walk. Meg's clothes were snagged and tattered from navigating thickets of wait-a-bit thorns. Her hands were scratched and bleeding, her patience frayed to the snapping point.

A glance over her shoulder confirmed that she'd lost sight of the railway camp. It was hidden now, on the far side of the hill. She was alone, the yellow savanna spreading before her like an endless sea.

Meg had viewed wild Africa from the safety of the ship and the rolling train and from the cluttered confines of the camp. But only now was she struck by its overpowering immensity. The golden landscape stretched as far as she could see in all directions, rippling with light under the great sunlit dome of the sky. Even on the mule, she felt frighteningly small and solitary, a meaningless speck in a vast ocean of grass.

She shaded her eyes and peered across the empty landscape. Trees grew in scattered clumps, towering acacia, bare of leaves to the level of a giraffe's highest nibbling reach. Half a mile away, a wildebeest herd flowed through a hollow in a living stream. On its flank, small dark spots—wild dogs—darted in and out, searching for the weak, the young, the stragglers.

There would be lions out here, too, Meg reminded herself with a shudder. Great, hungry brutes who'd like nothing better than to make lunch of Bowman's mule and polish her off for dessert. Senses prickling, she eased the rifle out of its leather holster and slid back the bolt. The gun was loaded, but so heavy that she could barely raise it to her shoulder, let alone hold it steady. Any self-respecting lion would have her before she could even take aim. She cocked the gun and laid it across her knees, feeling scant comfort in its weight. If only Cameron would appear...

Worry plucked at Meg's taut nerves as she scanned the landscape for any sign of human life. She saw nothing but a cloud of vultures circling a spot beyond the horizon. Never in her life had she felt more alone.

Damn you for this, Cameron MacKenna, she thought. Damn, damn, damn you!

Glancing at the ground ahead, she suddenly realized that the mule had wandered off the road. The trackless plain stretched before her as far as she could see. Panic swelled inside her—but, no, it was all right. There was the road, a stone's throw off her left shoulder. She jerked the reins sharply and gave the mule a frenzied kick. Snorting, the stubborn animal broke into a trot. Meg clung to the rifle, her rump bouncing smartly on the hard saddle.

They had nearly regained the road when the mule's weight caved in a shallow warthog den, dug into the russet earth. Suddenly all hell, in the form of a fear-crazed warthog, exploded beneath them. Out of the frenzied melee of squeals and kicks, the warthog emerged tearing in one direction, the mule in the other, with Meg clinging desperately to the saddle.

The mule was dashing full tilt away from the road now. Meg sawed frantically at the reins, but the terrified beast was out of control. She could only cling on for dear life as it leapt and bucked its way across the plain.

Suddenly, a second pighole, this one empty, caved in beneath the pounding hooves. The mule went down head-first in a flurry of dust. Wrenched out of the saddle, Meg flew forward over its neck. She could see the trampled, yellow grass rushing up to meet her. Then the whole world went black.

Cameron and the three boys came upon the dead man fifty paces off the trail. He'd been easy enough to find because of the flocking vultures. But he hadn't been dead long. The big, smelly birds had barely started on him, and even the lone hyena that skittered off at the approach of humans had yet to charge in for its share of the grisly meal.

Juma, the tall Somali who shot meat for the camp, had discovered the body a little earlier that morning. He'd come pounding back to the railhead to inform Cameron, who'd recruited two Parsi coolies with shovels and returned with him posthaste. The body of a native or Indian, perhaps, would not have caused such a stir. But this man was white.

He was lying facedown in the grass, with no visible wounds save what the birds had inflicted. His khakis were ragged and dirty, his boots worn to holes; but the hefty .577 Nitro Express rifle that lay alongside him was in spotless condition, as were the cartridges in his bandolier. A knife hung from his hippo-hide belt. His canteen was still a third full.

"Help me turn him over," Cameron said.

Juma seized a shoulder, Cameron a boot, and they rolled the poor devil onto his back. The vultures formed a flapping, hopping ring around the grim tableau. At a greater distance, the hyena, a young one, loped back and forth in a frenzy of uncertainty.

The dead man was a big, ruddy fellow with a walrus mustache, his balding scalp fish-white where his *terai* had covered it. His face was frozen in an expression of mild surprise, the mouth oddly twisted. Apoplexy, Cameron surmised. Or a sudden heart attack. Even out here, such things happened.

The Parsi boys had already begun to dig the grave. Cameron leaned over to wave the flies off the waxen face, and to cover the glassy eyes with his kerchief. As he did so, he felt an abrupt prickle of recognition.

He knew this man.

The memory slammed into place like a 750-grain slug. It had been more than three years ago, when the railway was still snaking its way across the parched Tibi Desert. This fellow—Harry Murchison was his name—had passed through the rail camp on his way to Mombasa. Trailing him was a long string of Wakamba porters, loaded down with elephant ivory.

Dazzled, Cameron had counted the tusks. There were sixty or seventy of them, some longer than he was tall. Their worth, Murchison had hinted, was more than Cameron could earn in a lifetime of laboring for the railroad. Over brandy, a lot of brandy, the burly hunter had recounted his elephant-bagging exploits in the Ugandan wilds around Lake Victoria—the spectacular kills, the hair's-breadth escapes, the heart-stopping thrill of being charged by six tons of screaming fury. Cameron had listened, burning....

He jerked himself roughly back to the present. That was a long time ago, he reminded himself bitterly. And here was Harry Murchison again, under circumstances far less grand. No ivory. No stories. No evidence anywhere of the fortune he must have made.

Cameron stripped off his shirt and spelled one of the Parsis at the shovel. Sweat poured down his body as he vented his frustration against the hard, red earth. By now, Meg would be awake and dressed. By now, she'd have discovered the divorce papers he'd signed and tucked back into her rucksack. When the train pulled out, she'd be on it. He would have no reason to see her again.

The sun was well above the horizon by the time the six-foot hole was deep enough to discourage predators. As Cameron lifted Murchison's shoulders to position him for the drop, he heard a papery rattle from the dead man's breast pocket.

Chiding himself for his own haste, Cameron signaled the two boys to wait. He'd be a fool to bury Murchison without checking for some indication of who his people were. Someone would have to be notified about the death. Letters, photographs, maybe an address book. These things would provide the only possible clues.

A quick rifling through Murchison's clothes yielded nothing but an empty leather billfold and a folded, yellowed sheet of paper. Cameron stuffed the two items into his own pocket, resolving to examine them later. Then, with the Parsis helping, he swung the dead man over the open grave and lowered him to the bottom.

Murchison's rifle lay on the short-cropped grass. With a fluid motion, Juma bent and picked it up, hefting its weight in his long, dark hands. "This is a fine gun, *bwana*," he said. "Very good for hunting."

Cameron glanced from the open grave to the gun. It was indeed a superb weapon, capable of dropping a six-ton elephant bull with the right well-placed shot. If only—

Cameron closed his mind to the rest of the thought. That time was behind him. He could not allow it to torment him now. Slowly he shook his head. "No. It's the one thing Murchison had left. We'll bury it with him." He took the gun from the dismayed young Somali and laid it alongside the body.

The vultures ringed the grave like scab-headed mourners, squawking their frustration at the loss of a meal. As the dirt clods thudded into the hole, they flapped away in twos and threes. By the time the burial was finished, even the hyena had slunk off over the horizon. There was no handy wood for a marker, but Cameron arranged some stones into a cross pattern on the fresh dirt. The three boys stood by in respectful heathen silence, while he mumbled what he could remember of the Twenty-third Psalm. Murchison hadn't struck him as a man who drew much comfort from religion, but one never knew.

Walking fast, they cut back to the road. The Parsis trotted on broomstick legs, balancing the shovels across their shoulders. Juma glided along behind a wall of silence, probably thinking of the buried gun. Cameron tramped along beside them, his own Martini rifle swinging from his hand. Despite everything, his mind churned with thoughts of Meg.

What a bloody fool he'd made of himself last night! He'd started out trying to show the woman he didn't give a damn about the divorce or her fancy gentleman friend. But somehow he'd gotten sidetracked and ended up in a jealous rage. In the heat of its fury, his resolve to keep his hands off her had gone up in smoke.

The color deepened in Cameron's sweating face. Even now, his body stirred darkly at the memory of her shameless mouth, her warm flesh melting against him through that thin, wet nightgown. No wonder he'd lost control.

Meg's wanton response—aye, that was the last thing he'd expected. If she'd slapped his face or puffed herself up like an outraged Queen Victoria, he could have dealt with it.

But the way she'd caught fire in his arms, fearlessly answering his caresses with her own.... Cameron cursed. Only his anger had saved him from even greater folly.

And folly it would have been. He had no illusions about loving Meg, nor about her loving him. What they'd experienced last night was a raw animal hunger that had nothing to do with love. Love was tenderness and caring. Love was two people wanting the best for each other, wanting to share life, to work and grow together.

He and Meg. Hell, all they'd ever done was snap and snarl at each other like a pair of surly mongrel dogs.

Cameron lengthened his stride, anxious to get back to the bridge and throw himself bodily into the work. Meg would be long gone by the time he returned to the camp. He would never see her again.

Aye, it would be a proper night to get very, very drunk.

By now, they were close enough to hear the ring of hammers from the railhead. Cameron was still lost in his own thoughts when he heard Juma whisper, "Look, *bwana*."

Cameron raised his eyes. Twenty paces ahead, next to the road, was Bowman's mule. The big brown beast was ambling toward the camp, pausing to munch dry grass between steps.

"Bloody hyena bait! What the devil—?" Cameron sprinted forward and caught the trailing reins. The mule appeared to be all right, but its slick hide was coated with dirt and bits of grass. One stirrup hung twisted from the saddle, and the rifle was missing.

"This mule has been down," Juma said.

Cameron could see that Juma was right. Still, the picture didn't make sense. The mule had never wandered away from camp before. And Bowman wouldn't be riding out here alone. Nobody would, unless—

Fear slammed into Cameron's gut like an icy fist. He imagined Meg, failing to see the signed papers, frantic to find him before the train left. He could picture her asking where he'd gone, then, when no one was looking, taking the mule . . .

The little fool! He groaned out loud. Where was she now? Lost? Hurt? Even dead?

Sick with dread, he ordered the Parsi boys to ride the mule back to the railhead and tell Bowman what had happened. He and Juma would backtrack the mule's trail to wherever it had fallen. Juma was the best tracker in the camp. If Meg was out there, they would find her.

Cameron could only pray that it would be in time.

A black fly droned lazily around Meg's head. When she did not move, it zoomed closer, seeking, perhaps, a drop of moisture from the corner of her eye or a bite of her soft, pink skin.

Folding its blue wings, it touched down on the rim of one nostril and began to crawl upward, toward the bridge. Suddenly, the nose twitched. The pale eyelids fluttered. Startled, the fly buzzed into the air again.

Meg moaned and opened her eyes. She was lying on her side, her cheek pressed to the prickly grass. Her body felt curiously flat, as if she'd splattered like an egg against the sunbaked earth, but when she stirred cautiously, there was no pain. No part of her seemed broken.

All the same, a sense of lethargic shock weighed so heavily on her that she could not summon the will to move. She lay there staring at nothing through a blur of yellow grass, remembering the mule and the fall. Remembering Cameron and the divorce papers. Remembering Jenny.

The buzzing fly landed on her ear. Meg twitched it away. The sun was molten on her skin. She could not lie here like this. She had to find Cameron. She had to be on that train. She had to get back to her daughter.

Her head swam as she raised up on one elbow to check the lay of the land. She was dizzy and disoriented, but if she could see some sign of the road, or the hill that hid the railway camp, she might be able to—

Meg's thoughts froze as an immense, rounded gray shape, as broad as the side of a house, loomed into her vision from the far side of a thornbush. Another, even larger, materialized behind it, then another, drifting along as silently as ghosts, moving at an angle in her direction.

Several heartbeats passed before Meg's shocked mind registered that she was seeing elephants.

Elephants.

Meg's paralysis dissolved into panic as she stared at them. Elephants—and not a hundred yards away.

Incredibly, the giants had not noticed her. The light wind, Meg realized, was blowing her scent away from them. But they were coming closer, a cow and two young bulls, trunks swinging gently between their massive ivory tusks. If the wind changed, if they spotted her...

Meg's horrified eyes could see more elephants now, trailing the three leaders. There were other cows, smaller bulls and half-grown youngsters. There were trotting baby calves, no larger than sheepdogs. A whole herd of elephants.

They appeared to be browsing, for their pace was unhurried, even meandering. Even so, their course was carrying them unerringly in her direction.

Heart pounding, Meg dropped flat behind the low, thin bush. Every instinct in her body shrieked *run!* But she'd read enough about elephants to know that running would be an invitation to death. The very sight of her, so close to their young, was sure to provoke a charge. And no human was fleet enough to outrace an elephant intent on killing.

She lay excruciatingly still. Now she could hear the elephants, their big bellies rumbling, their trunks whooshing air, their babies squealing. Oh, surely those huge fan ears could hear her, too. Her heart was a pounding gong, her breath a rasping bellows in her throat.

But the herd's pace was tranquil, almost leisurely. Closer and closer they ambled on their great, tree trunk legs, in a slanting line toward the spot where Meg lay frozen in an agony of terror.

Her face dripped cold sweat. The fly had been buzzing around her head. Now it landed on her cheek and crawled its tickly way toward the corner of her mouth. Another fly settled on her neck.

Meg let them crawl. She could not so much as flicker an eyelash now, or the elephants would notice her. She could only mold herself to the earth and pray that the fragile, fickle wind would hold.

Cameron and Juma had backtracked the mule's trail for nearly a mile when the young Somali froze like a hound on point.

"Tembo," he said softly.

Cameron's mouth went dry. Peering through a shimmer of heat waves, he scanned the horizon. Nothing. But Juma had instincts about such things. If he said there was elephant nearby, there would be elephant.

"Where?" He mouthed the word.

Juma pointed silently eastward, his arm following the line of mule tracks into the glaring sun. Cameron squinted hard, narrowing his eyes against the light. Aye, he could make out the herd now, as a cluster of dark blurs floating above the grass like ships on a yellow sea.

And Meg would be out there somewhere, all alone.

He motioned to Juma and they crept ahead. Cameron's emotions churned with each step. It was all his fault, he berated himself. If he'd awakened Meg before he left, if he'd put the signed papers in plain sight, where she could see them right away...

But this was no time to be sorry. Right now he had to *think*. He had to find Meg without spooking the elephants. There'd be time enough for blame-laying later.

He glanced at Juma. The Somali had wet a finger and was testing the wind. "It blows well for us now, *bwana*," he whispered. "But it could change."

"Come on." Cameron motioned him forward again. They ran as fast as they dared, keeping low as they dodged from one clump of cover to the next. The mule's iron shoes had torn up the red earth, making the tracks simple to follow here. But Meg, Cameron knew, would not be so easy to spot. Her khaki clothes and blond hair would blend perfectly into the yellow-brown landscape.

They were getting uncomfortably near the elephants now. Cold fingers of fear crawled along Cameron's spine, stirring the horror that had haunted his memory for three years. He steeled his mind against it, but again and again the question returned to torture him.

What if he had to shoot?

But shooting was out of the question here. Even in the face of a charge, neither the Martini nor Juma's old Snider had the power to penetrate to the depth of an elephant's vital organs. The most precise shot would do no more than madden the beast. Remembering Murchison's .577, lying now under six feet of earth, Cameron swore under his breath.

His eyes scanned desperately for Meg as he and Juma crouched behind a termite mound. *Hapana,* as the Swahili would say. Nothing. Maybe she wasn't even out here. Maybe she'd found the bloody papers, after all, and had gotten on the bloody train. Maybe Bowman's mule really had wandered off on its own and—

Juma touched his arm.

Cameron's eyes followed the long, black, pointing finger and saw her. She lay fearfully still against the ground, not a hundred paces short of the elephant herd. A stray breath of wind feathered a loose tendril of her tawny hair. No other part of her moved.

Anguish clenched Cameron's stomach into a cold ball. His fingers whitened around the rifle stock as he huddled behind the termite mound, his shallow breath matching Juma's. Meg lay directly between them and the herd. He could not go to her. He could not even call out. A charge would bring the elephants right over the top of her.

He wet a finger in his mouth and held it up to test the wind. At first, he felt nothing but the leaden stillness of the air. Then, he sensed a subtle cooling on the near side of his finger, the slightest movement of wind.

It was blowing from behind them now, carrying their scent, and Meg's, right toward the elephants.

Chapter Six

Meg could not feel the subtle wind shift. But she didn't need to. The reaction of the elephants told her everything.

Their meandering path had brought them to within fifty paces of the thornbush where she lay. She had plastered herself to the earth and was trying desperately not to breathe when their lumbering pace abruptly halted.

The sense of danger riveted the herd like an electric shock. The big bulls moved forward with the lead cow, snorting and stamping, wheeling back and forth to catch the strange scent. The others moved into defensive positions behind them, gathering the squealing babies into the herd's protected center. Trunks snaked the air. Great fan ears spread wide like monstrous bat wings, alert to the slightest twig snap or the softest rustle of dry grass.

Shouldering ahead of the others, the biggest bull raised his trunk and screamed a blood-chilling challenge. Meg dissolved in terror at the sound. Any second now, the elephants would find her, and her life would be over. Poor little Jenny would grow up motherless.

Stop it! she scolded herself. *You've come too far to lie here and be trampled! There has to be something you can do. Think. Think!*

That was when she remembered Bowman's gun.

Shifting her eyes, she spotted the rifle, lying in a grass clump about ten feet to her right. It was loaded and cocked, she knew. But could she get to it in time? Could she use it?

Meg weighed her chances. Her entire experience with guns consisted of one afternoon's target practice on the moor with Arthur and his valet. It took skill to hit an elephant in a vital spot—more skill than she possessed. She would be wiser to shoot over the beasts, and hope the sound of gunshots might startle the herd into turning tail. The odds of living through the next minutes were fearful, but at least she would die on her feet.

Her muscles tensed like a cat's as she calculated the distance to the rifle. Summoning all her strength, she lunged for the weapon and caught it, with a quick roll that brought her to an upright crouch.

She was in full view of the elephants now. The huge bull loomed in front of her, so massively tall that she could have stood upright under its belly. Its eyes were soot-black in their deep, wrinkled sockets. She could see the veins in its leathery ears, the black hairs bristling from its trunk.

There was no time for hesitation. Firing into the air and whooping like a banshee, Meg charged.

The big bull froze in elephantine surprise. Its trunk quivered in the air. She yelled and pulled the trigger again, aiming well over the bull's head.

No sound came from the rifle but a faint metallic *click*. Meg's heart shrank in despair as she realized the gun was empty. But no, there were more shots. Not her shots. They were coming from behind her, and there were shouts, men's voices.

The elephants were turning. The old cow wheeled decisively and led the herd away at a dusty trot. Only when they were at a safe distance did the big bull drop his menacing stance, turn and lumber off after them.

And only then did Meg, her knees almost buckling, turn around and see Cameron with a tall young African, both of them running toward her.

"You—you—" she sputtered. No more words would come. She was shaking so hard she could barely stand. Three long strides and Cameron was beside her. His hands clenched her shoulders, the fingers hard and hurting. His cobalt eyes withered her with their fury.

"You little idiot!" he grated. "What the devil were you trying to do, get yourself killed?"

"I—I was just—only—" Meg struggled for coherence, but even putting words in order was too much for her now. The terror of her experience washed over her like a flood. She covered her face with her shaking hands.

"If I weren't so bloody relieved, I'd turn you over my knee!" Cameron rasped. "What the hell were you doing out here, anyway? You should have stayed in camp and waited for the train!"

Meg felt a cold, slow anger building inside her. She let it grow, let it push away her fear. Lowering her hands, she glared straight into his eyes.

"You know very well what I was doing," she said icily. "You ran out on me without signing the papers. I had to find you before the train left."

Cameron groaned. His hands dropped from her shoulders. "Did you look for the papers, Meg?" he asked in a pained voice.

"No."

"You should have. I signed them early this morning and put them back among your things."

Meg gaped at him in a horror of comprehension. In the dead silence that followed, as if orchestrated by some perverse cosmic mind, a piercing whistle echoed across the bleak African landscape.

It was the whistle of a departing train.

Strained beyond limits, Meg's self-control shattered. "Oh, you—you—" She flung herself at Cameron, her fists flailing wildly at his chest. "You impossible...arrogant ...condescending...*bastard!*"

"Now, Meg—" He tried to fend her off passively, shielding himself with his arms, but she flew at him again and again, like an enraged hornet. "Ouch! Damn you, woman."

His hands flashed straight out, seizing her upper arms and pinning them to her body with a grip like an iron vise. He held her at arm's length, her feet dangling like a doll's, just off the ground.

"Now, you listen to me, Mary Margaret!" he rumbled. "If you hadn't gone charging away from camp like a cocked pistol, none of this would have happened!"

Meg glowered at him like a disheveled owl. She wanted to spit fire in his face, to order him to put her down this very instant. But her mouth would not obey her mind. The sun was blindingly hot, her whalebone corset a tight-laced torture device. She could not get enough air.

"Blast you…" She mouthed the words. Cameron's eyes swam like blurred blue gas flames in front of her face. She was floating in them, spinning, dissolving in their heat.

Then everything went dark as she collapsed between Cameron's hands.

Cameron ordered Juma to take the guns. Then, hefting Meg in his arms and cradling her against his chest, he began to walk. He strode out hard, ignoring the heat. Meg needed the shelter of the tent. She needed plenty of water to cool her burning skin. She needed care, and camp was a good three miles off.

Her face was beaded with sweat; that, at least, was a good sign. She'd be all right, he reassured himself. Too much sun and a good scare, that was all. But she'd scared him, as well. Lord, how she'd scared him!

His arms tightened around her. What a sight—dainty little Mary Margaret, charging a bull elephant as big as a house! By nightfall, the story would be a legend in the railway camp. By the time the rains came, it would be known all over East Africa. Aye, she had spunk and steel in her, his

Meg. No, not *his* Meg, he reminded himself bitterly. Never again his Meg. But he burned with pride all the same.

Meg moaned, her eyes still closed. Cameron lifted her a bit, allowing her head to roll gently into the hollow of his neck. Her warm weight was sweet in his arms, her fragrance like a summer day on the moor. For all the heat and flies and his concern about her condition, he felt a curious, protective pleasure in carrying her like this. A sense of timelessness, as if he were walking through a sunlit haze with no thought except that of keeping her safe.

As they came around the hill, however, the sight of the camp wrenched him back to reality. Aye, there were things to be dealt with, and he'd best think them out. The train was gone, and would not be back for at least three days. Once she'd had time to recover, Meg would make his life a torment. Maintaining their facade of marital happiness would be more of a strain than ever.

Cameron sighed. Meg had been right about one thing: it would have been simpler to tell Bowman the truth, that they were as good as divorced. But even the thought of exposing so private a matter to judgment and ridicule jabbed his male pride to the quick. Meg did not owe him a great deal, but one thing he would demand of her—that this miserable business remain their own secret.

Meg's clothes were soaked with sweat where her body nestled against him. Her cheeks were damp and flushed with heat. As Cameron's eyes traced the smooth contours of her face, he found himself wondering what their daughter would be like. Little Jennifer Jane. Jenny.

Oh, he knew she was blond like Meg, with his own blue eyes; his mother had told him that much. But he would know nothing more of her. He would never see her golden curls bouncing in the sunlight or see a smile teasing the dimpled corners of her mouth. He would never hear her laugh. Or hear her cry. He would not see her grow up, fall in love, marry. Those privileges, he supposed, would fall to Meg's new gentleman friend. As for himself, it was a little late for fatherly regrets. Losing Jenny was a tragedy of his own making. For all his pain, it was no worse than he deserved.

Meg quivered against him. Her eyelids twitched. Her lashes fluttered and raised. Cameron found himself gazing down into the violet centers of her eyes.

"What . . . happened?" she murmured in a small, bewildered voice. "Cameron, I feel so strange. . . ."

Cameron bulwarked his emotions behind a wall of gruffness. "You got too much sun, that's all," he growled. "Don't worry. We'll be back in camp soon. Everything's going to be all right."

Reassured, she sank back in his arms. Cameron lengthened his stride, driven by a seething frustration. Everything was going to be all right, he had told her. Fine words, but they rang like cheap Indian brass. Everything was *not* going to be all right, he knew. It was possible, in fact, that nothing would ever be all right in his life again.

For the next twenty-four hours, Meg did nothing but rest. She lay in the sweltering tent, only half-aware of the faces that peered at her through the swath of mosquito netting. There was Anthony Bowman, politely solicitous and probably ruing the loss of his quarters. There was a jaded young Hindu woman, pressed into service, no doubt, for a few rupees, who called Meg *memsahib* and brought her tea and rice.

And there was Cameron, his hands pressing wet cloths onto her fervid skin, his eyes fiercely tender, his mouth hard and silent. It was Cameron, she realized later, who had manipulated her out of her tight clothes and into her nightdress. And it was Cameron who had stayed at her side for the first few critical hours, forcing fluids down her burning throat.

He had lingered until she was out of danger. Then he had vanished, returning only for brief glimpses into the tent. Too hot to sleep, Meg had tossed on the bunk all afternoon, her feverish mind haunted by the sound of the long-gone train. It would be days, she knew, before the train returned. Days before she would see Jenny again and hold that small, sweet rosebud body in her arms.

Only when night came, with its blessed coolness, had Meg sunk into slumber. But even then, she was troubled by dreams of running after a vanishing train, running and running, with a herd of wild elephants trumpeting at her heels.

When she awoke the next morning, shaky but clear-headed, Cameron was gone from the tent. Only his bedroll, flung hastily into a corner, gave evidence that he'd spent the night there.

Meg tottered across the floor on unsteady legs, gathering up possessions that Cameron had scattered when he'd put her to bed—a boot here, a stocking there, her rumpled waist, her corset. In her rucksack, she even found the divorce papers, signed, as Cameron had said.

She stared at his forceful signature, feeling a vague sense of loss. Then, placing the papers on the bunk, she seized her hairbrush and began yanking it through the tangles in her sweat-matted hair.

As she stroked furiously, she thought about seeing Cameron that evening. She imagined him coming in late, grumpy, distant, saying as little to her as possible. She imagined the strain between them as they tried to maintain the facade of their marriage for yet another night. Gloom settled around her, as gray and insidious as a cobweb.

She found the scattered hairpins and began jabbing them into place as she twisted her hair into its customary knot. Why should she care how Cameron treated her? She had what she'd come for. All that remained was to keep her distance from him, and to keep her emotions locked away until the train returned.

She thrust a cloth into the washbowl and scrubbed her face till it stung. Looking back was nothing but a waste of time and emotion. From now on, she would look ahead.

She would think about Jenny and the fine life they would have when they got back to Britain and she became Mrs. Arthur Tarrington-Leigh.

Mrs. Arthur Tarrington-Leigh. Yes, it was all right to imagine it now that she had Cameron's signature on the papers. The very name carried an aura of power and respectability. Oh, no one would look down on her when that name was hers! No one would whisper about her sham marriage to Cameron or the fact that she had to take boarders into the house. And no one would ever hurt Jenny with their gossip, as they had hurt *her*. No one would dare.

Jenny. Something wrenched at Meg's heart as she pictured her daughter, curled among the quilts in fragrant sleep. The two of them had never been apart for so long, and to Meg the separation was as unnatural as being cut off from a part of her own body.

Oh, but this gloom wouldn't do! Jenny would be fine, she reassured herself. The Emir's house was clean and secure. Jenny would have the Emir's wives to spoil and pamper her. She would have Jehani's sons to romp with. And the vigilant Hassan would be there to keep her safe. Oh, everything would be all right. Surely it would.

Swallowing the lump in her throat, Meg gathered her scattered clothes and began jerking them on. If only she could will the train to hurry; but she was being foolish now. She had no choice except to bide her time and make the best of the situation. That included her relationship with Jenny's father.

She sat down on the bunk and began pulling on her stockings. Maybe tonight, when Cameron returned, they could relax and talk. Maybe they could even make it through the evening without fighting. After all, the papers were signed. What was left for them to fight over?

Meg's left stocking dangled limply from quiet fingers as the reality sank in. It was truly finished; Cameron had given her her freedom. All that remained of their marriage would end with the thud of a magistrate's gavel when she returned to Britain.

A shiver passed through Meg's body as she remembered Cameron's brutal arms pulling her into the tub, as she remembered the savagery of his kisses and the wet warmth of his golden skin against the palms of her hands...

But tonight would not be like that, Meg vowed. Tonight they would behave like civilized, sensible people. Nothing would pass between them except polite conversation.

Meg thrust her foot into the second stocking and jerked it up to her thigh. She had her boots in hand when she remembered how excruciatingly they had pinched her toes. For a moment, she was tempted to slip on the Indian sandals she'd worn aboard the train. Then she recalled what Bowman had told her about horrid little insects called *chiggas*. They lived in the African dust, and they burrowed under one's toenails to lay their eggs, causing the most awful festering. Careless people who exposed their feet could lose toes to chigga infestations.

Meg sighed painfully as she contemplated jamming her feet into the twin leather torture-boxes. There *had* to be something she could do to make them wearable. Her eyes darted about the tent and came to rest on the washbowl, half-filled with murky water.

Of course! She'd soak the boots down and walk in them until they dried. Wet, they would stretch to fit.

Without another thought, she snatched up the bowl and poured half the water into one boot, then the other. She was about to put her foot into the left boot when a wet, angry scorpion as long as her thumb came boiling out of the top.

Meg gasped, then sank back on the bunk, feeling faint. If she had put the boot on...

This would not do, she told herself firmly. A woman who had faced a whole elephant herd could not quail before a creature scarcely two inches long, no matter how deadly.

Seizing one boot, she whacked the crawling scorpion with the heel, again and again, beating it into the canvas floor. Only when the hook-tailed horror was crushed beyond any sign of life did she allow herself to shudder convulsively, lace on her soggy boots, square her shoulders and step outside.

She paused at the threshold of the tent. Once more, the African morning engulfed her, clear and blue and cool. As she gazed beyond the quiet camp to the golden plain, she felt a surge of pride in her own strength. She had faced danger and survived. She had seized destiny in her hands and shaped it to her own desires. Soon everything she had set out to achieve would be hers.

A stray breeze stirred her hair. Suddenly, inexplicably, tears welled up in Meg's eyes and she began to tremble.

Dinner—*chacula,* as the Swahili called it—was grilled eland tenderloin with the ever-present boiled rice, *chupattis,* warm beer and tepid coffee. Once again, Cameron and Meg, along with Cummings, were guests at Bowman's table. The two Englishmen ate with their usual gusto, and even Meg had managed a fair show of appetite.

Cameron, however, could not even swallow.

He toyed with the food on his plate, his eyes shifting to steal glances at Meg. She'd assumed a brittle gaiety tonight, a determined charm that she wore like a mask. Her laughter tinkled on the night breeze as she responded to one of Bowman's tiresome rowing-team stories.

"Oh, but that's so *funny!*" she warbled.

The story was not funny, Cameron groused. It had not been funny even the first time he'd heard it. But Meg did look beautiful tonight. Aye, she was well recovered from her ordeal on the plain. She had spent the day outdoors, exploring the fringes of camp, and her hair was wind-rumpled, her face glowing in the soft firelight. In deference to the heat, she had unbuttoned her high collar, revealing the smooth ivory curve of her throat.

Cameron battled his own response to her. He imagined building a wall between them, alternating blocks of anger, frustration, loneliness and resignation. He pictured that wall growing higher, thicker, shutting him off from sight and touch and emotion. Shutting him off from Meg.

Even so, the question that had tormented him all day bored through the cracks to gnaw and worry at his mind.

Should he tell her?

It had begun that morning, during a short break in the bridge construction. Cameron had paused to wipe his sweating face and take a long, deep drink of the muddy water in his canteen. Swallowing hard, to avoid tasting the foul stuff, he'd lowered his arm and reached up to wipe his mouth with his left hand. The motion had rattled the folded paper in the breast pocket of his shirt.

Only then did he remember taking the paper off Murchison's body. He had carried it with him, he realized, for the past twenty-four hours, but concern for Meg had wiped all thought of it from his mind. Now, however, he found himself suddenly curious.

Wandering away from the noise of the work gangs, Cameron had found a patch of secluded shade, sat down on a boulder and unbuttoned his pocket flap. The paper was dirt-stained and yellowed with sweat. It crackled like old parchment as he unfolded it, expecting to find some sort of letter.

It was not a letter.

For long moments, Cameron had gazed uncomprehendingly at the scrawled lines and marks. Then little by little, things began to make sense.

It was a map. With some kind of accounting in the margin.

Cameron moved his thumb to study the right-hand side of the paper. It was divided off into a long column of marks—each set of four crosshatched with a fifth. Numbers. A hundred, perhaps. What would Murchison have been keeping track of? Days? Weeks? No, the groupings weren't right. It had to be—

Cameron's hand tingled, as if the paper were burning his flesh.

Elephants.

Ivory.

He stared at the map. To the untrained eye, it would appear to be nothing but a maze of meaningless lines. Cameron, however, had seen much of East Africa in his early surveying and hunting days. As he studied the map, its landmarks began to emerge. The jagged mark at the top of the paper matched the craggy silhouette of Mount Kenya. The curved, sweeping line at the bottom—that would be a river, the Tana.

The mountain and river appeared to have been put on the map for orientation. The country in between was drawn with no attempt at proportion or scale. There were marks and outlines that Cameron did not recognize, probably because their real counterparts were not large. Every feature, however, seemed to center around a black *X* near the map's center. That, Cameron realized, was the spot Murchison had marked, the spot the legendary hunter had wanted to find again.

Cameron remembered how he and Juma had found Murchison, with no money, no porters, nothing of value on him but his elephant rifle. He shivered in the torrid air as the circumstance fell into place like the pieces of a jigsaw puzzle, to fit with a terrifying neatness.

A cache. An enormous cache of elephant ivory. For some reason, Murchison had been forced to leave it behind. He'd been on his way to Mombasa, with plans to hire a string of porters and head back for it, when death caught up with him. The ivory, assuming it was well hidden, would still be there, waiting for the first taker.

With shaking hands, Cameron had refolded the map and buttoned it back in his pocket. His old nightmare had come full circle, and the devil was there, waiting for him. Ivory. White gold. Enough to make a man rich beyond his dreams.

He ought to destroy the bloody map, he chastised himself. He ought to burn it to black ashes and walk away. But it was already too late for that. The map had rewakened the old dreams and hungers. It was already calling to him, and Cameron knew he would answer that call. He would answer it at the peril of his soul.

He glanced at the glowing Meg across the table. Tell her? Why the devil should he? Meg was in the process of divorcing him, to wed a rich lover who'd probably inherited his money without having to lift a manicured finger for it.

Why should he even *think* of telling her about the map? Did he want to impress her? Did he think it would make a difference to her, knowing that wild, worthless Cameron MacKenna was about to become a rich man? Did he think it would change her mind?

Cameron quaffed his warm, flat beer. No, he would not tell Meg about the map. Only a fool would want a woman who would change her mind for that sort of reason. And he was no fool.

His eyes traced Meg's snub-nosed profile, lingering on a spot of gold where the firelight danced on her cheek. Aye, let her go, he told himself. Send her packing, back to her fancy gentleman friend, and good riddance. What did it matter? If the map proved true, he'd soon have his pick of beautiful women. All a man could want.

The conversation had fallen into a lull, and Cummings failed to stifle a gap-toothed yawn. Surprisingly, it was Meg who rose first, signaling an end to the long meal. "So we'll be putting you out yet another night, I fear," she said, flashing Bowman an apologetic smile. "I can't tell you how sorry I am, or how grateful. My husband and I shall never forget your kindness." She slipped an arm through Cameron's, playing her part like Lily Langtry, he thought.

Bowman bobbed like a woodpecker. Cummings grinned and shot Cameron a furtive wink—aye, the foul-minded little blighter. Let him and the others think whatever they wanted. As for himself, the best he could hope for was that he and Meg would pass a civil night together. Their battle was over, and he was weary of it. In truth, it would be a relief to have her gone. Only then would he feel free to concentrate on the map.

How soon could he get away to go after the ivory? he wondered. He couldn't ask Bowman for leave before the rains, especially without explaining his reasons. Yet, the longer the ivory lay where it was, the greater the chance of someone else stumbling onto it. And resigning from his job was a calculated risk. If he was wrong, or if he arrived too late... Aye, the whole matter would bear some thinking over.

He slipped a casual arm around Meg's minuscule waist. "It's getting late, Meg darlin'. Time for bed," he murmured, guiding her steps toward the tent. She gazed up at him with an adoring smile, playing her part almost too well.

They broke apart self-consciously as the tent flaps fell shut behind them. The masquerade was over for now. They could stop pretending. Cameron found the oil lamp in the darkness, removed the chimney and lit the wick. Soft, yellow light flooded the darkness.

Meg was sitting on the bunk, hands hugging her arms as if she were trying to warm herself. Her big, violet eyes regarded him gravely. In the lamplight, her lips were as full and red as pomegranates. They parted hesitantly; then she spoke.

"I'm sorry, Cameron," she said.

"Sorry?" The question sounded more sarcastic than he'd meant it to.

"I've caused you no end of trouble. If only I'd found an easier way to do this."

"It's done." He gathered up his bedroll and shook it cautiously to check for scorpions. There were none.

"Please, this isn't easy for me..." She gulped hard, then stumbled on. "I know we've caused each other a great deal of hurt, but most of it's behind us. I'd like to part as friends, if that's possible."

Cameron groaned his exasperation, knowing what would likely follow. Why did women have this urge to talk an involvement to death, to dissect, examine and analyze? Why couldn't they just make a clean, quick end to it?

"Why? What's the point?" he asked coldly.

A shadow darted across her face, and Cameron knew he had wounded her. But she lifted her chin and continued.

"We have a child, a sweet, tenderhearted little girl. She needs to know that her mother and father don't hate each other."

"I don't hate you, Meg."

"I know," she said softly. "If you hated me, you couldn't have taken care of me the way you did yesterday."

Cameron, his throat tight and aching, focused his attention on laying down the bedroll. If only she would leave him in peace!

"I don't hate you, either," she continued. "I'm only doing what I must. Jenny deserves a better life. So do I."

Must? Then you don't love this man? Cameron bit back the question before it could escape his lips. Meg's relationship with her fancy gentleman was none of his business. "I'd have thought your father would leave you well off. He did have the finest house in Darlmoor."

"In Darlmoor!" Meg chuckled bitterly. "Judges don't make a great deal of money—not honest ones, at least, and my father was honest. He left me the house, but little else. I told you how I earn enough to keep bread on the table."

"Aye. But that won't be for long, will it now?"

Meg did not answer. She glanced down at her hands, looking, suddenly, as vulnerable as a flower. Cameron gripped a tent pole, fighting a senseless urge to sweep her up in his arms and batter down the walls between them with lovemaking. It was too late for that, he reminded himself sourly. Better that the walls remain in place, to protect them both.

She raised her violet eyes again. "I remember how you always talked about going to Africa. You were planning to become rich, shooting elephants and selling the ivory."

The map seemed to burn in Cameron's pocket. "Aye. The dream of a young fool," he muttered.

"What happened, Cameron?"

He ran a hand through his dust-matted hair, battling the nightmare that lurked like a dark monster in his memory. "That, my dear Mary Margaret, is a long story. Too long for tonight. You need your rest."

"I'm not tired." Her eyes were as curious as a child's.

"Meg . . ." Cameron felt the monster stir inside him, felt its black, awful heaviness. And suddenly he knew he would tell her. He had to. He had held it in too long.

Anguish quivered through his body. "It's not a pretty tale."

"That's all right."

He swung a canvas camp stool around to face the bunk where she sat, huddled like a little girl, with her legs pulled up under her skirts. "No one else knows about this," he said warningly, pausing to clear his throat.

"I understand. No one else will."

"All right then." Cameron sank tensely onto the stool and took a deep breath. "I did try ivory hunting. Once."

Lamplight danced in Meg's eyes like the fire in a pair of opals. Her lips parted, but she did not speak.

Awkwardly, Cameron began. "I'd been with the railroad about a year when I met a grizzled old Portuguese in a Mombasa bar. He said he was an ivory hunter, said if I'd work for him six months, he'd teach me all I needed to know."

The memory broke over him, releasing a flood of words. "Aye, you can imagine how I felt, Meg. It was like heaven dropping into my lap. I said goodbye to the railroad and we headed up-country, for Lake Naivasha, with a string of porters. On the way, the old man taught me how to shoot pot game and how to live in the bush. It was like a picnic—until we got into the elephants.''

Meg was leaning forward to listen. Cameron could feel his own tension building. He could feel the painful throbbing of a vein in his left temple. No, he thought, he should not have begun this story. But it was too late now. It came pouring out of him as if a dam had broken.

"You can't know how it was. I'd never been around elephants. I'd never realized how intelligent they are—like humans almost, but stronger, nobler in their own way. Meg, I've never talked about this before. People would think I was crazy. Maybe you will, too."

Meg shook her head. Her hand brushed his wrist, its light pressure cool and reassuring. He took a breath and plunged on.

"The old man was so cruel it sickened me. The first elephant he shot was a pregnant cow. When the natives cut her open, I couldn't stay—" Cameron broke off. He would spare her the rest—the memory, time after time, of disgracing himself behind the bushes, the horror of tusks hacked from still-living animals, of spurting blood and youngsters squalling beside their mothers, of screams that were chillingly close to human.

"It got worse," he said. "Worse than you can imagine. I'd have left if I'd been more confident about surviving on my own. As it was, I felt I had no choice."

Cameron drew a long, ragged breath, waiting for some reaction from Meg. She did not speak, but her eyes were moist with sympathy. So far, she'd shown no dismay at his lack of manly fortitude. But he wasn't through. He'd started this hellish story, and now he would have to finish it. When it was done, she would know him for what he truly was.

The flow of words had stopped. Now he had to force them out. "The old man did all the killing. But he'd trained me to back him up with a second rifle in case anything went wrong. Not that he really needed me. The old butcher was a crack shot, and he knew his business. We'd take four, maybe five elephants in a day, more when we found a good herd. I kept hoping I'd get used to it. I didn't. I only got sicker.''

Cameron suppressed a shudder. Aye, he'd spare her that as well: the cold-sweat nightmares, the tortures of self-doubt when he questioned not only his courage but his manhood. Even now, there were times when those doubts returned to haunt him. But those times were secret, too painful to share with anyone, least of all Meg.

She was waiting expectantly for the rest of the story. Lamplight glowed on her face and on the golden tendrils of her hair. Oh, she was all sweetness, all sympathy now; and for the space of a heartbeat, Cameron was tempted to lie. To keep that sympathy, to win her favor—but no. Favor falsely won would be as worthless as tin. He would tell the truth. She would despise him for it, but what did that matter? He had already lost her.

"We were out in the bush one afternoon when we came across a cow with a fair set of tusks, trailing a calf. She charged as soon as she caught our scent.'' Cameron could feel himself sweating. He gulped back the tightness that rose like poison in his throat. "The old man was ready for her. He took the time to aim at a vital spot. She was almost on top of him before he pulled the trigger.''

Meg had stopped breathing.

"There was nothing but a click. The gun had misfired. It was suddenly up to me—'' Cameron's voice broke. He'd begun to tremble. Meg's hand reached out to him, but his eyes warned her away.

"Lord help me, Meg, I froze. I couldn't shoot. I stood fifty yards off and watched while that elephant cow pounded the old bastard into bloody red jelly.''

Cameron could not go on. Overcome with self-loathing, he buried his face against his clenched hands. His shoulders heaved with emotion.

He sensed Meg's eyes on him and imagined her revulsion. Aye, she knew his shame now. She knew him for the miserable coward he was. She could go back to Britain and marry her gentleman in good conscience. As for himself, he would swallow what little remained of his principles and go after the ivory that Murchison had so bloodily won. He would meet the devil and hand over his soul. What did it matter? What did any of it matter now?

He felt her cool hand on his arm and the sweet pressure of her tightening fingers. "Cameron, it's all right," she whispered gently. "Don't torture yourself. Forget what's past and go on."

Cameron quivered under her touch, like a wild animal being stroked. He burned with need. He ached to reach out to her, to gather her in his arms and lose himself in her softness; to find her lips and bruise them with kisses until both of them were dizzy with desire; to strip away her clothes and rediscover every lush curve and hollow of her body. And to love her. Aye, love her until the past faded away and the terrible pictures in his mind became nothing but a blur.

But that was the last thing Meg would want, he reminded himself harshly. Oh, she was making a dandy show of compassion, but he'd already seen what an accomplished actress she was. He'd wager his life that beneath those sweet words and gentle touch lurked feelings of disgust, revulsion and pity. Well, he would have none of it!

Jerking away, he turned on her in a fury of self-condemnation. "Forget the past? You think your saying it makes it so, Mary Margaret? Rubbish! You don't know how it was! You feel sorry for me, that's all! Well you can take your blasted pity and go to—"

"Stop it, Cameron!" She was suddenly ice, and her words froze him. "I thought we could part as friends, but I can see that's not possible. You're so full of self-hate, so full of anger—"

"That's enough!" He glared at her. She glowered back at him. They faced each other in dead silence, like two bristling animals in the confined space of the tent. Cameron knew he'd spoken too hastily, but it was too late to retract his words, too late for any kind of understanding.

He turned away with a ragged sigh as the weight of hopelessness crashed in on him. "Let's get some sleep, Meg. Otherwise, all we'll do is tear each other to pieces."

She hesitated, then slumped on the bed, the fight gone out of her. "Blow out the lamp. I want to undress in the dark."

He did as she'd asked, then fumbled his way to the bedroll and stretched out with his clothes on. He could hear Meg taking off her waist and petticoat, hear the rustle of fabric and the shallow rush of her breathing.

The small, intimate sounds were torture. Cameron endured them as the seconds ticked by. At last, when he could stand no more, he pulled the blanket over his ears and shut her out.

Meg was awake when he left the next morning, but she lay still in the bunk, her eyes tightly closed. After last night, she and Cameron had nothing more to say to each other.

She had tried to end the relationship on friendly terms, but Cameron did not want friendship, sympathy or understanding. He wanted nothing except to hide behind his wall of hurt and rage, where no one could reach him.

Well, let him, Meg resolved angrily. She'd done all she could. Her conscience was clear.

All the same, as she lay there, she felt hollow inside, as if something had been taken from her and irretrievably lost.

Only when Cameron was well away from the tent did she begin to stir. Sitting up, she swung her legs off the bed, parted the netting and reached for her hairbrush. She stroked hard and fast, venting her frustration on her tangled locks. Her hand slowed, however, as Cameron's story returned to haunt her.

The brush lay in her lap, forgotten, as her mind painted pictures of the maddened elephant, the screaming, helpless old hunter, and Cameron staring in mute horror, his finger frozen on the trigger of the rifle.

Agitated now, Meg stood up, the motion sending her hairbrush tumbling to the floor. She would do well to forget the past and look ahead, she admonished herself. Yes, she would think about the train coming, perhaps tomorrow. She would think about being with Jenny again. Hastily, she rummaged for her clothes and began to dress.

She was weaving the last of the pins into her hair when her ears caught the faroff wail of a train whistle.

She froze in disbelief. No, she reminded herself, it was too soon for the train to return. She'd heard something else, a bird or an animal.

But when the whistle echoed across the plain a second time, its shrill tone was unmistakable. It was the train, and judging from the sound, it would soon be pulling into camp.

Meg flew to snatch up her things—her nightgown, her toiletries, her divorce papers. She did not know why the train was early or how long it would be here. She only knew that when it pulled out again, she would be on board.

She raced out of the tent, her bundle under her arm. Far down the track, she could see a plume of smoke and the chunky outline of the locomotive. Cameron had heard the whistle, too. He was running, pounding up over the rise from the bridge, sweat-drenched and panting.

A small crowd had gathered by the time the train chugged into camp and hissed to a stop. But something was odd about this train. Behind the locomotive and its tender was a single car, a plain wooden boxcar with high, narrow windows.

As the crowd stared, a side door on the boxcar slid open. The first person to step out, looking gray and ill and ten years older than when Meg had last seen him, was the Emir.

She ran to him. His hands clutched hers, the fingers sharp and curved like talons. "My dear..." he murmured. "My dear child."

Meg was suddenly light-headed with fear. "What is it?" she whispered. "Tell me."

The Emir shook his head despairingly. "It is your daughter. Your little Jenny. She has been stolen."

Chapter Seven

Meg felt nothing at first. She'd misunderstood the Emir, that was all. It sounded as if he'd said Jenny was stolen. But that couldn't be true. Jenny was fine. She was safe in Mombasa. They were going to be together soon.

The Emir clasped her hand harder. "I came as soon as I could. I want you to know that we are doing everything we can to get her back."

"No!" Meg felt as if the world had frozen around her and was splintering into jagged pieces. She was dimly aware that Cameron had come up behind her, but even he had become part of that shattering world in which nothing was real.

"It was that devil, Hassan," the Emir hissed. "If I had realized he was capable of such a crime..."

"Hassan?" The name penetrated where nothing else could. Meg's knees began to sag. She felt Cameron's hands gripping her elbows.

"Meg, what in heaven's name is going on?" he growled in her ear.

The Emir seemed to notice him for the first time. His grizzled eyebrows raised slightly. "You are the husband?"

Cameron's hesitation was barely perceptible. "Aye. That I am."

"Then this concerns you, as well. Your daughter has been stolen from my household."

Cameron's fingers tightened, hurting Meg's arms. "There must be some mistake. I only have one child. She's in Scotland."

"No, Cameron—" Meg twisted out of his grip and spun back to face him, her voice an anguished whisper. "Jenny came to Africa with me. I left her in Mombasa."

"Good Lord."

Meg saw the shock and the pain come together in his face, but there was nothing she could do. They stared at each other in helpless agony, neither of them able to speak.

Mercifully, the Emir broke the silence. "Mr. Mac-Kenna, you must get your wife to a resting place, where we can talk. I will tell you everything then. But first, if you could arrange food and water for my men...."

Only then did Meg's dazed eyes see past him, into the open boxcar. In its shadows, she glimpsed dark faces and the glint of shiny new rifles.

Cameron was barking orders to the cook boys. Then Meg felt him take her arm again, felt the hard, painful pressure of his fingers guiding her back toward the tents, to a shady spot where someone had placed three camp chairs. Frail and agitated, the Emir glided along beside them.

She was dimly aware of sitting down, of someone giving her tea. But it was Jenny her mind was seeing. Jenny, and Hassan's oily, reptilian eyes. Jenny, small and frightened, in terrible danger. Fear surged like bile into her throat. She wanted to scream out her helplessness, to fling her tea, her stupid, meaningless tea, to the earth. She wanted to strike out at anything, at anyone....

But rage would serve nothing, Meg reminded herself forcefully. She had to keep a grip on her emotions, to be calm and controlled. She had to find a way to help her daughter.

She turned to the Emir and steeled herself to speak. "You said it was Hassan. Tell us everything."

The old man sat very straight in his chair, though his face was gray and he looked to be at the point of collapse. He took a deep, ragged breath and began to speak. "Understand first that what Hassan did, he planned well. How I learned of all this, I will tell you later."

Meg could feel Cameron's presence in the chair beside her. She could feel the strain in him as he leaned forward to catch every word of the old Arab's quaint singsong speech.

The Emir glanced at Meg. "Remember, child, you left before dawn for Kilindini, before the household was awake. No sooner had you gone than he took her. His friends were waiting outside the wall—"

"His friends?"

"Slavers." The old man spat out the word. Meg felt her heart shrivel.

"So clever, that devil Hassan," the Emir continued. "By the time the rest of us awakened, he was at his duties. He told us you had taken your little girl with you. I thought it strange, but saw no reason to doubt him. Her sun hat and some of her clothes, you see, were also missing."

Meg stifled a cry. She remembered that last morning, kissing Jenny's dewy cheek, unaware of the peril that lurked in her very shadow. She had always understood that mothers had a sixth sense to warn them when a loved child was in danger. But she had felt nothing. Dear heaven, all the time she was riding the train, all the time she'd been here at the railhead, she'd had no inkling of the tragedy that had befallen her own daughter.

The Emir wet his throat with a sip of coffee. "As I said, we suspected nothing. Two days later, Hassan approached me saying that his mother had taken ill in Lamu and was dying. I gave him leave to go, of course—" The Emir's voice faltered. He pressed his fingers to his eyelids. "Forgive me. How could I know?"

Meg reached through her own pain to press the old man's wrist. "We both trusted him," she whispered. "But how could Hassan do this? Why?"

"Hassan had gambling debts. The men he owed money to were losing patience. All this I learned on the third day when a cohort of his, a wretch who needed money, also, came to me with the tale. For a price, he told me all he knew—but there's more, child. There were others, ordered to watch for the train and take you, as well."

"To take *me?*" Meg went cold. "Then you would never have known that I didn't have Jenny."

The Emir nodded gravely. "Hassan would no doubt have returned to my service. I would never have suspected his part in your disappearance."

Cameron leaned forward in his chair, as if he were dragging at invisible chains. Meg could feel the wall between them. She could feel his cold rage and his fear. "This monster, Hassan," he growled. "What's become of him?"

"He has disappeared, gone with the slavers, perhaps." The Emir's eyes burned with a hawkish ferocity Meg had not known he possessed. "If Hassan were in my power, he would die slowly, and with great pain, for bringing this disgrace upon my house!"

The vehemence of the old man's outburst shocked both Meg and Cameron into silence. The empty seconds gave Meg time to think, to count the lost days, to imagine what Jenny might be going through even at this moment. Once more, panic overwhelmed her, surging through every raw nerve. She burst out of her chair. "But why would they take Jenny? She's only a little girl—a baby!"

She felt Cameron's hand on her arm, felt his anguished fingers pulling her back into her chair. The Emir's eyes were points of pain in their weathered sockets.

"Would that I could spare you this," he murmured. "There are men so vile that your daughter's tender years would only enhance her value. A child of such beauty would fetch a fortune in the markets of Khartoum or Addis Ababa." His breath sucked in sharply as he added, "But we have time on our side. That is why I have come."

"The men you brought—you're going after the bastards!" It was Cameron who spoke.

The old Arab nodded grimly. Leaning forward, he picked up a stray twig and scratched out a crude map in the dust. "The man who sold me this information said the slavers had gone inland, following the old caravan trails that lead north, into the desert..."

His words faded as he continued to sketch. Meg watched, fighting to contain urges that, had she allowed them free rein, would have sent her rushing heedlessly onto the plain, screaming her daughter's name to the unhearing sky.

"These trails." the Emir continued, "weave and cross like the strands of a woman's braids. To track the devils from Mombasa, with three days' head start on us..." He shook his head, then suddenly jabbed the point of the twig into the map. "But here, at this spot, all the trails come together!"

"I know that place!" Cameron was out of his chair, crouching over the map. "Caravanners call it The Neck of the Jar. A narrow ravine, with the only drinking water in fifty miles." He had grasped the Emir's plan now, and made himself part of it. Meg knew he would be joining the search. "Aye, we can do it—cut straight across from here, and get there first. Then all we have to do is wait for them!"

Wait. Meg churned with helpless frustration. She wanted Jenny *now*, wanted her safe, wanted her back. "But how long?" she cried. "How many days before they'll be there?"

"Days?" Cameron gave the Emir a dismayed glance. "Meg, it's not a matter of days. We're talking in terms of weeks, a month at least—longer if they stop to pick up more slaves."

"As I said, time is on our side," the Emir soothed. "From here, the distance to the pass is no more than half—"

"But what about Jenny?" Meg was on her feet again, fear lashing her to a frenzy. "All those days, with those horrible men! All the things that could happen to her! She'll be terrified—"

"Stop it, Meg!" Cameron's eyes flashed coldly. "Things are bad enough without your losing your head!"

The Emir was kinder. "We cannot shorten the time, child. But the slavers will care for your Jenny well enough. Her value is too great to do otherwise."

Meg sank back into the chair and pressed her hands to her face. Fear, bleak and helpless, hung over her like a death-pall. Offering her life for Jenny's sake would have been easy. But to wait like this, day after day, doing nothing at all . . .

"I'm going with you," she said.

"Don't be foolish." Cameron, standing now, shot her a withering look.

"Jenny's my daughter. I have the right to go."

"My dear child, you don't know what you're asking," the Emir said gently. "Even with the honor of my house at stake, I myself am not strong enough for such a journey, and neither are you. I will be going back to Mombasa on the train. You must come with me."

"Go back to Mombasa? Go back and wait?" Meg shook her head stubbornly. "I can't. I have to go after Jenny. I'm her mother, don't you see?"

Cameron scowled darkly. "This is no bloody picnic. We'll be walking twenty miles a day, at least, through rougher country than you can imagine. You'd only slow us down, Meg. Is that what you want?"

Meg lifted her gaze to meet his hard blue eyes. "You heard the Emir. We have time to spare. Even so, I won't slow you down. You have my promise." At the sight of his unyielding frown, desperation exploded in her. "For the love of heaven, Cameron, I *must* go with you! If we find Jenny alive, she'll need her mother! I have to be there for her!" Quivering, she seized his arm. His flesh was like stone. "I'm coming whether you like it or not!" she said. "You can't stop me!"

Meg sensed his withdrawal even before he stepped backward, breaking her hold. His eyes were as chilly and remote as the moon.

"No, Mary Margaret," he said quietly. "I don't suppose I can."

Leaving Meg with the old man, Cameron walked back
toward the railhead. He moved like an automaton, his mind
churning with emotions he could neither understand nor
control. It was as if he had been flung headfirst into a bi-
zarre and unfamiliar world. The blazing blue sky was the
same. The sweeping yellow grassland was the same. But
everything else had become as mixed and twisted as the
images in a set of carnival mirrors.

He tried to sort the mess out, one element at a time. First
there was his daughter—Jenny. Not just a name now, but
a little girl in terrible danger. And he, who'd done little
more than spill the seed to give her life, was suddenly a father—*Jenny's* father—and her rescue had become more
urgent to him than anything in the world. He would move
heaven and earth, sacrifice anything he possessed, to see her
safe.

Then there was Meg. He was still reeling with the shock
of what she'd done to him. Not the divorce—that he could
accept, even justify. But to bring their daughter all the way
to Africa, only to hide her in Mombasa; to lie about it when
she knew he would want to see the child, that was unthinkable. Cameron could not understand it, let alone forgive
her.

With all his bitter, wounded heart, he willed her gone. He
willed her to change her mind, to get on the train and go
back to Mombasa with her old Arab friend. But he knew
better than to believe it would happen. Mary Margaret
Owen MacKenna was the most stubborn female on God's
green earth, especially where her daughter was concerned.
She would be a headache and a hindrance all the way to The
Neck of the Jar, but she would not turn back.

As Cameron strode down the hill toward the bridge, he could see Bowman, mounted on his idiot mule. It crossed his mind to ask for the loan of the beast so Meg could ride. But no, mules in the bush were more trouble than they were worth. They scared off game and drew big cats like fish in an alley. If Meg was determined to go along, she could walk like everyone else.

Bowman hailed him as he drew closer. "I say, Mac-Kenna, was that the train I heard coming in? It's not due till tomorrow, at least. Highly irregular, don't you think?"

Cameron squinted up at him through the glaring sunlight. "There's an emergency. I'm sorry, but I'll be taking leave for the next few weeks."

"What?" Bowman's thin voice jumped to a squeak.

"It's my daughter. Meg left her in Mombasa, and—"

"But you said your daughter was at home in Scotland!"

"Aye, and so I thought. My little wife is full of surprises." Cameron paused to breathe his way through a surge of anguish, then plunged ahead. "The child's been kidnapped. Sold to a slave caravan going north. I'm asking your leave to lead the search party going after her."

Bowman's eyes bulged in their pale, round sockets. "Stolen? And sold? Great Scot, man, that sort of thing doesn't happen to British children!"

"Nevertheless, it has." Cameron forced himself to speak calmly. "Do I have your permission to go? I would be gone for several weeks."

Bowman's head swiveled toward the half-finished trestle bridge, and Cameron knew what he was thinking. Anthony Bowman was a fine engineer, well trained and methodical. But he dealt with this job in terms of stresses, angles and grades: steel, timber and gravel. In his head, the work gangs existed only as tools. It had been Cameron who dealt with the Indian coolies as men: Cameron who solved their problems, disciplined them and kept them working. Now, faced with the prospect of losing him for so long, Bowman was visibly agitated. His hands twisted the mule's reins as he looked at the bridge, then returned his uneasy gaze to Cameron.

"I sympathize, old chap," he said. "But we've got a railroad to build. The whole British Empire is depending on us. You can hardly expect to just turn your back and—"

"Bowman, do you have children?"

"Of course not. Why, I don't even have a wife."

"Aye, I'd have guessed as much." Cameron sighed wearily. "Will you be wanting my resignation on paper, or would just saying it be enough?"

Bowman went pale. "But you can't just quit! Blast it, MacKenna, what about the railroad? I need you!"

"So does my daughter."

Bowman's eyes darted one way, then another. "But what about the work? How will I manage the crews? What will I do?"

Cameron was already turning to go. He paused just long enough to speak. "I hear John Patterson's finished with the permanent bridge at Tsavo. He's had his own share of coolie troubles, but since he shot those two man-eaters, the boys bloody worship him. Get him up here if you can. You won't find any better."

"But what—"

"My wife and I will be out of your tent by noon. We thank you for the use of it. Luck to you, Bowman."

Cameron turned on his heel and strode away. Behind him, he could hear Bowman sputtering his protests to the empty air. The devil with him. The devil with the railroad and the whole stinking British Empire. The only thing that mattered now was getting Jenny back.

And if—no, blast it, *when*—they found her, Cameron vowed, he would be more to Jenny than the absentee father he'd been in the past. Oh, Meg could have her gentle man friend. She could have a dozen gentleman friends if she bloody wanted them. But little Jennifer Jane was half his, and he would press his right to be with her. Whatever it took, whatever sacrifices he had to make, she would know him as her father. She would know that he loved her.

Burning with the most intense emotion he had ever known, Cameron paced up the hill toward the dirty sprawl of the camp. Meg, he knew, would be waiting for him.

Meg was in Bowman's tent, folding some dry clothes she'd rinsed out the day before. Her hands moved mechanically, smoothing a collar, creasing a sleeve ... *Dear God, what did it matter?*

The Emir was somewhere outside, eating a late breakfast with the men he'd brought. There were twelve porters and half as many *askaris,* or native soldiers, armed with new Martini rifles like the one Cameron carried. Meg had recognized them as Swahili, a coastal race sprung from a blending of black and Arab blood. Like other Swahili she'd seen, they wore tarbushes and baggy, nightshirt-like garments called *kansus.* Meg shuddered, remembering her first glimpse of their guarded eyes. Jenny's life, all their lives, could depend on these men. Had the old man misjudged them, even as he'd misjudged Hassan?

The morning sun was high by now. It shone hotly through the open tent flap, making a bright rectangle on the floor. The sound of hammers echoed incessantly from the railhead. Setting the clean clothes aside, Meg found her rucksack and dumped its contents onto the bunk.

Her fingers trembled as she sorted her possessions into two piles, one to pack, one to send back to Mombasa with the Emir. She'd already determined to take no more than what was absolutely necessary. Jenny's rescue might well depend on the haste of their small party, and the weight of extra items could slow them down. She would do her part, Meg resolved. She would carry her own load. She would keep pace with the men. And no matter what happened, she would not fret or complain.

The folded divorce papers crackled at her touch. Without hesitation, she thrust them onto the heap destined for

Mombasa. The Emir would keep them safe, and when this horror was over, they would be waiting.

A shadow fell across the blanket. Meg looked up to find Cameron in the entrance of the tent, silhouetted against the glaring sunlight. Her heart stopped.

She waited for him to speak, but he studied her in dark silence, his face a mask. Only his hands, clenched angrily at his sides, betrayed his emotions. Meg froze. For a long moment, they faced each other. Then Cameron reached up, seized the tent flap and jerked it down. Shadows closed around them, shutting out the sun and the squalid surroundings of the camp.

He took a harsh breath. "Let's have this out, Mary Margaret. Lord knows, I've told myself you've enough to bear already, and that I should hold my tongue. But some things need saying. Otherwise, they fester inside a body like poison."

Meg forced herself to meet his cold eyes and speak in a quiet voice. "All right, Cameron. Say what's on your mind and be done with it."

He glared down at her. Meg could feel the pent-up anguish inside him, seething and ready to explode. Anticipating the blow, she plunged ahead herself. "Go on, then! Try to call me worse than I've already called myself. It's all my doing. I should never have brought Jenny to Africa. I should never have left her, not even with people I trusted. What's happened is all my fault, and if we don't find her—"

"Spare me the self-flagellation, Meg," he growled. "I'm not impressed. And I don't care whose bloody fault it was. Jenny's gone, and blame-casting won't get her back." Cameron had begun to pace, his chest rising and falling with each furious breath. Suddenly, halting in midstride, he turned on her.

"It's you I don't understand! How could you do it, Meg? How could you bring Jenny all the way to Africa, then hide her from me?"

Quivering, Meg stood her ground. "I brought her on the ship because it was the only suitable choice. As for the rest, don't you know why I kept her from you? I didn't want her hurt, Cameron. I didn't want her to meet you, and then find out how little you care about her!"

"Meg—"

"Deny it! You didn't want Jenny in the first place! You've never wanted her!"

He glared at her as if she'd lashed him with a whip. "You could have given me some say in the matter," he growled. "As it was, you did everything you could to keep Jenny from me. You never wrote me about her or sent so much as a snapshot. The money I sent, you squirreled away for her future. Did you show it to her? Did you tell her where it came from?" He paused menacingly. "Not bloody likely! Even when you were in need, you were too proud to sully your hands with what I'd earned!"

Meg quivered as the words stung home. "You could have written."

"And you could have told me Jenny was in Mombasa. What was the real reason you kept it from me, Mary Margaret? Was it because I'm not a fine gentleman like your English friend? Because I've got dirt under my fingernails? Because you think my face might not be fit for a child's eyes?"

"Stop it, Cameron!" Meg turned away, afraid he would see how sharply he'd wounded her. "You're just being cruel! It's Jenny we've got to think of now—getting her back! The rest doesn't matter."

He caught her wrist and spun her around to face him. "Doesn't matter? Listen to me, Mary Margaret. How can we work together, even on this, if we don't trust each other? How can we be out there, week after week, with our lives in each other's hands, if this filthy quagmire of dishonesty is lying between us?"

Meg squared her jaw and forced herself to meet his seething gaze. "Being honest with you isn't easy, Cameron. You're an angry, violent man. When the truth doesn't suit you, you simply explode and blow it away."

Cameron's breath sucked in sharply, and Meg braced herself for another furious onslaught. Surprisingly, it did not come—except in the form of a tightly controlled sigh.

"Aye, a point well taken," he conceded with a hard edge to his voice. "Take it for yourself, then. Remember it when you hear what I'm about to say."

He paused to clear his throat. The scar on his face gleamed in the dim shadows of the tent. "This in the spirit of honesty, Mrs. MacKenna," he said. "You come here with your fine airs and treat me as if I'm not fit to polish your boots, let alone meet the daughter who's as much mine as yours. You judge what you see, without knowing—"

Meg was too distraught to endure a lecture. Impatiently, she burst out, "Cameron, can't this wait? Every minute we waste takes Jenny farther out of our reach."

"I know that. But hear me out. This has to be said." His voice was mechanical, frighteningly calm. "You may not believe this, Meg, but for the past four years I've considered myself a married man. I've been true to you."

Meg lowered her eyes, unable to meet the frankness of his gaze. Her emotions tumbled and churned: guilt, relief, dismay, confusion and a curious rage. Why was Cameron telling her this now, with their marriage beyond saving and their child in the hands of slavers?

"I always meant to come back," he said. "But not as the man you see. No, what I wanted was to return with my fortune and somehow make it up to Jenny and you for all the grief I'd caused. But the fortune—you know what happened. And no, I didn't write. But it wasn't because I didn't care. I had my reasons."

"Cameron, please—"

"Be patient, I'm about to get to the point," he said, his voice cold and hard. "You can have your divorce. You're bloody welcome to that, and to your fancy friends, as well.

But hear me on this one thing, Meg. I'm not giving up Jenny. She's my child, and if—no, *when*—we find her, I intend to fight for the right to be her father!''

"Her father! Why, you don't know the meaning of the word! Where were you when she had the colic and cried and cried for weeks on end? Where were you when she was hungry? When she needed changing and washing and loving? You were off chasing rainbows in Africa! Why, I'll wager you didn't give Jenny an hour's thought in four long years!''

Yes, her words had cut him. He glared down at her, color darkening his face. "I won't apologize for the way things have been. But a man can change.''

"Change? You?'' she snapped. "Have you any idea how much you'd need to change to be a fit father to that little girl?''

Cameron had gone rigid. "If you're talking about money, I've known fine fathers who had little to spare. But I won't always be poor, Meg. The day's not far off, in fact, when I'll have the means to give Jenny as much as your gentleman friend could provide. When that time comes, I'll demand my fair share of time with her. That's my right, and I intend to claim it, if I have to fight you through every court from Darlmoor to London!''

"You wouldn't!''

"I would!''

"Then, indeed, Cameron, you shall have to!''

They stood glowering at each other in the dim-shadowed heat of the tent. Cameron's scarred face was a mask of grim determination. Meg met the stony anger in his eyes with her own defiance. She would not have chosen for them to be enemies. But the battle lines were drawn, and would be, she knew, for the duration of their search. She needed his help now. But whatever the outcome, she would not give up half of her daughter's life to a man who had never cared.

As the silent seconds crawled past, Meg felt her outrage melting into despair. She thought of Jenny, lost and frightened, at the mercy of brutal strangers who cared for nothing but the profit she would fetch. She pictured her trussed like an animal, her golden hair matted with dirt, her clothes ragged and filthy, her clear blue eyes wild with terror.

Meg's head had begun to throb. Her knees had gone rubbery. She battled the urge to fling herself into Cameron's arms and sob out her anguish against his chest. She would find no refuge there, she reminded herself. The dark, inflexible man was her enemy. They would endure a temporary truce to search for their child, but beyond that she could expect no comfort from him. She would have no comfort anywhere until Jenny was found.

He moved at last, turning aside from her as if to go. "I've spoken with the Emir's men," he said. "We'll be leaving within the hour."

"I'll be ready," she said.

He raised the tent flap, then paused. "It will be ten times worse than you can imagine. Go back to Mombasa with the Emir, while you still can."

"No. I have to come with you."

The look he gave her blended fury, despair and resignation. "Then God help you, Meg," he muttered.

He stepped out of the tent and was gone without another word.

They left at midday, the equatorial sun pooling like molten fire on their shoulders. It would have been more practical, Cameron realized, to spend the coming night in camp and depart at dawn, but even the thought of waiting was unendurable. He had no wish to face Bowman again, or to spend another "civilized" night with his wife. They had to be moving, he and Meg, or they would be at each other's throats.

They walked single file, with three of the six *askaris* leading, followed by Meg, Cameron, and the other fifteen men. The first leg of their trek would take them along the well-worn trail to Machakos, where there was a small white settlement. The distance could be covered in an easy three days. Cameron could only hope that by then Meg would be exhausted enough to consent to stay there. The wild country beyond was fraught with more danger than he would wish on any woman.

He studied her now as she strode ahead of him, her *terai* perched squarely on her proud little head. Her rucksack bobbed between her shoulders as she walked. She looked small and weak and vulnerable. But he knew better, Cameron reminded himself sharply. This was a woman who would stop at nothing to get what she wanted. He would never trust her again.

Narrowing his eyes, he squinted past her into the stark, blue distance. As far as he could see, the savanna lay like a tawny blanket, ridged and wrinkled, dotted with tree clumps and isolated rocky mounds called *kopjes*. Zebras floated like illusions, appearing and disappearing through shimmering curtains of heat. A blue-and-orange lizard, almost underfoot, scuttled out of the path to vanish in the dry grass. Last year, by this time, the long rains had already begun. But there was no sign of them now. The sky was like polished turquoise, unflecked by even a single cloud.

The twelve Swahili porters carried the gear on their heads in sixty-pound bundles, while the *askaris,* flaunting their higher status, marched with rifles slung across their backs. They moved along in silence, their big, leathery feet plodding softly in the dust. Their stillness unsettled Cameron. In other caravan's he'd traveled with, the Swahili had been gregarious souls who laughed, joked and sang their way across the tedious landscape. But these men were of a different stripe. Mercenaries, Cameron surmised, hired by the old Emir for the grim work that was their specialty. He could only hope they knew how to use those shiny new guns, and that they would take orders when the time came.

When the time came. He tried to imagine his daughter in the hands of slavers. He could almost feel Jenny's terror, feel her pulse pounding like the tiny, tender heart of a bird. The protectiveness that came over him was so fierce, it made him dizzy. He tried to reach out to her in his mind. *Be brave, little one . . . your father is on his way.*

But it was no good. Cameron fell prey at last to a sickening sense of futility. Jenny was no more than a speck in a vast wild world that crawled with peril: drought, disease, wild animals, poisonous snakes and insects, murdering natives and unscrupulous whites. The odds of finding her alive, let alone getting her back, were infinitesimal.

He stared morosely at Meg's narrow back and the firm set of her shoulders beneath the twill jacket. She was striding determinedly, just managing to keep pace with the three Swahili in the lead. No, he concluded, she could not possibly understand about Jenny. Meg was new to Africa. She had only a vague, unrealistic idea of the horrors that lurked behind its savage beauty.

And he would not enlighten her, Cameron resolved. He would leave her the illusion that Jenny was safe and well somewhere, and that finding her would be only a matter of time. The truth would crush her. Even he could not be that cruel.

Piece by piece the plan fell into place. For the next three days, he would make things as pleasant as possible. Meg was not conditioned to long days of trekking. By the time they reached Machakos, she would be bone-weary. She would sleep deeply and well. When she awakened the next morning, he and the eighteen Swahili would be gone.

Meg would hate him for it. Aye, she would curse him to the heavens. But Cameron's mind was made up. It would be a kindness, he told himself. An act of mercy.

Chapter Eight

At dusk, they passed through a clump of tall trees. To Meg's relief, Cameron ordered a halt. As if by conjuration, the camp began to emerge from the bundles that had bobbed atop porters' heads through the long afternoon. There were blankets, plates, lanterns and cookpots. And there was one tent, to be shared, evidently, by the *bwana* and *memsahib*, unless Cameron planned to sleep outside with the boys.

Too weary to take another step, Meg collapsed against the trunk of a massive thorn tree on the far fringe of the camp. She swigged water from her canteen as she watched the activity, no longer caring that the water was muddy and crawling with suspicious-looking specks. Her muscles ached. Her corset chafed her ribs. Her feet were swollen and throbbing. Worst of all, her whole heart and soul cried out for Jenny.

These miseries aside, the afternoon would have been filled with wonder. Meg had seen giraffes grazing the high branches of an acacia. She'd watched breathless through Cameron's field glass as a cheetah streaked through the sunlight to bring down an impala. Her footsteps had stirred up clouds of white butterflies, and sent a covey of spurfowl into squawking flight.

She had learned some things, as well, about the dark men who marched with them. Twice that afternoon, their caravan had halted while the Swahili spread their prayer rugs, raised their lean haunches and bowed toward Mecca, just as she had seen the Emir do. And Hassan, she reminded herself with a shiver, although it seemed strange that a man capable of what Hassan had done would bow to any god at all.

Toward sunset, one of the *askaris* had shot a gazelle. Another man had sprinted toward the downed animal and slashed its throat with a flat bush knife called a *panga*. That, too, Cameron had explained, was a law of Mohammed. Any animal not killed in such a way was unclean and could not be eaten by followers of the Prophet.

Skinned and dressed now, the gazelle hung roasting over the cookfire. Rice steamed in big tin pots, and the cook was using a rusty fork to mix up what appeared to be biscuit dough. The aromas had begun to blend, wafting outward into the cool twilight.

Above Meg's head, the tree's thorny branches were etched ink-black against the purple sky. She closed her eyes and rested her head against the rough bark, not caring, even, whether there might be ants on it.

Evening crickets chirped in the dry grass. Drowsy now, she willed the sound to fill her head, driving out the pain of conscious thought. She could not think anymore. She needed oblivion. She needed rest.

A hyena, attracted by the meat smell, tittered from the shadows beyond the tent. Meg's eyes shot open. Darkness had closed around her like a heavy black fist. She could see stars through the bare branches, and she realized she'd been dozing.

The hyena whooped giddily, like a demented schoolgirl. Its cry sent jolts of panic screaming along Meg's frayed nerves. She scrambled to her knees. Yes, it was all right; she could see the fire, a scant two-dozen paces away. She hurled herself toward it, but she had gone to sleep with her legs bent under her. They were as numb as two wooden sticks.

She plunged forward and sprawled full-length on the ground, crushing her hat beneath her.

As she lay there in dazed consternation, she heard the sound of a stone thunking into solid flesh. The hyena yiped as Cameron's curse shattered the darkness.

"Out of here, you mangy beggar." He flung more stones. The hyena's maniacal yelps faded into the night.

By the time Cameron stepped into sight, Meg was sitting at the base of the tree again, brushing twigs off her jacket and trying to recover her lost dignity. He towered above her, legs planted wide apart in his high-topped boots. One hand balanced the rifle, barrel-up.

"Are you all right?" His voice was carefully neutral, neither warm nor cold.

"Quite. Only a little ruffled." Meg concentrated on punching the shape back into her crushed felt *terai*.

His chest rose and fell. "You ought to stay closer to the fire after dark. Hyenas may look and sound like fools but their jaws can shear off a man's leg, bone and all. Worse, they've got no fear of humans. Bloody spotted devils will walk right into a camp. That one was getting a little too close to suit me."

Meg shuddered, then hid her fear with a nonchalant shrug. "I suppose I should thank you for saving me," she muttered.

"Spare me the sarcasm, Meg. I just wanted to remind you that you can't go wandering around wherever you please here. This isn't Darlmoor."

"I should hope not! Look at the trouble I got into wandering around *there!*"

Silence from Cameron. Meg stared down at the dark blur of her hat, wondering whether he was amused, disgusted, or so obtuse as to have missed her meaning.

"It's all right," she said. "Jenny's the best—the best thing anybody ever gave me—" Her voice nearly broke at the end, but she held on. There were no tears.

"Meg..." His hand reached toward her, then paused, hesitant, in midair.

"Don't," she said.

He turned away. "What I really came for was to tell you that dinner's almost ready," he said, his voice stripped of emotion.

"I'm not hungry."

"You're a grown-up lass. I can't force you to eat. But you'll slow us all down tomorrow if you don't have the strength to keep walking."

"All right. Go on. I'll come in a few minutes."

He made no motion to leave. "I meant what I said about staying close," he said. "Don't even go to the bushes without somebody to guard you."

Meg sagged dejectedly against the tree trunk. "I'm too tired to go to the bushes. I'm too tired to go anywhere."

"Are you sorry you came?"

"You know better than to ask. I had to come."

Silence again. Then a long, weary sigh as he settled beside her, sliding his back down the tree. Cameron had been civil all afternoon. Too civil, Meg reminded herself. This was the man who had vowed to fight her for Jenny. She could not afford to trust him. Especially now, when she was exhausted, discouraged and aching with her own needs.

The night sky was speckled with stars, paling where the full moon rode low above the trees. Bats swooped through the darkness, their high-pitched squeaks blending with the cricket songs. Out on the plain, a jackal yelped, and was answered by another, perhaps its mate. Jackals mated for life, Meg had read. Well, jackals had simpler lives than people did. They didn't have to live apart. They didn't need money. They weren't capable of hurting each other the way human partners so often did.

Cameron had been true to her. All this time, he had been true to her.

She turned her head slightly, so that she could see him out of the corner of her eye. His profile was dark against the moonlit sky. His eyes were closed. He was tired, too, Meg realized. But Cameron's was a weariness of the spirit, born of discouragement and despair. He saw himself as a coward and a failure, living in the desolation of his own lost dreams.

Light from the rising moon gleamed on the scar that slashed the side of his face. A coward? Cameron had attacked a man-eating lion, with a shovel as his only weapon. Had he been moved by compassion for a helpless coolie, or by the need to prove his own manhood? Meg would never know.

He sat, now, with his back against the tree, his shoulder a finger's breadth from hers. She could feel the heat that radiated from his sun-darkened skin. She could sense the pain of his aloneness almost as acutely as she felt her own.

What would happen if she were to lean against his shoulder, or reach out and touch his hand? Would he respond to her? Would he gather her into his arms and hold her as she longed and needed to be held?

Her fingers stirred. They moved, paused. Don't be a fool, she admonished herself, jerking her hand back to her lap. Cameron was too proud to accept comfort, and too angry to give it. He would only rebuff her, and the evening would end with both of them hurt and sullen. She would be wiser to keep the distance between them, to maintain the unspoken truce that had settled in over the long afternoon. Caution—yes, that would be her watchword as far as Cameron was concerned.

Had he meant what he'd said about fighting her for Jenny? The possibility raised some frightening questions. Where would he get the money for solicitors? How would he prove that he could support and care for a child? Would he expect to shuttle poor Jenny back and forth between Africa and Britain? What about her schooling? And, most important, what could Meg do to prevent the whole ghastly arrangement? She would have to contact her solicitors as soon as—

She crumpled as the truth slammed home. What good were questions? Jenny was lost, and if they didn't get her back, the answers would not matter. Nothing in this world would ever truly matter again.

The tension that hung between Cameron and herself was so black that Meg could no longer bear it. She groped for a way to break the silence. "You never told me the rest of the story," she ventured.

"Story?" He stirred beside her, his shoulder brushing her arm. Meg tried to ignore the spark of warmth that the contact awakened.

"Your ivory-hunting adventure. What happened to you after the old man died?"

Cameron sighed dejectedly and settled back against the tree. "Not much to tell. I buried what was left of the poor bastard. Then I went back to camp, got the whisky chest and drank till I passed out. Crazy thing to do, but my mind kept seeing that old man, and hearing him scream...."

He lapsed into an uneasy stillness, and Meg knew that he was still reliving that awful vision. She battled the urge to touch him, to glide a hand along his shoulder and soothe the tension from his rock-hard muscles. Such a gesture would be foolish, she knew. Cameron did not want to be touched, at least not by her.

"What happened after that?" she asked.

"When I came to my senses the next day, I found myself alone. The native boys were gone. They'd taken the ivory and all the gear. Didn't leave me anything except a canteen and an old single-shot with a handful of cartridges... Hell, I should have died. I *would* have died if I'd had the sense to. As it was, it took me six weeks to get back to the railroad. By then, I'd come down with malaria and could barely walk. Spent a couple of weeks in the infirmary and went back to work."

Meg gazed up through the branches at the star-speckled sky. "Cameron, I'm sorry," she blurted out impulsively. "I've blamed you for not writing, and for not sending more money for Jenny. If I'd understood how bad things were for you...."

"Save your understanding, Meg. I don't need it anymore. And I need your pity even less!"

His cold, proud voice chilled her into silence. She sat as if frozen, arms hugging her knees. No, she reflected, the war between Cameron and herself was not over. They might declare an occasional truce, but it would not last. There'd been too much conflict between them, too much bloodletting for any chance of a lasting peace.

The cook had turned away from the fire. *"Chacula, bwana! Chacula, memsahib!"* he called in a high-pitched, melodious voice. Meg hauled herself to her feet before Cameron could rise and help her up. For now, at least, there was nothing more to say.

The tent, which they would share in separate bedrolls, was a far cry from Bowman's—not much bigger, in fact, than a kennel for a good-sized sheepdog. In terms of comfort, it provided little more than sleeping space. When Cameron saw it, he had nearly offered to spend the night outside with the boys. But no, he reminded himself, there were all kinds of dangers here, from snakes and scorpions to marauding leopards. Whether she wanted it or not, Meg would need his protection.

They'd eaten in silence, too tired and hungry to talk. And that, Cameron groused, was probably just as well. He'd behaved decently all afternoon, but now his veneer of civility was wearing thin, exposing the raw emotions beneath. His nerves twanged with irritation. He'd spent too many hours walking behind Meg, watching the swing of her legs, the sway of her hips and the tantalizing up-and-down shift of her round little buttocks through the trim khaki skirt. That constant view of her had kept him in a maddening state of arousal much of the afternoon.

He had fought the swell of desire with every weapon in his emotional arsenal—his anger, his pride, even his fears for Jenny. But that wild ache, that burning woman-hunger he'd resisted for so long, had not gone away.

Cameron had relived every wretched night of the past four years. He'd counted the times in Mombasa when he'd conquered the temptation to vent his lust for the price of a few rupees, only to give himself up at last to solitary release in a locked hotel room. It was a practice he despised, because it left him feeling so empty. But he'd had no acceptable alternative. Mombasa whores were notorious for disease. And as for his marriage to Meg, aye, that, too, had given him an incentive to stay out of the brothels. Though until today he'd never declared it, even to himself, he'd always thought in terms of going back to face her cleanly and honestly. It had given him something to hope for, something he hadn't wanted to spoil.

Lord, what a waste.

He stood now, outside the tent, waiting for her to finish undressing and crawl into her bedroll. He could hear her moving awkwardly inside the dark, cramped space. He could hear those now-familiar little grunts as she eased out of her corset. How could a woman walk all day in such a miserable contraption? How could she breathe?

He hoped Meg wouldn't want to talk. Talk wouldn't be a good idea tonight. It would be too easy to say things both of them would regret.

The fire blazed up as one of the boys piled on fresh sticks. The *askaris* and porters were already bedded down, lying as close to the flames as they could manage without getting singed. The night had cooled to a pleasant chill.

"I'm ready. You can come in anytime." Meg's whisper was husky and intimate in the darkness, but Cameron knew better than to take her words as an invitation. He unlaced his high boots, unfastened his belt and unbuttoned his shirt and trousers. As the clothes fell away, he crouched low and stepped into the tent, clad in his union suit and carrying his rifle.

His foot nudged Meg, where she lay along the left wall, her back toward him and her blanket pulled up to her chin. She did not respond to the accidental touch, but he knew she was not asleep. Her breathing, in the small, close space, was tense and light. Moving awkwardly, Cameron eased himself into his own bedroll and laid the rifle within quick reach. His right side lay against the canvas, but he was as near to Meg as if they'd been sleeping on opposite sides of a double bed.

He stretched full length on his back, his eyes staring upward into the darkness. Faintly, through the flap, the campfire's peaceful flicker danced on the rear wall. "Good night, Mary Margaret," he murmured.

"Good night, Cameron."

There was a long, expectant silence. He could feel her fear in the night. He could feel her need for comfort, as he felt his own. If only they could put their arms around each other. . . .

But that would only make matters worse. Meg might still be his wife, but she was as good as promised to another man. The water was muddied enough already, he told himself. Aye, leave it be.

The quiet seconds crept by. Cameron could hear her breath, coming now in tiny, muffled gasps. She seemed to be crying.

"Meg . . ."

"I'm . . . all right."

He fought the urge to touch her. "Meg, we'll get through this. All of us. Even Jenny." Lord, what a promise! As if by saying it, he had the power to make it so!

"She's so . . . little. So alone. . . ."

No, he could not stand it. "Stop it, Meg!" he growled. "Falling apart won't help!"

"I—I said I was all right—" She was making an excruciating effort to control herself. "I'm just tired, that's all. And worried. Oh, Cameron, why? Why Jenny?"

This time Meg broke. Giving up the battle, she lay huddled wretchedly beneath the blanket while her body trembled with heartrending sobs.

Torn, Cameron listened in the darkness. He'd resolved to keep his distance, but Meg's grief was more than he could endure. It was as if her pain were his own, as if she were crying his own unshed tears. Driven as much by need as by compassion, he reached out, slid his arms around her and gathered her gently against his chest.

She came without resistance, like a child needing shelter. Cameron cupped her protectively in the curve of his body, feeling the sharp little jerks of her ribs against his chest; feeling, too, the softly swelling buds of her breasts and the throbbing of her heart through the thin nightdress.

"It's all right, lass," he murmured against her hair. "Go ahead and cry. Let it all out."

She buried her face in the hollow of his neck and sobbed until his chest was slicked with her tears. Cameron held her tensely, battling her nearness with all his strength. Every instinct cried out to shelter and protect her. But he could not trust this woman, he reminded himself forcefully. She had rejected, betrayed and deceived him. To give in to his instincts would be like walking into the web of an alluring female spider.

He felt her begin to relax in his arms. Little by little, her quivering sobs subsided until she lay quietly against him, breathing deeply. She had cried herself to sleep.

Overcome by a disturbing sweetness, Cameron stretched out alongside her and closed his eyes. Meg slumbered in his arms, soft and warm and fragrant, the length of her body pressed lightly to his. In spite of everything, the feel of her was heaven. His mind protested drowsily that this was madness, but his arms would not let her go. In all his wild and lonely years, he had never known the simple bliss of drifting off to sleep with a woman beside him. He ached now with the poignant awareness of what he had missed.

Meg whimpered in her dreams and nestled closer. Cameron's lips brushed a stray tendril of her hair; then, unable to resist the lure of her softness, nibbled a tentative path along her hairline.

Her skin was musky with tears and sweat. He traced a tentative circle on her forehead with the tip of his tongue. The taste of her sent erotic sparks spiralling crazily downward all the way to his feet. His body warmed and stirred, straining the crotch of his union suit.

This was insane!

He found himself craving more. He wanted to taste her ears, her cheeks and lips, and pillage her mouth with his tongue. He wanted to rip away the senseless barrier of her nightgown and lick, nuzzle, nip and savor his way over every inch of Meg's delectable body.

His swollen desire lay like ironwood against her hip. The sensation was sweet torture. He endured it for the sake of her rest, but as the minutes crawled by, Cameron's frustrated emotions churned themselves into a rage. By heaven, this woman was his *wife!* He had every right to take her and—

But no, he had no right at all. He had never believed that words and laws gave one person the right to violate another's free will, not even in marriage. What he wanted so desperately was not a right but a privilege—one that could only be granted by love.

And as far as love was concerned...

Don't be a fool, he lashed himself. *She doesn't care a hang about you. She's only tired and lonesome and scared.*

Cameron sighed and eased his fevered body away from her delicious, curving warmth. Meg slumbered on, oblivious to his torment. He let her sleep. Tomorrow's trek would be twice as long as today's had been. She would need all her strength.

In the dim light, he could make out the pale square of her face and the dark smudge where her lashes lay against her skin. Her hair tumbled on the pillow, smelling of wind and sunlight. Little Meg had done all right today, he reflected. She'd trudged along without a complaint, keeping up with the men and demanding no special treatment. She had grit; he couldn't deny that. But the journey ahead would be too hard for any woman, to say nothing of the heartbreak that lurked at its end.

But he could not even let himself think of that. Whatever the odds, he had to convince himself that Jenny was alive, that she would be found and rescued. Otherwise, how could he stand to look into Meg's hopeful eyes?

Cameron's own weariness had begun to catch up with him. The small night noises from outside were blurring to a muffled sigh in his head, to rise and fall like the cadence of the sea on a northern shore. The cries of bats and nightjars had dimmed to a muted piping, like the sound of faraway seabirds.

Aye, he knew where he was now. He knew the place and the time. He knew the tawny-haired girl who nestled alongside him in a cradle of moonlit sand. And the hot hunger that pounded through every vessel in his body—that, too, was as familiar as breathing.

Cameron had lived this dream more times than he could count. But this time he sensed something was different.

He did not realize what it was at first. The girl lay on her back gazing up at the stars. Sand grains glistened like diamonds on her wet skin. One arm was raised to pillow her head, the posture thrusting the point of one breast straight up, like the peak of a silky little mountain.

They had romped like children in the surf, each accidental contact sparking a surge of response that rocketed through their senses, leaving them breathless. At rest now, they lay without touching, cloaked in a throbbing silence that was broken only by the rush of the sea.

Cameron ached with desire. He imagined brushing his palm across the petal-soft tip of her upthrust breast until it puckered like a raspberry, then nibbling at its sweetness until she moaned. He imagined more, aye, much more. Oh, he was no innocent. He'd tumbled his share of loose, willing lasses in winter haylofts and summer meadows, and once, just for the experience, he'd even visited a brothel in Aberdeen. But *this* girl, the judge's violet-eyed daughter, so pure that he wasn't fit to wipe her shoes...

Cameron quaked at the very idea of what he was thinking. Touching her, he knew, could mean the ruin of them both. But the desolation gnawing at his insides was more than he could stand. He was caged in a world where he didn't belong, where he wasn't wanted. And the only ease for his cold, lonely hunger lay alongside him now, on the moonlit sand.

He reached out with a tentative finger and stroked her lightly along the flat of her belly. Her skin was like polished ivory, sprinkled here and there with sand grains. She whimpered as his palm molded to the curve of her lean, young hip. He felt the quiver of her response all the way up his arm.

"Meg," he rasped, "if you want me to stop, girl..."

Her only reply was a tender brush of her hand along the side of his face. The explosion of sweetness inside him brought tears to his eyes.

Aye, such sweetness. Cameron knew what would come next. The dream had grown familiar in its pattern. With a shudder of exquisite anticipation, he turned, raised himself on his arms and shifted his weight above her.

That was when he knew.

The Meg gazing up at him was not the prim sixteen-year-old Mary Margaret who had haunted his dreams for the past four years. This Meg was a woman—her eyes sad and knowing, her body ripe now, for his love. This Meg was his wife. She was the mother of his child.

Something burst then, inside the hardened soul of Cameron MacKenna. As Meg's arms reached up for him, he felt his bitter anger shattering like ice in a spring flood, the fragments washing away in a torrent of tenderness. In its wake lay a sense of peace, a warm certainty that everything was as it should be. He had been lost all his life. Now, at last, he knew where he belonged.

Wild with joy, he caught her close. She embraced him with a little cry. Her hands tangled in his hair. Her ivory legs mingled with his, thighs eagerly parting to welcome him home. Neither of them had noticed that the moon was gone, or that the dark sea had begun to churn like a boiling cauldron. Even when the water crept up the beach to nibble at their feet with cold white teeth, they were so lost in love that they paid it no heed.

Only when one huge black wave came hissing up onto the sand did Cameron raise his head. By then, it was already too late. The water had swallowed them like a voracious monster. He felt it pull Meg away from him, sweeping her out of his reach. Then, as he struggled, it began to suck him down like a whirlpool into its terrible throat. The rush of the ocean filled his ears, growing louder until it became an animal sound, a guttural, coughing, leonine roar that shook the walls of the tent.

Cameron's eyes jerked open. He'd been dreaming, he realized; but the sound was real. It came from somewhere outside the camp. Not close—he began to breathe again as he realized that. But all the same, since Tsavo, the call of a hunting lion never failed to chill his blood.

He lay rigid as the sound died away, his body drenched in sweat. Darkness surrounded him, and the vague restlessness of early dawn. He raised up on one elbow and glanced at Meg. She lay curled like a child in her bedroll, fast asleep. A quiver passed through Cameron as he remembered the dream. The tenderness between them had seemed so real, he could almost have believed . . .

But *this* was reality, he reminded himself. A cramped, gloomy tent in the bush, a missing child and a wife who was counting the days until she could go back to Britain and marry her new lover. Aye, dust in his eyes, sand in his pocket and an ache in his gut from a hunger that had nothing to do with food, *that* was reality. And he had bloody little choice except to get used to it.

He raised the bottom edge of the tent flap. Outside, the stars were beginning to fade. In an hour's time, it would be light enough to strike camp and march.

Too restless to stay in bed, Cameron eased his bone-sore frame out through the flap, then reached back inside for his clothes and rifle. Meg lay as he'd left her, her breathing light and even in the shadows of the tent. He moved quietly, trying not to disturb her sleep. She would need all her strength today.

Outside again, he pulled on his trousers and stockings, then his boots. The native boys lay sprawled around the embers of the fire, every one of them asleep. Not good, Cameron reflected darkly. He would have to enforce some discipline on them, and the first step would be to make sure sentries were posted and the fire kept burning at night.

Stepping around their sleeping bodies, he laid a branch on the dying coals and stared into the flames that licked the dry wood. He dreaded the day ahead, the blistering sun, the flies, the torment of Meg's slender hips swaying in his vision. Lord, how he wished he could hate her! That would make it all so much easier.

But he could not hate her. She was so full of life and spirit that he could not even glance at her without feeling an ache in his throat.

The lion coughed again, this time from far up the *donga* that lay to the east. The sound made Cameron shiver. Lighting the end of a small branch, he strode to the edge of the camp and made a cautious circle. The flickering torchlight revealed a set of huge, fresh pug marks within a dozen paces of the tent. Aye, he would have to take the boys to task. That, or wait for tragedy to strike.

He strode back to the slumbering forms that ringed the fire in their ragged blankets. Africans had such a fatalism in the bush. What was meant to happen would happen, they seemed to think, and there was no use trying to interfere with destiny. He would do well to kick them awake right now and curse some sense into them, Cameron thought. But that would wake Meg, too, maybe frighten her, when she needed her rest.

It could wait, he decided, sinking down onto a thick log that lay a few paces from the fire. The day would begin soon enough as it was. In the east, the sky was already fading from ebony to pewter. Soon the birds would awaken, the chattering hornbills, the fat white-winged doves and tiny warblers that were like dots of sunlight. As the sun rose, they would be joined by francolin and guinea fowl, squawking in the long yellow grass. The early-dawn grazers—impala, gazelle, zebra—would materialize out of the blue-shadowed landscape. Cameron savored mornings in Africa. Mornings were the only time when the land seemed gentle.

Shifting on the log, he eased the map the old Emir had given him out of his hip pocket. He knew the way to Machakos, but beyond that point, the trail would be devious and obscure. He'd be smart to study it now, and become familiar with the landmarks.

Opening the map with care, he angled it toward the firelight. It was drawn with brownish ink on parchment so old and soft that it folded like linen. The writing was all in Arabic script, as unreadable as it was elegant. But the outlines were easy enough to follow. Here was Mount Kenya, there the curve of the Athi River—

Cameron stared at the map, his pulse jolting.

Murchison's ivory map was still in the breast pocket of his shirt. He retrieved it from the tent, pausing long enough to make sure that Meg was still asleep. Then he sat down on the log again to compare one map against the other.

Neither map was drawn to scale. Even so, it was plain that they showed the same area. Aye, here it was on Murchison's—two lines, indicating a narrow pass that could only be The Neck of the Jar. The ivory cache, Cameron calculated, would lie no more than two days' march from that point.

Sweating, even in the cool dawn air, he stood up, folded both the maps and replaced them in his pockets. It was unbelievable that he hadn't noticed the similarity before. But then, he'd been so caught up with Jenny's kidnapping, and with Meg . . .

Not that he could let it make any difference, he reminded himself harshly. Until Jenny was found, he had no business even thinking about the ivory.

All the same, he'd begun to pace. Back and forth he strode, outside the circle of groggily sleeping natives. The thought of so much ivory and what it could do for him was enough to make any man's blood churn. Oh, he might not be as wealthy as a duke or an earl. But if he invested the money wisely, he could be secure for the rest of his days. He could have a fine, comfortable house; land, if he wanted it; time and money for travel he'd always dreamed of.

More important, he would have respect. And he would have the means to provide well for his daughter. Aye, with money, no judge on earth would deny him the right to share Jenny's life.

Money. Money from ivory—white gold. The key to all the doors that had been locked to him.

But even the ivory could not interfere with his search for Jenny. He would keep the map buttoned in his pocket, Cameron vowed. He would not even unfold it, not even think about it, until she was safe.

He clenched his teeth, aching with genuine resolve. But even then, he could feel the map burning where it lay over his heart. Ivory. His for the taking. The killing was done for him, the blood washed away by time and rain.

Aye, the devil had returned. And he was waiting with a knowing smile on his evil face.

Chapter Nine

She would not cry again.

Meg repeated that promise as she walked behind Cameron in the cool dawn air. She had been weak and clinging last night, but no more. From here on, she would be steel. And no matter how hard the journey, she would not shed one more tear until Jenny was safe.

She'd said as much to Cameron at breakfast. He had avoided her eyes, and she sensed that last night was a time he, too, would just as soon forget. "There's nothing wrong with a few tears, Meg. You'll be fine," he'd murmured distractedly. Then he had turned away, his manner stating clearly that he had more important things to worry about.

She'd watched him as he got up and stalked over to where the porters were packing up the camp gear for the day's trek. For no reason she could fathom, he had been railing at them all morning in Maxim-gun bursts of Swahili. Dismayed, Meg had followed him with her eyes as she munched her breakfast of stale biscuits and cold, sliced meat. For the life of her, she could not see that the boys had done anything wrong. What was bothering Cameron this morning?

He walked ahead of her now, at his own insistence, shoulders grimly square. Today the pace was relentless. Meg found herself double-stepping to keep up with his long strides. She was already gasping in the tightly laced whale-

bone corset, but complaint was out of the question. She
had made herself a promise, and she would fall dead on the
trail before she'd break it.

The morning sun lay low above the horizon, flooding the
savanna with tones of honey and saffron. This was the time
for animals, and Meg saw them everywhere. By now she
could recognize the dun coats and humped shoulders of
wildebeest and the perky black stripe of the little gazelle
Cameron called a Tommy. She knew that the spectacular
jumpers were impala, and that zebra called to each other
with rubbery barking sounds, not unlike a child's bicycle
horn.

Smaller creatures, too, were becoming familiar. A honey
badger blinked and vanished into its den in the base of a
termite mound. A family of spur fowl, with red-masked
faces, scurried out of the path. Insects buzzed in the dry
scrub.

Jenny's innocent blue eyes had seen sights like this, Meg
thought. But what else had they seen? What terrors?

"Don't move!" Cameron's sharp whisper caught her in
midstride. Meg froze. Her eyes followed his gaze to a point
not sixty yards off the trail, where a cow rhino had lumbered out of the wait-a-bits, its massive head casting this
way and that for the scent of danger. Meg's heart dropped
as she saw the collie-sized calf trailing the rhino-mother's
left flank. A female with young, she knew, was the most
volatile of animals.

The cow snorted, swinging its long, black horn. Its pinpoint eyes squinted nearsightedly in the glaring sunlight.
Meg held her breath, throat tight, heart galloping. She'd
glimpsed rhinos from the train, but only now, in the open,
was she struck by the animal's primal power. Like an ar-
mored dinosaur, it exuded a savagery that made the little
string of humans seem as defenseless as worms. Even their
rifles were toys, peashooters against skin that hung like
granite slabs on the rocky mass of its body.

Moving only her eyes, Meg could see sweat trickling between Cameron's shoulder blades, soaking his khaki shirt. Her own fear was acid in her mouth as the seconds crawled past like sickly heartbeats.

Three little tickbirds bobbed skittishly along the rhino's spine. Meg watched them, her mouth cotton-dry. The birds would take flight, she knew, the instant before a charge.

It was the calf that shattered the tension. With a bawl of alarm, it wheeled and broke for the bush. Cameron's rifle swung to his shoulder. His thumb pulled back the hammer as the cow hesitated, horn swinging wildly. Meg stifled a scream.

Snorting like a locomotive, the monster dropped its head, then abruptly turned and crashed off into the thorns after its squalling offspring.

Relief washed over the caravan as the noise died away. Meg sank to the ground, her legs too weak to support her. Cameron lowered the rifle and mopped his dripping face with his handkerchief. The boys, for the first time in the journey, dissolved in nervous laughter.

"Well, now, Mary Margaret," Cameron grinned down at Meg where she'd collapsed on the trail. "You've faced down elephant and rhino. I'd say that makes you an old hand!"

Meg glared up at him, too badly shaken to enjoy the banter. "What—what would you have done if she'd charged?"

"Tried a scare shot over her head. This rifle packs enough wallop for cats and antelope, but it would never stop a rhino."

"And if she'd kept coming?"

"Why, my dear, I'd have run like blazes! And I'd no doubt have encouraged you to do the same!"

Meg shook her head in dismay. "You'd have just run off and left me to fend for myself!"

"Aye, I might have done just that. But I *will* be enough of a gentleman to help you up!" Cameron's laugh was rough and raw as he offered his hand. His fingers imprisoned Meg's in a hard, warm grip that tightened as he jerked her to her feet. For the space of a heartbeat, the contact held. His eyes blazed into hers like twin gas flames. Meg tried to ignore the responding heat surge deep in her body, but it was no use. She squirmed as the embarrassing warmth flooded her skin.

"Why, Mary Margaret, you're blushing!" Cameron's voice carried a sardonic edge. "From what I know of you, I'd never have believed it!"

Meg felt oddly light-headed. She tore her hand from his, the red deepening in her face.

He laughed again, a harsh sound that held no humor. "Young Meg, the judge's bairn! What a strange mix you are! Just when I start thinking I know you—"

Meg's glare cut him into silence. "I told you, I'm no bairn," she said crisply. "But you're right about one thing, Cameron. You *don't* know me—not as the person I truly am. And I don't suppose you ever will."

His eyes glazed abruptly, their fire chilling to ice. "No, Meg, for that matter, I don't suppose I ever *have* truly known you...except, of course, in the biblical sense of the word."

Meg's face flamed like a bonfire. "Why, you—you insufferable..."

Her words trailed off as she realized she was sputtering into empty air. Cameron had turned away, cutting off any chance of retort. Now he was striding up and down the line of *askaris* and porters. Some of them had dropped their gear to rest, hunkered on their bony haunches. They stirred as he barked at them in Swahili, stretching their limbs, hefting their sixty-pound burdens onto their heads and easing back into line. Slowly, the small caravan began to move again.

Meg strode vigorously behind Cameron, outrage charging her whole body with energy. Cameron MacKenna—what an insulting, irreverent barbarian he was! And what a girlish fool she'd been to have cherished any romantic dreams of him! Why, compared to a cultured gentleman like Arthur Tarrington-Leigh ...

Strange, how little she had thought of Arthur in the past four days. Even now, when she tried to picture his dear, gentle face, his graying blond hair and trig little moustache, the image blurred in her mind.

But that would change as soon as she left Africa, Meg reassured herself forcefully. When she and Jenny stepped off the steamer at Tilbury, into Arthur's waiting arms; when she whispered her answer in his ear, then everything would fall into place. All her plans would be fulfilled.

If only...if only... She fought back the fear that surged with each step. Jenny *had* to be all right. They *had* to find her and get her back safely. Without Jenny, there would be no reason to plan, or to even care about the future. There would be no reason, even, to go on living.

The prayer that Meg repeated over and over in her mind consisted of only one word.

Please.

By midafternoon, Meg was exhausted. Her feet were swollen. Her clothes clung crustily to her sweat-soaked body. Under the brim of her hat, locks of hair dangled in limp tendrils, curtaining a face that was streaked with orange dust. The dust, in fact, seemed to be everywhere. In her eyes, in her nose, her mouth and every moist crease of her skin. Worse, even, than the dust were the tiny red ticks that clung to the grass, waiting to leap onto any passing warm-blooded body.

The sun was a furnace, and Cameron had not called a halt in more than two hours. Meg was beginning to hate him. As his broad, khaki-clad shoulders bobbed ahead of her, she entertained herself by visualizing fantastically dire things happening to him: screaming cannibal women dragging him off to their feast; an enormous thirty-foot python squashing him in its coils—

This last delicious image was shattered by a warning grunt from one of the *askaris*. Meg squinted past Cameron's shoulder to see a dark blur emerging from the distant heat waves.

At first it was little more than a shadow, its outlines dancing in and out of focus. Only as the shape moved closer could she begin to make out its separate parts— elongated bodies, spears, painted shields. The still air carried the faint metallic jingle of approaching bells.

"Masai," Cameron said softly. "Looks like about fifteen or twenty of them."

Masai. Meg shivered in the torrid heat. She had read about the Masai. They lived on blood they drew from live cattle. They fought lions with spears to prove their manhood. And they were known to be the most savage tribe in all of East Africa.

She watched them materialize out of the heat waves. They were as lean as willow whips. Their bare skin, greased with fat and dusted with red ochre, gleamed like copper in the pounding sunlight. Their rawhide shields, painted in red-brown patterns, were large enough to cover their bodies. Their spears, Meg estimated, were eight feet long. Each man wore on his head the mane of a lion he had killed in single-handed combat. These were the *morani*, the proven warriors.

The *askaris* had unshouldered their rifles, but the Masai kept coming, moving along at a confident dogtrot. They were clearly unafraid.

Meg found her voice. "Why doesn't somebody shoot... in warning, at least?"

Cameron chuckled grimly under his breath. "Shoot? My dear Mary Margaret, if we make one hostile move, or harm one hair of their precious heads, no European in two hundred miles will be safe. Just let them come." His voice dropped to a low rasp as he added, "But whatever you do, blast it, stay out of sight and keep quiet."

The Masai were within fifty paces of them now. Meg could make out the individual features of their proud, handsome faces. Their lithe bodies were clad in skimpy leather breechclouts. Little Indian bells jingled on leather strings around their ankles. Their flat, bare feet stirred up puffs of orange-red dust.

The caravan had paused at Cameron's order, and the *askaris* had lowered their rifles as a sign of peace. Meg stood among the clustered porters, tense and quivering, as the wild strangers approached. The hair on the back of her neck bristled like a dog's.

The Masai halted a stone's toss away. Meg's breath caught as Cameron handed his rifle to one of the porters and walked out empty-handed to meet them. Only minutes ago, she had been mangling him in her imagination. Now her throat tightened at the thought of what a single spear thrust could do.

The *morani* stood like wiry bronze statues, waiting as he approached. Their preening, almost girlish postures were studies in arrogant grace.

Cameron stopped an arm's length from the foremost warrior and raised his right hand in salute. *"Jambo,"* he said, uttering the traditional Swahili greeting.

The Masai leader scowled disdainfully. He was older than the others, and his earlobes, distended by flat wooden plugs, dangled almost to his shoulders. He answered Cameron in a burst of harsh tones that even Meg could recognize as different from the musically flowing Swahili. Her heart sank. These Masai appeared to speak no language except their own tribal dialect.

As Cameron struggled to communicate with them, Meg could feel the tension rising. Eyes shifted nervously. Brown hands fondled spear shafts.

The *askaris,* too, were uneasy. Their fingers hovered on the triggers of their new Martini rifles. Meg knew they had orders not to fire. But what if one of them were to get jumpy? A single shot could touch off a bloodbath, and Cameron would be right in the middle of it.

She stifled a cry as the leader's hand stirred, raised and moved to Cameron's face. Cameron stood like stone as one leathery brown finger stretched out to trace the lion scar, following the path of each claw.

Like sun breaking through a cloud, the senior *moran* smiled, his mouth stretching wide to show the gap of two missing bottom teeth. As if on signal, the whole band came to life, chattering, pointing and reaching out to finger Cameron's scar. It was all right, they seemed to be saying. This stranger was a true man. Like them, he had braved the claws of death. His face carried the mark of the lion.

Only then did one of the porters, a timid fellow who'd been cowering behind his comrades, creep forward to volunteer something to Cameron. From what followed, Meg surmised that this porter had dealt with Masai before and spoke a few words of their language. An awkward dialogue began, with the porter translating from Swahili to Masai and back again, and Cameron tossing out a few English phrases for Meg's benefit.

The Masai, it appeared, were on a scouting expedition, seeking fresh pasture for their precious cattle. Their homeland was dry, the warrior said sadly. The rains were late, and the grass was dying. They had come a far distance, and everywhere it was the same.

A far distance. Forgetting Cameron's warning, Meg shoved her way through the ranks of nervous Swahili. "Ask them!" she burst out. "Ask them if they've seen a little girl."

But even as she spoke, Meg realized the hopelessness of the question. The Masai had wandered down from the hinterland, while Jenny's captors would be moving up from the coast. There was no chance that their paths might have crossed.

But now, for the first time, the Masai had noticed her. They stared, then began to point and whisper. Cameron glared at Meg. "Don't move!" he growled as the Masai leader broke from his band and walked toward her with a hitch-hipped gait like a cheetah's, half arrogant, half cautious.

Meg quivered as he lifted her hat and fingered a lock of her hair. His narrow eyes, the whites curiously yellowed, stared disdainfully into hers. Braced rigid against her own fear, Meg met his gaze without flinching. His skin was a reddish chocolate color, the cheeks crisscrossed by a fine peppering of ritual scars. His nose was broken, as if by an old blow; and he smelled of—what was that odor? Yes— Meg began to breathe again as she recognized it. The milk-musky scent of cattle hung about him, as warmly familiar as a Scottish barn. Somehow it made the savage Masai *moran* seem less fearsome—though only a little less.

Abruptly, he snorted, spun away and began firing questions at Cameron. Cameron's eyes glittered sardonically as he replied in Swahili, questions and answers funneling back and forth through the porter. This time he did not bother to translate into English.

The dialogue grew more intense. When the Masai turned back to Meg and pinched her upper arm, she realized they were talking about *her*. What did this wild man want? And what was Cameron telling him? She could fathom nothing, except for the twist of bitter amusement on Cameron's face.

"Cameron, what is going on?" she demanded.

He scowled blackly, his eyes warning her to keep still.

"Cameron—"

"Keep out of this!" he growled. "I'm trying to save your bloody hide!"

The Masai held up two fingers. Cameron shook his head and held up three fingers of his own, that spark of wry humor never leaving his eyes. The Masai was clearly becoming disgusted. Adamantly, he thrust three fingers in Cameron's direction, Cameron shook his head and held up three fingers of his own.

The Masai jabbed the blunt end of his spear into the earth and uttered what sounded like an oath. Then, with an exasperated grunt, he wheeled in the dust and stalked back to his *morani*. As if by invisible signal, the wild band resumed its brisk dogtrot, bells jingling, spear points dancing in the sun. Minutes later, without a backward glance, they had vanished over a scrubby rise.

Meg was still staring after them when she felt the cool touch of Cameron's canteen against her arm. "One good swallow," he said tersely. "Then we'll be getting on. I'd just as soon put some distance between ourselves and those lads."

Meg drank deeply, tilting her head back to let an escaping trickle run backward along one hot, dusty cheek. She felt Cameron's eyes on her as she lowered the canteen and wiped her mouth with the back of her hand. The porters were moving into place, hoisting the gear onto their heads.

"I think you owe me an explanation," she said as she fell into line behind Cameron. "What did that man want?"

He glanced back at her, eyes narrowed to slits. "Couldn't you guess? He wanted to buy you."

"Oh, rubbish!" Meg insisted hotly, hiding the prickle of fear that his words touched off.

He had turned away and begun to walk again. "I'm not joking, Meg. He claimed you had strong *dawa*—magic—because your hair was like a lion's and your eyes were like the flower that blooms after the rains. He wanted to sire a son by you, he said, a mighty warrior with your *dawa* and his bravery." Here there was a dramatic pause. "He offered me two goats in trade for you."

"Two goats!" Meg stumbled over a tuffet of grass.

"Oh, he was a shrewd one!" There was a distinct edge to Cameron's voice. "He claimed you'd be too weak to carry a decent load of firewood, and that your white skin would burn in the sun. He told me, in fact, that I'd be much better off with a good, strong Masai girl, if I wanted to come back to his *manyatta* and bargain for one."

"You told him, I trust, that women aren't meant to be bought and sold like livestock!" Meg responded coldly.

"Not exactly."

"Then I hope you at least told him I wasn't yours to sell!"

There was a barely perceptible pause. Then Cameron chuckled harshly. "No. He would have laughed at that. What I told him was that I wouldn't let you go for less than three cows."

Meg choked. "Of all the—"

"He did raise his offer to three goats," Cameron added in a voice he might have used to discuss wool prices in Aberdeen. "But when I turned him down, he called me a fool. He said that no woman on earth, not even a woman with *dawa*, was worth as much as three cows."

Meg managed a disdainful sniff. "Cameron MacKenna, that's the most ridiculous thing I've ever heard! What if he'd accepted?"

Cameron's long stride did not falter. "Why, then, my dear Mary Margaret, you would have yourself a new husband, and I would be the owner of three fine Masai cows!"

"Humph!" Meg said, trying to sound like the society matrons who graced Arthur's weekend soirees. "Humph! The very idea!"

She strode through the buttery afternoon sunlight, struggling to maintain what was left of her dignity. As the seconds passed, however, the corners of her rigid mouth began to twitch, subtly at first, then uncontrollably. Something quivered in her chest and bubbled upward, to pop out between her lips in the form of a giggle.

Cameron glanced over his shoulder, his eyes flashing in rough amusement. "Are you all right?" he asked.

Meg tightened her cheeks to keep the laughter in. "Oh, you were so—so dour! And that—Masai, he was—so—disgusted—" She was losing control, but she could not stop. "And when he squeezed my arm—my poor, flabby little muscles—"

It was no use. She doubled over, quaking and helpless. Her sides throbbed with laughter. Tears ran down her dusty cheeks, breaking the vow she'd made only that morning. The native boys had halted and were staring. It made no difference. She could not stop. She was getting hysterical, she supposed. Arthur would not approve. But then Arthur was half a world away.

Cameron's hands clasped her shoulders. "It's all right, Meg," he was saying in a worried voice. "It's all right, lass."

"Three goats! Three bloody goats!" she squeaked. "At least I know what I'm worth on the open market!" His face was a blur through her tears. Maybe he would slap her. Wasn't that what men did to hysterical women in books and stage plays?

But Cameron did not slap her. His hands were gentle as they lifted her chin, cradling her jaw between his warm, rough palms. His eyes were fiercely tender and so blue—as blue as an African twilight.

"Blast it, Meg!" He had probably meant to sound threatening, but his voice came out thick and husky. "Blast it, woman, I can't fathom you from one minute to the next!"

She was no longer laughing. Cameron's sweat-streaked face, the mouth disturbingly masculine, was too close to hers for laughing. The slight twist from the pull of the scar was sensual, almost devilishly so. If the porters and *askaris* were not there, she might even be tempted to stretch up and brush that twisted corner with her lips—no, with just the very tip of her tongue.

What in heaven's name had come over her?

Panic triggered all the safety latches in Meg's mind. She forced herself to remember who she was and why she had come to Africa. She reminded herself how much Cameron had hurt her in the past. She thought of Arthur and the future they could have together. To throw all that away on an impulsive whim... No! She would be a fool to even think of it!

Marshaling her will, Meg took a step backward. The movement broke the mesmerizing contact of Cameron's eyes, enabling her, at least, to speak.

"You know, Cameron, I wouldn't have put it past you to let that Masai have me!" she said flippantly.

His breath jerked inward, straining the shirt buttons across his broad chest. "Well, if I had, then heaven help the Masai!" he rumbled. "Heaven help any man moonstruck enough to take on a woman like you!"

He turned away and began to walk again, the whole caravan obediently keeping pace with him. Meg strode along in his wake, drained of laughter now, and weary from the long day's trek. Cameron's back and shoulders filled her vision. Her eyes traced the contour of each chiseled muscle through the sweat-soaked fabric of his shirt. As her mind began to wander, she imagined running her palm up the rugged furrow of his spine, tracing each hard bulge and curve until she reached the black hair that curled low on the back of his neck, then slowly tangling her fingers in those damp ebony locks and leaning forward to taste his salty ear with—

Meg jerked herself back to reality, forcing the image to shatter. What was wrong with her? Her child was in desperate danger, and here she was, unable to keep her mind off a man!

Maybe she was too tired to think straight, she speculated. Or maybe this untamed land, where every facet of life was visible in its raw, naked state, tended to lure everyone's thoughts into forbidden quagmires.

Or maybe it was Cameron.

Meg sighed as she watched his powerful body striding ahead of her. Cameron had grown up in four years. Hardship and danger had toughened him like harness leather left to sun and wind. The gentleness she remembered had evaporated in the African heat, leaving nothing behind, it seemed, but anger. His scarred face mirrored a hard, cynical soul.

And yet, Meg reflected, Cameron had not lost his power to stir her. He moved like a splendid, savage animal, with a lion's strength, a leopard's grace. He breathed and spoke with a primal energy that touched off mysterious quivers deep inside her body. Even the scar—yes, when she looked at him, she found herself wanting to touch it, to fit her fingertips into the grooves the man-eater's claws had left, and trace them down the long, flat plane of his cheek, to linger on that sensual twist at the corner of his mouth.

She remembered the night in Bowman's tent when Cameron had yanked her into the tub. Color flamed in her face as she recalled how his kisses had reduced her to a panting shambles in seconds. He had humiliated her then. Given the chance, he would try it again. And he would succeed, if she lowered her guard. She was lonely, frightened and vulnerable, a perilous condition for any woman.

She would not let him near her, Meg resolved. Not physically. Not emotionally. She would build a thick, high wall against him. Every hurt, every tear, every lonely night of the past four years would be a brick in that wall.

She would guard that wall with every weapon she possessed. Otherwise, Cameron would break through. And if that happened, he would destroy her.

Sunset hung in the sky like a tattered silk curtain that faded upward from crimson to violet-gray. An arid wind rustled the thorn trees and whispered in the parched grass. The air mingled the smell of dust with the musky odor of dried elephant dung.

Cameron stood outside the tent and listened to the night coming alive. Bats whistled through the darkening air. Hyenas, drawn by the camp smells, snickered in the twilight. The cook had spitted a half-dozen guinea fowl, taken late in the day, and propped them over the fire. They were just beginning to sizzle. Cameron's belly growled with hunger.

Behind him, sheltered by the open tent, Meg slept like an exhausted child. As soon as the boys had the canvas pitched, she'd flung down her bedroll and collapsed on it full length in her clothes, declaring that she would not move till morning. Within seconds, she had fallen fast asleep.

Cameron turned and gazed at her where she lay, one arm flung outward as if groping for something beyond her reach. In spite of everything, his heart went soft at the sight of her. She was a pretty woman, his Meg, even with dust-smeared cheeks and sweat-tangled hair. And she was strong, too, much stronger than he would have guessed. He'd pushed her hard all day, but not once had she fallen behind or asked him to slacken the pace. Not once had he heard her complain.

He knew what kept her forging ahead. He had seen too many females in the wild, protecting their young, *not* to know the power of those instincts. As long as Jenny was missing, Meg would not give up the search. Given free rein, she would drive herself through exhaustion, through danger, through sickness, to the point of her own destruction.

Tomorrow afternoon, if the day went well, they would reach the tiny European settlement at Machakos. The next morning, he would steal away early, leaving her behind. Meg would be frantic when she found him gone. She would rage at his betrayal, call him every foul name she could dredge up from the depths of her proper little mind. Sure as sheep come to water, she would never forgive him.

But that made no difference. Cameron knew what lay ahead, and he was determined to spare her what he could.

He stepped across the threshold of the tent and stood gazing down at her. She lay on her back, the sunset casting an amethyst glow on her small, tired face. Her childlike mouth looked as soft as a rosebud. Cameron ached with the sudden urge to bend down and brush the mauve petals of her lips with his own. The temptation teased at him. She would not know. She was sleeping so soundly that she would not even stir. He leaned closer, then caught himself in time. One taste of her, he knew, would only whet his appetite. His body would demand more, and more, until only one thing would be enough.

And Cameron knew that he would not be satisfied with stealing a kiss, or anything else, from a passively sleeping Meg. No, he would want her wide-awake, clinging to him and whimpering with a need as urgent as his own. He would want to crush her to his chest and feel her heart hammering against his; to part her mouth, and feel the responding tingle of her delicious little strawberry tongue.

Aye, that, and a hundred things more. But it would never happen. Not with his signature already on the divorce document, and Meg hell-bent on marrying another man.

Cameron thrust his hands into his pockets and stared out into the dusk. Outside, firelight danced on the walls of the tent, the boys hunkering within its safe, warm circle and chatting in their musical language. The savory aroma of the roasting birds blended with the smell of fresh biscuits, driving the skulking hyenas to frenzied giggles.

He ought to wake Meg. She would need food as much as she needed rest. Turning back to her, he paused, then sighed in defeat. She was so weary, and she slept with such sweet abandon, her lashes feathering darkly against her pale cheeks. He would ask the cook to save her something for later, Cameron resolved. For now, he hadn't the heart to disturb her.

Nor the fortitude, he admitted, watching the play of light on her throat above the loosened collar. There were times when even looking into those violet eyes was more pain than he could stand. Tonight, he sensed, was one of those times.

Aye, he would let her sleep, even in her clothes. He himself had slept many a night fully dressed. But as for her tight boots—no, that would not do. Her feet would swell, and walking the next day would be misery.

Crouching beside her, Cameron lifted one boot and nested it between his knees. Meg lay quietly, her breathing deep and even as he untied the dusty knot and began undoing the laces. He worked carefully, loosening the tongue, easing down on the dusty boot until it slipped off, leaving her small, warm foot, in its brown cotton stocking, cradled damply in his hands. For a moment, he let it linger, savoring the lightness of her bones, which were as fine and delicate as a gazelle's. He would welcome the chance to hold more than her foot, he thought. Aye, if he could, he would gather all of her into his arms and play with matching the curves and hollows of their bodies until they fit together like pieces of a Chinese puzzle. Then . . .

But he was only tormenting himself. If he had the brains of a cock bustard he would finish this business and get outside to supper.

Steeling his resolve, he gently lowered her stockinged foot to the blanket and lifted the other boot. For a breathless moment, Meg stirred, rolling her head and whimpering in her sleep. Cameron froze, then relaxed a little as he realized she wasn't waking up. *Easy, you fool,* he told himself.

Unfortunately, the second boot was more stubborn than the first had been. By the time he'd worked it loose, Cameron's imagination had heated to a simmering caldron of possibilities. The images that seethed in his mind would have made a gentleman blush. But then, he was no gentleman, Cameron reminded himself harshly. And the Meg he knew, for all her fine airs, was no lady. As long as he kept his thoughts to himself, he could think what he bloody well pleased.

And think he did, as emotions he'd been holding back all day burst through the dam of his weariness. He imagined leaning over her as he was now, lifting her petticoat and unhooking each garter, one by one; then sliding the thick stockings down her legs, inch by agonizing inch, to bare her satiny skin. He imagined starting at her feet with little nuzzling nips, tasting each rosebud toe with his tongue, then kissing his way along her arches to her slender ankles.

By now, he fantasized, Meg would slowly be waking up. Roused by his touch, her body would be quivering with sensuality. She would moan softly and twist against his hands, the pressure urging him to venture farther.

And so he would, but not in haste. He would take a wealth of time to fondle his way up the ivory contours of her calves to the thin lace ruffles that edged her drawers. He imagined slipping them gently down her legs, tugging them over her bare feet and tossing them aside to pool in a be-ribboned heap on the floor of the tent.

Aye, she would be ready for him now. She would be sobbing with anticipation, her lovely, wet woman-smell swimming in his senses. His own need would be a raging firestorm in his vitals; but even now, he would keep the pace as exquisitely contained as a ritual dance. He would court her body with the tenderest strokes of his lips and fingers until she writhed and cursed him in her fevered impatience. Only then would he—

A sound in the darkness shattered Cameron's thoughts. He was reaching for his rifle when he realized it was only the Swahili cook, coming to call him to supper. Meg was fast asleep, her brown-stockinged foot still resting between his knees.

"*Chacula, bwana.*" The cook's voice piped through the dusky twilight.

Cameron nodded, releasing his fantasy with a weary sigh as his arousal cooled. Meg slumbered on, her hands curled like a child's on the rumpled muslin pillow. Gently, he lowered her foot to the bedroll, then covered her with his own blanket so the breeze would not chill her. Her sleeping face was sweet in the golden firelight.

For the space of a long breath, Cameron stood in the doorway of the tent, gazing down at the delicate rise and fall of her chest. There was no denying how much he wanted her. But his chance was gone. He had frittered it away over the past four years, and now it was too late for anything but regrets.

Sometime tomorrow they would reach Machakos, a place of safety and rest. There would be settlers there, kind families who would welcome them with food and shelter. They would pass a pleasant afternoon, a restful night.

And there, the next morning, he would betray her.

Chapter Ten

The settlement at Machakos looked more like a ramshackle native village than a proper British town. Its scattered bungalows were built round and thatched in the Kikuyu style, or thrown together from wagon boxes, canvas and any other material at hand. Between properties, a network of thorn *bomas* defined boundaries and kept out marauding animals. There were no streets, no inns and only one shop, a run-down Indian *duka* built of scrap lumber and flattened steel drums. Some spindly acacia, sprouting up around a spring, lent a few mottled shade patches, lengthening now in the afternoon sun.

As the caravan neared the settlement, the first person Meg saw was a boy about eight years old, with mud-colored hair and a bumper crop of light brown freckles. He grinned, waved, then raced off to trumpet the news of their arrival.

Cameron, who was walking ahead, glanced back at Meg. "Be ready for a rousing welcome," he said. "These folk don't get many visitors. They're always glad for company."

Meg could see people coming out of their houses: farmers, traders, missionaries and government workers, some with their families. There were rawboned men in shirtsleeves, their faces sunburned leathery brown below their hat lines. The few women were young for the most part.

They were dressed in sun-faded gowns, their waists neatly cinched, their hair done up with combs. Their finery puzzled Meg until she realized that today was Sunday.

There were children, too, a dozen or so, in a variety of sizes. Shy toddlers peered from the sheltering folds of their mothers' skirts. Older boys and girls, lively as grasshoppers, darted among the *bomas* in a spirited game of tag. Meg ached for the sight of Jenny.

A woman about thirty, with light brown hair and a plain, pleasant face, bustled through the crowd to clasp Meg's hand. "I'm Clara Roberson," she said, her palm warm and hard with calluses. "You look all in, dear. You and your husband must rest and eat at our house. I've a big pot of eland stew on the fire, and there's all the room in the world at our table."

Here Clara paused to wave away another approaching woman. "You're too late, Nan! I've already invited them to our place!" Turning again, she linked an arm through Meg's. "Don't worry, you'll meet everyone soon enough. We're so cut off from the outside world here, you can't imagine what it means to have company. When a stranger shows up, there's always a scramble over who gets to play hostess. No, don't try to talk. You look too tuckered, even for that. After you've rested and had a cool drink, that's when I'll trouble you with questions."

While she spoke, Clara was propelling Meg toward a large thatched bungalow with a yard enclosed by a high *boma*. Glancing around for Cameron, Meg saw that he was talking to a short, wiry man with hair that matched the dusty straw roof of the house.

"That's my husband, Malcolm," Clara explained. "Don't worry, dear, we'll take care of you both, and your native boys, too. They'll have to camp outside the settlement, of course, but I'll have Malcolm take them a haunch of the eland he shot Friday. Goodness knows, we can't be letting it go to waste."

Clara's chatter had begun to blur in Meg's mind, but the pressure of her strong, brown hand was reassuring. Meg felt herself relaxing as she surrendered to the woman's friendly overtures. She felt as if she'd been at war, battling Cameron, her own fear and the perils of this harsh land. She had not realized until now how weary she was, or how much she'd needed a touch of simple kindness.

"You're in luck," Clara was saying. "Malcolm's brother and his wife were planning to come here and settle. We'd just finished building on a room for them, with a double bed, when we got word they weren't coming. He'd taken a position in Edinburgh—a pity, since Malcolm could have used his help. But all for the best, I'd say, with her such a frail little thing and not at all keen on coming to Africa.

"Anyway, now we have a nice room for visitors—nothing fancy, I'll grant you, but it's private at least, with its own outside door. Oh, and the bed's a fine one, with a real feather tick. I'll wager it's been too many nights since you and your husband slept in a good, solid double bed." Clara's laughter held no trace of awkwardness.

Meg blinked. Tired as she was, she'd lent only half an ear to Clara's good-natured patter. At this last revelation, however, her chest tightened in panic. For the space of a breath, she was tempted to confess the truth about herself and Cameron.

No, she checked her tongue. The truth would only trigger gossip and create extra bother for their hosts. Silence was the course of wisdom here—that, and keeping up appearances for the sake of these good people. As for the bed, once the lights were out, either she or Cameron could spend the night on the floor. If he didn't offer to do it, then she would.

She would have to. Otherwise, she would be lost.

Meg pressed a hand to her hot, dusty face, her knees turning to jelly as reality sank home. The truth was unsettling, even frightening, but it had to be faced. She was too exhausted to fend it off any longer.

For the three days that she and Cameron had been trekking together, her eyes had scarcely left him. She had memorized the cadence of his leonine stride and the deep, strong rhythm of his slumber. She had traced the curl of each black lock against his golden skin until she could duplicate their pattern in her dreams. She had watched him bring down an eland at two hundred yards, watched him dress the bloodied foot of an injured porter, and held her breath as he faced down a party of wild Masai, armed with nothing except his own courage.

They had shared the little intimacies of waking and sleeping. He had stood guard, his face decorously averted, whenever she went to the bushes. Only this morning he had used the medical kit to dab iodine on a long thorn scratch down the back of her leg, where she could not see to treat it herself. The accidental brush of his fingers on her bare skin had sent sparks rocketing through her whole body.

She was vulnerable. As vulnerable as the sixteen-year-old girl who had flung off her clothes to plunge naked into a moonlit ocean.

She remembered Arthur only with effort now, and even then his face was little more than a blur. Wild Cameron MacKenna had cast his spell again, and she was confused, frightened and lonely. Worse, she was so bone-weary that even the small dilemma of the bed was more than she could deal with. She would put it out of her mind until she'd rested and eaten, Meg resolved. Night was hours away. There would be time yet to muster her strength.

Clara guided her through the gate in the *boma,* toward the big, thatched bungalow. The yard, Meg noticed, was immaculately swept. Along one side, turnips, potatoes, carrots and cabbages sprouted in neat rows. "You can't imagine what it's like trying to garden here," Clara was saying. "The soil is wonderful, but what the drought doesn't get, the bugs and animals do! It's a constant battle to grow enough for the table—"

She broke off suddenly, with a little laugh. Her eyes were the color of cinnamon, and she had a generous sprinkling of freckles across her nose. "Heavens, how I do rattle on! Malcolm says there's no silence so big that I won't try to fill it with words, and I'll tell you, the silence out here can get mighty big! Oh, but Africa's a grand place, dear! Sunsets to break your heart! And the animals... I'd never leave this country! They'd have to drag me back to Scotland in chains!"

Clara paused as she looked Meg up and down. "Why, you poor thing, you look ready to drop! I'll show you to the privy, since you'll no doubt be wanting it. Then you can have a drink and a nice nap, as well as a bath before dinner."

Warmed by Clara's openness, Meg managed a wan smile. "The privy and the drink I'll take, thank you. But the nap and bath can wait. What I'd really like now is to help you prepare the meal."

Clara grinned, showing generous, uneven teeth. "Help? Why, to be sure! I can always use an extra hand, and it'll give us more time to visit! Come on!" She clasped Meg's arm and steered her toward the rear of the house, chatting every step of the way.

When Meg was ready, they set to work in the open-sided, backyard kitchen, peeling vegetables for the stew. By the time the last turnip slice had plopped into the simmering brown broth, Meg had poured out the story of Jenny's kidnapping.

She'd fudged, naturally, on her reason for seeking out Cameron in the first place. But the rest—Hassan's treachery, her own grief and guilt—was as true as she could tell it. By the time she'd finished, Clara's eyes were brimming with sympathetic tears.

"Oh, my poor, poor dear" was all she could say.

"We'll find Jenny, of course," Meg declared, thrusting out her chin in a determined show of bravery. "I know we will! We simply won't turn back until she's safe!"

"And if you don't find her?" Clara's gentle question jabbed like a cold blade.

"No! I can't even think of it!" Meg scrambled to fortify the dikes against her own fear. "Why, if I were to lose Jenny, my life would be over!"

Clara wiped her hands on her apron. Compassion deepened her pale brown eyes. "My dear Meg, you *must* think of it! If the worst happens, you must prepare yourself to survive and go on, for the sake of your husband, for the sake of the other children you'll have one day."

Meg pressed her lips together, biting back emotions that were too cruel to face. "No!" she whispered. "I couldn't! You don't understand—you couldn't understand."

Something flickered across Clara's plain face. Her hand reached out to clasp Meg's forearm. "Come for a walk with me while the stew simmers," she said softly. "There's something I think I should show you."

Cameron had visited settlers' homes before. Even so, the incongruity of such places never failed to amuse him. The Roberson house, like most, was fashioned of thatch, laid native-style on a framework of poles. The evening breeze blew right through the walls. Spiders and chameleons made their homes in the eaves. Inside, however, the house was furnished in faithful English style, with possessions hauled halfway around the world. Under the straw ceiling of the dining room, the Queen Anne table was polished to a dark gleam and laid with a cloth of Irish lace. China and pewter glistened in the candlelight.

The Robersons had dressed in their weatherworn best. Cameron glanced from one to another as they sat around the table awaiting grace. Malcolm Roberson was a man of quiet energy, with a lean, honest face. He had a bluntness about him that Cameron liked, a way of getting to the point of a matter without a lot of dithering. He'd come to Machakos to farm, but had admitted to Cameron that he was wearying of it. Two years of fighting drought, disease and locusts was taking its toll on him, and on his family.

As for Clara Roberson, she was no great beauty, but her plain face glowed with health and generosity. She was the kind of woman, Cameron reflected, who would bloom wherever she was planted. Malcolm was lucky to have her.

There were three Roberson children. The eldest was a shy ten-year-old girl who resembled her father and would be pretty one day. The second, a rowdy, freckled boy of eight, had shouted the news of their arrival that afternoon. The youngest Roberson was another boy, about three, with Clara's coppery eyes. There was a gap in years, Cameron observed, between the second child and the third. Aye, but he had seen too much of life here not to understand why. Africa was an unfeeling land, striking down the weak and tender. He tried hard not to think about Jenny.

Meg sat next to him at the table. As Malcolm intoned grace, Cameron stole a glance at her bowed profile. In the flicker of the candle flame, her skin glowed like mother-of-pearl. Her eyelashes lay dark gold against her cheeks, iridescent in the light, like the fine edge of a feather. Clara had lent her a lavender gown with a high lace collar—too large, but the delicate color would match the deeper hue of her eyes. As the prayer droned on, Cameron devoured her with his gaze, surreptitiously at first, then openly. Little Mary Margaret, he realized with a sinking heart, was one of the most beautiful women he had ever seen.

And the hell of it was, she was his wife.

The blessing ended almost without his knowing it, and the conversation turned to polite comments between bites of fresh soda bread and Clara's savory stew. By now, the whole settlement was aware of what had happened to Jenny, but this was dinnertime. Cameron knew their hosts would avoid such upsetting talk during a meal.

Meg spoke little and seemed lost in thought. At least she and Clara had made friends. That was good, Cameron observed. It would be easier to leave her tomorrow, knowing she was in kindly hands.

And leave her he would. He'd intended it all along, but after his conversation with Malcolm before dinner, he was more determined than ever.

They'd been seated outside on a crude bench, enjoying the last of the daylight. Cameron had unfolded the Emir's map and was using it to show Malcolm where he planned to intercept Jenny's kidnappers. Malcolm's ruddy forehead had furrowed in sudden concern.

"But that's Kikuyu country! It's a terrible risk you'll be taking, man!"

Cameron had shrugged off his worry. "I've dealt with the Kikuyu before. They're not so bad, as long as you treat them fairly."

Malcolm ran an agitated hand through his blond thatch of hair. "You haven't heard, then. Bunch of Kikuyu butchered a missionary up past Marunga last month. Witch doctors put them up to the job, or so I heard—claimed their god, *Ngai*, was angry, and wouldn't end the drought till they'd driven every foreigner from the land. Whole bloody country's on edge up there."

Cameron refolded the map. "For me, that can't make any difference. I've got to go. It's that, or give up all hope of finding my daughter."

"But to take a woman along..."

"Meg isn't going. She doesn't know it yet, but I've been planning all along to leave her here at Machakos. I'll give you a little money for her keep, and for the trouble of getting her back to the railhead." He had begun to fumble in his pocket, but Malcolm touched a restraining hand to Cameron's wrist.

"Never mind the money. Clara will be glad for the company. And Pioneer Mary's due in here any day. She'll no doubt be swinging over to the railhead for some trade. She'll be happy to take your missus along."

"Then it's settled!" Cameron's relief was like the lifting of a heavy load. He was acquainted with tough, red-headed Mary Wallace—Pioneer Mary—who drove her trade wagon alone through the African highlands while her husband tended store at Fort Smith. She kept her mules in line with a hippo-hide whip, and she could outshoot and outcurse most men. Nobody messed with Mary, not even the Kikuyu. Aye, Meg would be in good hands.

"When do you plan to tell her?" Malcolm asked.

"I don't. Meg's a strong-willed woman. If she knew, you'd have to clap her in irons to hold her back."

"I see." Malcolm ruminated on the implications of this. "Well, of course it's for her own good. But not a word to Clara, now, or your secret won't be worth spit on a brushfire."

Malcolm's words echoed in Cameron's mind as the meal continued. He was acutely conscious of Meg beside him, warm through her dress, and as fragrant as wildflowers after the first rains. Her hair was brushed gold in the candlelight, her lips soft and full, like a child's. Her amethyst eyes did not look at him. Not even once. It was almost as if she knew.

Blast it, he hated lying to her. He hated lying to anyone. But he could not risk her to the dangers ahead, especially now.

"What do you think about that, eh, MacKenna?" Malcolm's question jolted Cameron out of his reverie. He blinked uncomprehendingly. His host chuckled.

"It's Nairobi I was talking about. Not much more than swampland now, I'll grant you. But once the tracks get there and the railway sets up its headquarters, the town'll sprout like a crop of mushrooms! Wouldn't you say so?"

"Oh, no doubt about it," Cameron agreed. "A year's time, and Nairobi will be booming."

"I've been thinking," Malcolm said. "A man with some building skills could do right well for himself there." He glanced at Clara, as if he were about to make a momentous announcement. "I was a carpenter back in Glasgow. But I worked for wages there, and when we pulled up stakes for Africa, I swore I'd never do that again. No, what I'd really like to do is start my own construction company."

"But Malcolm." Clara laid a gentle hand on her husband's arm. "You're only one man. You'd need so much help."

"Aye, that I know. I was hoping at least to have my brother here, but..." He shrugged, sighed and turned to Cameron. "What about you, MacKenna? You've worked for the railroad. You ought to know a thing or two about the building trade."

"Why, I..." Cameron paused while the possibility fluttered like a hatchling bird in his mind. He liked Malcolm Roberson, and Nairobi, springing out of a bog on the Athi Plain, was bound to grow in the months ahead. With luck and hard work, a man in the building business might make good money.

Then he remembered the map in his breast pocket. It lay over his heart, burning like a brand. Ivory. His for the taking. Aye, he could almost hear the devil's laughter as he replied, "No, Roberson, I'm afraid I can't help you. I've other plans that can't wait."

Meg looked squarely at him then, for the first time that evening. Her eyes held little fire-darts from the reflected candle flame—and something else. Pain. Deep, heartfelt anguish.

She had hardly spoken since the meal began, he realized. For the past two days, she'd seemed in decent spirits, but tonight she looked as if the world had caved in on her.

Leave her alone, he admonished himself, you'll only make matters worse. But as Meg lowered her gaze to her plate, Cameron knew that whatever was troubling her, he could not just push the matter aside. He felt her hurt too keenly. For all her deceit, he cared for her—blast it—too much.

He would catch her alone at the first opportunity, he resolved. It could be that Meg would resent his intrusion and push him away. But he would comfort her while he could. Tomorrow, even that would be finished.

His chance came an hour after dinner. Clara was busy tucking the children into bed, and Malcolm was seated at the table with sheets of foolscap, sketching what looked like crude floor plans with a flat carpenter's pencil. Cameron knew Malcolm would enjoy talking about his ideas, but just as he was about to join him, Meg wandered in from the kitchen area, where she'd been drying the dishes. She was wearing one of Clara's old aprons, and was wiping her hands on its skirt.

Her face looked peaked and drawn as she crossed the room without speaking and vanished outside through the open front doorway. With a murmured apology to Malcolm, Cameron turned and followed her into the night.

He found her standing next to the bench where he'd talked with Malcolm that afternoon. Her hands hung at her sides. Her head lay back, resting against the thatched wall of the bungalow. Her eyes stared emptily at the stars.

Cameron moved into place beside her, close, but not so close as to risk making her uncomfortable. What could he say, with so much strain between them? Maybe nothing. Maybe, for now, just being nearby would be enough.

They stood for a time without talking, the night cool and alive around them. Meg's profile was as pale as chiseled ivory against the stars. Cameron could feel the distress in her. He could hear her ragged breathing in the darkness. The stillness between them grew heavy as he waited. He ached to reach out to her, to break the tension with a word or a touch. But that was for Meg to do. Forcing things would only raise more barriers between them.

Seconds crawled by, weighted by silence. Finally, Meg stirred. A shudder passed through her body as she spoke.

"I...went for a walk with Clara this afternoon," she began hesitantly. "We'd been talking about Jenny—"

Here her voice faltered, but she recovered and plunged on. "Clara took me to the graveyard, just outside the settlement. She showed me where her own little girl was buried—her own little girl who died of fever a year ago. She was just—Jenny's—age—"

Meg pressed clenched hands to her face. An anguished spasm shook her body. "I—I thought about it all afternoon. All this time, I've never let myself imagine not finding Jenny, not getting her back. But terrible things *do* happen, Cameron. Children die. All over the world, they die. Or sometimes they just disappear, without a trace, forever."

"Meg...Meg, don't." Cameron reached out, as if it was the most natural thing in the world, and gathered her into his arms. She came without resistance, her body quivering against his chest. Aching with his own deep needs, he cradled her close and rocked her like a child.

"Don't even think it, Meg," he whispered against her hair. "No matter how hard it seems, we've got to go on believing that Jenny's all right, that we'll find her."

"Clara's so strong. You've seen how she laughs and smiles. But I'm not like her, Cameron. Jenny's my whole life! I couldn't stand it—I couldn't go on—"

"Stop it, Meg...oh, Meg—" His fingers fumbled for her chin, and the next thing Cameron knew, he was covering her soft petal mouth with kisses. Gentle kisses, warm kisses. The feel of her lips was so sweet on his that he could have wept.

"Hold me," she whispered brokenly. "Oh, Cameron, I need to be held."

His arms tightened around her. Her body yielded to the pressure, curves nestling hollows as naturally as if each had been molded for the other. Cameron felt the delicate pounding of her heart. He felt the sharp little bones of her shoulders where his hand lay, and the spasmodic rise and fall of her ribs. He felt her pain, and he burned with the fierce desire to protect her, to cherish her, to possess her.

"My sweet, brave Meg...." he murmured into the fragrant shell of her ear. She shivered in his arms, clinging to him as if he were the only solid object in a world of shadows. Cameron fought the temptation to comfort her with lies. He would do everything in his power to rescue their daughter, but even he could not deny the bleak truth of what she had said. Terrible things did happen. Children did die; they cried and suffered and endured unspeakable terrors. And somewhere out there in the far darkness was a frightened, lost, precious little girl, the innocent creation of their folly. Suddenly, he, too, was afraid.

He cradled Meg against him, needing her strength as much as she needed his. His own fear was a cry in the night. He knew the horrors Jenny would be facing. He knew the staggering odds against her rescue, against her even surviving the perilous trek, against his catching the slavers at the Neck of The Jar, then freeing her alive. The chances were dismal. And as for what lay beyond... Aye, death was a kinder fate than the hellish abuse Jenny would suffer as the slave-toy of some depraved master.

Clasping Meg close, he thought of tomorrow, when he would steal away in the dawn and leave her behind. "Listen to me, lass," he whispered, his throat raw with strain. "There'll be hard times ahead for all of us, times when you'll curse me, when you'll even hate me. But whatever happens—Lord help me, Meg, I swear this on my life—I'll do everything I can to get Jenny back. Whatever it takes, whatever it costs—"

Her finger touched his mouth. "Hush. I know. I know." Her hand curved around the back of his neck, pulling his head down to hers. The lips that caught his were salty with tears, desperate in their urgency.

As he kissed her, Cameron reeled with the need that surged through his body. He'd thought that holding her, giving comfort, would be enough. But he was wrong. The loneliness of years exploded as raw desire that shook his vitals like a storm. Meg's mouth was as soft as blown silk, and wet with promise. Her corseted waist arched against him, crushing her firm breasts to his chest. Her hands taloned his hair.

Cameron was dizzy with wanting her. "Meg...." he whispered between urgent, gasping kisses. "Sweet Meg..."

He could feel the quivering response where her body pressed his, and the hot, hard surge of his own readiness. From some foggy recess in his mind, Cameron's pride cried out that this woman had rejected him, betrayed him, lied to him—but it no longer mattered. Nothing mattered but Meg, and the feel of her in his arms.

They froze suddenly at the sound of a footstep and the creak of the plank door on its leather hinges. Meg spun away from him with a little gasp. Swiftly she smoothed her hair and straightened her apron.

The door swung open. Clara stood in the pool of lamplight that spilled from inside the house. "There you are!" she exclaimed cheerfully. "I just came out to tell you that your bed's made up and ready. Malcolm and I could keep you up visiting all night. But we know the two of you have to get an early start tomorrow."

Your bed. Cameron swallowed hard. With so many other things going on, he hadn't given a thought to the sleeping arrangements. Now the implications of what lay ahead came crashing in on him. Kissing Meg in the moonlight was one thing, but the torment of his aroused body was proof enough that he could not be trusted alone with her, especially in the dark, delicious warmth of a real bed. And as for Meg herself...

He shot her a furtive glance. She was clasping Clara's hands, thanking the woman for her hospitality. The lamplight cast a glow on her tousled hair, swollen lips and flushed cheeks, which Clara, bless her, was pretending not to notice.

Cameron felt himself sweating in the cool night air. If he had any sense, he would take to his heels right now. He could spend the night camped with the Swahili boys, and pull out before dawn. A clean getaway with no risks. And no rewards.

He remembered Meg's unbridled response to his kiss, her body arching to his, her hands tunneling his hair. Was she bluffing, or did she truly want him? If he turned tail now, he would never know.

Aye, Meg was still his wife, and his lips stung with the taste of her passion. Tonight, Cameron resolved, he would see this thing through. If she was playing games, he would call her bluff and be gone for good. If she was not... His knees weakened at the thought of what that could mean. Meg, still loving him, still wanting him. The chance for a new life together.

He forced the thought from his mind, afraid to believe it could really happen.

Meg was still talking with Clara. Cameron stood in the shadows, listening to the sounds of night—the cry of an owl, the bleat of the long-eared Nubian goats milling inside their snug *boma*—as he probed the well of his courage. He had always told himself that love was something he didn't need. He'd told himself it didn't matter that Jock MacKenna and his big, ruddy sons had never fully accepted him as part of the family. He'd shrugged off the fact that all of hidebound little Darlmoor looked on him as a reprobate and a dreamer, that even his own bride had been forced to marry him.

He had told the world to go to hell, and built a world of his own behind the barrier of his pride. Only in the past few days had he come to realize what a bleak, miserable prison he'd created for himself.

And now it was all staked on a single throw of the dice. Meg had deceived him. He had ample reason to hate her. But now, seeing her through a haze of moonlight, Cameron realized how deeply he needed her love.

"Your room's got its own outside door," Clara was saying. "And it's on the opposite end of the house from the other bedrooms, so you'll have it quiet for sleeping. Get a good night's rest, and we'll see you in the morning."

With a parting smile and a swish of her skirts, she vanished into the house, closing the door behind her. Meg turned back to face Cameron, her heart drumming a wild tattoo against her ribs.

He stood in the shadows, waiting, she knew, for her to make the next move. Now would be the time to run, she thought. Now would be the time to follow Clara back into the safety of the well-lit parlor.

Her feet would not move.

What was happening to her? Less than a fortnight ago, she'd stepped off the boat at Mombasa with her future all planned—the divorce, her marriage to Arthur, a gracious, respectable life for herself and Jenny. Now, here she was, in the middle of nowhere, with Jenny tragically missing; and as for herself...

Meg shivered, chilled by the memory of that small, lonely grave she'd seen today. Clara's child. A lively, pink-cheeked little girl who had laughed, played, chased butterflies, only to have her life snuffed out like a candle in the wind. And somewhere, out there in the darkness was Jennifer Jane, whose days were meant to be filled with new toys, party dresses, pony rides and boundless love.

Meg gazed at Cameron, the night wind cooling lips moist from his kisses. She tried to think of Arthur, but his face had vanished from her mind. Arthur was not part of this. Jenny was Cameron's child, and it was Cameron who held her young life in his hands. Only Cameron was strong enough to save her.

And only Cameron was strong enough for what Meg needed tonight.

She remembered his arms in the darkness, the wild hunger of his kisses. And now, as she stood poised and quivering on the brink of temptation, Meg knew only one thing.

She could not go on without him. She needed Cameron more than she had ever needed anyone in her life.

The waning moon hung rich and full above the horizon, framing a lone baobab tree in the circle of its light. From the black plain beyond the settlement, the call of a leopard echoed like the sound of tearing silk. Meg hesitated, gathering her courage. Her body trembled with anticipation as she opened her arms.

Cameron crossed the space between them in three long strides. A tiny sob escaped Meg's lips as he caught her against him. She lifted her face to meet his kisses, tender, probing kisses that rippled through her like a flood, leaving her weak with longing. Her arms slid around his neck, pulling him against her so tightly that she could feel his pounding heart against her breasts.

"Oh, Meg...." he whispered between kisses. "I've needed you so much... for so long..."

Meg's lips parted in response, but her own emotions choked off her answer. She felt as if a frozen spring had begun to thaw deep inside the most protected part of her. Its sweetness trickled through her body, whispering its secret message: *trust him... love him.*

She closed her eyes, her mouth swelling to the firm mold of his lips. His hands moved gently up the curve of her waist, to knead her back and shoulders. They quivered with restraint, as if awaiting a signal from her.

Instinctively, her tongue stirred. Its tip feathered his mouth, flicking his lips, darting between his teeth. Cameron stiffened against her. A shudder ran through his body. Then, suddenly, he was crushing her hard against him, his kisses bruising in their power, wild in their unleashed urgency.

Responses too long confined exploded like rockets inside her. Her hands clasped his head, fingers tangling in his hair. Her tongue met his in a jumbled thrust-and-parry that sent hot, wet waves surging through her body.

She whimpered as his hand found her breast through the thin fabric of her gown. The pressure of his fingers was ecstasy. Meg fumbled wildly with her buttons, needing his touch against her skin, hungering for his hands, his mouth on her body, on all of her.

Yes, he knew—surely he knew. Cameron's lips seared a path down the line of her open bodice. Lost now, Meg clung to him, savoring the warm dampness of his breath in the cleft between her breasts. For the past four years, she had remained alone and untouched. *No more,* her heart whispered. *No more,* her throbbing body echoed. After tonight, she knew, she could never go back and face Arthur. It no longer mattered.

"Meg...oh, Meg, lass..." His free hand jerked her hard against his hips. She felt the solid ridge of his manhood quivering against her belly. Her knees buckled as she arched against him. He caught her in his arms, sweeping her up in a surging rush that carried them all the way to the bedroom.

By lamplight, they tore frantically at each other's clothes. Garments flew aside in total abandon, leaving a trail from the bolted door to where they stood at the bedside, locked in each other's arms.

Meg's touch devoured him. Her fingers furrowed the crisp, black hair that curled on his chest. Her tongue circled the puckered rosette of one tiny nipple, tasting his warm salty flesh. His lips were in her hair, his hands ranging hungrily over her bare skin. She whimpered with frenzied impatience as his fingers moved lower, along the curve of her pelvis. Her hips curled upward to meet his hand, offering him the intimate tangle of hair, the moist, secret slit beneath.

Cameron groaned as his fingers took their sweet possession. He arched her backward onto the bed, stroking with a silky touch that shimmered like moonlight through her body. His desire lay hard and swollen along her thigh. Meg's breath tore at her throat as she moved against him, her hips undulating in urgent little twitches, her body throbbing with need. "Love me, Cameron," she whispered hoarsely. "Love me...."

He shifted above her, trembling as her slick, pulsing softness parted to meet him. Like a long lost key finding its lock, he entered her, opening the doors of the past, bridging the lonely years as if they had never existed.

"Oh—" Meg clung to him, transfixed. Her hips curved upward, pulling him deeper into her warm, pulsing center. With a gasp that was almost a sob, he pressed home.

They moved together, now, in a rhythm as wild and timeless as the sea. Abandoning reason for trust, Meg gave herself up to him, to the exquisite tugs and tightenings, to the delicious quiverings that unfolded in her like the opening of a thousand flowers. She was his. Shamelessly. Completely.

Her hands clasped his buttocks, drawing him into her as she met each thrust of his powerful body. He caught her lips as their ecstasy mounted. Her senses were drunk with the taste of him, with the scent and feel of him. "Cameron—" she whispered as their rapture burst like a shower of comets. "I love you, Cameron—"

She felt him shudder, felt his wordless kisses on her face. He leaned away from her long enough to extinguish the lamp. Then, deliciously spent, they slipped into darkness together.

Cameron felt the dawn arrive. He felt it before the sun's first rays had paled the horizon, before the first bird had stirred in its nest. For a moment, he lay in the darkness, listening to Meg's soft breathing on the pillow next to his ear. Then, with excruciating care, he eased himself away from her satiny warmth and slid out of bed. It was time to leave.

His clothes, tangled with Meg's stockings and lace-trimmed underthings, lay strewn in a path from the door to the bed. Cameron collected them and dressed hurriedly, trying not to think about last night. If he truly let himself remember, he would never be able to leave her.

He froze as she stirred with a kittenish little purr, turned drowsily in the bed, quivered and lay still again. Cameron exhaled silently and continued buttoning his shirt. It was a rotten trick he was about to play on her, especially after last night. But he had no choice. Meg would never stay behind willingly, and he could not expose her to the dangers that lay ahead.

Bending from the waist, he tugged on his boots and jerked the laces tight. He'd ordered the boys to be up and packed before daylight. If things went as planned, they would be miles away by the time she woke up and missed him.

Aye, she would be furious. Cameron could only pray that she'd listen to Malcolm's explanation, and that she would understand and forgive. All his hopes and dreams hung on that forgiveness.

Dressed and ready to go, he stood in the doorway. He should have written a note to leave behind, he thought. But there was no time for that now.

Still, for the space of a long breath, he lingered, his eyes memorizing the shadowed contours of Meg's sleeping face and the tumble of her tawny curls on the pillow. Despite his resolve, Cameron's thoughts clung to the memory of last night's loving. Meg had given him back his manhood, he realized. She had opened the door to heaven.

He ached to lean over her, to brush back her hair and tease her ear with his tongue until she whimpered and stretched sleepy arms to draw him close, to begin again where they'd left off last night.

But no—he tore his thoughts away. For her own sake he had to leave now, while he could.

"I'll be back for you, Mary Margaret," he whispered, his throat raw with emotion. "Wait for me, lass. Trust me and believe."

His eyes blurred as he slipped out of the room and closed the door behind him.

Chapter Eleven

A finger of gray morning light probed a thin spot in the thatch. It teased at Meg's slumbering face, peppering her eyelids, tickling her nose.

Meg moaned drowsily, pulled the eiderdown over her head, and snuggled deeper into its feathery softness. She was still deliciously sleepy, and her naked body tingled with the memory of Cameron's lovemaking. Morning could wait a little longer.

One hand crept across the sheet, seeking Cameron's reassuring warmth. What a proud fool she'd been, thinking she could be content as Mrs. Arthur Tarrington-Leigh, when all the time it was Cameron she'd wanted! Dear, troubled, passionate Cameron, who needed her love as much as she needed his!

Everything was going to be all right, she fantasized, still half-asleep. First they would rescue Jenny, and then the three of them would go back to Scotland together. They would sell the house in Darlmoor and move to Aberdeen, or even Edinburgh, where Cameron, with his railway experience, would surely find good employment. Oh, maybe they would never be wealthy, but money wasn't essential to happiness. Seeing Malcolm and Clara together was proof enough of that. Perhaps one day, they could even—

Meg's fingers froze on the cool, empty expanse of sheet. Her eyes shot open.

Cameron was gone.

She sat bolt upright, eyes racing around the shadowed room. There was no sign of his clothes, his boots, his canteen or his rifle.

Clutched by panic, Meg leapt up and began scrambling for her scattered underthings. She found her drawers under the bed, her corset and camisole tossed over a chair, one stocking under the same chair, the other dangling out of her boot-top. Her face blazed hot as she remembered last night's rush to the bed, remembered the compelling urge that had swept away all common sense. The morning was dark and cold now, and last night seemed so far removed that it might have happened to someone else. Meg ran a trembling hand over the curves of her body, still feeling Cameron's touch, feeling his hands, his mouth, in places so intimate that it made her blush to think of them.

What had she done? she asked herself. Who was Mary Margaret Owen MacKenna now?

She stood naked on the straw mat, confused, frightened and shivering in the cold dawn. Until a moment ago, everything had seemed so right—she and Cameron together, facing a world that bloomed with hope. Now, suddenly, that world seemed alien, and even bleaker than before.

And where was Cameron? If he had truly gone off without her... Yes, it was a foolhardy thing she'd done last night. More than foolhardy. It was disastrous.

She yanked on her clothes, telling herself all the while not to panic. Cameron had gone to see that the boys were up and ready, that was all. He would be back for her any minute.

But even as she dressed, even as she scrubbed her face and cleaned her teeth, the feeling would not leave her that something was dreadfully wrong. Her hands shook as she twisted up her hair and retrieved the scattered pins to jab into the knot. The eyes that stared back at her from the looking glass were bloodshot and apprehensive.

The setting moon lay low and pale in the indigo sky as Meg stepped outside. She could hear no stirrings from the main part of the house. That, she told herself, was just as well. Much as she liked the Robersons, she would be in no mood for pleasantries until she knew what had become of Cameron.

She glanced around the yard, not really expecting to see him. Cameron would not have taken his gun and canteen if he'd planned on staying within the settlement. It was more likely that he'd gone out to check on the camp. She would look for him there.

Meg stepped back into the bedroom long enough to jam her own possessions into her rucksack and snatch up her hat and her own half-filled canteen. The grove where the porters and *askaris* had set up camp was only ten or fifteen minutes from the settlement. With luck, she could get there and back again before Clara and Malcolm had a chance to miss her. But just in case, she would want all her things along.

The eastern sky was fading to violet-pink, streaked with dry red clouds that would burn off once the sun was up. Meg slipped out through the gate in the *boma* and closed it behind her. The settlement was just beginning to stir. Here and there, smoke from outdoor kitchens curled into the sky, and Meg's nose caught tantalizing whiffs of frying bacon. But there was no one in the yards. Only a flock of tamed guinea fowl, scratching for their breakfast in the dooryard, saw her depart.

The morning air was rich with the smell of grass and alive with birdcalls. Meg could feel her spirits lifting as she strode along the trail. She'd been silly, worrying about Cameron, she told herself. He would be at the camp, of course, rousting out the boys. Once they were up and about, he would head back to fetch her. She would surprise him. They would laugh about it together.

She walked faster. Monkeys quarreled in a treetop, their chatter harsh and mocking. What if Cameron regretted last night? She imagined his eyes, cold and distant in the gray dawn air, their gaze shifting to avoid hers, his mouth a stubborn slit pulled down at one corner by the scar.

Last night she'd behaved like a wanton! She'd given herself to him shamelessly, without reservation! Cameron probably thought she did that sort of thing all the time! He probably even thought she'd done it with Arthur!

By now she was running. Her frantic eyes flashed this way and that, scanning the horizon. Where was the camp? She'd been sure it was just ahead, under those big thorn trees. But there were no tents, no cookfires, no people....

Sides heaving with effort, Meg burst into the campsite beneath the trees. She saw the circle of trampled grass, the charred remains of the fire, its ashes still sending up thin spirals of smoke.

She collapsed against a tree trunk, heart thudding as reality sunk into her senses.

Cameron had truly left her. He had meant to leave her all along.

She sank to the ground, out of breath and reeling with shock. She understood everything now. Oh yes, he had planned it from the beginning! Give her a taste of the trail, just enough to discourage her, then abandon her at Machakos, to the kindness of strangers! Malcolm had probably known about the plan since last night, maybe Clara, too. She could imagine them whispering about it behind her back.

Hurt, angry and betrayed, Meg slammed her fist into the dust. Yes, it had all been arranged. When she came weeping back to Machakos, Malcolm and Clara would explain everything, the danger, the hardship, and all that piffle about how Cameron had wanted to spare her. Oh, she could not go back and listen to them! She could not stand to look into their pitying faces!

And as for Cameron, his betrayal was the worst of all! To take her in his arms last night, to make love to her when he knew all along—

Meg sprang to her feet, driven by a fury of desperation. Going back to the settlement was out of the question now. She had to catch up with the caravan. Not because of her anger; not because of the lies and the betrayal. She could turn her back on those things and walk away. But she could not turn her back on her child.

Jenny was out there somewhere, frightened and in danger. Meg could not rescue her alone. For that, she needed Cameron. For that, she would endure Cameron's sarcasm, his arrogance and his lies. Nothing mattered now except being there when Jenny was found.

Meg took a calculated sip from her canteen. She had no food and only a little water, but the caravan could not be more than an hour or two ahead of her. The trail they'd taken led off through the dry grass. If she followed it without stopping to rest, she should catch up with them before nightfall. No matter what happened after that, she would not let Cameron send her back to Machakos.

She capped her canteen and tightened the lid. Then, squaring her shoulders, she struck out on the trail with long, determined strides. There could be fearful dangers ahead, but to imagine them now would be to lose her courage. She would think of Jenny, Meg resolved. Only of Jenny.

Cameron crouched in the darkness, staring into the flames of the campfire. *Chacula* was finished, and the Swahili were already settling in for the night, wrapped in the fine wool blankets the Emir had provided for them. They'd covered a good thirty miles today, he calculated, and he himself was exhausted. But the release of sleep would not come.

His fingers toyed with a twig he'd picked up from the ground, absently breaking it into fragments that he tossed into the blaze. Aye, he'd pushed the boys hard today. In his effort to cover distance, he'd driven them ruthlessly, never stopping for more than a few minutes at a time. They had not liked it. He had heard their grumbling and sensed their discontent. But he could not afford to spare them. He had to press ahead now, while he could, in case there were delays later on.

Cameron settled back on his haunches and closed his eyes, listening as the crackle of burning wood mingled with the sounds of the African night. Wind rustled the dry grass. The ever-present hyenas tittered from the shadows. A waning moon rode low above the trees.

Meg's face, her eyes like black-centered violets, floated in and out of his tired mind. He'd struggled all day to put that vision aside, but it had been a useless battle. She had haunted his every footstep.

Even now, his skin tingled from the silken pressure of her hands; his mouth stung with the memory of her kiss-swollen lips and darting tongue. Her musky woman-fragrance lingered like perfume in his nostrils.

Cameron remembered her ecstatic little whimpers as she welcomed him home to that warm, moist part of her where he had been too long a stranger. He remembered—

Damn! Cameron opened his eyes and tossed the half-crumbled twig into the fire. At this rate, he would be a raving madman by morning! He'd already made up his mind that he wanted a life with Meg. But first there were things he had to accomplish, urgent things that demanded the full measure of his concentration. Mooning around like a lovesick schoolboy would only make them more difficult.

At least he knew that Meg was safe. Angry or not, she would have no choice except to wait for his return. And if, by some miracle, he could come back with Jenny and—

A piercing female scream shattered his thoughts.

Cameron leapt to his feet. The sound had come from the darkness, perhaps fifty yards from camp. As he snatched up his rifle, he heard it again, its tone all too familiar, and intermingled, this time, with yelps and snarls.

There was no time to wake the native boys. Cursing under his breath, he raced toward the sound.

Aye, it was Meg. Once he'd cleared camp, he could see her clearly in the moonlight. She was fending off three hyenas with her tin canteen, which she swung like a mace from its long canvas strap. Her screams were not so much cries for help as shrieks of desperate rage.

He could not shoot. There was too much risk of hitting Meg in the melee of spotted bodies. Seizing the rifle's barrel and using the stock as a club, he plunged into the fray.

The boldest animal had just lunged for Meg. Her canteen caught the side of its head with a resounding whack, and the brute reeled to one side, dazed but not hurt. Another hyena, meanwhile, had seized her skirt in its massive jaws and was threatening to drag her off balance. Cameron swung the rifle with all his strength. Its impact cracked ribs as the hyena yelped and let go.

By now, all three attackers had reassessed the odds and were backing off. Intelligent and cowardly, they would look for easier prey somewhere else. As they melted into the nighttime shadows, Cameron seized Meg by the shoulders.

"You little fool!" He was limp-kneed with relief. "You stubborn, reckless—"

"Let go of me!" Her voice was an icy whisper. Her rigid body quivered with suppressed fury. "You conniving, deceitful opportunist!" she hissed. "You liar!"

Cameron's arms dropped to his sides. In the moonlight, he could see that her hair hung in dusty strings around her grimy face. Her jacket was gone, and her once-white shirtwaist was torn and filthy. Meg had been through thirty miles of hell, he realized. She'd walked all day alone in the blinding sun with no weapon, no food, and very little water. She was lucky to be alive.

His emotions had begun to spill over. "Damn it, Meg—"

"You were planning this all along, weren't you?" she snapped, glowering at him through tangles of hair. "Even when we were making love, you were planning to go off and leave me at Machakos!"

Cameron groaned. "Meg, it was for your own safety."

"Rubbish! You just didn't want to be bothered! Oh, but you weren't above having a little fun first! I could almost forgive you for the rest, Cameron. But not for that!" She was reeling with hunger and exhaustion.

If she hadn't been so angry, Cameron would have swept her up in his arms and carried her back to camp. "You didn't talk with Malcolm this morning?" he asked her.

"Not with Malcolm, and not with Clara, either! They'd only have tried to stop me. They were both in this with you, weren't they?"

"No," he answered swiftly. "It was all my idea. I warned Malcolm last night, but Clara didn't know anything about it."

She swayed slightly, like a child's block tower about to topple. Then, abruptly, she drew herself up again. "Why didn't you tell *me*, Cameron? I'm not a child that you can manipulate according to what you think is best!"

He took her arm, trying to support her as he steered her toward camp. Meg was so tired she was stumbling over her own feet in the darkness, but even then she tried to pull away from him.

His hand clamped onto her arm, almost hurting. "Listen!" he growled, suddenly out of patience. "I didn't tell you because I knew what you'd do! And I was right, you little idiot! Do you know what a bloody miracle it is that you survived out there today?"

"You had no right to leave me behind!" Meg's voice cracked with exhaustion. "Jenny's my daughter! She needs me, and I have to be here! Don't you understand?"

Cameron clenched his jaw, torn between the urge to shake her and a senseless desire to crush her in his arms. To his credit, he managed to keep his hands to himself. "You'll only slow us down," he grated. "And if you'd talked with Malcolm, you'd know that the Kikuyu are on the brink of an uprising. We're already deep into their territory."

"As if that would make any difference!"

"Damn it, Meg, I did it for your own good!"

"My own good!" She was weaving like a drunkard, straining against his hold on her. "And what about last night, Cameron? Was that for my own good, as well?"

Her words stung him like a lash. "You're in no condition to talk about last night," he said, thinking of how fast a man could tumble from heaven to hell. "When you've had food and sleep, then we'll talk."

She twisted out of his grasp and stood wild-haired and quivering in the moonlight, legs braced apart to keep herself upright.

"I'll say my piece now, and this is the last we'll speak of it!" she rasped. "I'll march with you, Cameron MacKenna! I'll share your food and even your tent, until Jenny is found! But hear this, because I mean every word of it—don't you touch me! Don't you ever touch me again!"

The weeks that followed were as bleak as any in Meg's life. Day after day, from first light till sundown, the little caravan plodded along the dusty highland trails. Breakfast was cold meat, cold biscuits and gritty coffee, all gulped in nervous haste. Supper was whatever meat had been gunned down that afternoon, often so tough and rubbery that she lacked the strength to chew it. Sleep was oblivion, or else it was wild, frightening dreams where Jenny vanished into the hollows of Hassan's skull-like eyes.

Meg was becoming hardened to the trail. Her body was down to bone and muscle; and she'd long since abandoned her useless, constricting corset to the fire. She marched now in her tattered twill skirt and one of Cameron's spare khaki shirts, gathered at the waist with a strip of petticoat. Her sun bleached hair, no longer twisted up and pinned à la mode, dangled down her back in a single braid that swung as she walked. The high-topped boots, which had once pinched so miserably, had since molded to the contours of her callused feet.

Even under more pleasant circumstances, the trek would have been grueling. But with the rains delayed, the land cried out everywhere for water. The trail was a ribbon of powdery red dust that sifted into eyes, choked off nostrils and invaded every crack and fold in the body. Only the trees were green, and even these had been nibbled bare as high as the game could reach. The sparse grass was as dry as broom straw, and Meg had learned to avert her eyes when they passed a dry water hole, where vultures clumped like blowflies on the dead and dying animals.

Now and again, they saw deserted native *shambas,* the huts empty, the maize stalks standing brown and withered in the little garden patches. Kikuyu, Cameron had told her when she'd asked. Where had they gone, these people who were reputed to be so fearsome? It was as if they had been swept off the face of the earth.

Cameron had been forced to ration the drinking water. Meg accepted her portion without complaint and did not ask for more, even when the midday heat raked her throat with thirst. The Swahili, however, were less stoic. They whined at every turn, and it was only with threats, curses, sometimes even punishment, that Cameron kept them in line.

Meg, who'd picked up a few words of their language by now, was beginning to worry about them. The Emir, she realized, had recruited them hastily from the slums and alleys of Mombasa. Anxious and distraught, the old man had not taken time to assess their characters.

The Swahili had been paid half their wages at the journey's outset, and were to be given the rest on their return, with an extra reward for Jenny's rescue. Only that—not loyalty, not even a decent concern for Jenny—kept them working. The porters were peevish and lazy. The six *askaris* were negligent in their duties and careless of their weapons. When danger threatened, they reacted like hyenas, brave only when the odds were in their favor.

But the drought and the natives were not the worst things Meg had to endure. No, that black honor went to Cameron, and the bitter silence that lay between them.

From dawn to dusk, the two of them scarcely exchanged words, scarcely even looked at each other unless it was to ask a question or growl an order. At night, he entered the tent only when he thought she was asleep; and he was always gone by the time she crawled out of her bedroll in the morning. Even when she *wasn't* asleep, Meg kept her eyelids tightly closed, her breathing deep and even. Feigning sleep was easier than facing Cameron's cold, polite gaze or hearing the tone of mocking deference he used when he spoke to her.

It wasn't fair, she thought as she plodded through the glare of numberless days. Cameron had lied to her. He had betrayed her trust. Now, it was as if *she* had been the betrayer, as if he were punishing *her* for his own wrongdoing.

Oh, she had meant it, for all her half-delirious rage, when she'd ordered him not to touch her. He'd taken advantage of a vulnerable moment, and she would never trust him again. But that aside, their child was lost. Meg needed his emotional support. She needed, at least, his kindness. Couldn't Cameron see that? Or was he punishing her, as well, for bringing Jenny to Africa and leaving her with strangers?

A dark cycle of fear, guilt, rage and self-castigation began to evolve in Meg's mind, grinding like a mill wheel as she moved through the blur of days. In her isolation, she felt helpless to break its power. This was how madness began, she told herself, and she knew that if nothing intervened, she would spiral downward into a yawning pit of despair, so deep that she might never struggle out again.

The trail was beginning to climb now. Two days ago, they had forded the Tana River. Its stream was so low that they'd crossed on dry stones, stopping only long enough to fill canteens and water bags from the murky pools that remained where the bed was low and shaded. The water was foul, but no matter. It would keep them alive.

Now, on the horizon, the spires of Mount Kenya thrust into the hot blue sky like cusps of a massive tooth. The mountain, sacred to the Kikuyu, appeared close through the diamond-clear air. But its nearness, Meg had discovered, was an illusion. They had been pushing toward it for days now, and still it loomed ahead of them, out of reach.

Meg had long since memorized their route on the Emir's map, but she'd had no comprehension of its scale. The trail, she knew, would skirt the mountain's western slope and drop down again into the foothills. By the time they reached The Neck of The Jar, Mount Kenya would be at their backs. Only now, as the days passed and the mountain seemed to move before them like a mirage, did she begin to understand the vastness of this land. It was as if the whole of England, Scotland and Wales could be dropped into its space and lost there, with no one knowing the difference.

And Jenny in all this wide expanse, she was no more than a pinpoint, a tiny, moving dot.

It was midafternoon of a long day's march when they came upon the slaughtered caravan. At first, it appeared that the vultures and the hideous marabou storks were flapping around another dry water hole. Only when they came up on the edge of a *donga* and found themselves gazing straight down on the awful scene did they realize what it was.

"Don't look!" Cameron seized Meg's wrist and whipped her roughly against him, holding her tightly so that she could not turn around and see. But Meg had already seen enough. There were between twenty and thirty dead men in the shallow wash. Three of them were Arabs. The rest were Swahili, their long white *kansus* soaked with blood. They'd been killed, perhaps two or three days ago. The air swam with black flies and with the odor of their swollen flesh.

Still grasping Meg with one arm, Cameron ordered two of the *askaris* down into the *donga* to investigate. Meg stood rigidly against him as they waited. She could hear the low, steady pounding of his heart against her ear. Her shoulder ached where he gripped it with his tense, hard fingers.

A terrible thought invaded her mind. "Jenny?"

"Don't be silly! They wouldn't have come this way from Mombasa!" he growled, and Meg, realizing he was right, felt a little of the fear go out of her. She stood in the clench of his arm with her face against his damp, musky shirt, torn between needing his strength and wanting to tear herself loose and run until she dropped from exhaustion.

The *askaris* returned swiftly. One of them carried a long-bladed spear, its point crusted with blood. Cameron gave the spear a quick glance. "Kikuyu," he said in a low, hard voice. "And these poor bastards are beyond our help. Let's go."

Keeping a rough grip on Meg's wrist, he drew her back from the edge of the *donga*. At his terse command, the porters hoisted their burdens, the *askaris* fell into line and the little caravan moved forward again.

Meg held her tongue for the next mile, staring fixedly at the blocky outline of Cameron's shoulders and the dark streak along his spine, where the sweat plastered his shirt to his skin. Behind her, the grim black birds squawked and wheeled above the *donga*. Death's ripe aroma lingered sickeningly in her nostrils. She thought of Jenny, and suddenly the awful silence was too much to bear alone.

She cleared her tight throat and took a deep breath. "Cameron, what do you think happened back there?" she asked.

He sighed raggedly. "Ambush, I'd say. The Arabs had muzzle-loaders, but from the looks of things, there was no time to use them. The fact that they hadn't scattered or taken shelter points to a surprise attack, and by enough Kikuyu to do the job in a hurry."

"But I don't understand. Why would they do it?"

Cameron's muscular shoulders rippled in a shrug. "Good question. I've never known Kikuyu to attack anybody who wasn't trying to harm them. But with the drought, who knows? We've seen their empty villages. If they're starving and desperate for supplies..." His voice trailed off, leaving the unspoken thought hanging like a lead weight.

"Then, they could attack *us,* too," Meg said, finishing his sentence in the calmest voice she could muster.

Cameron glanced over his shoulder, his eyes flashing indigo in the bright sun. "Aye, that they could. And there's more that you might as well know. Malcolm told me their witch doctors have been stirring them up, telling them their god won't end the drought till the foreigners are gone from the land."

"The Swahili aren't foreigners."

"No, but they work for the Arabs and Europeans. In Kikuyu eyes, that tars them with the same brush."

Cameron paused to let the words sink in before adding a note of reassurance. "There's probably nothing to worry about. We're well armed. The Kikuyu would think twice before they'd go up against this many modern guns. As long as we're careful—"

"Cameron, you knew all this at Machakos. Why didn't you tell me then?"

"Would it have made any difference?" He spoke without looking back at her. "Would it have stopped you from running after us like a stubborn little mule-head?"

"At least I could have made an intelligent choice! As it was, you treated me like a child!"

His back muscles stiffened, and Meg braced herself for an angry retort. To her surprise, it did not come. He was silent for a moment; then the tension eased out of him in one long breath.

"Aye, so I did, lass," he said quietly. "But I only wanted to spare you. Maybe after today, you'll understand why."

Meg felt a trickle of warmth melting away the edge of her frozen emotions. Its unexpected sweetness brought tears to her smarting eyes. "I understand," she said. "I still don't think it was right, but I do understand. In that, at least, you meant well, Cameron."

He did not answer her, but his silence seemed gentler than before, as if he was fearful of breaking this first tenuous thread to cross the chasm between them. Maybe the bitter weeks had been as painful to him as they had to her, Meg thought. Maybe he even—

But no, she'd had enough of building castles on her hopes. Cameron had wounded her cruelly, she reminded herself. She would be a fool to trust him again.

A dust devil swirled across the path, sucking at the earth and lashing the lifeless yellow grass. Meg closed her eyes against the stinging wind. Her throat had turned to sawdust. Her mind still screamed with the horror of what she'd seen back there in the *donga*. She quickened her steps, frantic to put it behind her.

The same thread of urgency seemed to run through the whole caravan. Cameron forged ahead at a relentless pace, and for once the porters and *askaris* kept up without grumbling. Danger, real or imagined, lurked in every shadow and crouched behind every rock and tree.

Meg could feel the fear that emanated from the men behind her. It hung in the air like a cold miasma that chilled her skin to goose bumps. Squaring her shoulders, she forced her mind to form a picture of Jenny's face. *Faster*, she ordered her tired feet. *Faster!*

They camped that night on a hilltop, surrounded on all sides by open savanna. Supper was leftover biscuits and the stringy remains of last night's topi. A cookfire, Cameron feared, might attract the wrong kind of attention.

Meg had collapsed on her bedroll and fallen asleep as soon as the tent was pitched. Today had been hard on her, Cameron reflected. It had been hard on them all.

He knew he ought to get some sleep himself, but his jangling nerves would not let him rest. He prowled the fringes of the camp, ears straining for the slightest sound, rifle cocked and ready. The Kikuyu might not rush a well-armed caravan by day, but darkness was a different matter.

The moon had come up, flooding the barren hills with its pallid light. The night was eerily quiet, but then, there were few animals here. Most of the grazers, along with the predators that hunted them, had migrated in search of water. Of those that had stayed, only a handful survived.

He glanced back over his shoulder at the camp. The boys were not sleeping, either. They sat hunkered in their blankets, talking in low tones. Aye, they'd been spooked by what they saw today. Cameron was not even surprised when one of the older *askaris* unfolded his lanky body, separated himself from the group and came walking slowly toward him.

"What is it, Kidogo?" Cameron demanded, knowing full well how the man would answer.

The tall Swahili glanced back at his cohorts. "They asked me to talk to you, *bwana*. This is bad country. We should not be here."

"In other words, you're afraid," Cameron retorted sharply. "Maybe you're all cowards."

"We are not cowards," the man answered with a touch of wounded dignity. "But we are not fools, either. If we do not turn back, we will all be dead men."

"You realize you'll get no more pay if you turn back."

"At least we will have our lives, *bwana*."

"And what about my daughter's life?"

Kidogo shrugged. The whites of his eyes gleamed yellow in the moonlight. "If we die from thirst or from Kikuyu spears, it will be the same for her. She is only a girl-child, *bwana*. Your *memsahib* is young and strong. There will be other babies for you. Maybe next time a son."

Cameron gulped back a surge of rage. Kidogo meant well, he reminded himself. Such fatalism was the way of his culture. "Tell the men I will double their wages!" he growled, thinking of his own savings, which were barely enough to cover such a promise.

Kidogo shook his dark head. "All the rupees in the world are no good to the dead, *bwana*. It is our lives we want."

Cameron gazed out across the moon-shadowed landscape to where the craggy, black outline of Mount Kenya loomed against the sky. He thought about the hellish massacre they'd passed a few hours before. He thought about Meg and the threat to her safety. He thought about Jenny, and he felt as if his heart were being torn to pieces.

Aye, there was something to be said for turning back. It would be easy enough to retrace their steps to the Tana River, follow its course to the coast and then hire a boat for Mombasa. Easy enough—except that Meg would never agree to it. And neither would he, Cameron realized, as long as there was one chance in ten thousand of getting Jenny back. Whatever the cost, she was his child, too. He could not abandon her.

Kidogo was waiting for an answer. Cameron kept his eyes on the mountain as he spoke. "Go back to your friends," he said. "Tell them I will shoot the first man who tries to leave. And—make sure they know this—I will shoot to kill."

Chapter Twelve

Mount Kenya filled the horizon now, its exposed lava crags jutting like sharp, black fingers against the cerulean sky. Squinting through the glare, Meg could make out the glaciers that lined its rugged hollows. Their icy whiteness mocked her windburned face and raw, dry throat.

Two days had passed since they'd come upon the slaughtered caravan. They'd seen no Kikuyu, but there'd been scattered signs of them: blackened campfires, still smoldering; charred animal bones; iron-headed arrows, their tips crusted with poison.

Tension weighted every moment of the trek. Each rock cluster, each *donga* they passed, lay dark with the threat of danger. The porters marched with eyes that twitched beneath their burdens. The *askaris* clutched their rifles so nervously that Meg began to fear the guns might go off by accident.

Cameron had not slept. His eyes were red-rimmed and bloodshot, his hollow cheeks coated with grimy black stubble. He answered Meg's questions in monosyllabic grunts, and snarled his orders at the men. His rifle never left his hand.

She watched him with dismayed eyes. Something was troubling Cameron, something that went far deeper than the threat of Kikuyu. At first, she'd dared to hope he would confide in her. But as time passed, he only withdrew deeper into himself. Now, as before, they scarcely spoke. She could feel the strain in him. Sooner or later, she feared, he would break.

As the trail climbed, the landscape evolved from grassland to thick bush. There were more animals here: baboons, colobus monkeys and flocks of miniature jade-green parrots. Rhino tracks crisscrossed the caravan path, and once they passed a heap of elephant dung, still steaming in the cool dawn air. Here on the skirts of the mountain, hidden streams trickled down from the glaciers to lose themselves in the tangled undergrowth. Birds and animals knew where to find these streams. Human travelers, alas, did not.

In some spots, the vegetation overgrew the trail, and the *askaris* had to hack through the thornbush with their long, sharp *pangas*. The caravan had halted at one such place under a searing midday sun. Meg was taking a disciplined sip from her canteen when the air was shattered by a gut-wrenching shrick.

One of the porters, who'd stepped out of sight to relieve himself, lurched back onto the trail, clawing wildly at his thigh. Reeling and blubbering, he staggered toward Cameron and collapsed at his feet. By the time Meg reached him, he was gray-faced and gasping for breath.

Cameron jerked up the man's *kansu*, exposing a set of ugly red marks on the side of his upper leg. "Cobra," he muttered, shaking his head. "Big one, too, from the looks of the bite. Damn!"

Meg had knelt to cradle the porter's head between her knees. She could feel the convulsive jerks as the swift-acting poison paralyzed his nervous system. She looked up at Cameron, her vision blurred by tears. "There's got to be something we can do!"

Cameron's red-rimmed eyes glittered with exhaustion. "Not this time, lass. He's a dead man."

The other Swahili clustered around them, their faces grim and resigned. They had seen such deaths before. Cameron gave them a few seconds to look, then snapped an order that sent them hurrying back to their work. Two of the men took their *pangas* and began to beat the bush for the cobra. They returned a few minutes later, dragging the dead snake by its tail. As Cameron had guessed, it was a big one, well over six feet long and as thick as Meg's wrist.

By then, the stricken porter was gasping his last tortured breaths. Meg supported him gently, her eyes swimming with helpless tears. This man, she remembered, had shown her small kindnesses—a splinter removed from her leg, a hand extended when she'd slipped crossing the Tana, her canteen filled from a hard-to-reach spring. She remembered these things as he died.

Cameron stood over her, his shadow blotting out the sun. "Leave him, Mary Margaret. It's over." His voice cracked hoarsely. He swayed with weariness as his big, brown hand reached out to pull her up.

Meg did not move. "He was a good man. I want him properly buried, Cameron. Promise me you'll see to it."

He hesitated, contemplating the dangerous delay, then acquiesced with a sigh. "All right, lass, if it matters that much to you."

Meg eased away from the dead man and allowed Cameron to help her to her feet. She could feel the taut cords of his fingers. His eyes glittered with strain.

Meg battled her own compassion. She struggled against the urge to surround him with her arms and hold him tight against her, each of them drawing strength from the other. Cameron would not welcome that, she reminded herself. He would push her away, or worse, endure her nearness in stony silence.

At his terse order, a pair of short-handled shovels emerged from the packs, and the porters began to clear away a patch of brush at the trailside. Emotionally drained, Meg sank onto a boulder to rest.

The ground was rocky, the porters weary and enervated. They scraped away at the shallow grave with so little spirit that Cameron began to grow impatient. Muttering something in Swahili, he seized a shovel from the nearest man and thrust it into the hard-packed soil. Dirt flew under the fury of his attack.

Meg watched him anxiously as he paused to strip off his shirt and fling it aside. Cameron had been driving himself too hard. His nerves were strained to the breaking point. If he kept on this way...

She forced the worry from her mind. She could not dwell on dark possibilities, or she, too, would snap. She had to think in terms of moving on, of finding Jenny and somehow being happy again.

Cameron's shirt lay in a discarded heap at the grave's edge, half-covered by a growing mound of earth. Meg leaned forward, stretched out her hand and tugged it loose. The garment was in sad condition, frayed, sweat-soaked and caked with dust; he'd given his spare shirt to *her*, Meg reminded herself. She would wash it for him when they came to water. Meanwhile, the least she could do was shake out the dirt.

Turning away from the gravediggers, she grasped the shirt by its tails and shook it briskly. A shower of dust, twigs and leaves settled to the ground. And something else. Meg frowned as she picked it up. It was a folded, yellowed sheet of paper.

She opened it without thinking. It was a map, not unlike the Emir's, but more crudely drawn. She recognized Mount Kenya, but the rest of it made little sense, especially the number columns jotted along one side in faded pencil.

Stifling her curiosity, Meg refolded the map. However mysterious it might appear, Cameron's possessions were none of her affair. She would put it back in his pocket and say nothing.

On inspecting the shirt, however, Meg saw that the single pocket was missing a button and coming unseamed at the bottom. Cameron could lose the map; and it was surely important to him, or he would not have carried it all this way.

She slipped the stained, yellowed paper into her own shirt pocket and secured the button. For now, she would keep it safe. She would return it to him when they made camp that night.

The grave was finished. The porter's limp body was dropped into the hole, his companions swiftly covering it with dirt. Cameron stood watching. His eyes were grim, his skin beaded with sweat. When the burial was done, he raised the canteen and took one deep, hard swallow. Then, catching up his shirt from the grass where Meg had left it, he jerked it on and jammed the tails into the waist of his trousers. He did not look at Meg, but she saw the torment in his face, as if he'd taken blame for the man's death and laid its burden on himself.

The caravan moved on, with one grumbling *askari* bearing the dead porter's load. A blackness hung over them all as they trudged up the winding trail. Even the birdcalls and the chatter of monkeys had taken on a hostile tone. Cameron found himself checking every footstep, and realized that the others were doing the same.

By nightfall they were all exhausted. But at least they'd managed to find a decent campsite. It lay in a sheltered ravine, screened by trees and overhung by a rocky outcrop where a lookout could be posted. There was even a tiny trickle of water running down the rocks into a pool the size of a soup tureen.

Cameron had decided to risk a fire. Just before twilight, he'd brought down a waterbuck—not his favorite game, but the boys needed meat to keep up their strength and their spirits. Maybe if they went to bed with full bellies, he would feel safe enough to get some rest himself. Lord knows, he needed it. He hadn't slept in two days for fear of waking up with a mutiny on his hands.

He sat now with his back against a boulder, watching the camp settle in. He knew his boys—at least he hoped he did. They were lazy, and not particularly brave. As long as he wielded constant authority, they would take the path of least resistance and obey him. But if he dropped his guard at the wrong time...

Cameron shuddered away the fog of sleep that threatened to engulf him. His eyes stared idly through the flames of the campfire, to where Meg was rearranging her rucksack in the opening of the tent. Having her along made everything harder. Looking after his own skin was worry enough, but the thought of what seventeen Swahili run amok could do to a defenseless woman...

Again he shuddered, this time in imagined horror. There had to be a way to buy the loyalty of these weak-willed rascals. Maybe if he told them about the ivory and offered them a share for their help, it would make a difference. It was a fearful risk, he knew, but it could buy Meg's safety, and ultimately Jenny's.

Cameron's hand moved instinctively toward his pocket, where Murchison's map lay folded over his heart. In this maddened world where even Meg had turned against him, the map, at least, had given him something to hope for. It was his key to the future, his one chance for a better life beyond these black days.

His hand brushed the weathered khaki, then froze. The pocket hung limp, its button missing and its seam frayed loose at the bottom.

The map was gone.

Meg was starved after the long day's trek. Even so, it wasn't easy to eat the stew the cook had prepared. The waterbuck meat was dark, tough and greasy. Worse, the well-meaning Swahili had seasoned the dish with some feathery herbs he'd found growing near the camp. Their taste reminded Meg of licorice, only stronger, with a bitter overtone that made her mouth pucker. She forced down each swallow. She had to eat. They all did. It was a matter of survival.

At least the dumplings, fashioned from biscuit dough and cooked in the thick broth, were edible. Meg picked them out of the stew, swirled them in the broth and ate them off the tip of her fork. Glancing through the flames, she saw Cameron doing the same. He did not look well, she thought. His face, ashen in the flickering light, wore a look of dazed shock, as if he'd just experienced some awful tragedy.

How long had it been since Cameron had slept? Days. If he did not rest tonight, he would drop from exhaustion. Meg sighed as she put down her bowl, unfolded her cramped legs and stood up to wander around the fire. She and Cameron might scarcely be on speaking terms, but somebody had to take him in hand before he drove himself to collapse.

She seated herself on a rock, an arm's length away from him. Cameron glanced at her, then turned away. He looked like death, Meg thought. This could not go on.

As she leaned toward him, determined to break the silence, something rustled in her shirt pocket. Only then did she remember the map.

She drew it out of her pocket, relieved at having found an excuse to approach him. "I have something of yours," she said gently. "Here, it fell out of your shirt."

His head jerked toward her then, the expression on his face so haggard and hungry that it made her gasp. Instinctively, Meg shrank backward. Her hand withdrew so quickly that his lunge for the map met empty air.

"Give it to me, Mary Margaret," he grated. "I'm in no mood for your teasing!"

Meg stared at him in numb horror. "No!" she heard her own voice saying. "Not until you tell me what it is! I have to know what would make you look at me like that!"

He hesitated. Meg sensed the conflict raging inside him, and suddenly she was afraid. It was as if some dark, violent stranger had invaded Cameron's body and was fighting for possession.

Impulsively, she reached out and seized his wrist. The corded muscles quivered like steel wires beneath his skin, but as her touch persisted, the tension seemed to go out of him. He exhaled sharply, his shoulders sagging. The eyes that looked at her now were merely tired.

"All right, Meg," he sighed. "I'll tell you everything. But inside the tent. Too many eyes out here. And too many ears. Some of these boys know more English than you'd suspect."

He rose wearily. Meg followed him back to the tent, where he lowered the flap and lit the lantern. The flame cast his face into stark patterns of orange light and black shadow. She crouched on her bedroll as he hung the lantern from a hook on the tent pole, paused, then sat down beside her. Wordlessly, she handed him the folded paper.

"Did you look at it?" he asked.

Meg nodded slowly. "I know it's a map. But I don't understand what it means, or why you've kept it a secret from me."

"Meg, it's... Blast!" His fist clenched around the map. "You wouldn't understand. You can't—"

"You promised to tell me." Meg spoke calmly, but she could feel her heart hammering against her ribs. Cameron was trembling like a man possessed, and she was afraid of him.

"All right." His rib cage jerked as he took a sharp breath. Then the words came churning out of him. "It's ivory, Mary Margaret. A small fortune, cached away and waiting, if the map's to be believed. I got it off a dead elephant hunter. He was on his way to the railhead, poor devil. He didn't make it."

Meg gazed at him, her heart sinking. Yes, it was the old dream. Ivory. A fortune in white gold, and this time with no need for the killing he'd hated so much. Another rainbow.

Oh, Cameron, she thought.

He read the dismay in her face, but it only seemed to feed his fervor. He leaned toward her, eyes burning. "You can't know how it's always been for me, Meg. Never quite belonging, never quite being good enough, not for my family, not for your father, not even for you, blast it! I've never had anything that I felt was truly mine. But this—" the map quivered in his fist "—if it's real, and if I can find the ivory, I can tell them all to go to the devil! I'll have my own piece of the world!"

Meg stared at him empty-eyed. Her thoughts were spinning like a maelstrom around a black center that was inexorably sucking her in, drawing her toward a conclusion so terrible that she quaked at the prospect of facing it. She remembered the map, and the jagged outline of the mountain that now loomed above them. No! something cried out inside her. Even Cameron could not be that monstrous!

But she had to know.

She forced her constricting throat to form the words. "The map—from what I saw of it, the mountain, the river—the ivory must be somewhere in this area."

"Aye, so it appears." Cameron's voice was guarded. "The map's not drawn to scale. Some of the markers are bound to be small and hard to find."

"And The Neck of the Jar?" She stared at him coldly. "Where does it lie from here, Cameron?"

"Another week's march, maybe more, in the direction we're going—" He stiffened abruptly as he caught the glint of stark rage in her eyes. "Meg, I know what you're thinking, and it isn't true! You're looking at a coincidence, that's all! You know that Jenny comes first!"

"Does she?" Anger, nauseating in its power, surged through Meg's body. Reeling from its impact, she attacked him without mercy. "You're lying to me, Cameron! You've been lying to me all along! This trek—this safari—isn't about rescuing Jenny at all! No, as far as you're concerned, this is just another of your bloody treasure hunts!"

"Meg—" His face had gone death-white in the yellow lamplight. His body swayed like a drunkard's. "Listen to me! You've got to believe—"

"If your intentions were so honorable, why didn't you tell me about the map?" she snapped. "Why did you keep it to yourself all this time?"

He glared at her in dark desperation. "You'd announced your intention to divorce me, remember? Maybe I figured the map was none of your concern. Or maybe, I was afraid you'd think I was using it to buy you back."

"To *buy* me back?"

"Isn't that what your English gentleman is doing?"

Meg would have slapped him then, if she'd had the strength. But for some reason, her arms would not move. "Jenny's loss played right into your hands!" she hissed. "Your own expedition, paid for by a frantic old man! And me—once you'd left me at Machakos, you planned to abandon your daughter—your own flesh and blood—and go after the ivory! Of all the greedy, contemptible—"

"Stop it!" His voice was a slurred growl. The light swam around him in sickening waves. "Don't you talk to me about greed, Mary Margaret. 'Twas your own greed that brought all this trouble on our heads."

"Don't...don't you try to put the blame on me." Meg's words echoed strangely in her ears. The walls of the tent seemed to be floating. "What you've done is...is unspeakable, Cameron MacKenna."

"And you..." His eyes were blurs in his face. His head lolled crazily. "If you'd only learn to...to trust..." The rest of Cameron's speech trailed off into nothing. He swayed, tried feebly to catch himself, then toppled sideways onto the bedroll. He quivered once, then lay still.

"Cameron—" Meg crawled toward him, dragging limbs that had become as heavy as concrete. Above her, the lantern shimmered with undulating waves of color. The tent vibrated around her in darkening circles.

She reached him with one hand. His shoulder was a rock, rooted to the earth. She could not stir him. That was when she understood. "Cameron...." she whispered with excruciating effort. "The stew...they drugged..."

The dark mist enfolded her like a smothering blanket. Meg dropped to the bedroll with a little moan, her head falling on Cameron's arm. She felt his flesh against her cheek. Then there was only blackness.

The crescent moon, ghostly pale, hung like a scimitar above the western horizon. In the east, breaking dawn washed the inky sky with silver. A monkey stirred on the branch of a camphor tree, yawned and went back to sleep.

Below, in the purple-shadowed ravine, a leopard crept down through the rocks. Its body rippled like liquid gold, mingling glints of newborn light with the black rosettes on its coat. Its cold jade eyes knifed the darkness.

The night had been long, the hunting sparse, and the big cat was hungry. The ravine was known to shelter baboons. An unwary one could be taken with a lightning bite to the neck, and dragged swiftly away before its cohorts caught the alarm.

The leopard eased lower now, its white-tipped ears alert, its tail twitching like a housecat's. Suddenly it froze. A growl quivered in its throat. Tawny hair bristled in a ridge along its spine.

The scent that wafted on the dawn wind was not baboon. This odor was bitter, mingled with the acrid tinge of smoke. It could mean only one thing—man.

The leopard bared its fangs in a breathy hiss, then resumed its stalk, bellying down the rocks with the silence of death. Humans sometimes kept dogs. Dogs made fine eating.

Fingers of silver daylight probed the ravine's thick foliage as the leopard flowed along a branch, to stare down at the deserted camp below. Its yellow eyes saw a solitary tent and a dead fire. No dogs. No people.

Curiosity warred with caution as the leopard edged closer. A charred animal carcass hung over the ashes, and for an instant the big cat was tempted to leap down and investigate. But just then, a noise came from inside the tent. A muffled groan broke the morning stillness.

The leopard flattened on the limb, suddenly wary. As the tent flap quivered, it made its decision. Swiftly it turned and melted back into the foliage. Seconds later, it was streaking up the side of the ravine, to lose itself in the tangle of rocks and trees. By the time the birds awakened, it was gone.

Cameron's first awareness was of pain. He groaned and raised an uncertain hand to his head. His temples felt as if they were being crushed in a vise. What the devil had happened to him?

For the space of a dozen long breaths, he lay still, his arm flung over his eyes. He felt the map, still clutched damply in his hand. Slowly the memory returned—Meg, her refusal to believe him, her anger—

Meg! Cameron's eyes flew open. He sat bolt upright, his heart pounding in sudden panic. If Meg had been furious enough to leave—

But he saw her now. She lay curled in the shadows beside him, fully clothed and sound asleep. Her breasts quivered softly with the motion of her breathing.

Still dazed, he sat watching the play of light on her face. His heart ached with unspoken tenderness. Brave little Mary Margaret. She'd been as mad as a hornet last night, he remembered. Not that he blamed her. After the way he'd behaved, what else was she to think? But she would soon know that he was telling the truth. Aye, she would know, when they reached The Neck of the Jar, and—

The silence hit him like a thunderbolt.

From outside, where he should have heard the stirrings of an awakening camp, there was no sound—nothing, ex-

cept birdcalls and the chatter of monkeys from the tree-
tops.

Cameron flung the tent flap aside and staggered out into
the gray dawn, his head reeling. The camp was deserted. No
porters, no *askaris,* no gear, no food, except for the waterbuck carcass lying charred and blackened across the smoking ashes of the cook fire.

Cameron gaped uncomprehendingly. This was a bad
dream, he reassured himself. Or maybe he'd fallen sick and
was hallucinating, the way he'd done after the lion attack.

As he came fully awake, however, the picture began to
clear. The frightened boys, the odd-tasting stew, the pain
in his head, which was fading now to a dull ache. *Bastards,* he thought. *Thieving, cowardly, treacherous bastards!*

Cameron's legs would not hold him. He sank down on a
log, his vision swimming. At least he and Meg were alive,
he reminded himself. At least the bloody rascals hadn't—

"Cameron!"

He turned at the sound of Meg's cry. She had crept to the
entrance of the tent and was staring at the empty camp in
horrified disbelief. "They're ... gone."

"Aye, lass, they're gone." Cameron's voice croaked
painfully in his raw throat. He would have made his way
back to her, somehow, and gathered her in his arms, but
after last night, he knew the gesture would not be welcomed.

She struggled to her feet, clutching a tent pole for support. "The stew," she said weakly. "I realized it when
you—*oooh!*" She pressed a hand to her eyes. "The whole
world is shaking!"

"Rest for a minute. It should go away soon." Cameron's own head was beginning to clear. He rose unsteadily
and surveyed what was left of the camp. It wasn't much.
The boys had taken all the food and cooking equipment,
the blankets, the ammunition, the medical kit, the large
water bags, and, of course, the guns. They had left little
more than the tent and what was in it: clothes and per-

sonal things, bedrolls, two tin canteens, the lantern, Cameron's knife, and his rifle, with a meager pocketful of cartridges.

Cameron cursed under his breath as he took grim stock of the situation. How long could he and Meg expect to survive out here alone on these scant supplies? It might have been a mercy if the deserters had killed them while they slept.

"We have to go on." Meg's flat voice came from just behind his shoulder. His heart contracted as he turned to look at her. Her thin, childlike face peered up at him through dank strings of hair. Her eyes were bloodshot and ringed by deep, purple shadows. The oversize khaki shirt hung like a shroud on her bones. Not until now did Cameron realize what a toll the past weeks had taken on her.

"We have to go on, Cameron," she insisted. "No matter what happens, we can't abandon Jenny."

"Meg..." He sighed painfully. There would be trials enough just following the river to the coast. As for going forward, it was madness now. They had no food, no medical supplies and no protection except his rifle and less than a dozen shells. The chances of rescuing Jenny had been minuscule before. Now they were almost nonexistent. As for Meg, his heart broke when he looked at her. She was trying to be strong, but he could tell she was nearing the end of her endurance. How could he risk this small, stubborn, tender woman to the dangers ahead?

But it was no use weighing alternatives. One glance into Meg's burning eyes was enough to tell him that. She would never give up the search. She would spend her last breath, if need be, trudging into the wilderness where her child had vanished.

And so would he, Cameron realized. Any other choice was unthinkable.

"We can't give up, Cameron!" she pleaded again. "We've got to go on!"

Cameron filled his eyes with her face. He could be leading her to her death, but they had no choice.

"Aye, lass," he replied softly, "of course we'll go on."

Days were blinding sun and searing wind. Nights were frigid, and filled with frightening animal sounds. The sixty-pound canvas tent had proved too taxing to carry, and so it had been left behind. Meg and Cameron slept huddled around a campfire, shivering in their bedrolls and starting awake at the slightest noise.

Much of the time, Meg's belly growled with hunger. Cameron had stripped the remaining meat from the water-buck and smoked it over the fire to make *biltong,* which did not spoil and was light to carry. Unfortunately, one could only eat so much of the leathery stuff before it became repulsive. Meg knew better than to complain, but she spent hours of each dreary, trudging day fantasizing about Yorkshire pudding, fresh-baked shortbread, scones with clotted cream and endless varieties of chocolate. She fantasized, as well, about hot baths with perfumed bubbles, warm, clean beds, carriage rides, waterfalls . . . and Jenny. Jenny beside her, laughing and romping, or curled in slumber with her thumb in her little rosebud mouth.

As the days crawled by, Meg created a whole world in her mind, a world that was warm, safe, familiar and happy. Dwelling in that world helped the hours pass. And it was easier than dealing with the reality of dust, wind, ticks, exhaustion and a man who had betrayed her faith.

Cameron still had the cursed ivory map, she knew. He never looked at it in her presence, but it was somewhere on his person, and on his mind, as well. Meg was no fool. She'd read about what could happen when men caught the glimmer of wealth. They went mad, like rabid dogs, forsaking their homes and loved ones, and taking terrible risks.

When she looked at Cameron, she realized he was no different from the others. For all she knew, he could still be plotting to abandon her—and Jenny—for the lure of white gold. After all, hadn't he deceived her before?

Recriminations tore at Meg like sharp-beaked birds as she trudged along beside him. *What about you?* she lashed herself over and over. *You're no pillar of virtue, either. You plotted to marry a man for his money! You were willing to risk anything to get what you wanted—even leaving Jenny in a strange place! And look at you now!*

That, for Meg, was reality—day after gruelling day, filled with mistrust and guilt. Living in her fantasy world had become a near necessity. It kept her from collapsing in despair. It kept her moving.

By now they had crested the foothills of Mount Kenya and were traveling on the downslope. Where the trees cleared, Meg could see out over the hilly plain below, a desolate mud-gray expanse, dotted with enormous clumps of black rock. It looked like hell on earth to her. But somewhere beyond the horizon lay the place Cameron called The Neck of the Jar. The place that held their one hope of rescuing Jenny.

When the *biltong* ran out, Cameron spent two of his precious rifle cartridges downing a kudu, a big antelope with massively curled horns, so beautiful that in a less desperate situation Meg would have wept at its death. Now, however, she realized that the kudu meant survival. As she helped Cameron drag the carcass to level ground and stretch it out for skinning, her only thought was of the wonderful fresh meat they would have.

By the time the skinning was done, Meg had gathered dry brush and built a fire, with two forked limbs stuck in the ground to support a spit. Cameron hacked off a generous chunk of loin, and minutes later the meat was sizzling over the flames, its aroma so delicious that it made Meg's head swim.

But there was no time to sit back and wait for the feast. Cameron was already carving more meat into strips for *biltong*. The smoking process, which took many hours, would demand a small mountain of firewood, and someone had to collect it.

Meg squared her shoulders and went to work. She could only hope that kudu *biltong* would be tastier than the greasy, half-rancid waterbuck had been.

She waded into the hip-high scrub, flailing away with a seven-foot limb to flush out snakes and any other creatures that might be lurking there. By now she was no longer fearful in the bush. There were dangers, to be sure. But one took sensible precautions, that was all. Most animals, even lions, would give you a wide berth if you made enough commotion to warn them. It was the startled ones that were prone to attack.

Singing in full voice, Meg bent to pick up the loose twigs she'd knocked to the ground. "... And for bonny Annie Laurie, I'd lay me doon and—"

Her voice shriveled to a croak as a long shadow fell across her hand. She froze, crouching, her heart in her throat. When the shadow did not move, she raised her eyes slowly, inch by trembling inch.

A man stood before her as if he had sprouted out of the ground—all long, proud bones, with skin the color of deep earth. A ragged leather tunic fell from one shoulder, exposing the stump of a missing arm. He wore nothing else except for a dirty string of cowrie beads knotted around his neck. Piercing black eyes stared down at Meg from the dust-caked mask of his face.

Behind him, trailing through the scrub, were three emaciated women with shaven heads. They wore scanty leather aprons, and their bare breasts hung like withered balloons on their bony brown rib cages. They were loaded like beasts of burden with household goods—calabashes, utensils, baskets—slung from leather tumplines that stretched across their foreheads, digging into the skin.

Meg's eyes shifted warily to the iron-headed spear clutched in the man's right hand. At his nod, she rose slowly to her feet. She knew better than to cry out, or even to look around for Cameron. It was too late for that. The Kikuyu had found them.

Chapter Thirteen

Meg could see more Kikuyu now, materializing like phantoms out of the bush: an older man, a youth, two half-grown girls and even a small child, peering from among the trees. There appeared to be ten or twelve of them, the remnants of a band, or perhaps a single family. And they didn't look ferocious, Meg thought, only tired, and terribly hungry.

"Move away from him, Meg!" Cameron had stepped into sight, his rifle aimed at the one-armed Kikuyu. "If he touches you, it'll be the last—"

"No!" Meg spun toward him, placing her body directly in his line of fire. "You can't shoot, Cameron! Look at these people!"

Cameron groaned in exasperation. "Get out of the way! I don't intend to shoot if I can help it. I just want them to know they're not welcome here!"

Her eyes darted from Cameron to the sad little band of Kikuyu. Their skins were stretched like rawhide over their knobby bones. The sockets of their eyes were dark hollows of hunger, and they moved with the listlessness of long-spent strength. Meg remembered the deserted *shambas* with their withered garden patches.

She turned back to Cameron. "Look at them," she said gently. "They're starving. Think how our meat must smell to them."

"Set them loose on that kudu, and there'll be nothing for us! Blast it, *think,* Meg! Think of where we have to go and what we have to do! I've six bullets left. I could spend them all in the days ahead and not bag enough meat to keep us alive!"

Meg's gaze found the youngest child, a small, naked boy. He was peering from between two trees with huge, frightened eyes. His matchstick legs barely supported his swollen body. He looked to be about Jenny's age, Meg thought. What if it were Jenny standing in his place, starving to death within the sight and smell of food?

She turned to Cameron with pleading eyes. "Please— there are children...."

Cameron muttered a curse. His shoulders rose, then fell in a long exhalation. Keeping the rifle leveled, he addressed the one-armed leader in gruff Swahili. After a tense pause, the man answered. He spoke the language haltingly, interspersing words with gestures and conveying much by the expressiveness of his long, intelligent face, which was dotted with ritual scars.

Meg's ears strained for phrases she knew. Yes, it was all right. Cameron was offering to share some of the meat. Two of the Kikuyu were to come forward and carry it off. The rest were to keep their distance. Everything was to be controlled and orderly, and there would be just enough—

An eager, high-pitched cry rose from one of the women. Suddenly, the entire band was surging forward, almost knocking Cameron over in their rush to the meat. In a melee of stabbing knives and plunging spears, they fell on the kudu. The loin that had been roasting over the fire vanished in seconds, along with the strips Cameron had been cutting for *biltong.* Frantic hands scrambled for shares as the starving Kikuyu crammed chunks of raw flesh into their mouths.

Suddenly, at a guttural command from the leader, the frenzy halted. Meg stared in amazement as the one-armed Kikuyu strode into the midst of the clan, lashing them with the anger of his voice. He was speaking in his own dialect, but it was not hard to guess that he was chastising them for their manners. No matter how hungry they might be, he appeared to be saying, Kikuyu did not behave like wild animals.

Cowed by his diatribe, the eaters backed away from the feast with downcast eyes, some licking meat juices from their fingers. Their leader turned with great dignity to Cameron, indicating that Cameron was to separate his portion of the meat first, the Kikuyu would take what remained and cook it over their own fire. Resigned to the loss, Cameron took his knife and carved off one hindquarter, leaving the rest of the carcass to be carried off by the jubilant natives.

An air of tense joviality had settled over the scene. With the edge of their hunger slaked, the Kikuyu were in high spirits. The women laughed as they gathered firewood, their grins showing teeth that had been filed to sharp little points. The children danced with anticipation.

Meg replenished her own blaze and used Cameron's knife to cut and skewer another chunk of meat. As she sliced the little that remained into *biltong* strips, she felt the first sense of peace she had known since leaving Machakos. Gloom and ill fortune had dogged their every step. She and Cameron were barely on speaking terms, able to give to each other in only the most minimal ways. Like automatons, they'd plodded through each day without thinking or feeling, each lost in an isolation that was growing more and more unbearable.

The Kikuyu women had begun to sing. Meg paused to rest for a moment, abandoning her senses to the primal rhythm of their chant. For now, at least, she did not regret the loss of the precious meat. Maybe this act of kindness would open some doors between Cameron and herself. Maybe, somehow, fate would at last begin to smile on them.

She could see Cameron now, at the edge of the clearing, deep in conversation with the Kikuyu leader. The two of them were pointing, holding up fingers, as if discussing time and direction. How thin and tired Cameron looked, how in need of kindness himself. His eyes were hollows of weariness. His dust-matted curls hung below his ears, and a ragged, unkempt beard blotted his cheeks and chin. In his own way, he looked almost as savage as the Kikuyu.

Abruptly, he broke off the conversation and began walking toward her. His image rippled through the heat waves of the fire. His eyes blazed a feverish blue. Meg sank back onto her heels and watched him come.

"Sit down and rest," she said, trying to sound friendly. "The meat will be a while yet."

"Meg, lass..." Cameron was staring down at her with an expression she'd never seen on his face before. If she hadn't known him better, Meg would have sworn he was close to tears.

"You're not angry with me for this, are you?" she asked gently. "I couldn't turn these people away when they were starving."

He lowered himself to a crouch, his eyes on a level with her own. Dear heaven, there *were* tears in his eyes.

"Cameron, what is it?" she whispered, suddenly afraid.

"These people—their leader says they came up from the south." His voice rasped with emotion. "Meg, they've seen Jenny."

Cameron watched her face, watched the wild play of emotion, from disbelief to joy, from joy to sudden fear. Then came the flood of questions. Where and when? Was she alive? Was she all right?

He gripped her hands hard. Her trembling fingers curled like talons into his palms.

"Aye, lass," he said softly, "it was three or four weeks ago, as nearly as the man can remember. As to where, it was far to the south, but he had no way of telling me more. His people heard the caravan coming, and they hid in the bush while it passed. They saw a small girl-child, he said, with honey-colored hair, riding a porter's shoulders like the daughter of a chief..."

A little sob tore loose from Meg's throat. Pulling her hands free, she pressed them to her face. Her shoulders shook with the ragged jerks of her breathing. Cameron ached to put his arms around her. But he could not bear the thought of her stiffening with distrust and shrinking away from him. Even now, his pride was too great for that.

After long seconds of struggling, Meg regained her self-control. "What else did they see? Tell me everything."

"It was a slave caravan. Four Arabs, one of them very tall—"

"Hassan!" The name hissed out of her, with a vehemence that made Cameron shiver. "What else?" she asked after a tremulous pause.

"They had a handful of Swahili porters with them, and about twenty black slaves, fastened together with wooden yokes—"

"Like animals!"

"Aye, you could say that." Cameron had seen slave caravans, and the inhuman way of keeping the slaves in line had wrenched his heart. The heavy lengths of wood, with collar-pieces at the ends, joined the poor devils in such a way that none could move independently of the others. Even when a slave died—which happened all too often—he was dragged along with the rest until someone unbuckled his body.

"The porters were carrying empty yokes, a great many of them, if the estimate is to be believed," Cameron continued. "That could only mean they planned on picking up more slaves along the way."

Meg's hands worked the fabric of her skirt, clawing in and out like a cat's in her agitation. "I keep thinking of what Jenny must have seen, all the horrible things—" Her breath caught brokenly. "Oh, Cameron, how could an innocent child bear it? What would it do to her mind?"

Cameron's throat constricted. "It won't help to dwell on that, lass. At least, if the devils are picking up more slaves, they won't be moving fast. That buys us more time to find them."

Aye, and what then? he wondered. *Just the two of us, and scarcely enough bullets for one loading of the rifle. What can we do against an armed caravan?* Black thoughts, and true. But he would keep them to himself. Meg's burden was sore enough already.

He tested the roasting meat with the blade of his knife. The outside, at least, was brown enough to eat. Carving off the first thin slice, he blew it cool and held it out for Meg. She accepted it with cautious fingers. The grateful glance she gave him forced home all the more how much he needed her warmth, her approval, and yes, blast it, her love.

These past few days had been a purgatory; needing Meg; marching beside her in wretched silence, too proud and too fearful to reach across the gulf that separated them. The memory of that night in Machakos burned his body every time he looked at her. He never walked beside her without aching to put out his hand and touch her hair, her shoulder or her lightly swaying hip. He never looked at her sleeping face without wanting to brush her cheek with his fingertip and whisper the tender love-words he had never spoken aloud. Exhausted as he was, he never lay down at night without wanting to gather her in his arms and love her—love away the pain, the weariness, the discouragement, until they both drifted into sweet oblivion.

Cameron carved a second slice of meat for himself, nibbling it with slow restraint. Strangely enough, he did not feel hungry. He only felt tired now, and so heavy-limbed that every move seemed an effort. A sense of foreboding stole over him as he edged closer to the heat of the fire, his skin clammy beneath his clothes. No, he resolved firmly, he could not be ill now. Meg needed him. Jenny needed him.

For their sake, he had to stay on his feet. He had to keep moving. All their lives depended on it.

He stared at the flames, willing their warmth into his body. From the nearby camp, he could hear the Kikuyu singing around their fire. The sound vibrated strangely in his ears. He would be all right, he reassured himself. He would be well and strong. He would take care of Meg. He would rescue his daughter—all this against impossible odds. The power was inside him; he had only to find it.

The fire swam before his eyes. Cameron shivered, blinked and forced himself to continue eating.

Meg awoke to a lavender sky. She yawned and rubbed her eyes, feeling rested for the first time in weeks.

"Time to get up, slugabed." Cameron was crouched next to the fire, tending to their meager *biltong* supply. His eyes were raw, his features sunk into blue-tinged shadows. He looked as if he'd scarcely slept. Still, he managed to give her a faint smile, the first she had seen on his face in many days.

"You should have awakened me!" she scolded him gently. "We could have been on the trail an hour ago."

"What? And disturb such a peaceful sleep?" He was making an effort to be cheerful, Meg realized, but the words rang like brass when she looked at him. His face was lined with pain, and his hand trembled when he prodded at the meat with his knife.

"Cameron, if you're not well . . ."

He shrugged off her concern. "It's nothing that won't pass. Come on, now, up with you! We've a long day's trek ahead of us!"

She wriggled out of her bedroll, stood up and stretched. Through the scrub, she could see the Kikuyu moving about their own camp. The little naked boy grinned at her and waved. Meg waved back, her mind seeing Jenny, bobbing along on the porter's shoulders—*like a chief's daughter,* the Kikuyu had said.

Where was Jenny now? Meg wondered. Was she getting enough to eat? Was she warm at night? Did any of those vile people who'd stolen her care enough to be kind?

She swallowed the ache in her throat. Cameron was right, it did not pay to dwell on such thoughts. But oh, if by the will of heaven she could somehow take Jenny's place; if only there were a way to take Jenny's pain and fear and loneliness upon herself.

Meg's balled fist struck her skirt. She turned back toward the fire, to find Cameron's eyes watching her, unspeakably weary those eyes, and curiously gentle.

"I'll do everything under heaven to get her back, lass," he said softly. "Whatever else you believe of me, believe that."

His voice touched her with unexpected warmth. Meg's gaze dropped to her hands. "Yes," she whispered, realizing to her amazement that she was beginning to trust him again. "Yes, I know you will, Cameron."

They left after breakfast, with the farewell chant of the Kikuyu echoing in their ears. As they zigzagged their way downward through the foothills, the dry landscape became as parched and desolate as the moon. Meg caught herself mentally gauging the meager amount of water in the canteens and counting the precious *biltong* strips in her rucksack. When she glanced at Cameron's pensive face, she knew he was doing the same. The Neck of the Jar could be days away yet, and there was no sign of water in any direction; no sign of life, even, except the lizards and beetles that scuttled across the sunbaked rocks.

Cameron, for the most part, labored along in silence. Just putting one foot in front of the other seemed to tax his strength today. His face was gray, his forehead jeweled with sweat. More than once, the smallest stumble sent him reeling. When Meg urged him to rest, however, he dismissed her concern with a defiant growl.

"Don't fuss over me like a mother! I'm all right. And even if I weren't, this is no time to quit. We've got to keep pushing ahead!"

From that point on, Meg held her tongue. She was sick with worry, but she knew better than to try to stop him. The same urge that compelled her own feet was driving Cameron. They had to reach The Neck of the Jar. They had to find Jenny.

As she walked beside him, seeing the agonized effort that went into each step, Meg realized how wrong she had been to doubt his intent. Cameron had never set eyes on his daughter, but the bond was there. To save Jenny, he would offer his life.

This new awareness touched a wellspring of tenderness in Meg. She found herself walking close to his side, matching her stride to his, feeling his every labored breath as her own. She caught herself wanting to reach up and blot the trickles of sweat that beaded his face, to slip beneath his arm and lend her support to his wavering steps. But she knew Cameron's pride would not allow that. He would crawl on his hands and knees before he would accept her help.

At midday, they took restrained sips of water and split one strip of *biltong* between them. By now, Cameron's eyes were swimming with fever. His hand could scarcely raise the canteen to his mouth, let alone hold it steady. Looking at him, Meg knew with a sinking certainty that he could not hold out much longer. They needed to find shelter now, or he would collapse in the hot sun, and she would never be able to move him.

She put out her hand and touched his wrist. The heat of his burning skin made her gasp. Too late she realized that she should have stopped him hours ago. She should have done something, *anything*, to keep him from breaking camp that morning. At least that way the Kikuyu might have afforded some help and protection. As it was, Cameron had become terrifyingly ill, and she was alone, with no medicine.

"What is it?" she whispered. "You must have some idea."

He nodded weakly. "Aye," he muttered in a slurred voice. "It's malaria that does this kind of thing to a body. I—I caught it three years ago, an' always thought myself lucky that it hadn't come back." He pulled off his hat and ran quivering fingers through his thick, black hair. "Forgive me, lass. I should never have let you come with me...." His voice shook. His body swayed like a tree in a storm. "Should've hauled you back to Machakos, while I had the chance...."

"No!" Meg sprang against him, catching his weight as he staggered. Her arms went around his chest. She held him fast against her, his heart pounding next to her ear. "No, Cameron," she whispered. "I would never have let you leave me. I would have followed you, no matter what."

His fever was a furnace. As its heat burned into her, Meg held him, willing her own strength to fortify his weakness, willing him, hopelessly, to be well. She clasped him close, sharing Cameron's frustration at his body's betrayal. Dear heaven, why now, when they were so close to the end of their quest? Why now, when so much depended on him?

Meg's churning mind struggled to recall what she'd read about malaria. A recent discovery had revealed that the tiny parasite was spread by mosquitoes. Infected people carried it in their bloodstreams for years, and recurrences could flare up at any time. These attacks were not necessarily fatal, but they could disable a man for days, even weeks, with chills and fever.

She fought back waves of panic. How would she care for Cameron with no medicine? How would she find food and water with him lying too ill to move? And Jenny... But right now she could not even think about Jenny. Without Cameron, everything would be lost. Saving him was up to her—and to heaven.

Her arms tightened around him. "We've got to find shelter. And it's got to be soon, while you can still walk."

"Aye." His voice was a fevered rasp. "A half mile or so back, we passed some rock ledges. There could be caves—"

"Sit down and rest. I'll go back and see." Meg slipped away from him and was off before he could argue.

Be careful! Cameron tried to call after her. But his muzzy brain could not make his dry mouth form the words. He slumped to the ground as she sprinted away, racked by a sudden spasm of chills. His fist slammed the dust in impotent rage. Never in his life had he felt so wretchedly helpless.

He battled to stay awake. Unconscious, he would be too heavy for Meg to move. Wherever shelter lay in this sun-parched hell, he would have to be able to walk there.

His eyes strained into the shimmering distance where Meg had vanished. She had all the spunk and courage in the world, his beautiful Mary Margaret. But even that would not be enough against the odds that faced her now.

He should have found shelter at the first sign of sickness. Cameron laid that blame on his own stubbornness. With so much at stake, his mind had refused to believe he could be having an attack of malaria. Now he and Meg had pushed themselves too far. Their desperate hope of finding Jenny had made fools of them both.

Cameron's ears echoed like the sound of the ocean, and he knew the sickness was rising swiftly in his blood. He willed his body to resist, but it was no use. By the time Meg reappeared, her blurred image dancing through the heat waves, he was already drifting into delirium.

"I found a cave!" Her voice echoed in his head like the cry of a seabird. "It's very small, but it will have to do. Come on, you've got to stand. You've got to walk." He felt her at his side. She had wedged herself against him, with his limp arm flung across her shoulders. Now she was struggling to lift his inert weight. "Come on!" she whispered, her knuckles jabbing his ribs. "Cameron, I can't do this alone! You've got to help me!"

Cameron's limbs were granite blocks. He groaned with effort as he willed his mind to concentrate on moving each muscle. Meg pressed close to him. He could feel the sweat-dampened sweetness of her body beneath his arm as she strained to help him stand. "That's it," her voice coaxed. "Now one step...then another. We're going to make it, Cameron MacKenna! If I have to drag you all the way through the bloody thornbush, we're going to make it!"

He leaned on her—perhaps the first time, since his boyhood, that Cameron had leaned on anyone. Her tough little body supported his every step, lending him strength. Her arms held him fast. Her tenderness penetrated his reeling senses. Sweet, brave Meg.... If they lived through this ordeal, Cameron vowed, he would battle the world to keep her with him. He would never let her go again.

If they lived.

By the time they reached the cave, Cameron was delirious. He staggered this way and that, stumbling over his own feet and muttering curses that blended elements of English, Hindustani and Swahili. Meg was exhausted from the effort of keeping him on the path. Her body was drenched in sweat. Her ribs were bruised from slamming against him, and her arms felt as if they'd been wrenched from their sockets.

The cave, as she'd told him, was small, no more than four or five paces from broad mouth to narrow rear, and scarcely tall enough for standing. Meg had taken time earlier to sweep the leaves, twigs and rodent droppings from its flat stone floor and to spread out her bedroll. When Cameron at last lay collapsed full length on the blankets, she sank against the wall and spared herself a moment to rest.

Cameron's ordeal was only beginning, she knew. In the days ahead, his body would be racked with chills and fever. For much of that time, he would be as helpless as a babe. He would need constant care. He would need food. Even more urgently, he would need water. Dear heaven, how would she do it all?

She closed her eyes, trying to ignore the thirst that burned like hot sand in her own throat. She had already checked the water in the canteens. Hers was, at best, a third full. Cameron's was even lower. His fever-dehydrated body would need all the water they had, and more. There would be none to spare for her.

At a sharp moan from Cameron, she opened her eyes. He was lying rigid as ice, his body shivering violently. "Meg, darlin'..." he whispered through clenched, chattering teeth. "I'm so cold...so cold...."

She touched his cheek. His flesh was fiery. Heart pounding, she jerked his own bedroll from his pack, shook it out and tucked it tightly around him. "You're all right," she whispered. But the feel of his burning, quaking body made lies of her words.

"Cold..." he continued to mutter, though he was swathed in blankets on a blistering African day. Sick with fear, Meg lifted the covers, edged in alongside him and enfolded him in her arms. "It's all right," she murmured against his hot chest. "I'm holding you, Cameron. I'll warm you."

His ribs, lean as pitchfork tines, heaved beneath her fingers. Meg tightened her arms around him, locking him to her. Her legs intertwined with his. As her lips tasted the salty skin in the V of his open collar, she willed her own strength to flow into him.

"Rest, my dearest love," she murmured, the words coming as naturally as if she had been speaking them all her life. "Rest and get well. I'm here. I won't leave you."

His body jerked against her in a spasm of malarial chills. Meg had no way of knowing whether Cameron heard her. But no matter; it was for herself she had spoken. For years the words had been locked inside her, imprisoned behind walls of wounded pride. Now, while there was still time, she needed to set them free.

Her arms tightened around him. "I love you, Cameron," she whispered fiercely. "Heaven help me, I've loved you all my life. If only you hadn't made it so hard." Trembling with him now, she pressed her face into the salt-matted hair of his chest. "Please get well," she breathed against his heat-ravaged body. "Please, my darling, I have so much to tell you . . . so much to give you."

Cameron's only answer was another racking chill. Meg cradled him tenderly with her body, whispering frantic little phrases of love and comfort. What a blind fool she'd been to ever think she could be happy with Arthur, when it was Cameron she loved. It had always been Cameron. He was flesh of her flesh, soul of her soul. Why had it taken so much heartbreak to make her see it?

Even that night in Machakos, Meg had not realized the depth of her own feelings. She had *needed* Cameron then, in the most urgent way. But she'd been so involved in her own wants, so caught up in the physical bliss of having him, that she'd grasped little of love's true meaning.

That night seemed like years ago now. And, yes, she understood. At least, she had reached a beginning.

She lay tightly against him, eyes closed in wordless prayer that her discovery had not come too late. Cameron's illness was frightening under the best conditions. Here, with no medicine and almost no water, he faced dismal odds. She would do everything in her power to keep him alive, but she could not do it alone. She would need a miracle.

Cameron whimpered as another chill shook his frame. Meg pressed her desperate warmth into his bones, feeling each agonized tremor as her own. Her lips kissed the fevered pulse along his throat. "Hush, my love," she whispered, her eyes wet with tears. "Lie still and rest. I'm here."

Cameron's chills diminished after the first three days, to be replaced by a fever so high that he seemed to be burning alive. Meg had stripped away his clothes, and he lay naked on the bedroll, covered only by her own discarded muslin petticoat. His heat-parched flesh was as dry as the land that surrounded the tiny, shadowed sanctuary of their cave.

He drifted between delirium and sleep. Meg hovered over him, fanning his tortured body with her *terai* and dribbling water between his cracked lips. He no longer seemed to know her. Even when his bloodshot, blue eyes stared directly up at her, there was no recognition in them, no cognizance of where they were or how they had come to be here.

Sometimes in his sleep, he cried out for his mother. At other times, during the worst of his nightmares, he moaned a name that sounded like *Gonzalvo*, which Meg could only guess to be that of the old Portuguese who'd been trampled before his eyes. Not once did he speak her name or Jenny's. It was as if the present had been erased from his mind.

On the rare occasions when she dared leave him, Meg spent her time exploring the ledges around the cave. For all her hopeful searching, she'd found nothing but blistering rocks, withered grasses and leafless clumps of thornbush. Behind her, the lava-black spires of Mount Kenya jutted against a flame-blue sky. Before her, the land was a dreamscape of desolation, scared of life.

She sank down on a rock and stared out toward the bleak horizon, her body screaming with thirst. Her own canteen was empty now, and Cameron's contained only a few more swallows of water. Once that was gone...

But she could not even think about dying. Not while Jenny was out there. And she *was* out there. The Kikuyu had seen her with the hell-merchants of the slave caravan. The very thought of Jenny alone with those evil men...

Meg shuddered away the terrible vision. She would never abandon hope, she vowed. She would widen her search for water and not give up until she found it. As for Cameron, she would not let him die. She would bind him to life, and they would search out their child together. Anything was possible if she willed it strongly enough!

Burning with resolve, Meg sprang to her feet. Sun-sparks danced in her throbbing head. Her limbs dangled limp and lifeless from their sockets, like a rag doll's. Her throat crackled like hay when she breathed.

Find water! she commanded herself. One foot moved, then the other. Her swimming vision narrowed on a dry stream furrow at the foot of a ledge. She lurched toward it, falling on the spot. *Dig!* she ordered her inert hands. Her nails clawed the ground, wearily at first, then with frenzied desperation. She gasped with effort. Her fingers bled into the dry gravel. Deeper and deeper they scraped, pulling the dirt up between her knees like a dog, until her arms could reach no further. Shaking with exhaustion, she collapsed on the heap she'd made, with her head hanging over the edge of the hole.

Nothing. She'd found nothing but dust and rocks and a few tangled roots. The earth was as dry two feet down as it was on the surface. As far as Meg could tell, it was dry all the way to the center of the planet.

She did not have the strength left to cry.

That afternoon, the wind began. Yowling like a monster, it swept in from the east, choking the air with red African dust so thick that it blotted out the sight of the sun.

Meg crouched beside Cameron in bewildered terror. Never, not in Africa or anyplace else, had she experienced wind like this. It was as if physical laws had been suspended, and the whole universe was howling past the cave's sheltered mouth.

Stirred perhaps by the weather change, Cameron was unusually restless. He tossed and moaned on the bedroll, his cracked lips working to form words that would not emerge from his throat. His fever-glazed eyes darted wildly about the cave, seeming to see everything but Meg.

Where were his thoughts now? she wondered. It had been days since he'd shown any sign of knowing her or of knowing where he was.

She had given him the last drops of water at midday, resolving to go out and search for more when the sun was lower. Then the wind had sprung up out of a slate-blue sky, trapping her in the cave with its stinging fury. That had been hours ago. Now, as twilight turned the dusty sky to an apocalyptic blood-red, she slumped to the floor and bowed herself to fate. She had done all she could, but it was not enough. Hours from now, a day or two at most, she and Cameron would both be dead of thirst.

As for Jenny... Meg's vision blurred as she gazed out over the crimson landscape. Closing her eyes, she willed her thoughts to fly across the unknown distance. *Goodbye, my little one. Be strong wherever you go. Remember who you are and where you came from. Remember how much we love you.*

Swallowing the ache in her throat, she turned back to where Cameron lay on the bedroll. His eyes were closed now, his breathing deep and regular. What a mercy it would be if he could sleep peacefully through the end, free of pain and fear.

The red daylight deepened to purple as the sun sank into the storm. Soon there would be nothing outside except the roaring blackness of night. Meg lay down alongside Cameron, her head resting on his shoulder. Anyone who came upon them later would find them like this—together.

She slid an arm across his bare chest, drawing him closer. "I love you, Cameron," she whispered. "I never stopped loving you, even when we let so much pride come between us. I was always yours, my dearest. I always will be. I love you. Never forget that."

Cameron stirred beside her. She felt his arm move, felt the light touch of his hand stroking her hair. Meg's heart leapt with sudden joy. Yes, it was all right. He had heard. He knew.

She closed her eyes. Peace filled her mind as she drifted gently off to sleep.

Chapter Fourteen

Cameron awoke to dead silence. The air around him was as still as glass and as black as the grave. He stared wild-eyed into its darkness. Good Lord, where was he?

His heart was pounding. Its rhythm echoed like a gong, overflowing the confined space. His right hand stirred, groping for anything that might be solid and familiar. He tried to move his arm, but he could not lift it. It was weighted by something warm and soft and breathing.

Meg.

Aye, it was all coming back now. The malaria. The cave. The hideous nightmares. And all the while, her violet eyes floating in the mist above his face. Her hand, and the touch of wetness on his lips. Sweet Meg. He owed her his life.

Rousing a little, he made a gentle effort to twist his arm free. But he was too feeble to move even her slight weight. Her sleeping body held him fast.

Cameron sank back onto the bedroll and tried to assemble his wits. He was naked, he realized, and his skin was tingling with sweat. Aye, his fever had broken. The attack was over. But he was as weak as a newborn lamb. Great heaven, how long had he been here? How had Meg managed to keep him alive?

Thirst raked his dry throat. He remembered the canteens, and how low they'd been, even before his illness. Meg, he realized with a lurch of his heart, would have to have given almost all the water to him. Otherwise, he would have died.

"Meg..." Her name rasped in his throat as he struggled up onto one elbow. His free hand nudged her shoulder. He heard her breath catch in her throat, but she did not move.

"Meg, wake up." Fear shot adrenaline into Cameron's system. He sat up in panic, yanking his arm out from under her. She whimpered drowsily, then fell back in a stupor.

"Blast it, Meg!" Frantic now, he caught her against him. Her dehydrated body was weightless in his arms. His eyes, darting about the cave, caught the glint of a tin canteen in the darkness. He snatched it up. Empty. And the other canteen, wherever it was, he realized would be the same.

He lifted Meg's face, his parched lips kissing her forehead, her closed eyelids, her mouth. Her body shuddered in response. She moaned, but she did not awaken.

As he held her, Cameron's memory began to clear. He saw her bending over him with the canteen. He felt her warmth beside him, heard her voice whispering words of love.

By all that was holy, he could not lose her now!

Wild with frustration, he stared out at the darkness. There was no water within easy distance, he knew. Maybe somehow, tomorrow, if she lived through the night...

But no, it was hopeless. Without water, neither of them would be strong enough to leave the cave. They would die right here, together.

He clasped her close, battling the urge to howl like an anguished beast. To lose her now, when they had finally stumbled through the morass of their pride and found each other.... Sweet heaven, no! He would do anything, give anything to save her.

Cameron pressed his face to her tangled hair, whispering in frenzied regret. "Oh, Meg, lass, forgive me. If I hadn't been such a stubborn fool, I could've had you and

Jenny and a whole world of love. Now I'm losing it all. And I'm just beginning to understand what it means.''

A sound penetrated his senses. A faint, distant rumble. What was it? Cameron stiffened, instantly alert, ears straining in the darkness.

Seconds crept by before he heard it again, louder this time, and unmistakable. His pulse skipped a beat, then began to race as the celestial growl rumbled across the sky.

Thunder.

The rains.

The rains!

Lightning forked through the blackness, splitting the heavens with an ear-shattering boom. Cameron felt Meg flinch in his arms, but her eyes remained closed. He kissed her frantically, his lips grazing her temples, her cheeks, her soft, cool mouth. "Hold on, lass. Stay with me," he murmured as another lightning flash flooded the nightmare landscape with ghost-blue light.

The thunderclap that followed seemed to rip the sky apart. The ground trembled with anticipation as the drops began to pour, not gently, but all at once, in solid, driving, roaring sheets.

The rains!

Cameron dragged his body and Meg's to the mouth of the cave. Thrusting out a hand to catch the life-giving water, he splashed her face and throat, then drizzled more between her parched lips. His heart leapt as she stirred and moaned in his arms.

A lightning flash illuminated her eyes. She blinked, sputtering the water he'd given her. "Cameron, what—"

He caught her close. "It's rain, my love! More bloody rain than you've ever seen in your life!" He reached out to trap more water in his hand. She sucked it eagerly from his palm, then reached up to brush his face with her fingertips.

"You... Cameron, you're..." She struggled for words that would not come. Her eyes glowed with joy.

"Aye, the fever's broken, lass! I'm all right! We'll win this fight yet!"

Wordlessly, she buried her face against his chest. For a long moment, she did not move. Then, suddenly, she was struggling away from him to crawl onto the ledge that jutted beyond the cave's mouth. The rain lashed and pelted her, soaking her hair and clothes, beading on her upturned face.

"It is! It's rain!" Meg's voice gurgled as she cupped her hands to catch the downpouring water and scoop it into her mouth. She drank with wild abandon, heedless of the stinging drops.

"Come back in here, you little fool! You'll catch your death!" Cameron grimaced as he recognized the absurdity of his own words. Ducking under the lip of the cave, he joined her on the ledge. The raindrops smarted like buckshot on his naked skin. He filled his hands, his mouth, his belly. They were both drunk on rain!

Meg had revived like a flower. She knelt on the ledge, back arched, face lifted, arms spread to the sky like some pagan rain-worshiper. A flash of lightning illuminated the fine-cut planes of her face. She was beautiful, Cameron thought. No, she was glorious.

Impulsively, he seized her waist and pulled her against him. She came, desperately eager, fingers catching his head, taloning his hair as she pulled his face down to hers. Her wet lips opened to him as they kissed—kissed dizzily, wildly, achingly in the driving African rain.

"Meg..." he whispered, lost in her. "I love you, Mary Margaret. Did I ever tell you that?"

They lay in the darkness, Cameron cradling Meg in the crook of his arm, her damp head nestled against his shoulder. Their legs entangled sweetly beneath the blankets. Rain drummed on the rocks outside.

He closed his eyes, savoring the silk of her skin against his. Never, in his whole lonely, frustrated life, had he known so much love. He could have been totally content at this moment, if only...

Meg sighed raggedly, breaking the warm silence. "Jenny..."

"I know, lass. We'll leave as soon as we're able."

She raised her head anxiously, eyes large and fearful in the darkness. "When? Cameron, we've already lost so much time, nearly a week."

"Aye, and all we can do is pray that we're still ahead of them. But they'll have to hole up for the worst of the rains, just as we will. That should buy us a few days, at least, to get our strength back."

"We can't wait! We have to try—"

He silenced her soft lips with a brush of his finger. "Meg, love, we wouldn't last a mile in our condition, especially in the rain. We've been given a second chance, but I doubt we'll be given a third." Cameron smoothed a lock of damp hair back from her face. He knew she wanted other words from him, words of bold, reckless determination. But he was through taking foolish chances. He loved Meg too much to risk her life again.

Her head settled back onto his shoulder. "Cameron, I'm afraid," she whispered. "I'm afraid for Jenny."

"So am I, lass." His hand stroked her damply tangled hair. "But we'd be no good to her like this. We have to be strong enough to get her back, and to take care of her."

She shivered against him. "What happens if we're too late?"

"We shouldn't be. The bastards have had farther to come than we have, and picking up more slaves should delay them even longer. So will the rains."

"You didn't answer my question, Cameron." He sensed the fear in her taut little voice. "What if they reach The Neck of the Jar ahead of us?"

Cameron hesitated, knowing that neither choice—to turn back, or continue on into the hellish northern desert—would end in anything but heartbreak. He knew what Meg wanted to hear, but he could not lie to her. "Wait and see," he said gently. "There's no sense making that decision before it's needed."

Meg settled quietly against him once more, her cheek petal-soft on his chest. Cameron pulled the blanket protectively around her. She would not speak of the matter again tonight, he knew. But he could feel the strain in her, the instincts that compelled her to follow her lost child, the primal urges that would not let her rest.

Outside in the darkness, the storm lashed the bare rocks with a sound like the fall of endless tears. Cameron drew his wife close. "Sleep, lass," he murmured, nuzzling her temple. "Close your eyes and listen to the rain. I'm here."

Overnight, the land began to transform itself. New grass carpeted the earth like moss-green velvet. In the low spots, where water pooled, clouds of tiny insects appeared. Swallows and nightjars materialized out of the air to feed on them. Frogs filled the twilight with their symphonies.

Meg spent her waking hours in a state of rapt astonishment. "I don't understand!" she exclaimed to Cameron. "Where did all this life come from? The land was dead!"

"Dead? No, only sleeping, lass. And the wake-up's just beginning. You'll see."

Like a reenactment of Genesis, the miracles unfolded. Leaves emerged on trees that had been lifeless sticks only days earlier. One morning, Meg spotted an eagle and a flock of marabou storks. The next afternoon, she realized that the moving shadow she saw in the distance was a herd of migrating wildebeest. Late that same night, the roar of a hunting lion rumbled across the plain like distant thunder.

Every day, for hours on end, the rain poured down. When the storms grew fierce, Meg and Cameron huddled in the shelter of the cave. The waiting gave them time for napping in each other's arms, for poignant, tender lovemaking, and for long, quiet talks. They whispered about their lives in the years they'd been apart, and about their love. But they did not speak of the future. Until Jenny was found, or her fate known, the future was a closed door.

Because soaked garments took so long to dry, the two of them spent much of their time naked. Meg soon lost all trappings of modesty. It seemed natural now to wander as bare as Eve in this emerging Eden, clad only in her boots, with her hair falling in a tangled, tawny web over her breasts. She grew to savor the kiss of wind on her skin, the tickle of sunlight, the myriad sensations that a body could experience without the barrier of clothing.

Britain, with its inflexible social conventions, seemed as far away as the moon. How could she ever feel at home in such a place again? Meg wondered. After what she had known here, how could she ever go back to being prim little Mary Margaret of Darlmoor?

Her eyes followed Cameron shamelessly now, as his body moved through patterns of dappled sunshine. She loved watching the play of light on his clean-muscled limbs. She loved tracing the pattern of crisp, black hair, from the broad, curling patch on his chest to the dark line that arrowed down his belly to frame his manhood in luxuriant shadow. She loved his strength; she loved the easy, supple grace of his every motion. And most of all, she loved the feel of his warm golden skin pressed to hers when he caught her in his arms.

These few brief days were the most bittersweet Meg had ever known. She and Cameron had found paradise together. But with Jenny in peril, every moment of delay held its own purgatory.

Oh, she understood the wisdom of waiting till they were stronger. Precious little good they'd be to Jenny if they could not get her to safety. But rational arguments meant nothing when Meg's every instinct cried out for her daughter. Jenny's innocent blue eyes haunted her thoughts, drawing her like a magnet toward the distant horizon, toward the place caravaners called The Neck of the Jar.

Every hour of delay racked her with anxiety. Only Cameron's love, and his tender patience, made the time endurable.

Meanwhile, the two of them could not afford to be idle. The *biltong* had fed them for the first few days, but it would not be enough. When he was able to stalk game, Cameron used one more cartridge to shoot a wildebeest. While he hacked the tough, stringy meat into strips, Meg scoured the sheltering ledges for any firewood the soaking rains had missed. The precious sticks she found kindled a tiny blaze, to which larger, damper pieces could be added.

Day and night, the fire had to be tended, and the meat strips rotated on their smoking racks. Meg sat her last watch in the dark hours after midnight, while Cameron slept. Clad in her boots and Cameron's khaki shirt, she huddled beside the flames, listening to the night sounds beyond the cave.

Jackals had found the remains of the wildebeest carcass. They yipped and sang as they tore at the bones, their high-pitched cries vibrating through the darkness. Weeks ago, their exuberant chorus would have sent chills up Meg's spine. Now the sounds were no more than a friendly element of the night. She could even be glad, in fact, that the hungry little creatures had found a meal.

She stirred restlessly, stretched and prodded the fire with a stick. The meat would be done by morning. Once it was packed, she and Cameron would be breaking camp to set out for The Neck of the Jar.

Tired as she was, Meg could not relax. Like a soldier on the eve of battle, her body seethed with nervous anticipation. The waiting, the helpless frustration, would be over at last. But a fearful truth lay at the end of their safari.

Would they find Jenny alive? Would they find her at all?

Meg stared into the glowing coals, her mind grappling with all the things that could go wrong. She and Cameron could fail in their rescue attempt. They could lose Jenny. They could lose their own lives.

She jabbed the stick into the embers, sending up a shower of sparks as she imagined finding the slave caravan, only to discover that Jenny had not survived the trek. Even worse, perhaps, she imagined arriving at The Neck of the Jar to find nothing; waiting, week after fruitless week . . . for nothing.

Cameron stirred behind her. His arm circled her waist, drawing her against the lean curve of his body. "We'll take this one step at a time, lass," he said gently. "Besides hoping, that's all we can do."

"I know." Meg fumbled for his hand, curling her small, rough fingers into his big, protecting palm. "But when I think about Jenny, when I try to measure the odds . . ."

"Don't try, Meg. You can't measure the odds. And it won't help." He had spoken firmly, but his voice softened as he added, "Lie down and get some rest. The meat's nearly done. Those coals are hot enough to finish it without your tending them."

His hand tugged insistently. Stretching out alongside him with a sigh, Meg molded her curves to his lean hardness. She needed Cameron tonight. The days ahead loomed dark and uncertain, and she was afraid.

His arms tightened around her. His throat moved against her hair as he whispered, "Whatever we have to face out there, it won't be easy. But we'll get through it, love. We've got to. We owe each other that much."

Meg pressed her face into the roughness of his chest, taking refuge in his warmth. Cameron was trying his best to understand. But how could he? He had never known Jenny. He had never heard her laugh, or seen her running through the heather with sunlight on her hair. He had never leaned over her bed to savor the sweet, milky child-fragrance that rose from the nest of her blankets.

Jenny was Cameron's daughter, and he cared for her unseen because he was good and kind. But he could not know Jenny's special magic. He could not know who and what she was.

He could not understand what it truly meant to lose her.

"Meg?" He had drawn back a little, to brush her cheek with a tentative finger. Only then did she realize that there were tears trickling down her face.

"Oh, blast it, I'm sorry, Meg." He bent his head to kiss away the salty droplets. "Forgive me, lass. I meant to comfort you, but I should have known better. There'll be no comfort for you or me. Not until our little girl is safe."

Meg closed her eyes and gave herself up to his kisses. His lips were like cool silk on her skin, soothing the raw, stinging pain of her tears. Strange, how she had once thought him rough and hard. In truth, Cameron was the gentlest man she had ever known.

Her body arched against him, aching to lose itself in his tender warmth. Tomorrow loomed dark with unknown fears. But tonight they were safe; and she needed him, suddenly, with a desperate, urgent hunger that took her breath away.

Love me, her heart whispered, and it was as if Cameron had heard. His arms caught her close. His kisses flamed with desire as he drew her fiercely beneath him. Meg's breath caught in a little sob as her body opened to his passion. Yes, she would love him tonight. She would love him to the depths of her soul.

She would love him as if it were the last time.

Cameron paused in the shade of a termite mound to study the Emir's map. By his reckoning, The Neck of the Jar lay scant hours away. The trail, however, was not easy to follow here. At best, it was faint and little-used. Now the rains and the lush, new grass that followed had all but wiped it out. He was having to rely more and more on distant landmarks.

"Are we all right, do you think?" Meg had plopped on the ground, her hat askew and her legs stretched in front of her. They'd been marching hard for nearly two days, and the drain on her stamina was beginning to tell. Cameron's heart tightened with worry as he gazed down at her. She had not recovered from their ordeal as fully as he'd expected. Her face looked pinched and drawn, and only that morning she'd been unable to keep down her *biltong*. He'd have been smart to insist on a longer rest at the cave, but he'd already waited as long as he dared.

Shading his eyes, he scanned the sun-blurred horizon. "Aye, we seem to be on course. That far range of hills is marked on the map, and I've set us on a bearing with that notch. But I can't see a sign of the trail."

Meg sighed wearily. "Then all we can do is go on."

"It won't hurt to stop a bit, lass." Cameron stalled, hoping she would rest longer.

"No, it's all right. I'm ready." She lifted her canteen and took a quick, hard swallow, wiping her mouth on the back of her hand. Her face was pale and lightly beaded with sweat. Cameron resolved to try to bag some game before dark. Maybe fresh meat would restore her appetite.

His fingers locked around her small, rough hand as he pulled her to her feet. His Meg. He would give anything to spare her what lay ahead. But he knew better than to try. It was not in her to hold back and leave the danger to him.

She struck out with long, determined strides. Cameron matched his pace to hers, mentally counting the rifle cartridges in his pocket. There were so few left. Could he spare even one to shoot meat?

"Look!" Meg's voice shattered his thoughts. "Up ahead! It's a water hole!"

Cameron followed her gaze to a spot that glinted like a mirror in the hot afternoon sun. "It's just a rain pond," he said as they came closer. "See how the grass grows all the way to the edge? A regular water hole would have a muddy bank, and there'd be animal trails. This will be gone once the rains let up."

"Water is water." Meg tossed off his explanation with a shrug. "I'm going to splash my face and fill the canteens."

Cameron frowned cautiously. "All right, then. But be careful. Water tends to attract dangerous animals."

He watched, rifle at the ready, as she filled the two canteens, then bent to splash her face, her throat and the tops of her breasts. His heart broke as she sat up smiling, beads of water sparkling on her skin. In this raw, perilous world, his Meg was as vulnerable as a flower, and as precious. Losing her would be too much for a man to bear, he thought. It would be worse than dying.

Suddenly, Cameron was afraid.

She saw the shadow cross his face. "Are you all right?" she asked softly.

"Aye. I'm all right, lass. Let's see if we can find the trail before dark sets in." He took the canteens, gave her a brusque hand up, and turned away before she could look at him again and confirm his fear. For several minutes, they strode side by side, without speaking.

"Cameron?" Meg's small, husky voice broke the silence. "If—*when* we find Jenny, have you thought about how we'll get her away from the slavers?"

"Aye." Cameron nodded wearily. "I've racked my brain. But there'll be no way of knowing what's best until we've caught up with them. They'll have us outmanned and outgunned, but if we can sneak into their camp at night, or ambush them somehow, without risking Jenny—"

"The ivory map," she said, her voice taut with quiet excitement. "It's still in your trouser pocket. We could use it to bargain for her, Cameron. We could use it to get Jenny back!"

"Aye, that we could." He spoke mechanically, the ramifications of what she had said flashing through his mind. "But even that idea's not foolproof," he added swiftly. "The bastards we're dealing with have no honor. They could kill us, and take the map, as well."

"Not if you threatened to destroy the map first." Meg's voice had taken on a note of steel. "These men are greedy, Cameron, and they're gamblers by nature—at least Hassan is. If the ivory's really there, it could be worth a thousand times what they'd get for one fragile little girl."

"You may be right. But that's not a decision we can make till the time comes." Cameron spoke evasively, avoiding her eyes. In truth, he had been wrestling with the same plan for weeks, but he had yet to come to terms with it. Oh, it was not a matter of choosing between the map and Jenny. Faced with that, there'd be no question—his daughter would come first. But if there was a way to hold on to his dream, to have Meg and Jenny *and* a fortune in ivory...

Cameron stared into the distance, his emotions churning. With the ivory, he could give Meg and Jenny the life they deserved: a fine house, beautiful clothes, servants, holidays abroad, the right friends. That kind of life was important to Meg. It was so important that she'd been ready to divorce him for it.

That was the crux of his dilemma. Without the ivory he had nothing—he *was* nothing. Meg would have no reason to stay with him; and even if she did, how could he support a wife and child? Even the job with the railroad was gone now. He had resigned, and there was no guarantee they would hire him back. What could he promise a woman like Meg, or provide for a little girl like Jenny?

The map was his only hope.

They came over the top of a rocky hill. Cameron was still wrapped in his own thoughts when he felt Meg's touch on his sleeve.

"Down there," she said in a hushed voice. "Cameron, it looks like...a road."

Jolted by her words, he stared at the green-speckled plain below. There it was, like a thin scar gouged across the landscape, not a true road, but a broad, well-worn caravan path.

Meg shaded her eyes against the low afternoon sun. "That can't be our old trail, can it?"

"No, lass. You're looking at one of the main caravan routes. See, back that way, where it swings off to the south? And look, there's another trail coming into it, and another."

Her breath caught sharply. "The Neck of the Jar."

"Aye, we must be close." Cameron's throat was so tense that every word was an effort. "Come on. That road should take us there in no time."

They descended the hill at a controlled pace, like a team of tightly reined chariot horses. Beside him, Cameron could hear the labored rush of Meg's breathing. He could feel her fear and sense her anticipation. The past weeks had been cushioned by uncertainty. Now the truth loomed over them, black with possibilities.

Even with the rains, the caravan trail was like kiln-fired terra-cotta. Centuries of trudging, bare soles had polished its surface to a hard patina that showed no trace of footprints. Cameron inspected the ground carefully, but there was no way of knowing when the last travelers had passed.

"We'd best get moving," he said. "The sky's clouding up again. With luck, we'll reach The Neck of the Jar before the rain hits. The Emir mentioned something about ancient caves there, carved into the rock."

"Wonderful! I've grown downright fond of caves!" Meg's attempt at lightness rang hollow. Her reed-thin voice trembled as she spoke. Cameron reached out to support her with his arm, but she shook her head adamantly. "I'm all right," she insisted. "Let's go on."

They had traveled, perhaps, half a mile, Cameron slowing his pace to spare her, when he saw her body stiffen abruptly, as if she'd received an electric jolt.

"Meg, what the devil—" He clasped her arm, but she twisted away from him with a little strangled cry. In the next instant she had swerved off the trail and was sprinting toward a tattered, red object that fluttered from atop a huge thornbush.

Cameron hesitated, cursed, and then went pounding after her. By now, Meg had plunged into the thorns. They tore her clothes and left raw, bleeding scratches on her skin. Heedless of the pain, her hands clawed upward through the awful tangle. By the time Cameron reached her, she was hanging half-suspended in the branches. Tears streamed down her face as she clutched her prize, crushing it close against her breasts.

He had drawn his knife and was moving in to cut her loose when he realized what it was.

It was a hat. A child's straw sun helmet, lined with faded red felt.

Blood trickled down Meg's thorn-gouged arms, but she felt no pain. She gripped Jenny's hat—*Jenny's hat*—in her hands as Cameron hacked away the thorn branches and gently pulled her free. Her clenched fingers would not let go of it, even as he lowered her to the ground and began cleaning her bleeding scratches with his wet handkerchief.

He did not have to ask her what it was.

As she looked up into his grim blue eyes, Meg realized what he was thinking. "They've already passed this spot," she said in a choked voice. "That means they're ahead of us!"

"Aye." His gaze inspected Jenny's hat. "But not far ahead. The hat's dry and still in good condition. It couldn't have hung there through the last rain." He took a deep, rough breath. "We can catch them, lass. And we will."

He continued to wipe at Meg's wounds as he spoke, pausing every few seconds to moisten the cloth. Meg was wild with impatience. "Hurry!" she breathed. "Cameron, please."

"We've got time." He worked with maddening care. "Night's coming on soon. They'll be making camp, maybe at The Neck of the Jar. If the rain doesn't pin us down somewhere, we'll just keep moving till we find them."

He scowled pensively at her, and Meg knew what he was thinking. She hadn't felt strong since they'd left the cave, and now she was exhausted. How long could she keep up the grueling pace without rest?

"I'll be all right," she insisted, clutching Jenny's sad little hat. "For the love of heaven, Cameron, we can't waste any more time!"

He squeezed the last drop of blood-tinged moisture out of the kerchief and jammed it into his pocket. "Let's go, then. But promise me one thing. If you get to the point where you're too tired to go on, Meg, have the common sense to tell me. You won't help Jenny by collapsing on the trail."

Meg nodded her assent. "Let's go."

Cameron set a moderate, steady pace. Frantic with anticipation, Meg fought the urge to plunge ahead of him and race down the trail. She would only burn out her strength, she warned herself. The caravan could be miles, and hours, away. The important thing now was to keep moving.

The afternoon melted into twilight. Clouds roiled across the rising moon. The evening breeze smelled of rain.

Meg trudged along at Cameron's side, still clasping Jenny's hat to keep up her courage. It was dangerous being on the trail after sundown, with no campfire to keep preying animals at bay. Earlier, they'd passed within a stone's throw of a lion pride, feasting on a downed zebra. Their hungry snarls and the snap of crunching bone had sent chills through Meg's body. Later, through the darkness, they'd heard the death-squeal of a warthog and glimpsed the spotted flash of a leopard.

Cameron walked with the rifle cocked and ready. Now and again, he would start at some sound in the darkness. Meg would shrink against his side, senses prickling as the tip of the barrel swung in a slow arc, then dropped when the danger failed to materialize.

Her body cried out for rest, but she sealed her lips against complaint. They could not stop. Jenny was just ahead of them. They had to reach her. The trail had begun to climb again, winding upward through clumps of stark, black rock, when Cameron suddenly froze.

"Take a deep breath," he said. "What do you smell?"

Closing her eyes, Meg inhaled. The acrid odor on the wind was faint but unmistakable. Smoke. A campfire.

She met Cameron's gaze, her pulse suddenly racing.

"Listen to me," he rasped. "Once we've figured out where they are, we're going to find a safe place and leave you there while I go closer to investigate. Promise me— promise me *now*—that you'll keep quiet and stay put."

"Cameron!" The protest exploded in her, drowning the voice of reason, which whispered that he was right. If trouble broke out, her exhausted state would only make her a hindrance. But how could he ask such a thing now, when all her motherly instincts were driving her toward Jenny?

He glared at her in the darkness, moonlight glinting on his grim, scarred face. "I won't risk you, Meg! Promise me now, or we don't budge from this spot!"

The smoke smell was stronger now. Its bitter odor swam in Meg's senses as she lowered her gaze, sighed and nodded her resignation. It was for the best, she told herself. She would see her daughter soon enough.

But even as they crept through the moonlit darkness, silent as panthers, her instincts screamed against the promise she'd made.

The trail dropped abruptly. Meg could see that a narrow ravine lay ahead of them, and she knew without asking that this was The Neck of the Jar. Firelight flickered on its high, rocky walls. The aromas of meat, rice, ash cakes and exotic spices drifted upward on the night wind.

Cameron caught her arm. "This is far enough for you," he whispered. "You'll be safe up here in these rocks."

Meg bit back the temptation to argue. She was running on adrenaline now, and her nerves were frayed to the snapping point. Maybe if she rested now, she would be of more use later.

After a quick search, Cameron selected a narrow niche, sheltered on two sides and overhung by a jutting ledge. "Wait here," he ordered her. "I'm going to circle down through those big rocks on the left-hand side of the ravine. They should give me enough cover to get close."

Meg slipped into the place he'd shown her and sat down. "Be careful," she whispered through the pain of her tight throat.

"I will, lass." His hand closed around hers for an instant before he turned away. He took a few steps, then abruptly moved back toward her. "Take this," he said, handing her the rifle. "It's loaded. If anything goes wrong, fire it."

"But, you'll be unarmed!"

"I'll have my knife. Don't worry." He was gone again before she could protest, leaving the rifle in her hands.

Meg pressed her back against the rock and tried to rest. The night flowed around her, alive with sound and motion. Wind moaned through the ravine, stroking her face with cool, damp fingers. Thunder rumbled faintly above the distant hills. A bat fluttered through the darkness, floating past her face like a ghost.

Time passed so slowly that even her heartbeats were like the leaden tick of a steeple clock. Though she knew it was only minutes, it seemed as if Cameron had been gone for hours.

Meg strained her ears for the slightest sound from the ravine, but she heard nothing, nothing but the wind and the faint animal noises that were part of any African night. She stood up and stretched in a torment of restlessness. The man she loved was down there, alone, in danger and armed with nothing but his hunting knife. And Jenny, her baby, was down there, too. She was close enough to see and hear, almost close enough to touch.

Only half aware, Meg was moving forward, leaning to one side to balance the heavy rifle as she threaded her way down through the rocks. Cameron had gone left; she would go right. She knew she was breaking her promise. She knew there was a chance she'd wind up sorry. But she no longer had the power to stop.

Chapter Fifteen

Meg could see the firelight clearly now. Its orange glow flickered on the jagged walls of the ravine, casting shadows that danced like goblins in the darkness.

Tantalizing aromas rose from the pots on the cook fire, but food was the furthest thing from her mind now. Desperate for a glimpse of Jenny, she inched along the treacherous slope. A clump of rocks jutted against the moon, blocking her view. If she could reach them, she calculated, she would have a clear, safe vista of the camp below.

Bracing herself with the rifle stock, she edged her way over a jumble of loose boulders. Once her foot slipped, and the crunch of shifting rock rang out like a gunshot in the night. Meg froze in the shadows, expecting to hear the entire camp erupting in alarm. But nothing happened. Maybe the sound had not been as loud as she'd imagined.

She crept forward again, wondering if Cameron had heard her. He could be anywhere on the opposite side of the ravine. Or, by now, he might have even returned to her hiding place and found her gone. She knew he would be upset, but the urge that drove her now was too compelling to resist.

At last, the jutting formation was within reach. Meg pulled herself onto solid footing and collapsed, panting, in the shelter of the massive rocks. From here, she had a clear, protected view of the ravine's bottom.

Far below, the camp was settling in for the night. A half-dozen Arab-style tents were pitched in a semicircle around the fire. Meg could see the slaves, huddled like a dark spill on the open ground. There were thirty or forty of them, and the firelight glinted on the irons that shackled their raw legs to a single long chain. The yokes that kept them in line on the march lay stacked like cordwood along the camp's edge.

Three Swahili guards, whips coiled at their belts, lounged around the fire. Two Arabs sat smoking as they played some sort of game on a rug outside one of the tents. Meg saw no one she recognized—no sign, even, that this was indeed the caravan that had taken Jenny. Her heart sank as she realized that she could watch all night and still learn nothing.

Then, as she watched, a tent flap parted, and a gaunt, familiar figure strode out into the firelight. Even from a distance, there was no mistaking who it was.

Hassan.

The rage that galvanized Meg's body was so overpowering it almost made her faint. Her hands gripped the rock's fractured edge until the palms were sticky with blood. Hassan's long, skeletal face, with its hooded eyes, had haunted her dreams for weeks. But not until now, as he stood in her very sight, did Meg realize how much she hated the man. She had trusted Hassan with her most precious treasure—and he had betrayed her with a reptilian coldness that made her flesh crawl.

The rifle's cool weight lay against her side. Meg hefted the gun to her shoulder, with the barrel resting across the top of a boulder. Deliberately, she pulled back the hammer. The sight bead quivered in its notch as she brought the muzzle into line with Hassan's lank body. Her finger tensed on the trigger. *She could shoot him,* she realized, startled by the vehemence of her own emotions. She could kill him—and she would, she swore, if anything had happened to Jenny.

She lowered the weapon with shaking hands. She would be a fool to shoot now. The camp would be thrown into pandemonium, imperiling Cameron and destroying any chance of saving Jenny. But in that brief heartbeat, with Hassan in her sights, Meg had known she was capable of killing him. It was a frightening discovery.

Her eyes followed Hassan as he swaggered across the camp. Gone was the fawning attitude he'd displayed as a servant. Now he strutted like a peacock, his hands fondling a long, black whip. The slaves shrank in their shackles as he strode past them to settle beside his two cohorts on the rug.

Leaning forward, Meg peered over the edge of her hiding place. Only now did she realize that this spot had been used as a sentry point by other caravans that had camped below. A narrow path zigzagged downward through the brushy boulders, all the way to the bottom of the ravine.

Her pulse skipped a beat and broke into a canter. She could get closer. Maybe close enough to discover some sign of Jenny.

Uncocking the rifle, Meg crept out from between the rocks. The moon had emerged through an open patch in the clouds. Its light lay like platinum on the path as she slipped from shadow to shadow. Her heart slammed a wild tattoo against her ribs. Her palms were clammy where they clasped the rifle stock.

By now, she was so close that she could hear the crackle of the fire. Screened by a patch of thornbush, she dropped to the ground and bellied her way forward. The camp was clearly visible through the black filigree of thorns. Meg's ears caught the mutter of voices and the click of gaming pieces. The odor of tobacco mingled with the rich aromas of meat and spices.

One of the Swahili guards strolled past, so near that Meg's eyes could trace the bush-scars on his thin, black legs. He paused, spat in the dust and turned away. Until he was gone, she lay as still as death. Even then, her eyes darted about the firelit circle in a desperate search for her child.

But there was no sign of Jenny. If she was with the caravan at all, Meg realized with a sinking heart, she could only be inside one of the tents. There would be no way of knowing for sure until the camp broke at dawn.

Racked by disappointment, Meg began edging backward into the shadows. Cameron would be worried, maybe angry, as well, if he returned to find her gone. Perhaps if she hurried, she could get back to where he'd left her before—

A voice shattered her thoughts—a tiny distant voice, as sweet as a spring warbler's. Meg's ears had picked up no more than a single musical tone, but its familiarity wrenched her heart.

She looked up, afraid to believe what she saw. Not forty yards away from her, Jenny had come out of a tent. Jenny—her face smudged, her clothes torn and dirty, her hair a tangled golden nest. Sweet heaven—*Jenny!*

In that first blinding second, Meg could see nothing but her daughter. As her vision cleared, however, she realized that Jenny was not alone. A squat, sullen Swahili in a dirty brown *kansu* had emerged behind her. Meg's throat constricted with a jerk as she saw that he was holding a thin rope, attached by a ring to a leather collar around Jenny's small neck.

Jenny was tethered like a pet monkey.

Meg choked back a cry of helpless rage. She could not reveal herself now, or all would be lost. She could only watch in silent anguish as Jenny and her captor walked purposefully across the camp, moving at an angle toward the spot where she lay.

Meg's eyes inspected her daughter from head to toe. Aside from being ragged, uncombed and dirty, Jenny appeared to be physically well. And she walked before the wretch who held her with the grace of a tiny queen leading her lackey.

She paused now, to glance back over her shoulder and say something to the Swahili in her clear, childish voice. Meg, who was close enough to distinguish words by this time, was startled to realize that Jenny was not speaking in English. In the long weeks of the journey, her quick, young mind had picked up the tongue of her captors. The awareness tugged at Meg's heart. Cameron's daughter had inherited more from her father than his arresting blue eyes.

The two of them were coming closer now, headed toward an opening in the thornbush a dozen yards to Meg's right. Jenny was skip-hopping in an impatient little dance that Meg recognized at once—and only then did she realize what was happening. The Swahili was escorting Jenny into the bushes so the little girl could relieve herself. For the few minutes it took, they would be secluded from the camp's view.

The chance was a gift of providence.

Meg's muscles tensed as she gathered her body into a crouch. The gun hung cold and heavy in her hands. She could not shoot without alarming the camp. But the rifle's thick stock would do as a club, if she could find the strength to swing it.

Clasping her hands around the barrel, Meg crept forward. She would have only one chance to strike home. If the blow was weak or badly aimed, there would be no time to recover.

Through the tangled thorns, she could see Jenny and her captor. They had halted in a sheltered, open spot, surrounded by bushes. Jenny glanced around at the Swahili and uttered an imperious command in her tiny, bell-like voice. Obediently, he turned his face away. His hand, however, kept a tight grip on her tether as Jenny pulled down her drawers and squatted in the moonlight.

Meg sprang like a cat. The swinging rifle butt caught the Swahili in the side of the head, cracking his cheekbone. Dazed by the blow, the man reeled and staggered. Jenny's tether dropped from his hand.

Jenny had frozen in midcrouch. She stared at her mother. "Run, Jenny!" Meg gasped. "Run up into the rocks!"

The Swahili was still on his feet. Pain-crazed, bloodied and bellowing, he turned on Meg. His face twisted like a wounded animal's as he gathered himself to rush her.

Praying that Jenny would obey, Meg swung the rifle again. But she had spent her meager strength on the first blow. The gun stock glanced harmlessly off one powerful black shoulder. The Swahili grinned malevolently as he lumbered toward her.

Meg caught a glimpse of Jenny flashing off into the darkness. She breathed her thanks. Then she turned to face her enemy like an antelope at bay, backing, dodging, side-stepping in a frenzied effort to cock the rifle and fire it.

It was no use. By now, others from the camp had heard the struggle. They were all around her, closing in like a ring of wild dogs. Their faces were floating blurs in her vision, half-lost in the swirling darkness. The rifle seemed as heavy as a tree. It was almost a relief when someone wrenched it from her hands.

Meg staggered one way, then another as the world spun around her. Her legs were too weak to bear her weight. She struggled feebly as rough hands clutched at her arms. The sickening odors of tobacco, sweat and garlic flooded her senses. She was vaguely aware of being shoved, pulled and lifted. Then the stars came crashing in on her.

As she sank into oblivion, the last face she saw was Hassan's.

Cameron had seen everything. From his vantage point on the far side of the ravine, he had watched Meg's capture in helpless despair, fingers clenched frantically on the hilt of his hunting knife.

He'd cursed himself for not having kept the rifle, though even that, he realized now, would have been of little use. There were too many of the bastards, and there'd have been too much danger of a shot hitting Meg. He'd had no choice except to watch in mute anguish, groaning inside as they cornered her like a spent animal and dragged her limp body toward the tents.

At least the brutes hadn't raped her on the spot—he was thankful for that. But he knew the kind of men who had her, and what they could do. Meg was in terrible danger, and he was sick with fear for her. But even Meg could not be his first concern now.

Steeling his emotions, Cameron moved stealthily out of his cramped hiding place and headed up the slope. Someone else was in danger, too—a little girl, alone and frightened in the darkness. And no matter what happened down in the camp, he knew what Meg would want him to do.

As he circled along the ledges, he caught glimpses of the camp below. Meg was nowhere in sight, but two of the Swahili were lighting torches to go after Jenny. Desperately, Cameron lengthened his stride, doing his best not to dislodge the loose, slippery scree that covered the slope. He could not afford a noisy misstep that would give away his whereabouts. Not when the two most precious lives in his world were at stake.

Bats shrilled above the muted roll of thunder as he recrossed the trail at the head of the ravine. Here the ground was solid, and out of earshot from the camp. He could run; and run he did. His lungs heaved with effort. His ribs throbbed. His pulse hammered as he scanned the side of the ravine, a maze of jutting rocks and moonlit shadows. One tiny, terrified child. She could be anywhere. And time was running out.

From below, flickering torchlight danced up the slope. There were at least two men, maybe more, and they would likely be armed. The slavers were smart enough to realize that Meg couldn't have come this far alone.

Cameron paused for breath, his thoughts galloping. Aye, they would know someone was out here. But they would be expecting a band of armed rescuers, not one lone man. He needed a way to use their ignorance, to twist it to his own advantage.

He could see the torches clearly now. The two men had parted and were winding separately among the rocks. He had to act swiftly, before either of them flushed out Jenny. *Stay hidden, little lass,* he pleaded silently as he bent to pick up a fist-sized stone. *Stay quiet until I can find you.*

Aiming carefully, he flung the missile hard onto the loose scree that lay in scattered patches, interspersed with scrub, on the slope. The impact set off a clatter of slithering shale that caused both torches to jerk, swing sharply, then move toward the sound.

Pressing in closer, Cameron snatched up another rock and tossed it onto a different slide area. Again the torches leapt and wavered. Cold sweat poured down Cameron's body. He meant to create a diversion, to confuse the searchers and lead them away from Jenny. But he had no idea where Jenny was. What if he was leading them *to* her? He prayed silently, teeth clenched, as he forged through the darkness.

A lightning bolt split the crown of the sky, flashing ice-blue on the bleak hillside. Thunder boomed its low rumble, and Cameron felt the first drops of moisture on his face. By now, he was on the slope, zigzagging in a downward path toward the moving torches. Somewhere in the darkness below, a little girl quivered small against the danger. He could feel her terror as acutely as he felt his own. He could almost hear the frantic *pit-pat* of her tiny heart, mingled with the newborn rain.

Keep still, Jenny... Your father's coming...

Lightning forked again as he plunged through the scrub. The misty rain was slowly dousing the torches. They glowed red, like cheroot stubs in the night, as he paused to hurl another stone, aiming it far down the slope this time, to clatter on the rocks behind the searchers.

Again the red dots paused and wavered. Cameron heard voices. Then he saw them separate, one to weave downward toward the sound, the other to continue the upward search for Jenny.

By now, Cameron was a third of the way down the slope. The crimson stub of the moving torch bobbed ever closer. He crouched behind a clump of thorns, his right hand clenched on the handle of his long-bladed hunting knife. Above the patter of the rain, he could hear the sound of crunching rocks and harsh, rasping breath.

Lightning ripped the darkness with an earsplitting crash. Below him, in the flare of white light, Cameron glimpsed a tiny, pale figure huddled in the lee of a huge boulder. Scarcely daring to breathe, he edged forward.

The nearest Swahili had seen Jenny, too. Dropping the torch, the husky native lunged in to cut off her escape. Cornered like a mouse, Jenny cringed mutely as he swooped in on her, his arms curved high like the wings of a monstrous, black owl.

The rain-slicked *kansu* clung wetly to his muscle-ridged back. Cameron narrowed his focus to that brutal back, selected a vital spot between the third and fourth ribs and struck with all his strength. Time stopped as he felt the blade penetrate cloth and skin and muscle to pierce the vital organs beneath. The Swahili stiffened, gurgled and collapsed like a felled tree. His body slid partway down the slope, its sound muffled by the driving storm.

Cameron faced his daughter. Jenny stood erect in the rain, water trickling off the pale tangles of her hair and gleaming like moon-beads on her long eyelashes. Cameron's throat constricted in an agony of tenderness. His first attempt to speak emerged as a muffled groan.

Jenny gazed at him with regal calm. Her eyes took in the bearded face, the raking scar, without the slightest trace of fear.

"Are you my father?" she asked in a voice that was like a clear silver bell.

Cameron struggled for words. "Aye, my brave little lass," he rasped, "I'm your father."

She stood poised and quivering like a butterfly in the rain. "I knew you would come!" she whispered. Then, with a little sob, she flung herself into the open circle of his arms.

Chapter Sixteen

Meg opened her eyes to the sound of rain. The first thing she saw was the flicker of lamplight on the dark canvas wall of a tent. The second was Hassan.

He was sitting cross-legged on a mat, a few feet from where she lay, as if he had been guarding her. But his eyes were closed. His head drooped in sleep. A breathy snore bubbled on his thin lips.

Meg's eyes darted to the viciously curved dagger that hung from his belt in its beaded scabbard. If she could reach it before he awoke...

She lunged for the knife, only to be wrenched backward and almost strangled by her own momentum. Too late she realized her hands, neck and feet had been tied to a tent pole behind her, in a devilish fashion that caused the ropes to tighten painfully whenever she moved. She lay quivering now, her back excruciatingly arched in an effort to keep the thin, rough rope from cutting off her breath.

Hassan's snoring had stopped. His hooded eyes twitched and opened. They gazed unblinkingly down at her, with no more expression than a cobra's. His lips curled in a cold smile.

Meg glared up at him from her twisted position, her jaw clenched against speaking. She knew he was waiting for her to beg, to plead with him to untie her. But even that small satisfaction was more than she would give him.

He laughed at her resistance, a hollow sound, without humor. "So," he declared, "I have lost one little fish and caught a bigger one in its place."

Meg gaped at him in astonishment. Not only had Hassan revealed that Jenny had indeed escaped, but he had done so in accented but fluent English.

"My first master, Mustafa, had me schooled in your language," he said, relishing her surprise. "He had hopes that I might prove valuable as a spy against your countrymen. Alas, he did not live long enough to put me to use." Again that cold, dark smile played around his lips, showing the glint of his gold tooth. "In my years with the Emir, I helped myself to the English books in his library. Oh, the old fool did not know. He looked on me as a faithful dog, with no thoughts of my own. His ignorance served me well. Under the protection of his house and his name, I have dealt in slaves for years."

"You're a monster!" Meg hissed, straining against the prickly hemp that raked her limbs and neck. "That old man trusted you! I trusted you, Jenny trusted you."

"Then you are all fools." Hassan's eyes had darkened under the shaggy ridge of his eyebrows. The oily cadence of his voice, however, remained unbroken. "But you—you owe me a debt, *memsahib.*" The title dripped sarcastically from his tongue. "Had I not saved her, your daughter's bones would even now be scattered on the bottom of the harbor."

"Your treachery cancels all debts!" Meg snapped.

Hassan's gaze flowed arrogantly over her twisting body. His eyes glittered in the lamplight—not so much with lust, she sensed, as with power. Something in him fed on seeing her helpless and in pain. Had he taken the same pleasure in Jenny? The possibility made Meg's stomach lurch.

"What—did you do to my daughter?" she demanded, struggling to sit up, then collapsing, half-choked with the pain of the jerking ropes.

Hassan's long-jawed face was as impassive as jade. "Whether or not you choose to believe it, *memsahib*, the child was well cared for. I saw to everything, even the protection of her innocence."

"Of course!" Meg gasped, feeling ill. "She was worth money to you!"

"As you, too, will be in time. What a pity you are not younger and a virgin. As such, your beauty would fetch a king's ransom in Marsabit. But even so, I plan to dispose of you for a handsome price."

"Let me up. I'm going to be sick," Meg protested weakly.

He looked beyond her, as if he had not heard. "You were unwise to send your child off into the darkness. There are snakes in those ledges, and they hunt at night. Leopards, also, I am told." His black gaze riveted Meg with sudden displeasure. "Of the two men I sent after her, one did not return. His life will be added to your debt, *memsahib*."

Meg's eyes closed as a wave of relief washed over her. The missing man—yes, that would surely be Cameron's doing. She could dare to hope, now, that he'd found Jenny, as well, and that both of them were safe.

"Your debt is a heavy one. . . ." Hassan had drawn his knife. Meg's heart stopped as the razor-sharp blade neared her throat. Its point skimmed her flesh, leaving a stinging, crimson thread.

Smiling at her terror, Hassan gave the blade a deft twist, slicing the rope that constricted her neck. Meg whimpered as her screaming muscles collapsed. Her wrists and ankles were still tethered to the tent pole, but at least she could stretch out to an endurable position.

"Rest now," Hassan murmured darkly. "Soon enough the time will come for you to repay me. I protected your daughter's innocence because it enhanced her worth. You, *memsahib*, have no innocence to protect."

Meg shrank back against the wall of the tent. "No!" she whispered in a strangled voice. "I'll die before I let you near me!"

Hassan's laughter echoed in the shadows, blending eerily with the rain outside. "Do not flatter yourself, dear lady. When I sell you in Marsabit, I plan to spend my profits on a graceful young boy, a Greek perhaps, with flashing black eyes and skin like golden honey."

For the space of a long breath, Hassan's eyes glazed with anticipation. Then he rose, unfolding his body's full, gaunt height until his embroidered cap brushed the ridgepole of the tent. "Meanwhile, you will make yourself of use," he hissed, turning toward the closed flap, then pausing. "There are others here, men of less refined inclinations, to whom I owe...debts. These they will cancel in exchange for your nightly favors. And by day you will earn your keep, as well, tending and feeding the slaves."

Meg glared her defiance, struggling mutely against the ropes that held her prisoner. The rough hemp sawed into her flesh, leaving raw, bleeding rings around her wrists and ankles. At least she had freed Jenny, she consoled herself. Whatever happened now, she would bear it, knowing her daughter was safe.

Hassan had raised the tent flap. Rain swept in through the opening on the cool, dark wind. Meg gulped at the fresh air, battling the nausea that roiled in the pit of her stomach.

Turning toward her once more, Hassan caught up the lantern. Its light gleamed like devil-fire on the jutting planes of his face. "One thing more," he added with a chilling smile. "We know there are others out there in those rocks, others who would try to set you free. Do not think they will succeed, *memsahib*. Our trap is set, with you as the bait. As Allah so wills, all who come against us will fall into it."

The flap fell as he slipped out into the night, leaving Meg alone in darkness.

Writhing and jerking, she struggled frantically against the ropes that bound her. But it was no use. After a string of futile minutes, Meg collapsed, exhausted, on the mat. A single tear trickled down her cheek to drip onto the sweat-stained fabric. What was the use?

Hassan had been right about more than one thing. Cameron would try to rescue her. The slavers would be waiting for him, and from what Meg knew of Cameron, he would not be taken alive. Jenny would be left alone and unprotected. She would have no choice except to return to the hell of the slave camp.

Meg's fingers balled into desperate fists. If she could get word to Cameron, insisting that he take Jenny and leave.... But Cameron would not listen, she knew. As long as he believed she was alive, he would try to rescue her; and he would fail. They had come all this way, the two of them. They had found each other, found Jenny, only to lose everything in the end.

Only her death would persuade him to leave. Only her death would save the two dearest people in her world.

The tent was growing stuffy again. The sour air, rank with the odors of sweat, tobacco and rancid grease, had begun to turn Meg's stomach. She clenched her teeth to keep from retching. What was the matter with her? She'd felt queasy for days, and didn't seem to be getting any better. Why, she hadn't been so nauseated since before Jenny was—

Great heaven, it couldn't be!

Meg lay thunderstruck, her eyes staring up into the darkness. How could she possibly be carrying Cameron's child?

A reproachful little moan escaped her lips as she counted the weeks since her last menses. Of course it was possible! More than possible!

Quivering with fresh determination, Meg steeled herself for the ordeal ahead. She had thought of dying. That was out of the question now. A new life had begun. She owed that life every chance for freedom.

The rain drizzled on through the night and into the next morning. Cameron had spent much of the time with Jenny, huddled inside one of the caves that honeycombed the ledges above the ravine. Here they had eaten, talked, worried and dozed. Here he had experienced his first hours of being a father.

Jenny lay asleep now, curled like a kitten on the bedroll, her mouth tugging softly at one wet, pink thumb. Crouched at the cave entrance, Cameron watched the play of morning light on her tangled curls and wondered how he could have lived so long without her. That reckless night on the beach had produced a miracle, a small bundle of laughter, curiosity and tenderness that had thoroughly entrapped his heart.

Cameron could no longer imagine life without his daughter. But Jenny's presence had placed him on the horns of a nightmarish dilemma. He stared out at the rain, his mind sifting frantically through the alternatives.

Meg was down there in the camp, at the mercy of monsters who dealt in human misery. The slavers would keep her alive for her value; he felt confident of that much, at least. But the thought of what she might endure at their hands almost drove him to madness. To spare her, he would take any chance, run any risk, without a thought for his own safety.

But there was Jenny.

He glanced back at her over his shoulder. She stirred in her sleep, making tiny animal whimpers as she dreamed. Sweet little Jenny. If anything was to happen to him, she would not last a day in the bush. Alone, her only hope of survival would lie in returning to the camp. Even with Meg at her side, the odds against reaching safety were fearful. There was no getting around reality. Jenny needed her father.

Cameron gulped back the tightness in his throat. He could not communicate with Meg. But he knew without asking what she would say. To risk his own life would be to risk Jenny's. That was something Meg would never stand for. She had entrusted Jenny to his care. Whatever the cost, he could not violate that trust.

He gazed out at the ravine through the gray curtain of rain, his nerves screaming with suppressed urgency. Meg's time was running out, and he was alone, with no gun and no ally except a four-year-old child.

He had only one resource left. One ace in his pocket. And the time had come to use it.

The stiff leather collar chafed Meg's neck as she moved across the camp. Its weight was worsened by the thirty-foot chain that ran from a locked ring at its back to a stout pole near the firepit. The arrangement was as humiliating as it was miserable. But at least it gave her the freedom to be outdoors in the fresh air and to be active.

A pockmarked Swahili with a rifle lounged in the entrance of a tent, his eyes watching her every move. Inside another tent, the four Arabs, Hassan among them, continued the furious gambling game that had raged through the rainy night and into the morning. Meg had no need to wonder about the stakes. Hassan had made that clear enough. She could only pray that the gaming would go on until she could lay the foundations for her escape.

The rain had faded to a fine mist. With a half day's good weather remaining, it would have made sense to break camp and march. But everything awaited the end of the gambling marathon.

The Swahili yawned and scratched his armpit as Meg crossed to the fire and spooned thick, gritty rice gruel from a big iron pot into a calabash made from a dried gourd. Hassan had ordered her to feed the slaves, and feed them she would—with more than gruel.

She filled the calabash and started back through the camp, chain clinking behind her through the gooey orange mud. In the night, she had wondered briefly why the camp was not flooded by the heavy rains. Now she saw the reason. Many years ago, along the far side of the ravine, a drainage ditch had been dug to divert the runoff. Countless seasons of rain had washed it to the depth of a chasm, through which a torrent of muddy, red-brown water boiled and rushed.

Keeping a safe distance from its crumbling bank, Meg picked her way toward the slaves. There were thirty or forty of them, all males, huddled wet and shivering under the shelter of an overhanging ledge. She approached them with apprehension. Over the past weeks, these men had received bestial treatment from their captors. How would they react to a foreign woman in their midst? Would they attack and tear her to pieces?

She needn't have worried. Most of the slaves were so ill and dispirited that they scarcely seemed to notice her. They showed little interest in anything except the rice, which they clawed out of the calabash with their bare hands as she passed, and crammed into their starving mouths.

Their shoulders were bleeding and festered where the wooden yokes had rubbed them raw. Their ankles, too, were ringed with blood from the leg irons used to chain them together in camp. Their bodies, many bearing whip marks, crawled with lice, and more than half of the men were visibly sick. Those with the strength to raise their heads showed tragic eyes in which the spark of life had all but died.

Meg struggled to keep from breaking into tears. Her aim had been to offer these men hope, to rouse them to rebellion against the brutes who held them captive. But she had not counted on the depth of their misery. Her plan, if it worked at all, was going to take more time than she'd expected.

The calabash emptied as fast as she could refill it from the rice pot. Again and again she slogged back through the mud for more. As she fed the men, she tried to whisper as much encouragement as her limited Swahili would allow. If she could give them the will to rise up against their captors, there might be hope for them all.

But the words were beyond her. How did one say *Have courage* in Swahili? How did one say *There are many of you and few of them. You could take them by surprise?*

Meg struggled with the barely-familiar language, her stumbling phrases meeting nothing but blank stares from the few men who had the spirit to raise their eyes. She was about to give up in despair when one of the slaves, older than the others, with crusting whip marks on his back, answered her in halting English.

"I worked for missionary, *memsahib.* We know what you want. But how can we fight? We are weak and sick. We have no weapons. We are chained so that none can move without the others. How, then, can we fight men with whips and guns?"

"Surprise them," Meg urged. "Use what you have— your hands, your chains, whatever you can take from the slavers. When you fight, fight as one man, all of you moving together."

The slave shook his head. "How can we be one, *memsahib?* Some of us are enemies. Our tribes have fought since we were children. We speak with different tongues. You are only a *mzungu* woman who knows nothing of these matters. Keep to your woman's work, and leave this talk of fighting to the men."

Meg drew herself up tall and cold. "I see no men," she said disdainfully. "I see only slaves."

She turned her back and stalked away, chin thrust bravely forward. Inside, she could feel her own strength crumbling. The slaves had been her only hope. But they would not fight. They would not even listen to her.

As she paused by the fire, Meg's attention was riveted by an uproar of cheers, hoots and groans from the tent where the gambling was in progress. A moment later, the flap opened, and the four Arabs, stretching, blinking and rubbing their stiff haunches, staggered blearily into the daylight.

Two of them, clearly the losers, wore disgruntled expressions. One hawked and spat in the fire as they shuffled off toward their own tents to get some sleep. The third man, small and wiry, with a black wart on his nose, appraised Meg with glittering, bloodshot eyes. His mouth dropped open to let his tongue glide wetly across his lips. Meg shuddered as his hands shaped an obscene gesture, the meaning of which even she could not miss. She would die, she told herself, before she let him lay a finger on her.

But she could not die. Not while she carried a precious new life inside her body.

Behind him, Hassan had emerged from the tent, a weighted coin pouch in his hand and a triumphant leer on his face. He snapped a barrage of orders at the Swahili guard, then wheeled back toward Meg.

"We will stay the night here. But I expect Suleiman will not wish to wait until dark to claim his winnings. You will go with him now."

"I will not!" Meg stood glaring and defiant at the end of her chain.

Hassan raised one shaggy eyebrow. His bony fingers fondled the coils of his long, black whip. "It appears that you have little choice, *memsahib*. You will go on my orders, or you will be beaten and dragged to Suleiman's tent."

"I will not go." Meg quivered with determination as she steeled herself against the pain she knew would follow. She would not submit, she vowed. She would not become like those poor, cringing slaves, without hope, pride or spirit.

Hassan growled his impatience. "Stubborn English bitch! You have much to learn!" He seized the chain an arm's length behind Meg's collar, snapping her around with a force that left her choking. For a paralyzing instant, his chilling black eyes bored into hers. Then his hand shot up, its motion a blur as he struck her hard across the face.

Meg staggered. Bubbles of light danced in her vision as she sagged into the strangling collar. Her tongue tasted blood. But her head came up again, to meet Hassan's gaze with proud defiance. "You do not . . . own me," she grated through the raw pain of her throat. "No one can own me!"

Hassan hissed with rage. For the space of a heartbeat, Meg expected him to strike her again. She braced herself for the blow, but it did not come. Instead, with a snarl of disgust, he spat into the mud at her feet and thrust her chain, along with the whip, into Suleiman's hands.

"I've no patience for this!" he growled. "Suleiman has won you for the night. Let him be the one to teach you manners! I will take my enjoyment in watching."

He snapped his fingers, and the hovering Swahili produced a wineskin and a folding leather camp stool. Seating himself like a sultan, he squirted a thin red stream into his open mouth. A trickle ran down his chin to mingle like blood with his gray-peppered beard and dribble onto his soiled *kaftan*. He muttered a grinning aside to Suleiman in Arabic before turning back to Meg.

"Now, my proud English mare," he declared with a lascivious smirk, "it will be my greatest pleasure to see you broken and mounted."

Suleiman was still gripping Meg's chain. Small, but strong as cable wire, he spun her around and jerked her hard against his body. His hot eyes blurred in her vision with the hideous black wart on his hooked nose. His breath reeked of garlic.

As she struggled against him, Meg could feel the jut of his lust through the rough cloth of his robe. Summoning all her strength, she jabbed her knee upward between his legs. Suleiman yowled as hard bone crunched into his unprotected manhood. He reeled backward and doubled over in agony. Hassan wheezed with laughter as Meg fled to the limit of her chain and crouched there like a cornered leopardess.

Hurting and humiliated, Suleiman turned on her. Pinpoints of rage flamed in his eyes as he uncoiled the whip. Expertly, his arm went up. The leaded tip hissed through space.

Suddenly a large, black shape hurtled downward as if from the sky itself, to land, with a sickening crunch and a splatter of mud, almost at Hassan's feet.

Suleiman froze. Hassan choked on the wine. Meg stifled a scream as she realized what she was seeing.

The Swahili guard who'd gone after Jenny last night lay dead in the mud, his rigid corpse already gathering flies.

"Hassan!" Cameron stood at the top of a high, overhanging ledge, shouting at the top of his lungs. "All we want is the woman! Set her free, and the rest of you can go!"

It was a fearful bluff. He could only hope the slavers had no way of knowing he was alone, except for Jenny. Cameron risked a swift glance to make sure the little girl was where he'd left her. His eyes glimpsed her blond head twenty yards down the ravine, at the top of big, loose rockslide. She was sitting tensely, arms and legs tucked close against her body like a cat's. He felt a tug of fatherly pride. If Jenny was afraid, she hid it well.

Hassan was standing now, staring up into the ledges. Cameron had shouted at him in Swahili, but he answered in surprisingly good English.

"Brave words! But I hear only one voice! Show yourself if you dare!"

Cameron's heart dropped. Aye, he should have known it would not be easy. He glanced at Jenny again, and at the long limb jutting from the base of a carefully stacked rockpile at the top of the slide. *Wait*, the shake of his head told her.

She returned his gaze with eyes that matched his own. Cameron tried to be reassured by her calm. Inside, however, he was sick with worry. Jenny had her instructions, and she seemed to understand. But she was so young and small. How much could he expect of her?

The rest of the Arabs and Swahili had come out into the open to gather in a curious circle. Near the firepit, Cameron could see Meg, crouching like a staked animal. His hand clenched on the handle of the knife as he let the thought of freeing her drive all distractions from his mind.

"Hassan!" he shouted. "I have a trade to offer you! What do you know about a man named Murchison—an ivory hunter?"

"Murchison." Hassan indulged in an arrogant pause. "I know he shot more ivory than any man in Africa. And I know he never had money to show for it. I heard rumors that he had a cache of ivory that he kept in a cave, but no one ever—"

"Murchison's dead. He left a map."

Hassan stiffened, and Cameron knew his words had struck home.

"I found the body," he said. "I have the map. You already know my price."

"You're bluffing again, you English cur!" Hassan glared malevolently up at the ledges.

"No, the map is real. Do you want to see it?"

"Come down here!" Hassan growled.

"Only if my wife goes free." Cameron edged downward through the maze of jutting rocks, keeping out of sight. Jenny would have to manage on her own now.

"How do I know the ivory is there?" Hassan demanded.

Nervous sweat trickled down Cameron's body. "You don't. No more than I do. But I understand you're a man who enjoys a gamble."

"Come down here where I can see you, son of a dog!" Hassan was dancing with impatience. The sun had come out, and the rain-soaked ground steamed like a caldron. Cameron felt as if he were looking down into a scene from hell, with Hassan in the devil's role. He was frantic with fear for Meg, but he forced himself to speak calmly.

"Send up the woman with one unarmed man."

"No. You come down! When I see you and the map, she goes free!"

"On your word of honor?"

"On the grave of my mother!" Hassan snarled his acquiescence.

For the space of a heartbeat, Cameron hesitated. He had every reason to be distrustful. But Meg was so near he could almost feel her. And he was tired, so damnably tired that his head was swimming. It would be so easy, he rationalized. All Hassan wanted was the map. Minutes from now, everything would be all right.

He fumbled for the map, and for the matches he kept in a tiny, sealed tin. "I'm coming," he called out. "But no tricks, or the map goes up in smoke."

"Come, then!" Hassan shouted back. "Come and take this worthless hellcat off my hands!"

Cameron left his vantage point and moved down through the rocks. Relief washed over the shoals of his caution like the waves of a sweet, warm sea. He clasped the folded paper in his hand; but it was as if he had already let the map go. Incredibly, the feeling was wonderful.

For weeks, he had spun his dreams around the map and what its treasure would buy him—possessions, power, respect, even love. Lord, what a fool he'd been. Respect bought with money was an illusion. Love bought with money was a travesty.

Meg's love was no travesty. It was pure and true and honest, a treasure beyond value.

He thought of the ivory, gathering cobwebs in its hidden lair. He heard the gunshots and screams that had bought it. He saw the great, intelligent beasts collapsing on their massive legs, their tusks crumbling the red earth. He saw the skinners swarming like ants onto mountainous gray bodies that still pulsed with life.

The map was death; Cameron knew that now. Once it had possessed him. But it would never possess him again. The ivory might make him rich beyond all dreams. But weighed against Meg's vibrant young life, and the sweetness of her love, it was as worthless as dust.

As for the future, he had two strong arms and a world of possibilities. He would work harder than he had ever worked in his life. His family might not live like royalty, but they would never know want. They would have food on their plates and a good, solid roof over their heads. And Meg would never have to take in boarders again.

Cameron felt as if the sun had risen inside him. He was striding swiftly now, eagerness overriding judgment.

Soon she would be in his arms.

By the time Meg realized what was happening, Suleiman had seized the collar around her throat. His strong, smelly hand clamped her mouth, choking back the warning scream that would have alerted Cameron to the trap.

She watched in helpless horror as the two Swahili guards, armed with sharp-bladed *pangas,* slipped into their hiding places on either side of the trail. She knew exactly what was about to happen, but she was powerless to stop it.

Hassan gave her a sidelong leer. "Your husband is an even bigger fool than I'd hoped," he murmured. "But I doubt he would make a good slave. Too much of a troublemaker. No, my proud one, you will watch him die."

Meg thrashed vainly against Suleiman's steel grasp. She struggled to bite the fingers that choked off all hope of crying out. But his hand was as tight and hard as an iron vise on her mouth. There was nothing she could do.

Cameron was tramping confidently down the path, making no effort to hide the crunch of gravel under his boots. Meg's heart stopped as he appeared between two jutting boulders, the map in his hand.

He saw her. He knew.

But it was too late. Cameron dived for cover as the two Swahili jumped him in a melee of flying blades and fists. Hassan had clearly given orders that he be taken alive, or the *pangas* would have hacked him to ribbons. As it was, by the time the two husky Swahili subdued Cameron, blood was dripping from cuts on his face and arms.

Hassan picked up the map where it had fallen to the ground. As he examined its markings, his eyes narrowed to slits of pure greed. He strolled over to where Cameron stood glowering in helpless rage, arms pinioned by the two guards. Lifting one contemptuous eyebrow, he spat in Cameron's face.

"That for all English!" he hissed. "I have no further use for you. Alive, you will be nothing but trouble. You will watch as Suleiman takes your woman. Then I will enjoy seeing you die."

Cameron's chin lifted as he flung his remaining strength into a shout that echoed off the sides of the ravine.

"Now, Jen—"

The word ended in a grunt as a rifle butt slammed into his midsection. Cameron sagged, fighting for breath. Hassan leered in triumph. Suleiman laughed, his breath hot in Meg's ear.

The sound from the ledges above them was not loud at first. It began as a rattle of cascading rock that grew to a clatter, then crescendoed to a roar as the vast bed of loose scree began to slip.

For an instant, all attention was riveted upward. Suleiman's hand had slackened. Meg glimpsed a tiny blond head, safely above the slide. She bit hard into the Arab's palm and, with all her strength, drove her elbow into his belly.

Suleiman's breath whooshed out. Meg rolled clear as he doubled over, gasping. She could see Cameron struggling with the guards. He had knocked one of them down and was wrenching the *panga* from the other. Flat, sharp-edged chunks of shale were singing into the camp like bullets.

With the pandemonium at its height, the slaves charged. Joined at the ankles by their long chain, they moved in a single, clanking line that cut through the camp like the blade of a scythe, mowing down everything in its path. Tents collapsed. The pole that held Meg's chain was torn from the ground, setting her free. Battling to reach Cameron, she was caught up and swept toward the far side of the ravine.

The slaves whooped and chanted, snatching up fallen weapons as they pushed their panicked captors toward the brink of the deep-cut chasm where the red-brown floodwaters rushed. Suleiman screamed as he toppled over the edge and disappeared.

Meg had managed to tumble free of the line. Seeing one of the guards go down with a rock gash in his head, she dived for the rifle that had dropped near his body. Her fingers clawed through the mud to reach and grasp the slippery stock. Seconds later, she was staggering to her feet, the mud-spattered weapon cold and solid in her hands.

She levered open the breech. The rifle was loaded and ready to fire. She glanced up to see Hassan crawling half-dazed out of the wreckage of a toppled tent, the map clutched in his fingers.

The anger that flamed up inside Meg was sickening in its intensity. Her hands quivered with fury as she lifted the gun to her shoulder and pulled back the hammer with her thumb. Her breath came in tiny, sobbing gasps as her index finger found the hard, smooth steel of the trigger.

"Hassan!" She spat out the name.

He started. His eyes widened in surprise as he turned and saw her.

"Look at me, you monster!" she hissed. "I want to see your face as I kill you!"

Hassan had risen to his full height. He stood facing her, his back to the drainage channel. A slow smile slithered across his face. "Kill me, *memsahib?* Brave words. But no, I think you will not do it."

Meg's finger quivered on the trigger. "And why shouldn't I? You betrayed me, you stole my daughter."

"But, *memsahib*," he said in a cajoling voice, "do you not understand? I, Hassan, have been the instrument of your fate."

"What?" The tip of the rifle blurred in Meg's vision. She readjusted the bead to cover his heart.

"*Think*. Your daughter—if not for Hassan, she would be dead. Your husband—if not for Hassan, you would have divorced him and gone back to Britain. Do you not see? All that is yours now, you owe to me. And for that reason, *memsahib*, I cannot believe you will fire that gun."

Meg swayed on her feet, dizzied by the man's strange logic. Incredibly, she realized, Hassan was right. And he knew nothing of her new secret, the tiny life-spark she carried inside her body, the life that would not exist, except for—

"Meg!" She heard Cameron's frantic shout from somewhere behind her, and she realized that Hassan was moving away from her, edging backward along the brink of the chasm.

"You see?" Hassan's voice was like honey, sweet, oozing and hypnotic. "I knew you couldn't—"

His face froze in sudden shock as the rain-saturated bank gave way beneath his weight. Time seemed to stop as his feet trod thin air. Then, with a shriek, he sank into the cascade of mud and rocks.

For an instant, his empty hand clawed at the bank. Even then, he might have saved himself, but his other hand was gripping the map and would not let go. The very last thing Meg saw of him was that frenzied fist, clutching the crumpled piece of paper. Then Hassan was gone.

"Meg!" She heard Cameron's voice and felt the sweet strength of his body as he caught her close. As the careening world slowed around her, she realized that the rock-slide had stopped. The slaves had found the keys and were unfastening their shackles.

Her arms locked around Cameron's waist. She clung to him, overcome suddenly by a strange sense of peace. Unbidden, her thoughts drifted back in time to an evening in a moonlit garden, and the words of a wise old man. She could almost hear the Emir's silvery voice.

"... It is the unplanned that makes us strong... the unplanned that teaches us the true meaning of happiness."

Meg blinked back a freshet of tears. How foolish she had been that night, in her resolve to seize destiny and mold it to her wishes. How could she have known what was in store? How could she have foreseen that her journey would end here, with everything as it was meant to be?

But her journey had not ended at all, Meg realized with a little shiver of contentment. In a larger sense, the journey was only beginning.

Cameron lifted her chin and gazed into her face, his eyes burning with love. "Come, lass," he whispered hoarsely. "It's finished here. Let's find Jenny and go home."

Epilogue

Nairobi
June 14, 1900

Cameron paced the platform, alternately glancing at his watch and peering down the track. The train was not late, but Meg and the children had been in Mombasa visiting the Emir for a week. Without them, the house was as quiet as a mausoleum, and he was wild for the silence to end.

Thrusting the watch into his pocket, he stared through the gathering twilight, where the gleaming lines of the narrow-gauge railway arrowed across the Athi Plain. How had he survived so many years of being alone? he wondered. How had he existed without the love that was so much a part of him now?

Behind him, a vermilion sunset cast the skyline of the growing town into stark, black relief. Malcolm Roberson had been right about Nairobi. With the arrival of the railroad, the place was booming. Homes, government buildings, stores and hotels were rising up everywhere, and the construction firm of Roberson and MacKenna had as much business as it could handle.

Cameron indulged in a contented sigh. Next to marrying Meg, going into partnership with Malcolm had been the best decision of his life. To his own amazement, he was already on his way to becoming well-off. Life was so good, in fact, that he found himself pausing from time to time, shaken by the fear that this was all a dream.

The long blast of a whistle broke into his reverie. Cameron's pulse quickened as the squat, wood-burning locomotive chugged into view. By the time the passenger cars pulled alongside the platform and the train hissed to a stop, he was growling with impatience.

The first one out of the open car was Jenny. She shot across the platform to fling herself against him with the force of a small, beribboned hurricane, hugging his neck and peppering his scarred cheek with kisses.

Looking past Jenny's shoulder, he could see Meg making a more cautious descent, with six-month-old Duncan sleeping in the crook of her arm. She looked weary but radiant, in a plumed hat and a deep violet gown that matched her eyes. Snatching Jenny up with one arm, Cameron strode across the separating distance, caught Meg's waist with his free hand and pulled her tight against him. Her subtle fragrance surrounded him like a dearly familiar cloud. He closed his eyes, lost in the bliss of having her home again.

Young Duncan, as dark as Jenny was fair, stirred, whimpered and settled back in to slumber as Meg met her husband's lips with a hungry, nibbling kiss. "Don't wake this little mischief," she whispered. "He's all ready for bed, and I'm hoping he'll sleep through the night."

Cameron caught the spark in her eye. Meg's remark had been innocent enough, but he knew she was anticipating the warm, private darkness of their bedroom as much as he was. Aye, he'd been aching for her all week. He would be ready. More than ready.

Jenny tugged at his ear. "We saw giraffes!" she piped. "And Jehani has a new baby girl! Her name is Fatima, and she's so tiny—" Her voice broke off as she hugged him again. "Did you miss us, Daddy?"

Cameron's throat tightened as he circled his family in his arms. "Aye, that I did, Jennifer Jane," he whispered. "I missed all of you."

*   *   *   *   *

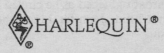

HARLEQUIN®

Weddings, Inc.

Harlequin Books requests the pleasure of your company this June in Eternity, Massachusetts, for WEDDINGS, INC.

For generations, couples have been coming to Eternity, Massachusetts, to exchange wedding vows. Legend has it that those married in Eternity's chapel are destined for a lifetime of happiness. And the residents are more than willing to give the legend a hand.

Beginning in June, you can experience the legend of Eternity. Watch for one title per month, across all of the Harlequin series.

HARLEQUIN BOOKS... NOT THE SAME OLD STORY!

WEDGEN

MILLION DOLLAR SWEEPSTAKES (III)

No purchase necessary. To enter the sweepstakes and receive the Free Books and Surprise Gift, follow the directions published and complete and mail your "Win A Fortune" Game Card. If not taking advantage of the book and gift offer or if the "Win A Fortune" Game Card is missing, you may enter by hand-printing your name and address on a 3" X 5" card and mailing it (limit: one entry per envelope) via First Class Mail to: Million Dollar Sweepstakes (III) "Win A Fortune" Game, P.O. Box 1867, Buffalo, NY 14269-1867, or Million Dollar Sweepstakes (III) "Win A Fortune" Game, P.O. Box 609, Fort Erie, Ontario L2A 5X3. When your entry is received, you will be assigned sweepstakes numbers. To be eligible entries must be received no later than March 31, 1996. No liability is assumed for printing errors or lost, late or misdirected entries. Odds of winning are determined by the number of eligible entries distributed and received.

Sweepstakes open to residents of the U.S. (except Puerto Rico), Canada, Europe and Taiwan who are 18 years of age or older. All applicable laws and regulations apply. Sweepstakes offer void wherever prohibited by law. Values of all prizes are in U.S.currency. This sweepstakes is presented by Torstar Corp, its subsidiaries and affiliates, in conjunction with book, merchandise and/or product offerings. For a copy of the official rules governing this sweepstakes offer, send a self-addressed, stamped envelope (WA residents need not affix return postage) to: MILLION DOLLAR SWEEPSTAKES (III) Rules, P.O. Box 4573, Blair, NE 68009, USA.

SWP-H494

Harlequin® Historical

Looking for more of a good thing?

Why not try a bigger book from Harlequin Historicals?

SUSPICION by Judith McWilliams, April 1994—A story of intrigue and deceit set during the Regency era.

ROYAL HARLOT by Lucy Gordon, May 1994—The adventuresome romance of a prince and the woman spy assigned to protect him.

UNICORN BRIDE by Claire Delacroix, June 1994—The first of a trilogy set in thirteenth-century France.

MARIAH'S PRIZE by Miranda Jarrett, July 1994—Another tale of the seafaring Sparhawks of Rhode Island.

Longer stories by some of your favorite authors.
Watch for them this spring, wherever
Harlequin Historicals are sold.

HHB1G2

HARLEQUIN SUPERROMANCE®

TIRED OF WINTER?
ESCAPE THE WINTER BLUES THIS SPRING WITH
HARLEQUIN SUPERROMANCE AND

MARRIOTT'S

Camelback Inn

RESORT, GOLF CLUB & SPA

Mobil Five Star, AAA Five Diamond Award Winner
5402 East Lincoln Drive, Scottsdale, Arizona 85253, (002) 948-1700

April Showers brings a shower of new authors! Harlequin Superromance is highlighting four simply sensational new authors. Four provocative, passionate, romantic stories guaranteed to put Spring into your heart!

May is the month for flowers, and with flowers comes ROMANCE! Join us in May as four of our most popular authors—Tracy Hughes, Janice Kaiser, Lynn Erickson and Bobby Hutchinson—bring you four of their most romantic Superromance titles.

And to really escape the winter blues, enter our Superromantic Weekend Sweepstakes. You could win an exciting weekend at the **Marriott's Camelback Inn, Resort, Golf Club and Spa** in Scottsdale, Arizona. Look for further details in all Harlequin Superromance novels.

HARLEQUIN SUPERROMANCE...
NOT THE SAME OLD STORY!

HSREL3

HARLEQUIN®

Don't miss these Harlequin favorites by some of our most
distinguished authors!
And now, you can receive a discount by ordering two or more titles!

HT #25551	THE OTHER WOMAN by Candace Schuler	$2.99	☐
HT #25539	FOOLS RUSH IN by Vicki Lewis Thompson	$2.99	☐
HP #11550	THE GOLDEN GREEK by Sally Wentworth	$2.89	☐
HP #11603	PAST ALL REASON by Kay Thorpe	$2.99	☐
HR #03228	MEANT FOR EACH OTHER by Rebecca Winters	$2.89	☐
HR #03268	THE BAD PENNY by Susan Fox	$2.99	☐
HS #70532	TOUCH THE DAWN by Karen Young	$3.39	☐
HS #70540	FOR THE LOVE OF IVY by Barbara Kaye	$3.39	☐
HI #22177	MINDGAME by Laura Pender	$2.79	☐
HI #22214	TO DIE FOR by M.J. Rodgers	$2.89	☐
HAR #16421	HAPPY NEW YEAR, DARLING		
	by Margaret St. George	$3.29	☐
HAR #16507	THE UNEXPECTED GROOM by Muriel Jensen	$3.50	☐
HH #28774	SPINDRIFT by Miranda Jarrett	$3.99	☐
HH #28782	SWEET SENSATIONS by Julie Tetel	$3.99	☐

Harlequin Promotional Titles

#83259	UNTAMED MAVERICK HEARTS	$4.99	☐

(Short-story collection featuring Heather Graham Pozzessere,
Patricia Potter, Joan Johnston)
(limited quantities available on certain titles)

	AMOUNT	$	
DEDUCT:	10% DISCOUNT FOR 2+ BOOKS	$	
	POSTAGE & HANDLING	$	
	($1.00 for one book, 50¢ for each additional)		
	APPLICABLE TAXES*	$ _____	
	TOTAL PAYABLE	$ _____	
	(check or money order—please do not send cash)		

To order, complete this form and send it, along with a check or money order for the
total above, payable to Harlequin Books, to: **In the U.S.:** 3010 Walden Avenue,
P.O. Box 9047, Buffalo, NY 14269-9047; **In Canada:** P.O. Box 613, Fort Erie, Ontario,
L2A 5X3.

Name: _____

Address: _____ City: _____

State/Prov.: _____ Zip/Postal Code: _____

*New York residents remit applicable sales taxes.
 Canadian residents remit applicable GST and provincial taxes.

HBACK-AJ